Dear Reader,
The Ruby Mountains of Nevada have always intrigued me. They are an isolated oasis in the vast western desert. Little has been written about the area, for it was off the track of westward migration in the nineteenth (and twentieth) century. Even with their abundant water, the mountains weren't a magnet for settlers.

The few people who were drawn to the vast silence of the Ruby Mountains were attracted by the desolate splendor of the land. Some of those people were outlaws. Others were hermits or prospectors. Still others were people with a dream. They saw in the springs and creeks of the mountains enough water to build ranches in the midst of wilderness.

Once I saw the Ruby Mountains and the amazing Ruby Marsh, I knew I would have to write about the land and the kind of men and women who built a dream that has endured until today.

Autumn Lover is my celebration of a unique place, and of a man and a woman who were strong enough to love. The characters are my own creation, but the land is as real as love itself.

Elizabeth Lowell

Autumn Lover

AVON BOOKS  NEW YORK

AUTUMN LOVER is an original publication of Avon Books. This work has never before appeared in book form. This work is a novel. Any similarity to actual persons or events is purely coincidental.

AVON BOOKS
A division of
The Hearst Corporation
1350 Avenue of the Americas
New York, New York 10019

Copyright © 1996 by Two of a Kind, Inc.
Front and inside front cover art by Fredericka Ribes
Inside cover author photo by Phillip Stewart Charis
Published by arrangement with the author
Library of Congress Catalog Card Number: 95-94906
ISBN: 0-380-76955-7

First Avon Books Printing: April 1996

AVON TRADEMARK REG. U.S. PAT. OFF. AND IN OTHER COUNTRIES, MARCA REGISTRADA, HECHO EN U.S.A.

Printed in the U.S.A.

RA 10 9 8 7 6 5 4 3 2 1

for Mike Greenstein

he knows why
thanks

1

" I hear you need a ramrod who can handle a gun."

The voice out of the darkness startled Elyssa Sutton. She hoped her face didn't show the lightning stroke of fear that went through her.

The stranger had come out of nowhere, without warning, soundless as a shadow.

She looked toward the man who stood at the edge of the ranch house porch. He was a dark silhouette just beyond the golden lantern light pouring through the windows. Beneath the brim of his hat, his eyes were like clear black crystal, as emotionless as his expression.

A winter storm would look warm by comparison to this man's eyes, Elyssa thought uneasily, biting her lower lip.

On the heels of that thought came another.

Yet he's compelling, in a dangerous kind of way. Almost handsome.

Next to him other men would seem like boys.

Elyssa frowned. She had never particularly noticed men. They were simply wastrel sons of titled Britons,

1

or sailors, or soldiers, or cowhands or wranglers or cooks.

Or raiders.

In the months since Elyssa had returned to America against her uncle's wishes, she had encountered more than a few renegade white men. The Ladder S was a remote ranch in the Ruby Mountains. It drew prospectors, Spanish treasure hunters, wagon trains of hopeful settlers on the way to Oregon—and the renegades who preyed on all of them.

The Culpeppers were the worst of a bad lot of raiders.

If anyone can stand up to the Culpepper gang, this man might, Elyssa thought wryly. *Question is, who gets rid of the ramrod after he gets rid of the Culpeppers?*

"Miss Sutton?" the stranger asked, his voice deep.

When he spoke, he stepped into the lantern light, as though he sensed her unease at not being able to see him clearly.

"I'm thinking," she said.

Elyssa let the silence grow while she openly studied the stranger. She wondered if she dared accept the challenge he presented.

The thought made Elyssa's mouth go dry. She licked her lips and took a deep breath. Then she concentrated on the man who had appeared out of darkness, instead of wondering at her own reckless impulse to meet this man on his own dangerous ground.

A thick, straight, dark mane of hair came down to the stranger's collar. His face looked tanned, with vague squint lines around the eyes and a neat, dark mustache above a well-formed mouth.

His black pants and jacket were clean, tailor-made, and had seen hard use. It was the same for his pale gray shirt, which was clean and rather worn. The shirt fit well to the masculine wedge of wide shoulders and narrow waist. A faded black bandanna was tied loosely around his throat.

Behind the stranger a horse stamped and blew softly through its nostrils. Without looking away from Elyssa, the man reached back and stroked the animal's neck with long, soothing motions of his gloved hand.

His left hand. His right hand—which had no glove— stayed where it had been, near the six-gun he was wearing at his side. Like his clothes, the stranger's gun was both worn and clean.

And like the man himself, the weapon had an aura of harsh use about it.

Yet for all the stranger's hard eyes and dark presence, Elyssa noted that he handled his horse gently. She approved of that. Too many men in the West treated animals as though they felt no pain from spur or lash.

Like Mickey. If I didn't need every hand, I'd send that swaggering fool packing, even though Mac thought the world of him. But I do need every hand.

Now more than ever.

The stranger's horse shifted, bringing the saddle within reach of lantern light. There was a rifle in a scabbard, and what looked like a shotgun in another scabbard on the far side of the saddle.

There was no silver on the guns or saddle, no fancy trimmings, nothing that would catch and reflect sunlight, revealing the man's presence.

What looked like a Confederate officer's greatcoat was tied behind the saddle on top of a bedroll. Whatever rank the stranger might have held had been stripped away from the greatcoat as ruthlessly as the saddle had been purged of shiny decorations.

The horse itself was a big, rangy, powerful blood-bay stallion that would have cost three years' wages for the average cowhand.

But then, the stranger obviously was no average cowhand. He was waiting for her response with the indrawn stillness of a predator at a water hole.

Such stillness was unnerving, especially for someone whose spirit was as impulsive as Elyssa's.

"Do you have a name?" she asked abruptly.

"Hunter."

"Hunter," Elyssa repeated slowly, as though testing the sound on her tongue. "Is that your name or your profession?"

"Does it matter?"

She closed her lips against the retort that was on the edge of her tongue. She had been told often enough that she was like her dead mother, impulsive and intelligent in equal and sometimes conflicting parts.

This man's deep stillness brought out in Elyssa a reckless desire to pry beneath his composed surface to the heat and seething life of him.

But life had taught Elyssa that recklessness could be very costly.

Warily Elyssa measured the cool reserve in Hunter's eyes. A deeply feminine part of her wondered where he had been and what had happened to take from his soul all but ice and distance . . . and an echo of pain that cut her like a razor.

Why should I care about this man's past? Elyssa asked herself fiercely. *He evaded whichever Culpepper was on guard out in the pass, and that's more than Mac with all his hunting skills managed to do.*

That's all I should care about. Hunter's skill.

Yet it wasn't all Elyssa was concerned about, and she was too intelligent not to know it. This man drew her as no other ever had.

Nervously she licked her lips and took another deep breath.

I should tell him to leave.

"Do you want the job?" Elyssa asked, before common sense could make her change her mind.

Black eyebrows rose in twin, oddly elegant arcs.

"That fast?" Hunter asked. "No questions about my qualifications?"

"You have the only qualifications that matter."

"Guns?" Hunter asked sardonically.

"Brains," she retorted.

Hunter simply looked at her, waiting silently for a better explanation.

"I didn't hear shots," Elyssa said, "so you got past whichever Culpepper was sitting at the opening to the valley or in the pass itself, all set to empty saddles."

Hunter shrugged, neither confirming nor denying Elyssa's words.

"How did you sneak by the dogs?" she asked.

As she spoke, she looked around for the black-and-white border collies that usually were the first warning of any strangers near the ranch house.

"I came in downwind of them," Hunter said.

"You were lucky."

"Was I? The wind has been blowing down out of the canyon behind the house for days."

Silently Elyssa conceded that Hunter was right. The autumn wind had been usually steady. For the past week it had flowed down the many canyons of the Ruby Mountains in a cool rush that smelled of piñon and rocky heights.

Then she realized that Hunter was watching her as closely as she was watching him.

"What makes you think I'm not a member of the Culpepper gang?" he asked calmly.

"Too clean."

The corners of Hunter's eyes tilted slightly, heightening the faint lines.

Elyssa had a feeling that was as close as this man came to a smile, so she smiled in return.

Although Elyssa didn't realize it, the smile transformed her. It gave an animation to her face that was startling.

Whereas before she had been a fairly pretty blond female with wide eyes and a pleasant voice, now Elyssa was a temptress with hair the color of moonlight, blue-green eyes radiant with sensual possibilities, and a body that set a man to thinking about what it would be like to get past all the buttons and muslin to the sultry flesh beneath.

Abruptly Hunter looked away.

"Missy, why don't you tell me more about the job? Then I'll decide if I want it."

His voice was clipped, almost rough. As he spoke, he snapped the reins between his fingers. It was the action of a man who wanted to be going about his business without further interruptions.

Missy. As though I was a child, Elyssa thought.

The word and the gesture rankled. It reminded Elyssa of her English cousins. They had been haughty and dismissive of the ill-born American girl who just happened to be a blood relative.

But not the right kind of blood. Not all of it.

In her cousins' eyes her plainsman father had been little better than a savage.

"I'm not a little miss," Elyssa said, no longer smiling.

Hunter shrugged.

"You look real little from here," he said.

"You'll sleep in the ranch house with us," Elyssa said curtly.

He nodded with absolute indifference.

Elyssa wondered what Hunter would have done if she had told him that he would sleep in her bed. Then she looked at his remote, watchful eyes and doubted that anything she said would have changed his reaction.

Little miss.

The thought irritated Elyssa even more. It increased the reckless temptation to bait Hunter into something other than male aloofness.

She had gotten rather good at that kind of baiting during her years in England. It had been her revenge for being treated as little more than a downstairs maid with a come-hither smile.

"For your information, Hunter," Elyssa said distinctly, "I'm no more a little girl than you're a little boy. I'm twenty."

"You look more like fifteen."

"The last foreman I hired was shot to death in the bunkhouse three weeks ago," Elyssa added gently.

Hunter showed no reaction.

"That's when Mac went for help," Elyssa said.

"Did he get any?"

"We heard a lot of shots. Mac didn't come back, but his horse did. There was blood on the saddle. Still want the job?"

Hunter nodded as though the fate of other men had nothing to do with him.

"I take back what I said about brains," Elyssa said.

Hunter gave her a cool black glance.

"The house might not be any safer for you than the bunkhouse was for the last ramrod," she said, speaking slowly, as though to an idiot.

"I understand."

"Do you? You don't look like a man expecting to die."

"I'm not."

Belatedly the border collies caught a strange scent and started barking. Three of the dogs dashed up from behind the house. Two others raced out from the dark ribbon of willows along the creek beyond the barn.

"Dancer, Prancer, Vixen, hush!" Elyssa commanded.

"Comet and Donner, that goes for you, too!"

All five dogs stopped barking.

Hunter looked at the rangy, long-haired, black-and-white animals seething around the two people.

"They don't look much like reindeer to me," he said.

"What? Oh." Elyssa smiled, remembering. "A few years ago, there was a litter born just before Christmas."

"Where's Dasher and Cupid?"

"A hawk got Dasher when he was barely five weeks old. We already had a cat named Cupid, so we moved on to Vixen."

The dogs circled Hunter and his horse, sniffing. Then they looked at Elyssa. She waved her hand. The dogs trotted off in whatever direction they had come from.

"They might bark at you a few more times," Elyssa said, "but they won't attack anything except four-legged predators. They're cattle dogs, not guard dogs."

"From what I've heard, the dogs can't have much cattle work left on the Ladder S," Hunter said dryly.

Elyssa didn't argue. The raiders had been systematically stripping her ranch of livestock.

In another month she would be bankrupt.

Hunter is right, she thought unhappily. *I need a ramrod who can handle a gun.*

"Do you have anything but meadow hay for my horse?" Hunter asked. "Bugle Boy has come a long way on grass."

"Of course. Follow me."

Elyssa stepped off the porch.

"No need," Hunter said. "I take directions well."

"Somehow I suspect you give directions a lot better than you take them."

Black eyebrows lifted again.

"Are you always this sassy?" Hunter asked.

"Of course," Elyssa retorted. "Uncle Bill has called

me Sassy since I was old enough to crawl onto his lap and tweak his beard.''

Hunter watched while Elyssa stepped past him into the darkness. She paused to speak softly to his horse along the way. The clean, subtly female scent of her caressed Hunter's nostrils, shortening his breath until he could barely force air into his lungs.

Like sunlight on a meadow, Hunter thought hungrily. *Clean and sweet and hot.*

Hot most of all.

With narrowed black eyes, Hunter looked at the girl who was even now walking away from him.

In the moonlight Elyssa's hips swayed delicately against the fragile silk skirts of a dress that had been stylish in England two years ago. The layers of cloth lifted on even the smallest puff of wind, revealing the pale glow of stockings beneath.

Hunter forced himself to breathe deeply despite the vital tightening of his body at the sight of her slender calves caressed by delicate cloth and moonlight.

Cool off, soldier, he told himself curtly. *She's just another empty young flirt, like Belinda. All big eyes and girlish sighs and a soft pink tongue sliding along her full lower lip.*

I should have known better than to take the bait the first time Belinda offered it, but I didn't.

I damn well know better now.

And it was my kids who paid the price of my learning.

Bleakly Hunter shoved aside the savage truth that he had married the wrong girl. It was in the past, untouchable.

Like the war that had taken everything from Hunter but his life and that of his brother.

Dead and buried, all of them, Belinda and Ted and Em. Nothing I can do about it except what I'm doing—

tracking Culpeppers and sending them to judgment just as quick as I find them.

Wonder how Case is getting along. Hope to God he hasn't found more Culpeppers than he can handle.

But Hunter wasn't truly worried about his younger brother. Case had gone into the War Between the States a boy and come out a man who was as closed and hard as flint, and even less forgiving.

"Hunter?"

The gentle, husky voice whispered through the darkness like a caress. Hunter's blood surged despite himself.

"Don't get your water hot," he said.

Great advice, he told himself sardonically. *You be sure to take it yourself.*

With a muttered curse Hunter set off after the girl who had gotten under his skin with the speed and heat of nettles.

Holding Bugle Boy's rein in his left hand, Hunter followed Elyssa through moonlight and shadow. A steady, cool wind blew around them. Elyssa didn't stop walking until they were across the dusty ranch house yard.

A weathered paddock fence seemed to grow out of the night in front of them. Thirty feet beyond, a hip-roof barn loomed. The mingled scents of horses and hay and dust flowed out of it. Nearby a pipe dripped water into a trough whose surface dimpled and shimmered with moonlight at each added drop.

It was obvious to Hunter that the Sutton ranch was no rawhide operation slapped together with equal parts laziness and hope of better days to come.

The Ladder S had been built to last by a man who cared about the future. In addition to the solid two-story house made of sawed wood and logs, there was a sturdy log bunkhouse, a barn with several paddocks close by, a large corral, a small orchard, a smokehouse, and a big kitchen garden.

From the corral and paddocks came the steady rippling sound of water being piped into troughs for the animals to drink. From the garden came the scent of earth and water and herbs. To Hunter it was a perfume more seductive by far than the cloying magnolias Belinda had preferred.

Hunter's measuring eyes probed shadow and moonlight with equal intensity. He was searching for both danger and confirmation of what he had heard about the Ladder S ranch.

So far, everything matched Case's reports and the information Hunter had gathered himself. The ranch hadn't changed from the description one of the soldiers assigned to Camp Halleck had given Hunter last week:

The Ladder S is as unexpected and beautiful in this howling wilderness as a girl born of aristocrats on her mother's side and restless plainsmen on her father's side.

But the army won't be riding by the Sutton place for a while. The major is dead set on mapping passes and getting himself some redskins, and the Indians leave the marsh pretty much alone at this time of year.

Hunter also knew what the soldier had been too discreet to say. The major in question was an out-and-out drunk, a man embittered by being assigned to the primitive West instead of the civilized East or the prostrate South.

There was no doubt that the Ruby Mountains of the newly created state of Nevada were a wilderness barely touched by man. Nor had Elyssa's parents chosen to settle near the northern end of the peaks, where wagon trains headed for Oregon passed nearby as they followed the uncertain course of the Humboldt River.

Instead, the Suttons had settled amid the wild, desolate beauty of the east side of the Ruby Mountains. Behind the ranch house rose steep, rugged, jagged peaks.

The pass through the Rubies that could be negotiated by wagons was far to the south.

There were two other passes, but they were useful only to a man on horseback. Driving cattle through them, especially while under fire from the likes of the Culpeppers, would have been impossible.

Passes, wagons, cattle, outlaws . . .

Hunter had studied all of them when he realized that the Culpeppers were planning to go to ground in the Rubies. The war, and a bad marriage, had taught Hunter to control his potent, deep-running passions. He had become a careful man. A disciplined man.

A deadly man.

Now Hunter studied the outline of the Ruby Mountains against the glittering stars. He fixed it in his mind so that he could orient himself along the mountain range no matter what the light. It was a night-fighter's trick, or an explorer's.

Hunter had been both.

At least water won't be a problem, he thought. *This place is a remote oasis in the middle of one hell of a desert.*

No wonder the Suttons chose it.

And no wonder the Culpeppers want to take it, now that someone else has done all the backbreaking work of hammering a ranch out of the wilderness.

Though surrounded by desert, the Ruby Mountains were themselves not dry. Their high peaks raked moisture from the winter clouds and gave it back as runoff in the spring and summer. All the rills and creeks and streams on the east side ran down to the Ruby Marsh, flooding it with water and life.

Then the melt stopped and the desert closed in until little was left of the marsh but miles of tawny reeds and small, hidden clearings around clean pools.

Most of the clearings were protected by stretches of

mud too deep to cross. The remainder provided water and good grazing for cattle. But the paths through the tawny reeds changed with each rain. Today's clear trail was tomorrow's deadly bog.

Even the Culpeppers hadn't been brash enough to take on the rustling, seething mystery of Ruby Marsh.

The marsh acted like a moat protecting the east side of the Ladder S lands. The mountains provided protection on the west side. The south was open to anyone willing to make a long, dry ride around the mountains. So was the north.

The Culpeppers were not only willing to make the ride, they kept a man posted somewhere back up on the shoulder of the nearest peak, watching the Ladder S.

No cattle had been permitted to leave the Ladder S. No new men had been permitted to get to the ranch, where they were desperately needed as cowhands.

A sound stitched through the long exhalation of the wind. In the instant before Hunter identified the source of the noise, he turned, drew and cocked his six-gun.

Just a horse rubbing his neck on the paddock fence, Hunter told himself.

Smoothly he slipped the gun back into its holster before Elyssa could even turn toward him.

"Is something wrong?" she asked.

"Just getting used to the sights around here."

"And the sounds?" she asked dryly.

Hunter made a sound that could have meant anything.

"If you have any questions, ask," Elyssa said. "That rattling you heard was just Leopard bumping against a loose railing. He scented you and your horse."

As they walked closer, Leopard whinnied and pranced, eyeing the strange stallion just beyond the fence.

Hunter's right hand drifted closer to his six-gun once more. Nothing he had heard about Elyssa Sutton's stallion was reassuring. Hunter had no intention of letting his well-trained, well-bred stallion be chewed up in a fight with an ill-trained rogue stud.

"Leopard, huh?" Hunter said, disapproval naked in his voice. "Is he the spotted devil everybody over at Camp Halleck is talking about?"

"That collection of ill-sawn timber and crooked logs can barely be called a camp," Elyssa said crisply. "But I guess that my stallion might be a topic of idle conversation."

"Spotted horses aren't that rare."

"Leopard is. The enlisted men were quite impressed when their commanding officer mounted Leopard."

"Rough ride?" Hunter asked, though he knew full well what had happened.

"The man lived. It was more than the pompous fool deserved. I told the captain that Leopard wasn't one of the horses we planned to sell to the military."

Hunter looked at the stallion without comment.

"The *gentleman*," Elyssa said with scornful emphasis, "told me he would simply commandeer Leopard and pay in army scrip, and I should get out of the way so that men could do men's work."

The contempt and anger in Elyssa's voice made Hunter suspect that the captain had gotten a rough ride from more than the spotted horse.

Elyssa is just like Belinda, Hunter thought. *Dead spoiled. No thought for what other people might need, even the army that protects her.*

"Paiutes and Shoshones both are looking for scalps," Hunter said. "The army needs all the men and horses it can get just to protect the settlers heading west along the Humboldt River."

"So the captain said. I think people would be better protected if someone cut off his supply of liquor, and that of his superior officer as well."

Hunter looked again at the stallion silhouetted against the night. If the soldiers at Camp Halleck were to be believed, Leopard had not only thrown the captain, the stud had tried to stomp him flatter than a shadow.

Bugle Boy blew through his nostrils and tugged at the reins, smelling grain in the big barn beyond.

Hunter tensed. He expected Leopard to take Bugle Boy as a challenge and start throwing himself at the paddock rails.

Leopard simply stood and breathed audibly, drinking the strange scents. Then he blew out and fixed his attention on Elyssa once more.

"Heard he's a killer," Hunter said.

"The captain? I doubt it. The fool probably doesn't know the loud end of a gun from the quiet."

"I meant the stud."

"Leopard is a lamb with me."

Elyssa's voice was soft and vibrant with affection for the huge stallion.

The horse whickered and pushed his nose through the poles in the paddock toward Elyssa. She bent and breathed into Leopard's nostrils. His ears pricked and he whuffled over her cheek and chin, taking in her scent and her breath.

She laughed softly.

The sound went through Hunter like lightning through darkness. He couldn't help wondering what it would be like to be stroked and murmured over so sweetly, to mingle breaths and then bodies until sweetness turned to fire.

With a silent curse, Hunter forced his attention back to the big spotted stallion.

Leopard's mane and tail were black, full, and very long, proclaiming his ancient Spanish bloodlines. His head was elegantly shaped, black, and held proudly.

High on the stallion's muscular neck, small ovals of

white appeared among the black hair. The white ovals increased along the deep chest and shoulders and barrel until they consumed the black background color. By the time the stallion's flanks were reached, white was the dominant color. Large black ovals stood boldly against white on the horse's rump and hind legs.

The equine eyes watching Hunter over the paddock railing were wide, black, as unblinking as the night itself. Hunter had the feeling that Leopard was sizing him up as surely as he was sizing up the stud.

"Sixteen hands?" Hunter asked.

"You have a good eye."

"Do you use him for stud?"

"Of course."

Hunter grunted. "Chancy."

"What?"

"Using a killer for stud. Likely he'll throw colts as vicious as he is."

"Leopard isn't vicious!"

"Tell that to the soldiers."

"They had no right to rope Leopard and throw him and blindfold him so that—"

"He couldn't kill the rider he unloaded into the dirt," Hunter finished coldly. "Probably the only smart thing that fool captain did."

With that, Hunter turned from the stallion to Elyssa. She stood in the moonlight and wind, her skirts swirling like an earthbound cloud. Even in the dim light, the flat, impatient line of Elyssa's mouth was visible.

"In any case," Hunter said in a clipped voice, "the army has every right to conscript suitable mounts, no matter whose pet the horse might be. The Paiutes have been raiding along the Oregon Trail."

"Or Culpepper trash dressed as Indians have been raiding."

"Either way, the army has its work cut out."

''We've had no trouble with Indians here.''

''Yet.''

Hunter's certainty rankled Elyssa. Impulsively she pushed away from the paddock and confronted the dangerous stranger.

''I'm surprised to hear you take the army's part,'' Elyssa said.

''Why?''

''Not so long ago, they were your enemy. Or,'' she added rashly, ''did you get that greatcoat behind your saddle from a Confederate officer whose luck ran out?''

''I don't steal from the dead.''

Hunter's voice was calm, soft, and all the more dangerous for it.

''That's not what I meant,'' Elyssa said.

''Then what did you mean.''

It wasn't a question. It was a demand.

''That you purchased the greatcoat,'' Elyssa said, ''the same way Mother and Father purchased furniture and farm animals from settlers on their way west.''

Hunter just looked at her.

''It happens a lot,'' Elyssa pointed out. ''Most of the people who go west can't believe what Nevada will be like. My English cousins thought I was lying when I talked about rivers that dried up long before they reached the sea, and lakes that evaporated into salt crystals every summer.''

Finally, curtly, Hunter nodded, accepting that Elyssa hadn't meant to insinuate that he was a grave robber.

Yet it was an effort for Hunter not to show the fury that had swept over him when Elyssa had seemed to describe him as no better than the crows and carrion eaters who descended after a battle to pick over the dead.

Like the Culpeppers, Hunter thought, *meaner than snakes and twice as low.*

Barely human.

No. Not even barely. The devil's own, corrupt to the center of their black souls.

What other kind of creature could do what they did to helpless women, and then sell their terrified children to Comancheros for the price of a fancy ruffled shirt?

There was no answer to Hunter's silent question.

There had been no answer since the moment he came back from war and discovered that everything he fought for had been raped and murdered, utterly destroyed by rebel raiders.

Culpeppers.

Southerners, like Hunter. That was the worst of it. Betrayal upon betrayal.

Slowly, soundlessly, Hunter let out his breath. He hadn't felt this depth of rage since he had learned his children's fate. But thinking about it wouldn't help. It just got in the way of doing what had to be done.

Take the Culpeppers back to justice.

Dead or alive.

Nothing could be allowed to interfere with that. Nothing at all. Not memories. Not rage. Not regret.

And certainly not a spoiled, sassy girl like the one standing in front of Hunter right now. Another Belinda, knowing only her own wants and to hell with anyone else.

"All right, Miss Elyssa Sutton," Hunter said neutrally, "you're not having trouble with the Paiutes or the Shoshones. Yet. What are you having trouble with?"

"Culpeppers."

"Culpeppers," Hunter drawled. "Heard of them. They seem to have more kith and kin than Russian royalty."

Elyssa grimaced.

"Royalty?" she repeated sarcastically. "Hardly. They have less breeding than lice."

"Even hell has a hierarchy. Which devil is in charge here?"

"Mac said it was the oldest one. Abner."

Tension snaked through Hunter.

He had followed the trail of Ab Culpepper and his murderous kin for more than two years and a thousand miles. Yet each time Hunter closed in, Ab slipped like smoke through Hunter's fingers.

And then Ab went on to raid and rape and murder more unsuspecting settlers.

It will end here, in the Ruby Valley, Hunter vowed. *Soon.*

Deliberately Hunter ran Bugle Boy's reins through his fingers, trying to still the savage eagerness that came when he realized how close he might be to getting his hands on the man who had sold Ted and little Em to an early grave with the Comancheros.

"Miss Sutton," Hunter said softly, "you've just hired yourself a ramrod."

⌒2

$\mathcal{F}$or an instant Elyssa had the distinct feeling that Hunter was giving an order rather than accepting her offer of employment.

Nonsense, she told herself stoutly. *It's just his way. Comes from too many years of giving orders.*

It will do him good to take a few.

"That fast?" Elyssa asked archly, echoing Hunter's earlier words.

He shrugged.

"What about pay?" she pressed.

"Is it a problem?"

Elyssa made an exasperated sound.

"You don't even know what I want you to do," she said.

"Kill Culpeppers."

Elyssa swallowed. "I'm not a—a—"

"Scalp hunter?" he offered, his voice bland.

Bugle Boy tugged again at the reins, wanting to be fed and watered and rubbed down.

"Easy, boy," Hunter said, stroking the horse soothingly. "It won't be long now. The little miss will make up her mind before the moon goes down."

"Mr. Hunter—"

"Just Hunter," he interrupted. "The war burned out

20

all the formality in me. Hunter is the name I go by now
—first, last, and middle.''

Impulsively Elyssa couldn't help wondering what else
had been burned out of Hunter by the war. Softness,
certainly.

But not all kindness.

He handles his horse gently, she reminded herself.
Surely that speaks of an inner tenderness.

*And surely I'm soft in the head to even think it! That's
one hard man standing in front of me.*

Yet that was just what Elyssa needed at the moment.
A hard man.

''Mr. Hunter—Hunter, that is—''

Elyssa made an impatient sound and started all over
again.

''I'm hiring you to round up livestock with a Ladder
S brand and take them over the mountains to the army
at Camp Halleck. Along with the cattle you'll be driving
eighty head of green-broke mustangs, also to be delivered to the army.''

''By what date?''

''Thirty-seven days.''

''Thirty-seven days.'' Hunter whistled softly. ''You
left it kind of late, little girl.''

''My name is Miss Sutton,'' she said through her
teeth. ''If you can't remember that, Elyssa will do
nicely. I don't answer to 'missy' or 'little girl.' Do you
understand me?''

''Touchy little thing, aren't you?'' Hunter asked.

Elyssa's temper flashed, but she controlled her tongue.
Her English cousins had taught her with cruel precision
just how her reckless temper could be used against her.

''I don't enjoy strange men being familiar with me,''
she said.

''In a few days I won't be a stranger.''

''You are rude.''

"I'm blunt, Sassy. I don't have any patience for little girls who think that big eyes and swinging hips are all a man wants in a female."

"You arrogant, overbearing—"

"No doubt of it," Hunter interrupted impatiently. "Now, do you want this job done or do you want to spend the next thirty-seven days praying for a gentleman gunfighter who also knows how to lead men into battle and round up cattle between skirmishes?"

It took every bit of the control Elyssa had learned at the hands of her cousins, but she managed not to say what she dearly wanted to: *Go to hell, Hunter. I don't need you.*

But Elyssa did need Hunter, and she knew it.

So, obviously, did he.

"I want the job done," Elyssa said distinctly. "Then I want to see you mount up and ride off Ladder S land."

"No problem there. I've got better things to do than herd cattle for a spoiled child."

"I hope you lead men better than you judge women," Elyssa retorted.

Bugle Boy nudged Hunter hard enough to lift a smaller man right off his feet.

Hunter was barely budged.

"Follow me," Elyssa said curtly. "Your horse has waited long enough for water and food."

Hunter followed Elyssa's swirling, scented silk skirts along the paddock fence, paced every inch of the way by Leopard. Yet despite the stud's fearsome reputation, he made no offer to pick a fight with Hunter's stallion. Leopard was like the ranch dogs, curious about the new scents of man and horse.

Well, at least the devil has some manners, Hunter thought. *Wish I could say the same for his mistress.*

Sassy to the core.

As Hunter walked, he watched the quick-tongued girl

who had looked at him first with apprehension, then with a frank feminine appreciation he was doing his level best to turn into distaste.

Looks like I'm succeeding, Hunter told himself. *Last thing I need is another girl like Belinda rubbing against me until I can't think for the heat in my blood.*

I'm here to get Culpeppers, dead or alive.

For that, I'll need my wits about me, or I'll end up killed before the job is done.

The rattle and screech of a heavy barn door sticking to its iron railings drew Hunter out of his bleak thoughts. Just in front of him, Elyssa was pushing and shoving against the creaking barn door.

Hunter's left hand shot past her cheek. He pushed once. The door complained some more and then slid obediently aside.

"Need some grease on those door rails," Hunter said.

For a moment Elyssa was too rattled to answer. The sheer male strength of Hunter had unnerved her. She could still feel the heat and coiled power of his body close to hers. He had pushed the door aside as though it weighed no more than her silk skirt.

"We're out of grease and I haven't wanted to risk going to the settlement," Elyssa said huskily.

"Try some of that scented soap you're wearing. It's good for more than making men come to a point when you walk by."

Elyssa's head turned around sharply.

Hunter was close, so close that she could see the gleam of reflected moonlight in the dark centers of his eyes and the subtle flare of his nostrils as he drank her scent.

Then Hunter turned away abruptly, freeing Elyssa from his intense, sensual interest.

Without a word Hunter led Bugle Boy through the barn door. Then he waited while Elyssa struck a match to light the small lantern that hung by the door.

The smell of sulfur was sharp against the mellow scent of hay and horses. The clink of the glass chimney sounded loud in the silence.

"You can put Bugle Boy in the big stall at the end for now," Elyssa said, her voice uneven. "There are loose rails in the fence on the east paddock. After I get the fence fixed, you can keep your stallion there, unless you would rather stable him."

"I'll see that the fence is sound."

Elyssa went to the grain bin and returned with a brimming gallon measure to Bugle Boy's stall. The grain made a hushed, whispering sound as she poured it into one side of the manger.

She was reaching for the pitchfork when Hunter's arm shot by her and grabbed the heavy wooden handle.

"Give that to me," he said. "It's more likely you'll stab me or yourself than the hay, what with those long skirts swirling around your ankles like hungry cats every time you move."

"Thank you." Elyssa smiled impulsively. "I think."

Hunter bit back what he wanted to say, which was that a girl with a smile like Elyssa's had no business being alone in a barn at night with a strange man, much less taking care of his horse.

That was what truly disturbed Hunter. He had expected Elyssa to stand aside and be alluring while he did what was necessary for his horse.

But she hadn't stood aside. She had gone to work as though used to it.

She got the alluring part right, though, Hunter thought sardonically. *Even Belinda couldn't put Sassy in the shade.*

Especially with that smile.

Cursing beneath his breath, Hunter rammed the pitchfork into a mound of hay that was piled just below the trapdoor that opened into the hayloft. Soon the manger was full.

Hunter put Bugle Boy in the big stall and took off saddle and bridle. He groomed the stallion with strong, rhythmic sweeps of the brush.

Elyssa pulled her silk shawl more closely around her shoulders against the chilly night air. She knew she should go back to the house, but something about watching Hunter work over his horse held her in the hushed silence of the barn. There was a natural grace and economy to his movements that pleased her.

And there was real strength.

Lord, and here I thought Mickey was strong. He has a lot more sheer bulk than Hunter, but no notion of how to put it to best use.

"Before you work the cattle or catch mustangs, you'll need to round up some Ladder S horses," Elyssa said after a time, thinking aloud.

"Are they broken?"

"Some of them, but most haven't been ridden since the men started leaving."

"Then they're probably running with mustangs by now."

Elyssa sighed. "Yes, I'm afraid so."

"When did your hands decide to drift?"

"Spring roundup."

"Before branding?" Hunter guessed.

"How did you know?"

"It's easier to rustle unbranded calves."

Elyssa made an unhappy sound.

"Are you sure it's Ab Culpepper stirring the pot around here?" Hunter asked.

"Mac mentioned the name several times."

Elyssa's mouth flattened into an unhappy line when she thought of Mac. Though she had never been close to the crusty old woman hater, he had been a part of her childhood just the same.

First Mother. Then Father. Now Mac.

Thank God that Penny seems to be getting over that ague that's been wearing her down. I can't run the Ladder S alone.

"Any others?" Hunter asked.

"Other what?"

"Culpeppers."

"Oh." Elyssa frowned. "I couldn't tell from what Mac said whether Abner is here or coming here soon. The man comes and goes without notice."

Amen, Hunter thought sardonically. *That old boy is as hard to pin down as swamp gas.*

"Horace and Gaylord," Elyssa said slowly. "Mac told me they were here all the time. More Culpeppers are expected soon. Rumor has it that they're east of here, somewhere in the Rocky Mountains."

The line of Hunter's mouth shifted in the lantern light. The slight curve was far too hard to be called a smile.

"Maybe," Hunter said. "And maybe some of those Culpeppers are buried up Colorado way."

A chill went through Elyssa.

"Your doing?" she asked.

"No. I got there too late to be useful. A man called Whip did the honors, with help from his woman."

The line of Hunter's mouth softened as he remembered. His brush slowed in its sweeps over Bugle Boy's glossy hide.

"Quite a woman, too," Hunter said. "Eyes like sapphires and a walk that no man would ever get tired of watching."

"Do tell," Elyssa said tartly. "Of course, I have it on excellent authority that men want more than big eyes and swinging hips from a female."

Hunter gave Elyssa a narrow look.

She gave it right back. She didn't know why Hunter's admiration of another woman rankled.

But it did.

"What help will the army give me?" Hunter asked, brushing his stallion briskly again. "It's their future beef being stolen, after all."

"Precisely what I pointed out to that insufferable captain."

"Was that before or after Leopard tried to flatten him?"

Elyssa's lips tightened.

"After," she said reluctantly.

Hunter grunted. "Figures."

"What does?"

"You couldn't hold your tongue even to save your ranch."

"I disagree," Elyssa said through her teeth. "I'm holding my tongue right now. Admirably. In fact, I will apply for sainthood by the next mail!"

Hunter made a sound that could have been a cough or a strangled chuckle. Because his hand was smoothing over his mustache at the time, it was hard to tell.

"So there won't be any help from the army," Hunter said after a moment.

"No. As the captain pointed out to me in generous detail, the livestock will still exist. The army simply will purchase them from a different owner."

"A true officer and a gentleman," Hunter said ironically.

"I will defer to your superior judgment in the matter."

"That would be a first."

Elyssa bit her tongue.

"How many head of cattle carry the Ladder S brand?" Hunter asked.

"Before I left for England, Father said there were nearly a thousand."

"How many now?"

Elyssa's eyelids flinched. It was an involuntary response to the sinking in her stomach that came whenever she thought how close she was to the crumbling edge of disaster.

"I don't know," she said starkly.

"Guess."

"I can't."

"Why?" Hunter asked.

"Mac never told me."

"Try counting them yourself."

"I tried," Elyssa retorted.

"Too much work?"

"Too much Ab."

"What?"

"Ab caught me away from the ranch house just after spring roundup. I haven't dared ride out since."

Hunter's gut clenched. He knew precisely what kind of evil Ab could wreak on a girl's soft body.

"Did he hurt you?" Hunter asked.

The promise of unleashed hell in Hunter's voice shocked Elyssa. She swallowed once, then had to swallow again before she could trust herself to speak.

"N-no," she whispered. "Leopard is very fast."

"So are those racing mules the Culpeppers ride," he said, but his voice was neutral once more.

Elyssa let out a long breath as Hunter resumed brushing Bugle Boy's muscular haunch. For a few moments he had looked like a man poised on the edge of violence.

"The mule wasn't much on hurdles," Elyssa said.

"What?"

"I jumped Leopard over ravines and deadfalls and boulder piles and creeks. Ab's mule couldn't stay the course."

The thought of Elyssa racing headlong over the rough country made Hunter's heart hesitate, then beat with redoubled speed. He didn't know why the thought of her in danger should affect him so fiercely, but he couldn't deny that it did.

"That was a fool thing to do," Hunter said bluntly. "You could have broken your horse's leg."

Elyssa didn't disagree. Even now the thought of that wild ride made cold sweat gather at the base of her spine.

But nothing made her feel as cold as what her fate would have been if she hadn't outrun Ab Culpepper.

"Damn," Hunter muttered. "You don't have the sense that God gave a goose. You never should have been out alone in the first place."

Hunter walked around Bugle Boy and went to work on the stallion's other side.

"Someone had to do the count," Elyssa said.

"What about your cowhands?"

"They left," she said simply.

"How many do you have now?"

"Oh . . . three, at last count. Depends on how their Dutch courage is holding out," Elyssa added wryly.

"Just three? A ranch this size could use four times that many hands."

"Finally we agree on something," Elyssa said beneath her breath. "I will treasure the moment."

Hunter looked at her over Bugle Boy's back.

"Did you say something?" Hunter asked, his voice bland.

Elyssa cleared her throat and decided that baiting Hunter was tempting, but not very bright.

"I agree that the Ladder S could use more men," Elyssa said. "In fact, when Mother and Father were alive, we had thirty hands for the busiest times of the year. In the winter we had fewer, of course. It depended on how many cattle we were holding over.''

Hunter was silent for a moment. Then he pinned Elyssa with night-dark eyes.

''Do you have enough money to hire at least seven more men at gunfighting wages?'' he asked bluntly.

Elyssa's stomach tightened again. Money wouldn't be a problem if the cattle and horses were delivered to the army on time.

If they weren't, she would be bankrupt.

''I can pay,'' Elyssa said tightly. ''But the men will have to work cattle, too.''

Hunter nodded. The brush moved in long strokes over Bugle Boy's bloodred hide.

''The kind of men I'm looking for won't mind pushing cows,'' Hunter said.

''There is a problem.''

''Just one?''

''Until this one is solved, the rest can't be,'' Elyssa retorted.

''I'm listening.''

''Another moment to treasure,'' she muttered.

Hunter's head came up.

Elyssa started talking. Fast.

''The Culpeppers are scaring away the men who would normally look for work here,'' she said.

''So I've heard.''

''Even the Turner clan off to the south is staying away, and Turners have worked autumn and spring roundups on the Ladder S for years.''

Hunter nodded.

''That doesn't worry you?'' she asked tartly.

He shrugged.

''But how will the men get through the Culpepper gang to be hired by the Ladder S?'' Elyssa demanded.

''Same way I did. By using their heads. Or in a group, using their guns. Either way, they'll come.''

"You sound very certain."

"Cash jobs are hard to come by out here. A man can make more money in a month at fighting wages than he can in a season of pushing cows."

Elyssa sighed and rubbed her arms, feeling the night chill through the heavy silk shawl. She wished she had the shawl's cost in plain old homespun wool.

But she didn't. There was no money for more suitable clothes for her or paint for the house or for anything else that wasn't essential for the ranch's survival. The Ladder S was all she had in the world.

And she was very much afraid she had already lost it.

"I wish Mac were still here," Elyssa said unhappily. "He liked women even less than you do, but—"

"Smart man."

"—nobody knew the Ladder S the way he did," she said, ignoring Hunter's interruption. "Every ravine, every spring, where the grass was good and in which season, even the marsh. He knew all of it."

"Didn't do him much good against the Culpeppers, did it?"

Hunter lifted one of Bugle Boy's big hooves and began cleaning it with swift movements of a hoof-pick.

Slowly Elyssa shook her head, blinking against the tears that burned at the back of her eyes.

"I tried to find Mac," she said in a husky, ragged voice. "As soon as I heard shooting, I grabbed the shotgun and rode Leopard out of here at a dead run."

"Don't blame yourself," Hunter said. "It probably was all over before you even tightened Leopard's cinch."

"I didn't bother."

"I beg your pardon?"

"With a saddle," Elyssa explained. "Or a bridle."

"Girl, only an idiot would ride—"

"I didn't even find where Mac had fallen," Elyssa said, not hearing any words but her own. "I searched until a thunderstorm broke and washed away the tracks. Then I quartered the land until it was too dark to tell trees from rocks."

"You *are* a fool! What if the Culpeppers had found you?"

"I was afraid Mac was lying injured out in the storm, maybe even dying," Elyssa said tautly. "I couldn't just turn my back and leave him to the cold rain."

"Getting grabbed by the Culpeppers wouldn't have helped Mac one damned bit. But you didn't think of that, did you? All you thought of was tearing around in the rain like the heroine of some fool dime novel."

Elyssa's mouth turned down at the corners. She watched as Hunter went to work cleaning another of Bugle Boy's hooves.

"You're going to love Penny," Elyssa said wryly. "She said the same thing, and more besides."

"Who is Penny?" Hunter asked, though he already knew.

But it was the sort of question that a man new to the area would be expected to ask.

Hunter wanted Elyssa to go on thinking he was just one more gun-handling drifter looking for work. If she knew he gave a damn only about tracking down Culpeppers, not about the fate of the Ladder S, Elyssa would likely fire him before he even started.

Then there would be merry hell to pay getting within rifle range of the Culpeppers.

Hunter had learned in the past two years that the Culpeppers left men watching their back trail. The only way to get close to the gang was to blend into the landscape.

The ramrod of the Ladder S would be invisible.

"Penelope Miller is kind of an aunt," Elyssa explained, "like Mac was kind of an uncle. And Bill, too."

"Kind of?"

"Penny was my mother's . . . companion, I guess. She cooked and sewed and cleaned, but she was always more than a hired housekeeper."

Hunter looked over his shoulder at Elyssa. She had the silk shawl clutched around her shoulders like a suit of armor.

Women sure put stock in finery, Hunter thought, remembering Belinda.

And they sure do sulk when they don't get fancy clothes.

Hunter dropped Bugle Boy's hoof and picked up another. Caked dirt flew as he went to work with the pick.

"Penny is like family," Elyssa said. "It was the same for Mac. He was no blood relation, but he was a great friend of Father's. And Bill's, too. Without Mac, the Ladder S would have fallen apart long ago."

Hunter barely heard. He was still thinking about Belinda. When he realized it, he was angry with himself.

Living in the past does no good, Hunter thought. *It can't bring back the dead.*

But it just might prevent me from making the same mistake twice. Elyssa is just like Belinda was, a lip-licking little flirt.

I'd better never forget it, no matter how hot Elyssa makes me with her scent and swinging hips.

"Bill," Hunter said, dragging his attention back to the matter at hand. "Would that be Bill the Hermit?"

"That's what some people call him."

"But not you."

"No," Elyssa said. "He's a good man, despite . . ."

Hunter heard the softness in Elyssa's voice and wondered just how friendly she was with good old Bill.

Even though Hunter knew it was none of his business, he found himself too curious for his own comfort.

"Despite what?" Hunter pressed.

Elyssa hesitated. Then she pulled her shawl more closely around her throat.

"Every man has his blind spots," she said finally.

Especially if big-eyed little girls are involved, Hunter thought sardonically. *More men have gone to perdition on the swing of a woman's hips than any other way.*

"Besides the Culpeppers, is anything else troubling your ranch?" Hunter asked. "Drought or bad water or not enough feed to carry stock through the winter?"

Again, Elyssa hesitated.

There had been small things, more annoyances than troubles, really. A wagon axle that broke, spilling hay into the wind. A mower whose blades were so badly dulled they ruined more hay than they cut. A dead cow in the little reservoir on House Creek, which forced them to haul water all the way from Cave Creek until the fouled spring cleared.

Just bad luck, Elyssa told herself. *If you complain of it to Hunter, he'll think you're a spoiled, whining little girl.*

"No," she said firmly. "No other troubles. So many cattle have been run off that wintering over the rest—after we fulfill the army contract, of course—won't be a problem."

"How many go to the army?"

"Three hundred is the minimum. We're their only local source of livestock."

"How many head of breeding stock do you have?" Hunter asked.

"I don't know."

"Guess."

"Fewer than two hundred."

Hunter looked at Elyssa, wondering if she knew just how close to the edge the Ladder S was skating.

"If you have to sell cows instead of steers to meet the army contract," Hunter said, "you'll be between a rock and a hard place when it comes to increasing your herd. Or can you afford to buy more breeding stock?''

''If I don't meet the contract, I'll have barely enough money to buy supplies for Penny and myself for the winter,'' Elyssa admitted.

Hunter was frowning as he went to work on another of Bugle Boy's hooves. Lack of breeding stock would doom the Ladder S as surely, if more slowly, than Culpepper raids.

Not my problem, Hunter told himself curtly. *I came here for Culpeppers, not to manage some sassy little flirt's life. She'll find some nice, gullible fool of a boy to do that for her.*

Hunter released the hoof and smacked Bugle Boy on the haunch, signaling the end of the grooming. The horse looked up momentarily from eating, snorted, and buried his muzzle deep in the grain again. Hunter checked the bucket hanging over the side of the stall, saw that the water was fresh, and turned to Elyssa.

''So,'' Hunter said. ''It's just Culpeppers troubling you.''

''Just?'' Elyssa made a disgusted sound. ''If you say that, you don't know Culpeppers. Those ruffians are the worst of a bad lot of renegades set on the loose by the end of the war.''

''So I've heard.''

Without looking at Elyssa, Hunter unlatched the stall door and motioned her through.

Although the opening was big enough for three men to stand side by side, Elyssa paused before walking past Hunter. He seemed to fill the doorway. She would have to go very close to him to get by.

The thought made her pulse kick.

Did he plan it that way? she asked herself.

Hunter waited with an air of thinning patience.

Don't be silly, Elyssa told herself. *Hunter has made*

it quite clear that he finds me even less attractive than the English lords did. They, at least, were angling for a mistress.

All Hunter is angling for is a smack on his unshaven cheek.

Head high, gripping the silk shawl with one hand and her flimsy silk skirts with the other, Elyssa swept past Hunter.

There was a distinct ripping sound as her skirt caught on a nail.

3

$\mathcal{E}$lyssa was jerked to a stop. Instinctively she threw out her hands for balance. The silk shawl slithered off one shoulder as she windmilled her arms, teetering on the edge of falling.

A hand clad in black leather closed around the colorful shawl, saving it from a descent to the fragrant stall floor. Simultaneously Hunter's right arm closed around Elyssa's body just above her waist.

She made a startled sound as she was lifted off her feet without warning. Her legs started flailing.

"Hold still before you rip your skirts right off," Hunter said curtly. "Or was that what you had in mind?"

Elyssa made another ragged sound.

The feel of Hunter's naked right hand just beneath her left breast made Elyssa feel light-headed. The warmth of his hand seeped through the thin layers of silk dress and chemise. Her heart kicked frantically. She dragged at breath but couldn't get enough air into her lungs.

"Hang on," Hunter said, backing up a step.

Abruptly his grip shifted.

Elyssa forgot about trying to breathe and clung to Hunter. The weight of her breasts was supported on his hard forearm while he bent, still holding her, and eased silk free from the nail.

The heat of Hunter was like a brand on Elyssa's soft flesh.

"Let go," a deep voice said right next to her ear. "You're free now."

But Elyssa wasn't. She was held motionless by Hunter's lean fingers curling across her ribs, brushing against the lower curve of one breast. Her heart was hammering so fiercely she was afraid Hunter would hear it.

Then she realized he wouldn't have to hear her wild heartbeat. He could probably feel it against the naked skin of his right hand.

Elyssa tilted her head and looked back over her shoulder at Hunter, trying to see his eyes. It was difficult. His eyelids were half-lowered, shielding his eyes.

Yet she sensed he was looking at her breasts and feeling their weight against his arm.

An odd, shimmering sensation went through Elyssa, as though she had stepped naked into a pool of warm water. Suddenly her nipples tightened and pushed against the silk in twin, hard peaks.

Hunter's breath came in with a swift ripping sound.

Elyssa turned more toward him, struggling softly against his strength, determined to see his eyes. When she succeeded, the glittering intensity of his glance sent a strange wave of weakness through her. She sagged against him.

Then her own breath came in raggedly. The quintessentially male flesh pressed against her hip was rigid, unmistakable even to a virgin.

"Hunter?" Elyssa whispered, her voice uneven.

"Stand up or I'll drop you."

The contempt in Hunter's voice was like being dumped into ice water.

"I didn't mean—" she began, only to have her voice break. "You didn't have to—"

"Stand up."

Hastily Elyssa straightened her legs, only to find that her knees were still wobbly. She took a half-step, stumbled, and grabbed the nearest thing for support.

It was Hunter, of course. The word he said under his breath made her wince.

"What the hell is going on here?" demanded a harsh male voice from the darkness beyond the stall.

Hunter looked up. A big, heavily muscled young man was striding down the aisle between the stalls, coming toward Hunter and Elyssa. He was wearing a six-gun on his hip and carrying a coil of rope in his hands.

The rope worried Hunter almost as much as the six-gun. He knew exactly how much damage a rope used as a club could do in close quarters.

Without making a fuss about it, Hunter took a step away from Elyssa, giving himself room to fight.

And the angry flush on the young man's face told Hunter that it might easily come to blows.

"Who—oh, it's you, Mickey," Elyssa said, glancing away from the young man.

Cautiously Elyssa shook out her skirts. Nothing snagged. She took a step. Her knees didn't buckle.

She let out a soundless sigh of relief.

"Did you want something?" Elyssa asked.

When no answer came immediately, she looked up. Mickey was staring blatantly at her breasts.

The knowledge both embarrassed Elyssa and made her angry.

A flush bloomed on her cheeks as she snatched her shawl off Hunter's arm. With quick, jerky motions she wrapped the silk around her shoulders, concealing her breasts from Mickey's pale blue eyes.

Then Elyssa realized that she hadn't minded one bit when Hunter had looked at her with male hunger.

Her hands fumbled, nearly dropping the shawl.

"You can bet your little tits I want something,"

Mickey said roughly. "I want to know what the hell you're doing rolling around in the hay with some damned stranger!"

"You overstep yourself," Elyssa said icily.

"The hell you say!"

Ignoring Mickey, Elyssa knotted the slippery silk in place around her shoulders.

The young man's arm shot forward. His broad fingers closed around Elyssa's upper arm with such cruel force that she cried out. He leaned forward until his face was only inches from hers.

"I'm tired of your uppity ways," Mickey snarled. "You've been sashaying around, promising me all kinds of things with your eyes and hips, and now you're giving them away to a no-account drifter."

The reek of alcohol on Mickey's breath was enough to make Elyssa's stomach lurch. She had learned to hate that smell since she had come back and found Bill hell-bent on drinking himself into an untimely grave.

"Let go of me," Elyssa said distinctly.

"Not until I'm good and ready. It's time you learned who's boss around here!"

"I am," Hunter said.

As he spoke, Hunter dropped his left hand onto Mickey's right shoulder. It could have been a gesture of goodwill, one man to another.

But it wasn't.

"I'm Hunter, the new ramrod of the Ladder S."

Though Hunter's tone was easy, his grip wasn't. Beneath the supple riding glove on his left hand, his fingers probed, discovered, and then ground nerve and tendon against bone.

Mickey let go of Elyssa for the simple reason that his hand no longer had any strength.

She stepped quickly beyond his reach. With shaking fingers she rubbed her bruised flesh.

"Who are you, boy?" Hunter asked gently, bearing down even more.

"Mickey," the younger man gasped. "Mickey Barber."

Hunter eased the pressure on Mickey's right shoulder. There was no possibility of a gunfight for the moment. Mickey couldn't have held a gun in his numbed hand.

"Well, Mickey Barber," Hunter drawled, "the reason I'm ramrod and you're not is real simple. You haven't figured out yet that there's no point in getting your kettle all aboil over a little flirt like Miss Sutton."

Elyssa spun toward Hunter so quickly that she nearly stumbled.

"Some girls," Hunter continued matter-of-factly, "just don't know they're alive unless some fool boy is admiring them."

"I am not a flirt," Elyssa said between her clenched teeth. "Nor am I a girl. I am the owner—*and boss*—of the Ladder S."

Hunter's slate-gray glance raked over Elyssa. Though he didn't say a word, she knew he was remembering how her breasts had felt against his arm, how her heart had raced beneath his palm, and how her hip had pressed against his suddenly erect flesh.

A combination of anger, embarrassment, and passion flushed Elyssa's cheeks and tightened her throat, making it impossible for her to talk.

Without a word, Hunter turned away from Elyssa as though she didn't exist.

"Now," Hunter drawled to Mickey, "you don't look like a fool boy. You look like a strapping young lad who puts in a day's work for a day's pay."

Elyssa waited for Mickey to give the rough side of his tongue to Hunter. To her surprise, the younger man simply nodded a bit sullenly.

"Thought so," Hunter said with satisfaction. "Nice rope you have. Mind if I look at it?"

Before Mickey could react, the rope was in Hunter's left hand.

"Braided leather, not hemp," Hunter said admiringly. "A true *la reata*. Takes a good *caballero* to handle a lariat."

"It belonged to a Mex that came here looking for work," Mickey said.

"I'll bet the man is a top hand."

Mickey shrugged. Then he winced at the pain in his right shoulder.

"I sent him packing," Mickey said. "We don't need chili eaters on the Ladder S."

"What?" Elyssa asked, startled. "When was this?"

The young man's pale glance slid from Elyssa's lips to the shawl wrapped around her breasts. The look was that of someone counting his possessions. But very little of Elyssa's breasts showed beneath the loose silk.

Mickey's expression told her that he had liked it better the other way.

"Yesterday," Mickey said.

"Why didn't you send for me to interview the man myself?" Elyssa demanded.

"No need to bother your pretty head, Miss Elyssa. Specially not over no Mex."

"Mr. Barber, you have the finesse and intellect of a rockslide," Elyssa said. "My orders were clear: If a man can ride, rope, and shoot, I want to hire him."

"He was a—"

"Mexican," Elyssa finished for Mickey. "Some of my finest hands are Mexican. Or were, until the troubles started."

"Cowards," Mickey said.

"Don't be more stupid than God made you," Elyssa said impatiently. "They had wives and children to protect. I couldn't have them on my conscience. I told them to find work on a safer ranch."

She gave Mickey a disgusted look and turned her attention to Hunter.

"Hunter, you are to hire men without regard to anything except their skill with rope, horse, and gun. Is that clear?"

The corner of Hunter's mouth shifted just a little bit. It could have been the beginning of a smile.

Or it could have been impatience with Elyssa.

"Yes, ma'am," he drawled. "Except for one thing."

"What's that?" she asked instantly.

"Booze. I won't hire a man with alcohol on his breath. In fact, there will be no tanglefoot in the bunkhouse while I'm ramrod. A drinking man can get himself killed, and a lot of good men with him."

Elyssa looked at Mickey with new comprehension.

"Yes," she said succinctly. "I agree."

"You do that and you won't have a man left on the place by sundown," Mickey said belligerently.

"Oh, I'll have a *man* left on the place," Elyssa said. "His name is Hunter."

"Like I said," Hunter muttered, giving Mickey a look, "there's just no need to get your water hot over a flirt. It's something age teaches you, boy."

Elyssa's mouth flattened.

Mickey simply looked sullen. "I'm foreman of the Ladder S."

"Not anymore," Hunter said mildly.

"Not ever!" Elyssa said. "I never asked you to be foreman, Mickey. I didn't like the way you acted toward some of—"

"Chili eaters," Mickey snarled. "I should have run them off sooner."

Appalled, Elyssa understood too late what had happened to her best hands.

"You're fir—" she began.

"You're one of three hands we have left," Hunter said, cutting across Elyssa's words, "so I'll give you a chance to make it up to Miss Sutton. Do the work of two men, pour the booze into the privy, and you've still got a job. Understand me?"

Mickey started to argue, looked at Hunter's eyes, and held his tongue.

"I'll be checking out the bunkhouse," Hunter said. "If I find any booze there, I'll be purely pissed off and you'll be walking out of here with no pay in your pocket."

Sullenly Mickey nodded.

"Go on to the bunkhouse and sober up," Hunter said. "Tell the other hands I'll talk to them in the morning."

Mickey gave Elyssa an angry, baffled look before he turned and stalked back down the aisle.

As soon as the sound of his footsteps faded, Elyssa turned on Hunter.

"I don't care if Mickey is the last hand between here and the Great Salt Lake," Elyssa said tightly, "I won't stand for him lording it over anyone who is smaller, kinder, or a different color than he is. If I had known what he was doing to Shorty and Gomez and Raul, I would have—"

"Gotten somebody killed," Hunter finished succinctly. "Or were they gun handlers?"

"No."

"Mickey is."

Elyssa looked startled.

"How do you know?" she asked.

"The soldiers over at Camp Halleck were talking about it. Said your young beau was fast to draw and quicker to shoot."

"Mickey? My *beau*? Never!"

"That's not what they're saying around Halleck."

"I'm not responsible for loose talk."

"Flirts have to take the talk as it comes."

Elyssa took a slow breath, fighting her temper. When she spoke again, her voice was cool, remote, the voice she had learned to use with good effect on her English cousins.

"You will believe whatever you wish to believe about me," Elyssa said evenly. "However, you will not insult me in front of others again."

"Or I'm fired?" Hunter asked sardonically.

"Precisely."

Hunter's black eyes narrowed. He was an excellent judge of men. It was one of the skills that had made him a good officer. If Elyssa had been a man, Hunter would have believed she meant every word.

But Hunter wasn't a good judge of women. He had proved it when he married Belinda.

"You'd lose the ranch just because your nose is out of joint?" Hunter asked.

"You have a higher opinion of yourself than I do. I'm not at all certain you can save the ranch."

"We'll make a deal, Sassy."

"I don't like that nickname."

"I'll keep it in mind."

"But you'll use it anyway," she said.

"Probably. Are you going to fire me over it?"

"No."

Hunter narrowed his eyes, surprised again.

"I believe you mentioned a deal," Elyssa said. "What is it?"

"I'll round up your cattle and horses. You stop flirting with the men. It's death on morale."

"I have never flirted with Mickey or any other hand."

"Mickey doesn't seem to think so."

"Mickey doesn't think at all."

Hunter made an impatient sound. "Men don't think

when their blood is hot. Women know that, and use it against men.''

''You have a sour view of women.''

''I have a realistic view of the fair sex,'' he said ironically.

''Rather like my view of the *un*fair sex.''

''That being?''

''If a man wants a woman and she doesn't want him, it's her fault. If a woman wants a man and he doesn't want her, it's her fault. If a man marries the wrong woman, it's her fault. If a woman marries the wrong man, it's her fault. If a man beats a woman, it's her fault. If a woman—''

Hunter held up his hands.

''I surrender,'' he said, almost smiling.

''I doubt it.''

The beginning of a smile vanished from Hunter's face as though it had never existed.

''You're right, Sassy. I won't surrender again to a girl. Ever. The price is much too high.''

The contempt in Hunter's voice made Elyssa flinch.

''I'm not a girl and I never asked you to sur—'' she began.

''So if you're planning on swinging your hips to see me come crawling, don't hold your breath,'' he said over her words. ''Hell will freeze solid. If I ever marry again, it will be to a woman, not to a spoiled little girl who doesn't know her own mind.''

Hunter's words rang in Elyssa's mind with dizzying force.

If I ever marry again. Ever marry. Again.

''You're married?'' Elyssa asked, stunned.

''Not anymore. She's dead.''

''In the war?''

''Close enough.''

Elyssa opened her mouth to ask if Hunter had any

children. Then she looked at his bleak eyes and decided it was time to return to the original subject.

"I would rather Mickey drew his pay and got off Ladder S land," Elyssa said.

"You quit flirting and he'll straighten out."

"As I never encouraged Mickey's attentions in the first place, I doubt that he will 'straighten out.' "

So did Hunter, but he saw no point in discussing it with Elyssa. Hunter had seen other boys like Mickey during the war, young and randy and willing to ride roughshod over everything in their path. Brawlers like Mickey had their uses in battle, if they could be controlled.

And the Ladder S was headed toward one hell of a battle.

"If Mickey doesn't work out, I'll fire him," Hunter said. "Until then, we need every hand."

Unconsciously Elyssa rubbed her upper arm where Mickey had grabbed her.

"If he touches me again," she said, "I won't wait for you to fire him. I'll do it myself."

Hunter glanced at Elyssa's arm.

"Quit teasing him and he'll quit grabbing," Hunter said roughly.

Elyssa felt her temper sliding away. Rather distantly, she wondered what it was about Hunter that got beneath her skin like poison ivy.

"Go to hell, Hunter."

"What?" he said, shocked.

"Go. To. Hell."

Each word was cool, separate, distinct.

"If you were a man—" Hunter began.

"Thank God I'm not," Elyssa interrupted curtly. "I'm tired of being held responsible for their damned childishness."

"Little girl, you're asking to have your mouth washed out with soap."

"If you do it, don't ever turn your back on me afterward."

Hunter gave Elyssa an icy, measuring glance. It didn't take any special insight to see that she meant every word.

By now, Belinda would have been sniffling and stamping her little foot, beside herself with pique. Then she would sulk for hours. Days, sometimes.

God, a girl can make life tedious for a man.

Wonder what Elyssa does when she loses her temper. Scream and swear like a fishwife?

"In a snit, are we?" he asked, almost smiling, curious.

It was a look Elyssa had seen on her cousins' faces when they thought they had her on the run. It took the fire out of her reckless temper as nothing else could have.

"We?" she asked with false gentleness. "I think not. I'm quite calm, thank you. We can discuss what I want you to do as foreman tomorrow, over breakfast. Perhaps you'll be over your, er, *snit* by then."

With that, Elyssa lifted her skirts to keep them clear of the barn floor and walked away from Hunter.

Hunter watched. Blood slid hotly through his veins with each of her steps. He told himself it was anger.

The vital hardening of his body told Hunter that he lied.

Soft, filmy, clingy skirts should be outlawed, Hunter told himself. *So should girls with swinging hips, sea-colored eyes, and hair the color of a harvest moon.*

If I had the sense that God gave a gosling, I'd mount up and ride out of here.

But I won't. If I stay here, I'll get the rest of those murdering Culpeppers.

Unless she fires me first.

The thought made Hunter frown. If Elyssa fired him, he would have no excuse to hang around the Ladder S. He needed to appear like a man interested only in cattle, not Culpeppers.

Damn! I'd better go and see if I can smooth her ruffled feathers.

But by the time Hunter secured the stall door, blew out the lantern, and hurried outside, Elyssa was gone.

"Elyssa?" Hunter called quietly.

Nothing came back to him but silence.

Then there was a flickering of light near the house as a door opened. It closed with a finality that echoed back through the night to the barn.

Any smoothing that got done would have to wait until morning.

4

Well before dawn of the next day, Elyssa was up and working in the kitchen, measuring flour for bread. Beneath an apron made of flour sacks, she was wearing another of her English country dresses.

This one was a sea-green silk. Irish lace filled in the deep neckline. Once there had been a luxurious fall of lace from each wrist, but no longer. She had removed the filmy stuff the first time it dragged through the kitchen fire, threatening to burn the dress and her with it.

Humming a waltz softly to herself, Elyssa sifted and measured. Her movements were rhythmic and graceful, as though she were dancing. Her skirt swirled lightly and then clung with each motion of her hips. The deep, gathered scallops of the skirt were marked by red silk rosettes. The color was repeated in the flounced scarlet petticoat that peeked through between the gathers.

Elyssa's English cousins would have been shocked that she wore only a single scarlet petticoat beneath her full skirt instead of the customary crinoline. Like filmy Irish lace, the hoops and stiff fabric of a crinoline simply got in the way of the ranch work.

But then, everything about me horrified my high-nosed cousins, Elyssa remembered wryly. *Mary Eliza-*

*beth nearly fainted when she found me in the estate's
herb garden.*

When her cousin had discovered that Elyssa was picking herbs rather than flowers and—horror of horrors—
actually planning to use them in a bread of her own
making, the outcry was intense.

*They would have made less fuss if they had found me
naked in the hayloft with a stable boy.*

A sound from the lower bedroom next to the kitchen
made Elyssa glance up. Moments later Penny hurried
into the kitchen. Her gingham dress was faded and
stained with age, but like Penny herself, the cloth was
as clean as a new coin.

Hastily Penny reached for an apron and tied it around
herself.

"Sorry, I overslept," she said.

"It's all right. You've been under the weather lately.
Make the coffee, would you? I never can bring myself
to add enough beans to turn it into Missouri mud."

Smiling, Penny reached for the tin that held coffee
beans. She poured a handful into the coffee mill and
turned the crank. The harsh yet companionable sound of
coffee being ground soon filled the ranch kitchen.

As always, a pot of beans simmered at the back of
the stove, basic rations for men who worked cattle. But
the Ladder S had a tradition of feeding its hands better
than most ranches, so there was bacon sizzling in a pan,
dried fruit stewing in a pot, fresh biscuits baking, and
fresh bread in the making.

Because Elyssa kept a kitchen and herb garden that
would have been the envy of many a small estate, the
Ladder S food had more savor than was common. Some
of the cowhands might not have appreciated the difference, but Elyssa did.

Humming beneath the sound of the grinder, she
snipped up a final sprig of rosemary, added it to the

bread dough, mixed well, and turned the dough out of the bowl onto the flour-dusted counter to knead.

"Such a pretty tune you're humming," Penny said as she paused in the noisy grinding. "What is it?"

"Just a waltz I heard before I left England. I don't even remember the name, but I woke up this morning humming it."

"Don't you wish sometimes that you were still in London with all those teas and fancy balls?"

"No," Elyssa said. "I didn't belong there."

"Sometimes I think Gloria missed it."

"My mother was born there. I was born here."

"But you look just like she did."

"Not really." Elyssa kneaded bread energetically. "In any case, it's only skin-deep."

"That's more than enough to draw every man's eye," Penny said with faint envy.

"Not every man," Elyssa said, thinking of Hunter. "Not the men who are worth having."

The line of Penny's mouth said that she disagreed, but she spoke no more about it. She emptied out the small drawer of the coffee grinder into a pot, added more beans, and went to work again.

Elyssa sifted a bit more flour onto the counter and returned to kneading with quick, smooth motions.

By the time the dough was ready to divide into individual loaves, Penny had ground up a third batch of beans and was putting the coffee on to boil. Occasionally she gave sideways looks at Elyssa, as though waiting for her to speak. Finally Penny couldn't wait any longer.

"I thought I heard someone ride in after dark last night," Penny said, her voice subtly strained. "Was it Bill?"

"No. It was a man called Hunter. Our new foreman." As Elyssa spoke, she cut the dough into four loaves.

"Truly?" Penny asked. "Will he be able to help us?"

"Unless I kill him first."

Penny looked up from the stove. Her brown eyes were wide.

"I beg your pardon?" Penny asked.

"The man is rude."

"Oh. Then why did you hire him?"

"Why do you think?" Elyssa said, shaping loaves vigorously. "We need him."

"If only Bill . . ."

Penny's mouth flattened and her voice faded into silence.

"If wishes were horses, beggars would ride," Elyssa said succinctly.

Penny looked down at the stove and said nothing.

"Ruddy hell," Elyssa said under her breath. Then, gently, "I'm sorry. I didn't mean it as harshly as it sounded."

Elyssa came quickly to the stove and hugged Penny.

"All I meant was that Bill can't help anyone right now, even himself," Elyssa said softly. "I know how hard it is on you to see your very old friend being such a ruddy stupid bas—er, so stubborn."

Penny nodded and made a stifled sound. Tendrils of shiny brown hair slid out from beneath her gingham cap and clung to her cheeks. Her eyes brimmed with sudden tears.

Elyssa felt an overwhelming tenderness toward the older woman. Normally Penny was as steady emotionally as a rock. But the longer Bill's drinking went on, the more tightly strung Penny had become. Then had come the ague that Penny couldn't shake off.

And on top of it all were the Culpeppers, gathering like vultures around the dying Ladder S.

Don't think about it, Elyssa told herself. *I can't fix the Culpeppers now. But I can comfort Penny, who has lost as much of her childhood as I have in the past two years.*

"Hush now," Elyssa said gently. "It will be all right. Just because Bill hasn't been by here for a while doesn't mean he has been dead drunk in his cabin all that time."

Penny nodded but said nothing.

Carefully Elyssa blotted Penny's eyes with the corner of her apron.

"Oh, dear," Elyssa said. "I'm leaving little flour tracks all over your face."

For a moment Penny closed her eyes. Then she took a shaky breath and hugged Elyssa.

"Maybe the flour will blot out the freckles," Penny said.

"Then I'll wipe off every speck of white. I love your freckles."

"Only because you don't have them. Even though you go outside in the sun without your hat."

"Not very often," Elyssa said. "Too much sun makes me look like one of Lord Harry's boiled lobsters."

"Such beautiful skin you have."

Penny looked at the younger woman enviously.

"All cream and pink," Penny continued. "Like your mother's. Hair like spun flax and eyes like blue-green gems. Just like hers."

"So you say. Personally, I think you're quite wrong. Mother was an unusually beautiful woman. I'm not."

"That's not what all the men think."

"Tell it to the English lords. They thought I was about as comely as a wart."

Penny shook her head in disagreement.

"I know the kind of woman who attracts men," Penny said emphatically. Then she added sadly, "And I know the kind who doesn't."

The tone of Penny's voice said that she considered herself one of the unattractive women.

Frowning, Elyssa turned to kneading a second batch of dough. While she worked, she thought of what it must have been like for Penny to grow up in the shade cast by Gloria Sutton's sun.

"A man who looks only at the outside of a woman isn't worth having," Elyssa said after a time.

"That's the only kind of men there are."

"For heaven's sake, Penny. You've turned down half the hands who ever worked on the Ladder S!"

"They only looked at me after they gave up mooning over your mother. *If* they gave up."

Tight-lipped, Penny ground harder on the coffee beans. The combination of sadness and acceptance in her expression told Elyssa more than words.

"Who was he?" Elyssa asked.

"What?"

"Who was the man who couldn't see past Mother to you?"

Penny went very still for an instant. Then she poured the last measure of ground coffee into the pot on top of the stove and added more wood to the firebox. Soon the water went from simmering to a hearty boil.

"What was it about this new ramrod—what is his name again?" Penny asked.

The crisp, no-nonsense voice was the old Penny.

Elyssa let out a breath she hadn't been aware of holding. If Penny came apart under the strain of outlaws and an old friend who drank too much . . .

It didn't bear thinking of.

We've lost too much to lose each other, too, Elyssa thought. *Father. Mother. Mac. Uncle Bill, in all the ways that matter.*

I can't lose Penny.

"Hunter," Elyssa said quickly, accepting the change of subject. "No mister. No last name. Or maybe no first name. He didn't make it clear."

"Is that why he struck you as rude? You know it's the western way to be informal."

Elyssa's cheeks pinked with more than the heat of the stove. She could hardly explain about the snagged skirt and Hunter's forearm under her breasts and his eyes watching her nipples stand so hard against the soft cloth.

Just thinking about it was unsettling. Talking about it would embarrass both her and Penny.

"Sassy?" Penny asked, using the old childhood nickname.

"Hunter accused me of flirting with Mickey."

"Don't you?"

"Of course not! In the time that I've been home, have you ever seen me so much as smile at that bullheaded wretch?"

"No, but from what Mickey said, I assumed you did a lot more than smile."

"What? When was he talking about me?"

"Every time he goes for supplies to the settlement or visits the Dugout Saloon up north."

Is that why Hunter is so scornful of me? Elyssa asked silently. *Has he heard all the talk?*

The answer was obvious. Hunter had heard the gossip. And he had believed it.

"Mickey has no right to talk about me," Elyssa said, her face pale. "I can't help what his lusts are. I want no part of them, or of him."

Penny looked over at the girl, caught by the emotion in Elyssa's voice.

"Don't worry," Penny said gently. "There used to be a lot of talk about your mother, too. Just talk. It didn't hurt her."

"She was married to the man she loved," Elyssa pointed out. "What if she had been single and a man who interested her wouldn't come close because he wanted nothing to do with a little flirt?"

Penny looked into the oven and pulled the biscuits out to cool.

"Is that why you're wearing silk and lace?" Penny asked. "To catch the new man's eye, even though he's rude?"

"I beg your pardon?"

"That dress makes you look like an angel freshly fallen from heaven."

"Bother." Elyssa's cheeks flushed. "I've been wearing my foolish English clothes because I don't fit into the clothes I left behind and there's no money for more sensible clothes."

Penny smiled, then laughed softly, not quite believing Elyssa's denial. Penny's smile was like the woman herself, generous and warm, bringing light to even the darkest corner of life.

Elyssa peeked at the other woman over her shoulder and began smiling too.

"Every time I see you smile," Elyssa said, "I know all over again why my mother grabbed you off the street in Saint Louis and brought you west. 'Nine years old and a smile like Christmas,' she always said. You should smile more, Penny."

"Not much to smile about lately, I'm afraid. It's not like the past."

"I miss my mother, too." Elyssa sighed. "And I miss Father, though not as much. He was always off after gold somewhere. It's Bill I remember teaching me how to ride and shoot and hunt and work cattle."

Penny's expression became even more unhappy. She, too, had been taught many wonderful things by Bill. As a young girl she had worshipped the ground beneath his big feet. She still did.

"Maybe we should get together, grab Bill, and bring him back here," Elyssa said. "Hunter has forbidden any alcohol on the Ladder S. In a few days we would have our old Bill back. He certainly never used to drink so hard."

A sad smile was Penny's only answer. She looked at the headstrong girl who was like a sister to her. Elyssa reminded Penny so much of the equally headstrong woman who had rescued a nine-year-old from cruel city streets and headed west with her for a better life.

And for a time, life indeed had been better.

"You should have sold out to Bill when he offered," Penny said.

"Why?"

"You could have gone back to England and lived quite well."

"I hated England," Elyssa said.

"What about New York or Boston or Los Angeles or San Francisco?"

"I don't care much for cities. The sky is the color of coal smoke and the streets smell of sewage."

Rather savagely, Penny forked cooked bacon out of the frying pan. She sliced more bacon, wielding the big knife as though killing snakes.

Elyssa watched her with sideways glances, wondering why Penny was so upset.

"What about Bill?" Penny asked abruptly. "You care for him, don't you?"

"You know I do."

"Then sell him the Ladder S! Maybe having a real ranch to run would make him drink less. And maybe if he didn't see your pale hair and fine eyes, he would be able to forget the past."

"What are you talking about? What is in the past that so bothers Bill?"

Bacon hissed wildly as it hit the frying pan. With a muttered word, Penny wrapped her apron around the heavy iron handle and moved the pan to a cooler part of the stove.

"Besides," Penny said, ignoring the questions. "You're like your mother in more than looks. You don't belong out here. You belong in a castle somewhere, with people waiting on you hand and foot."

Elyssa gave Penny a startled look, then laughed out loud.

"Whatever gave you that idea?" Elyssa asked.

"Something Bill said."

"Bill knows me better than that."

"Not when you're wearing silk. You look so much like your mother it's . . . heartbreaking."

"Rubbish," Elyssa said emphatically. "I've seen pictures of Mother. I've seen myself in the mirror. You would have to be blind drunk to think we looked alike."

The instant the words were out of Elyssa's mouth, she regretted them. Penny was even more upset by Bill's turn to the bottle than Elyssa was.

"Blazes," Elyssa said. "Why are men so stupid?"

The outer door to the kitchen closed softly.

"Are you talking about any man in particular?" Hunter asked.

Elyssa made a startled sound and spun toward him.

"Don't you believe in knocking?" she asked.

"I did, but nobody noticed. Too busy talking about the sins of men, I guess."

In the cozy ranch kitchen with its golden lantern light and delicious smells, Hunter looked startlingly male. The width of his shoulders brushed against the doorframe. He was so tall that he had to duck beneath the lintel, even though he was carrying his hat in his hand. His hair was clean, thick, black as a starless night.

Hunter's gunmetal eyes took in Elyssa's clothes with a glance that said he knew she had dressed for him. The look reminded Elyssa of the searing moment when she had been closer to Hunter than to any man in her life, ever.

And how much she had liked it.

Despite the pounding of Elyssa's heart and the sudden, vivid color of her cheeks, her voice was cool and controlled when she turned to introduce Hunter.

"Penny, this is Hunter, the new foreman," Elyssa said. "Don't bother calling him mister. He doesn't believe in formality. Hunter, meet Miss Penelope Miller."

"A pleasure, Miss Miller," Hunter said, bowing very slightly, his voice gentle.

Penny smiled suddenly and dropped a small curtsy.

"Please call me Penny," she said. "Everyone else does."

"For a smile like that, and a cup of coffee, I'll call you the Queen of Sheba."

Penny laughed out loud, delighted.

"I'll hold you to it," she said. "Welcome to the Ladder S."

Elyssa stared, unable to believe that the polite, soft-spoken, gently teasing man in her kitchen was the same rude gunfighter who had called her a flirt and all but caressed her breasts in the silence of the barn.

And I let him.

I can't forget that part of it. I let him!

Unhappily Elyssa looked from Penny to Hunter. He was taking a cup of coffee from Penny, smiling at her over the rim, and complimenting her on the strength of the brew.

For all that Hunter noticed Elyssa, she might as well have been a grease stain on the floor.

Is this what Penny meant? Elyssa asked herself. *Is this how she felt when some idiot male couldn't see past Mother to her?*

Elyssa looked again at Penny, seeing her in a different way. At thirty, Penny was as fresh and appealing as a daisy. She had an honest face, a generous mouth, and faint lines of life and laughter around her wide brown eyes.

Most of all, in any man's book, Penny had passed beyond the age of girlhood. She was a woman who had grown strong on the frontier of a wild land.

Elyssa thought of Hunter's cutting words—*If I marry again, it will be to a woman, not to a spoiled little girl who doesn't know her own mind.*

The thought that Hunter might just have found his woman was a chill moving beneath Elyssa's skin. Even as she told herself that she shouldn't begrudge Penny whatever happiness she could find, the nasty taste of envy soured Elyssa's tongue.

In that instant she understood just how deeply she was attracted to Hunter. Thinking of him with another woman was like having the ground cut out from beneath her feet, leaving her with no support.

My God.

Is this what it was like for my mother, this sudden, overwhelming desire for just one other person on earth?

Is this why an English aristocrat left her solid gold luxury and disgraced her family and abandoned her country . . . all for a man who was only slightly less wild than the land he loved?

In the end, though, Mother got the man she loved.

Am I going to be like Penny, an old maid who wants only the man who didn't want her?

"What do you think?" Penny asked.

With an effort, Elyssa focused on the other woman.

"About what?" Elyssa asked.

Penny smiled. "Wool-gathering about ballrooms and carriages again?"

The faintly scornful look Hunter gave Elyssa put the world right back under her feet. She straightened her spine and returned the cool look.

"You think more about England than I do," Elyssa

said crisply to Penny. "My thoughts are about problems closer to home."

"Hunter suggested that we bake enough bread for several weeks," Penny said.

"It will go moldy."

"Better moldy bread than none," Hunter said succinctly. "I'll hunt antelope and deer every chance I get. Can you jerk meat?"

"Of course," Elyssa said. "I can hunt, too."

Hunter's black eyebrows rose, but he said nothing.

"But the men prefer to eat beef," Elyssa said.

"We can't spare any more steers until we know how many you have," Hunter said bluntly. "In any case, you should have enough rations on hand to withstand a siege."

"We aren't going to war."

"Yet," Hunter said in a clipped voice. "But we will, Sassy. Bet on it. I put Mickey to work making some water barrels. Seems he was apprenticed to a cooper before he ran away from Boston."

Elyssa barely heard. She was still hearing Hunter's certainty that it would come down to a range war in order to hang on to the Ladder S.

Ever since Mac had been murdered by the Culpepper gang, she had been afraid of just that.

"You should have given that spotted stud to the army," Hunter added, seeing Elyssa's dismay. "Then they might have worried about protecting the Ladder S as well as the immigrant trains."

"The stud wasn't all the captain wanted," Elyssa said.

Hunter's eyes narrowed. "You?"

"Yes."

Hunter shrugged. "So you should have given him a little of what you were giving Mickey. There's plenty to go around. Ask any 'working' girl."

Elyssa's temper flared.

"All I ever gave Mickey was orders," she said hotly.

"Uh-huh," Hunter said.

His expression said he didn't believe her.

"Miss Penny," Hunter said, his voice polite once again, "would you show me to an empty bedroom? Sassy said I was supposed to sleep in the big house."

Taken aback by Hunter's attitude toward Elyssa, Penny just looked at the younger woman questioningly.

"I told him to sleep inside because I didn't want him shot to death like the last foreman," Elyssa explained without looking away from Hunter. "Now, however, the idea has a positively wondrous allure."

Penny looked startled and amused at the same instant.

"Put him in one of the empty rooms upstairs," Elyssa said ungraciously. "The stairway creaks so much that no one can sneak up on him no matter how loud he snores."

"I don't snore," Hunter said.

"Father used to say the same thing. But you know how it is when a man gets older, don't you, Hunter?"

Hunter's eyes narrowed.

Penny was horrified.

"Sassy," Penny said, using Elyssa's childhood nickname, "shame on you. You know how touchy men are about their age. Besides, Hunter is younger than Bill, and Bill is ten years younger than your father."

"Any man who thinks I'm a little girl must be old enough to snore," Elyssa said sweetly.

"I see," Penny said, hiding her smile. "Well, you'll have a chance to find out. I'm putting him in the room next to yours."

Uneasiness and something else streaked through Elyssa.

"My parents' room?" she asked. "Why?"

"It has the only bed big enough to hold him," Penny said matter-of-factly.

Elyssa opened her mouth to argue, then shrugged.

"If you snore," she said to Hunter, "that big bed is going straight to the nursery at the far end of the house. You'll love the rainbows and butterflies Mother painted on the walls."

An odd look went over Hunter's face, a shadow of agony that touched Elyssa despite her anger with him. She wondered if he had lost children as well as his wife to the war. It would certainly explain the pain she had sensed beneath his ruthlessly controlled surface.

"Never mind about the nursery," Elyssa said quietly. "If your presence bothers me, I'll sleep downstairs with Penny."

The fact that Elyssa somehow had sensed his grief nettled Hunter. He didn't like being transparent to a girl like her.

"I'll survive," Hunter said curtly. "I don't need special treatment from the local flirt."

Penny's breath went out with an audible rush. The antagonism between Elyssa and Hunter was strong enough to touch.

And so was the desire.

The sound of men's voices carrying across the yard came as a relief to Elyssa. She began putting thick coffee mugs and crockery plates on the long table that ran down one side of the kitchen. In other times, Mac and Bill and John, Gloria and Penny and Elyssa, had sat there, talking about the land or the cattle or the turning of the seasons.

"Better hurry getting settled in," Elyssa said without looking at Hunter. "The last man to the breakfast table has to clean the stables."

The back door of the kitchen opened as she spoke. Mickey, Lefty, and Gimp crowded in, elbowing to be the first to sit at the long table.

Elyssa gave Hunter a sideways look. Then she smiled. "Oh, dear," she said. "I guess you're last. After breakfast, I'll be glad to show you where the manure fork is."

Hunter didn't doubt it.

5

$\mathscr{H}$unter handled a manure rake the same way he did everything else—cleanly, quickly, and with no extra motions. He also did the job without resentment, a fact that the two oldest ranch hands noted and approved.

Cupid, the marmalade barn cat, watched from a nearby manger. Five black and orange kittens nursed hungrily, undisturbed by the commotion. Cupid's wide yellow eyes probed the shadows for tiny movements. Though quite full at the moment, the cat was a predator to the marrow of her delicate bones.

As Gimp walked unevenly down the center aisle, seemingly intent on getting a bit of grain for the horses in the corral, Hunter glanced up from his work. Gimp nodded to him and hitched along a little faster.

Lefty was walking next to his friend. Both cowhands were in their fifties. Both were gray-haired, and their faces were weathered by sun and storm. Their clothes were the same, faded and frayed. Their boots wore the marks of long use in stirrups. Spurs jingled softly at their heels.

Each man showed the unmistakable signs of a lifetime spent around large, unpredictable animals. The cowhands moved stiffly on legs bowed from saddles. Their hands were thickened by calluses, and scarred from burns left by ropes and branding irons.

Both men were short one finger. It was the cost of learning never to put your hand between a lariat and the saddle horn when a thousand pounds of angry steer is on the other end of the rope.

Except for Gimp's stiff leg, there wasn't a nickel's worth of difference in the two men's appearance.

"Just getting some grain for my best horse, ramrod," Gimp explained.

"Got a stiff bridle here, and the saddle soap is in the back cupboard," Lefty offered.

Hunter knew the two men were more interested in sizing up the new ramrod than they were in saddle soap or grain. So was Elyssa, who was watching him from the corner of her eye while she groomed Leopard.

Leopard watched Hunter, too, but without real interest.

"Do what you have to," Hunter said, "but I want those ten head of cattle I saw up in the piñons brought in closer before sunset."

"Yessir," Gimp said.

"We'll jump right to it," Lefty agreed.

Bugle Boy put his head over the stall door and watched the two strange men with pricked ears and calm eyes.

The cowhands passed quite close to Bugle Boy's stall door, because Leopard's stall was directly across the aisle. The men gave the spotted stud a wide berth.

Hunter's horse neither shied nor laid his ears back at the strangers walking close by.

"Nice stud hoss you have there," Gimp said admiringly.

"Big, but easygoing, like," Lefty said, glancing across the aisle. "Not like some other studs I could mention."

Leopard was standing in the center of his large stall, watching the men. His ears weren't back, but there was an elemental alertness about him that spoke volumes to men who knew horses.

"If you and all the other hands hadn't roped, thrown, spurred, and repeatedly tried to break Leopard's spirit while I was in England," Elyssa said, "he wouldn't watch you like a cat at a mousehole now. He has good reason not to trust men."

"Huh," was all Lefty said.

"Huh," echoed Gimp.

"Huh yourselves," she retorted. "You just don't like admitting there's more than one way to break a horse. Quirts and spurs don't work on an animal like Leopard."

"Yes, ma'am," both men said.

There was no real heat on either side of the disagreement. The subject had been aired thoroughly since Elyssa had come back to the Ladder S and confounded the men by riding the savage stallion with little fuss and no danger.

Leopard's unfailing gentleness with Elyssa still surprised the old cowhands, who were fond of predicting dire results from the stallion no man had been able to stay on top of. It galled their pride that a slender girl could do what tough, experienced men had failed repeatedly to do—ride the spotted stud that had a fearsome reputation as a man killer.

Uneasily Gimp looked over the stall at the big horse and the fragile-looking girl. Wearing the green silk dress, a blacksmith's leather apron, and leather gloves, Elyssa was bending over Leopard's left rear hoof, cleaning it with a blunt steel pick. Flashes of scarlet petticoat burned like fire in the dim light of the stall.

Gimp shook his head and muttered beneath his breath about foolish girls and man-killing studs.

"Huh," was all Elyssa said.

Hiding a smile, Hunter bent over the manure rake and forked the last dirty straw into a wheelbarrow. He had worked with men like Gimp and Lefty before, old bachelors who complained about everyone and everything, including the friends they had known since they were knee-high to a short horse.

Hunter knew the complaints weren't serious. They were just the cowhands' way of being alive.

"S'pose you want me to shoe that spotted devil again," Gimp muttered.

"How did you guess?" Elyssa asked, straightening.

"Combing cows out of them mountains is hard on shoes, and you'll be doing a bunch of it."

"Shoeing Leopard won't be necessary," Hunter said clearly. "She won't be taking him out of sight of the house."

"I can trim and file his hooves for you," Elyssa said, ignoring Hunter. "I'm just no hand with a hammer."

Bugle Boy's stall door opened and shut with emphasis. Hunter strode across the aisle.

Gimp and Lefty looked at one another and went back down the aisle with surprising speed. They had learned during breakfast that the little boss and the new ramrod didn't see eye to eye on a whole lot of subjects, especially if it involved Elyssa showing the Ladder S to Hunter from the back of a horse.

"Let me know who wins," Gimp said just before he vanished into the yard.

Elyssa gave the empty doorway a disgusted look. Quickly she peeled off the leather apron, traded the hoof-pick for a brush, and led Leopard into the paddock. The stud wore neither bridle nor halter nor rope. She controlled him with no more than a tug on his mane and a low-voiced command.

"Running away?" Hunter challenged from the aisle outside Leopard's stall.

"Leopard likes to be outdoors while I groom him."
Elyssa smiled slightly. "Do feel free to join us."

To Elyssa's surprise, Hunter opened the stall door and
walked through it into the paddock.

Leopard turned his head and flattened his ears in blunt
warning.

"Easy, boy," Hunter said soothingly. "I'm not planning to hurt one hair of your spotted hide."

Elyssa almost didn't recognize Hunter's voice. Instead
of the abrupt, abrasive tone she was accustomed to hearing from him, he was using the same beguiling voice
that he had used with Penny.

I could get used to that voice, Elyssa thought. *It's like
being stroked with a black velvet glove.*

The thought made her tremble slightly, secretly.

Leopard stamped and flicked his ears.

"Gently, Leopard," Elyssa said in a low voice. "It's
all right. Not a rope or a blindfold in sight. I'm here,
boy. No one is going to hurt you."

For the space of several slow breaths, Leopard measured Hunter with feral eyes. Then the stud blew through
his nostrils, shifted position so that he could keep an eye
on Hunter without turning his head, and slowly relaxed
his ears.

Elyssa's voice crooned praise, joined by Hunter's
much deeper voice. Leopard's ears flicked as he listened.
After a few minutes he blew again, stamped one foot,
and nudged Elyssa to get on with the grooming.

"You do love being petted, don't you?" she said.
"Well, I love petting you, so we're even."

Still singing Leopard's praises, Elyssa began brushing
the tall horse.

Though Hunter said nothing, he was impressed by
Elyssa's ability to get past the stud's wariness.

After several minutes passed, it became clear to Hunter that Leopard was far more interested in being

groomed than in stomping anyone. Slowly Hunter moved his right hand away from his gun belt.

"How did you get him to trust you?" Hunter asked.

"It started when he was born," Elyssa said, brushing Leopard's glossy hide. "Mother's prize Arabian mare was bred by a mustang stallion that had escaped from the Shoshone."

"So that's where Leopard got his spots," Hunter said. "The Shoshone trade with the Nez Percé, who are the best horse breeders this side of Ireland. Their Appaloosas are famous among plainsmen."

"That's what Bill said. Mother was too distraught to listen when she discovered what had happened."

"Because the foal wouldn't be purebred?"

"Partly. But mostly because the mare was too old to be in foal. She died when Leopard was born."

Hunter whistled softly. "Did you get another mare to accept him?"

"No. Leopard was born out of season. There were no other mares nursing foals."

Silently Hunter looked at the big stud. If Leopard had gone through a tough time as a foal, it didn't show now. The horse was big, well made, obviously powerful.

"What did your mother do?" Hunter asked.

"She was going to shoot the foal rather than watch it starve, but I begged her to let me try to save him."

With a remembering kind of smile, Elyssa brushed the stud's broad, shiny barrel. Leopard gave a sigh that was almost a groan and half-closed his eyes, obviously relishing the feel of the brush.

"I washed Leopard down with a warm, slightly rough rag, acting like it was his mother's tongue," Elyssa said. "Then I helped him stand, and helped him up when he fell, and rubbed him all over with that rag and talked to him all through the day and night."

With an intensity Hunter could barely shield, he

watched the expressions chase across Elyssa's face—
sadness for the dead mare, pleasure in the foal, amusement at his attempts to stand, and above all, love for the
dangerous stud who was standing half-asleep beneath
her gentle hands.

Belinda never liked animals, Hunter realized. *Not like
this. Belinda chose a horse for its color and a cat because it matched her trousseau. I thought it was amus-
ing, then.*

Judas Priest, but I was stupid.

Still am.

*Otherwise I wouldn't be getting hard just watching a
flirt groom a horse.*

"What did you feed him?" Hunter asked, his voice
almost rough. "Sugar mash?"

"We had a cow that was fresh, because my mother
loved butter and cheese. Penny and I rigged a bottle of
sorts. At first, Leopard wouldn't have anything to do
with it."

The stud shifted his weight. He turned his head and
lipped at a strand of long, pale hair that had escaped
from Elyssa's hastily made chignon.

Without breaking the easy rhythm of the grooming,
she tucked the hair back out of reach.

Leopard stretched his neck and pulled the chignon
apart with his agile lips.

Laughing, scolding Leopard gently, Elyssa balanced
the brush on his spotted buttocks, swept up her hair in
both hands, and knotted it at the back of her neck once
more.

Hunter let out a slow, hidden breath. He tried to ignore the sudden heavy running of his blood. It would be
a long time forgetting the sight of all that silky, flaxen
hair tumbling wild and free down Elyssa's sea-green
dress.

And her hands, so quick and graceful.

What would it be like to have those hands all over me? Hunter thought.

Then, savagely, *I'm a fool for even thinking about it.*

"That's how I got Leopard to drink," Elyssa said, picking up the brush once more.

Hunter made an encouraging sound. He didn't trust himself to speak. He knew his voice would be too deep, too husky, rough with the force of the desire pouring through his body.

"I dipped a strand of hair in milk and tickled his lips with it," Elyssa explained. "After a while, he got the idea and started sucking on the hair."

Hunter looked at the big stud and tried to imagine him as a feeble colt. It was impossible.

"Within a few days I had him on a proper nipple," Elyssa said, "but he never forgot. He loves to lip my hair, as though he expects milk and honey every time."

Hunter said nothing. He was too busy thinking what it would feel like to pull apart the loose knot of the chignon and bury his face in Elyssa's clean, sweet-scented hair.

And then he would reach beneath the silk to find even softer, sweeter flesh.

Elyssa would let me, just like she let me in the barn.

God, I've never had a woman respond like that, all in a rush, her breathing as sudden and ragged as mine.

Night after night, she would be a wildfire burning for me, hot and unrestrained. I would be the same for her, burning her all the way to her hungry, sensual soul.

A hidden shudder of desire went through Hunter as he thought about it . . . the girl and the night and the fire.

In one way, at least, Elyssa is different from Belinda. Belinda was calculating. Elyssa is too reckless to be wise.

Sex would be good with her. So damned good. Maybe even worth marrying for.

Hunter heard his own thoughts and went cold.

Haven't I learned yet? he asked himself scathingly. *Did Ted and little Em die for nothing?*

Shocked and angered by his own unruly sexuality, Hunter faced again the consequences of having chosen the wrong girl as a wife, just because she made his blood run hot and wild.

How can I even think of shackling myself to another Belinda? he asked himself. *A sexy little girl in woman's clothing.*

A girl who traded the lives of her kids for a fast poke from the neighbor while her husband was fighting a war a thousand miles away.

Too young. Too spoiled.

Too weak.

But I married her, and my kids paid for my stupidity.

There was no arguing with that icy reality.

Yet still Hunter wanted Elyssa with a force that left him shaken.

It made Hunter furious—with himself, with the situation, and most of all with the girl who wore a silk dress in a stable and gave him sideways glances from hungry, sea-green eyes.

"But it was nip and tuck for a while," Elyssa said, stroking Leopard's neck with her hand.

When Hunter said nothing, she glanced at him from the corner of her eyes. The cold set of his mouth made her wince. She looked back at Leopard.

"I spent the next month in the stall with Leopard fulltime," Elyssa said hurriedly. "I kept him warm when there was ice on the marsh and the wind blew fit to freeze hell itself. When spring came I just spent nights in the stall until he was old enough to be weaned."

"How old were you?"

The harsh tone of Hunter's voice drew another sideways glance from Elyssa and renewed interest from Leopard.

"Thirteen," Elyssa said.

"At that age most girls are trying out silks and fans."

Elyssa shrugged. "I never got the hang of fans. My highborn cousins thought it was hilarious."

"Highborn cousins? Around here?"

"No. Mother's relatives. Lords of England. She hoped I would marry one of them. I didn't, but I lived with them from the time I was fifteen until I came back this spring."

As Elyssa spoke, she brushed down Leopard's muscular buttocks with quick, strong strokes.

"Why didn't you marry one of them?" Hunter asked.

"They thought everything about me that wasn't disgusting was quite funny."

"Figures," Hunter said sardonically. "You couldn't snaffle off a rich husband, so you came running home with your tail between your legs."

Elyssa's temper flashed. It had been bad enough to watch Hunter be cream-pie-nice to Penny. Taking insults from him now was more than Elyssa could bear.

"Catch," she said, firing the brush at Hunter.

Before his hands snatched the brush out of the air, Elyssa vaulted onto Leopard. Her silk skirt flew up above her knees and the scarlet petticoat seethed like flame around her thighs. Impatiently she jammed the cloth beneath her legs and urged Leopard toward the gate.

Instantly Hunter moved to cut Elyssa off from the paddock gate.

"Where the hell do you think you're going?" Hunter demanded.

"Anywhere I please."

Elyssa spun Leopard away from Hunter with a touch of her hand on the stallion's powerful neck. An instant later the big stud was cantering toward the paddock fence.

Leopard went over the fence like his namesake, not even tickling the six-foot rails with his hooves. He landed lightly on the other side and danced in place, plainly wanting to run.

Motionless, Hunter watched Elyssa. Silk skirts and petticoat climbed halfway up her thighs. Her legs were long and lithe. Their womanly curves reminded Hunter of just how taut and full her breasts had felt against him.

With no warning Leopard gathered himself, took three strides, and leaped back into the paddock. Though the horse landed only a few feet from Hunter, he didn't back up an inch.

"Have I made my point?" Elyssa asked in a clipped voice.

"What point was that?" Hunter asked.

His voice was somewhere between harsh and husky, and blood beat visibly in his neck. He hoped that Elyssa couldn't see it, or the blunt male flesh that was swelling beneath his trousers with each heartbeat.

"You were hired to oversee the Ladder S, not me," Elyssa said. "I will go where I please, when I please."

"No," Hunter said before he could think better of it.

"I beg your pardon?"

"Now, that's something I'd like to see, you begging me."

"It won't happen," Elyssa assured him gently. "My cousins and their highborn friends tried for years to break me. They had time and cruelty on their side. You haven't a chance, Hunter."

"Not enough time?"

"Not enough cruelty."

"Don't be too sure of that, Sassy."

"How long have you owned Bugle Boy?"

Hunter blinked, surprised by the change of subject.

"All his life," he said slowly. "Why?"

"He bears no marks of quirt or spur. Nor is he head-shy. He has the confidence and calm nature of an animal that has been well and gently cared for since birth."

Again Hunter was surprised. He measured the easy way Elyssa controlled Leopard without benefit of bridle, saddle, or even a piece of string.

The knowledge that she could have run off and left Hunter in the dust was galling.

Whatever else, she's a hell of a horsewoman, Hunter admitted reluctantly to himself.

"In sum," Elyssa continued, "you are rude, arrogant, stubborn, and hardheaded, but not cruel."

Leopard gave a little leap, as though his patience was at an end. Clearly the stud wanted to jump the fence again and have a good run.

Just as clearly, Elyssa did too. A slight pressure of her hand pointed Leopard toward the fence again.

"Hold it!" Hunter said. "Just because you're in a snit, you can't head off at a dead run."

Elyssa's temper slipped.

"Really?" she asked coolly. "How will you stop me?"

"Penny depends on you," Hunter said in an icy tone. "If you kill yourself racing that damned stud over rough country, Penny would be at the mercy of strangers for the roof over her head and the food on her plate."

Penny, Elyssa thought starkly. *I should have guessed. Hunter wasn't worried about me at all.*

With outward calm Elyssa concentrated on the golden grasslands slanting gently down from the mountains to the tawny marsh below. After a few slow breaths she was certain she could control her temper.

I need this arrogant male creature, Elyssa reminded herself bluntly. *I have to keep telling myself that.*

I need Hunter.

And if that means watching him court Penny, so be it. I took a lot worse in England and never sniveled, so why does Hunter's contempt cut me so deeply?

Because I want him to like me, that's why. I want him to use that black velvet voice on me.

But it wasn't something Elyssa was going to say out loud.

"Are you listening?" Hunter demanded.

Distantly Elyssa nodded. The slight motion was enough to send her loosened hair rippling like moonlight over the green silk of her dress.

"I won't work for a spoiled girl who gets in a snit at everything I say," Hunter continued.

Again Elyssa nodded.

Again the motion set her hair to sliding softly against her breasts. With quick, impatient motions she gathered up the flyaway strands and knotted them at her neck once more.

"I won't work for a girl who sulks, either," Hunter said.

Elyssa turned and looked at him.

The look told Hunter that Elyssa wasn't sulking. Her eyes were distant. They had a primitive calculation that reminded him of Leopard.

The challenging, sexy, admiring light in her eyes had vanished.

Good, Hunter told himself. *It's about time she stopped looking at me like she was wondering what it would be like to get on me and ride.*

"What are you thinking?" he asked.

Hunter wondered if Elyssa was as surprised as he was by the question. He shouldn't care and he knew it.

If the question surprised Elyssa, she didn't show it. Her face had assumed a distant, lady-of-the-manor expression that irritated Hunter.

"You don't want to know what I'm thinking," Elyssa said after a moment.

Hunter's mouth flattened.

"Just as I thought," he said. "You're still in a snit. There's one thing a spoiled girl can't stand, and that's the truth."

"If you say so."

"I just did, didn't I?"

Elyssa said nothing.

"Damn," Hunter said finally. "I hate it when a girl sulks! What the hell is going on behind those green eyes of yours?"

"I'm thinking."

"About what?"

"A simple truth."

Hunter waited for Elyssa to explain.

And waited.

And waited.

"All right," he said roughly. "What is this simple truth of yours?"

"I need a man who can sneak past the Culpeppers, control Mickey, protect Penny and myself, and get those cattle to the army. In brief, I need you, Hunter. Therefore, I will have to suffer your unwarranted tirades until I no longer need you."

The calm, clipped summation surprised Hunter. When angry, Belinda hadn't been capable of anything more thoughtful than tears, flounces, and pouts.

"Are you going to cross me at every opportunity?" Hunter asked.

Elyssa watched Hunter with level sea-green eyes.

"Are you going to insult me at every opportunity?" she asked calmly.

"Only when you act like a spoiled little girl."

"I suspect that in your eyes I am incapable of acting any other way, no matter what I do."

Hunter resettled his hat with an impatient motion of his hand.

"Are you saying that my judgment is wrong?" he asked with deceptive gentleness.

"Yes."

"I disagree."

"I know, just as I know that you disliked me from the moment you first saw me."

Hunter said nothing. If Elyssa hadn't figured out that he was violently attracted to her—and just as violently opposed to being attracted to her—he wasn't going to point it out.

"What I don't know," Elyssa added, "is why you agreed to work for me at all."

Hunter went still. He needed the appearance of being the Ladder S ramrod. Otherwise the Culpeppers would get word that the Texans who had been dogging their trail for two years had finally caught up.

"I need the job," Hunter said roughly.

"Why?"

"Money."

"I don't think so."

Again, Elyssa's cool assessment of the facts startled Hunter.

"You haven't even asked how much I'll pay you," she pointed out.

"I'll get my pay."

"By taking the ranch from me?"

Fury ripped through Hunter. The effort it cost him to keep his temper was shocking.

He, who prided himself on his discipline.

"Listen, little girl," Hunter said in a low, deadly voice, "in Texas I had a ranch five times the size of the Ladder S, a ranch my brother and I built with our own hands. I don't need to steal from orphans to get what I want."

The tangible outrage in Hunter made Elyssa's mouth go dry. She tried to speak, swallowed, and tried again.

"All right," she said. "You'll get paid three dollars a day and fifty cents for every mustang delivered to the army. Is that agreeable?"

Hunter nodded curtly.

Elyssa let out her breath in a soundless sigh.

"We'll ride out over the ranch and count cattle as soon as I pack a lunch for us," she said.

"No."

"Then I'll just pack a lunch for me."

"No need," Hunter said. "You won't be riding anywhere with me."

"Talk about snits . . ." Elyssa shrugged. "Fine. I'll take the north half."

"You won't be riding anywhere, period. It's not safe."

For a long moment there was only silence and Elyssa's patient blue-green eyes.

"Hell," Hunter snarled. "You're going to ride out as soon as my back is turned, aren't you?"

"Of course."

"Just to prove you can," he said with contempt.

"No, Hunter. To count cattle. *My* cattle."

He grunted.

"If you're so worried about Penny's future," Elyssa continued sweetly, "it would be clever of you to ride along with me so that I don't get hurt. Wouldn't it?"

Hunter looked at Elyssa's smile—two rows of hard white teeth and not one bit of warmth—and knew that he had lost this round.

"If Leopard won't tolerate a saddle and a bridle," Hunter said, walking away, "ride some other horse."

Hunter disappeared into the barn before Elyssa realized that she had won. She was still savoring her victory when the dogs started barking.

A Culpepper on a huge sorrel mule was riding up to the ranch house as though he owned it.

ᘓ6

$\mathcal{E}$lyssa's first thought was that her shotgun was in the house rather than in her hands.

But then, I didn't expect a Culpepper to come calling in daylight, brazen as a cat at milking time.

Quickly Elyssa glanced around. No one was in sight.

If Hunter was aware that something was wrong, he wasn't advertising it. The door leading from Leopard's paddock to his stall was open and empty.

Abruptly Elyssa realized that she was sitting in bright daylight with her skirts halfway to her waist. She slid off Leopard in a whirl of emerald and scarlet silk.

When she hit the ground, her knees buckled. Only then did she realize how frightened she was.

The flurry of color as Elyssa dismounted caught the Culpepper's interest. He reined the mule past the kitchen garden, ignored the house, and headed straight toward the barn. The mule moved over the dusty, hoof-scarred ground with a peculiar, gliding gait that was both fast and easy on the rider.

Three more horsemen trotted into view behind the mule. They fanned out slightly, each watching a separate area of the ranch. The men looked and acted like former soldiers.

Rebel raiders, Elyssa thought starkly.

Fear ran nakedly over her skin, leaving a cold trail of gooseflesh that even the hot sun couldn't warm.

Surely the Culpeppers aren't so brazen as to attack in full daylight, no matter how peevish the army captain is feeling toward the Ladder S at the moment.

The dogs' barking rose to a frenzy.

The temptation to run into the barn was great, but Elyssa didn't give in to it. She suspected that the raiders were like her English cousins and other predatory animals—a show of weakness only encouraged them.

In any case, her legs were shaking too much to be trusted with anything beyond holding her upright.

Hunter, where are you? Elyssa asked silently, desperately. *Can't you hear the dogs?*

Nothing came in answer to her questions, not even so much as the sound of stealthy movement from the barn.

She was alone and the yard was full of raiders.

Hunter! I need you!

Yet no sound left Elyssa's lips. If Hunter was deaf to the dogs, her own screams wouldn't make any difference.

It took every bit of Elyssa's courage to appear relaxed and confident while the breeze blew through the paddock fence and a Culpepper rode up to the barn as though he owned the Ladder S and everything on it.

The man's clothes were trail-worn and dirty. Beneath the grime were the outlines of Confederate army trousers, boots, and jacket. Like the mule, the rider was long-boned, lean, and dusty.

Unlike the mule, the Culpepper had pale blue eyes and a beard that needed trimming. His manners could have used a little polish as well. The look he gave Elyssa was as crude as a hand up her skirt.

"You the owner of this spread?" the rider asked curtly.

"Yes," Elyssa said, just as curtly.

"I be Gaylord Culpepper. I come to buy you out."

"No."

The rider's eyes narrowed. He leaned forward slightly as though he didn't believe he had heard her correctly.

The mule stamped. Its long ears twitched and swiveled, tracking the sounds of the dogs as they paced between the intruders and the cottonwood trees that lined the nearby creek.

"I ain't askin', missy," Gaylord said.

"Good, because I'm not selling."

Gaylord looked around, paying special attention to the barn. It was clear he didn't believe Elyssa would be so brave unless there was an army hidden somewhere close by.

Elyssa sincerely wished there was. But there wasn't. All she had was her quick tongue, her trembling legs, and a sincere desire to be somewhere else.

Anywhere else.

"Well, that's a damn shame," Gaylord said. "We done got our hearts set on this place, and what Culpeppers want, Culpeppers get."

"I understand your dilemma."

"Huh?"

Elyssa said the first thing that came to her mind, hoping to distract the raiders until someone could grab a gun and distract them in a more meaningful way.

"I, too, love the Ladder S," Elyssa said quickly. "I couldn't bear to leave the ranch. Surely you understand?"

"Uh . . ."

"Exactly," she agreed instantly. "You should set your affections in a different direction. I hear that the Northern Territories are quite rewarding for, er, individuals such as yourself."

"Too cold."

The temptation to suggest hell as a warm alternative was great, but Elyssa resisted it.

"Texas is reputed to—" she began.

"No," he interrupted impatiently. "We done been there. Folks ain't friendly like."

"Perhaps they simply didn't know you well enough."

"Damn mean-spirited folks, them Tejanos. Git all riled up when a man has a little fun. Track him through hell an' high water an' never give up no matter what. It's right tiresome being dogged like that, I tell you."

Elyssa tried to look sympathetic. She doubted that she was successful.

"So I'll do it yer way," Gaylord said, "though I'll take some awful funnin' from the boys."

Elyssa blinked. She hadn't expected to be able to talk a Culpepper out of anything, much less the Ladder S.

"Thank you," she said. "I'm very grateful. The ranch is my whole life."

"Ya oughta be grateful," Gaylord retorted. "Ain't every day a gal gets hitched to a Culpepper. I s'pose you want a preacher an' all thet folderol. Lordy me, them boys will just bust a gut laughin'."

A distinct sense of unreality engulfed Elyssa, as though she was looking at the world through the wrong end of a spyglass. For a moment she was reminded of the Lewis Carroll story that had been all the rage when she left London.

This is how poor Alice felt, Elyssa thought.

Perhaps I should offer to serve tea to this mule-riding Mad Hatter.

The thought almost made Elyssa laugh aloud, but she was afraid if she opened her mouth, a scream would come out. Her appearance of calm was only that—appearance.

In truth, fear was drawing Elyssa tighter and tighter.

She felt as though her bones would break if she made an incautious move.

"I didn't make myself clear," Elyssa said carefully. "I have no intention of marrying you."

"Fine by me. I don't hold with leg shackles none. But if'n it ain't me, it be Ab, an' he's a mean 'un with the gals. Little bit of a thing like you won't see Christmas hitched to him. God's truth."

Elyssa swallowed over the bile rising in her throat.

"Mr. Culpepper," she said with desperate calm, "I am not of a mind to marry anyone."

The rider nodded vigorously.

"I hear ya talking," he said. "Prob'ly best thet way. The boys is gettin' restless. Knowing a sportin' gal come with the ranch will settle them some."

"What in the name of God are you talking about?" Elyssa asked, her voice thinning.

"Well, ya ain't leaving the ranch, an' ya ain't the marrying kind, so thet leaves the sportin' life, don't it?"

Gaylord slapped his thigh hard enough to raise dust.

"Mighty fine life," he crowed. "Migh-ty fine!"

The mule's ears swiveled, then resumed tracking the dogs that were circling fifty feet out from the men, barking wildly.

Elyssa stared at the Culpepper who was crowing like a tone-deaf rooster.

"I tole Ab ol' Gaylord would get this ranch for the boys an' not raise the kind of ruckus thet brings them Yankee soldier boys on the run."

Without warning Gaylord stopped congratulating himself on his cleverness and looked Elyssa over with a blunt sexual calculation that turned her blood to ice.

"An' here Ab is always funnin' 'cuz he thinks ol' Gaylord is slow and dumb like a stump," Gaylord said.

Elyssa caught herself just as she would have agreed with him.

"Ab's always sayin' how Pappy's juice was just plumb wore out when he finally got me on Turner's littlest gal. Lordy, she was a fighter for such a young'un. Ab still smiles when he thinks on it. Course, it were his first gal. Pappy was just breakin' her in like for him."

Dimly Elyssa realized she was holding her breath. She forced herself to breathe. At the same time she worked *not* to understand what Gaylord Culpepper was saying.

The mule walked closer to the paddock fence, urged by its rider.

"Hope ya got stayin' power," Gaylord said. "Me an' the boys is plumb ready."

Warily Elyssa backed away from the fence. A show of courage was one thing. Foolhardiness was quite another.

Only a fool would stay within reach of Gaylord Culpepper.

"Now, don't go to backin' up," Gaylord complained. "I ain't gonna throw ya an' mount ya right off. I just wanna get a feel of them teats. They shore look—"

"No," Elyssa said harshly.

"Thet don't sound friendly."

With shocking speed, Gaylord shot off the mule's back and onto the paddock fence. Elyssa barely got beyond range of his long arm in time to avoid his grasping fingers.

Leopard reared and flattened his ears, plainly warning Gaylord what would happen if he came into the paddock.

Gaylord got back on his mule and looked at the stud.

"Folks say this 'un is a killer," he said.

Elyssa said nothing.

"Huh. Well, Ab had a mind to ride him, but he ain't here an' I am, and I be plain pantin' for a feel of them teats. Call him off 'fore I kill him."

Gaylord might have talked in slow rhythms, but there

was nothing slow about the way he reached for his six-gun.

"No!" Elyssa cried.

Behind her a rifle fired, drowning out her cry. The bullet landed between the mule's front feet, startling it into rearing.

Gaylord stuck in the saddle with the same ease that he had reached for his gun.

"Holster that gun or die," Hunter said.

Elyssa barely recognized Hunter's voice. There was no emotion in it, simply a cold assurance of death.

The silence was so complete that she could hear the sound of Gaylord's gun being returned to the holster.

There was a shout from one of the men behind Gaylord. He lifted his hand slowly, waving them off.

"I was just funnin'," Gaylord said plaintively to Elyssa.

But there was nothing plaintive about the calculation in his pale blue eyes. They searched the darkness where the door to Leopard's stall was.

Elyssa looked too.

Hunter was invisible.

"Fun's over," Hunter said flatly. "Ride out and don't come back. If I see you or your men on Ladder S land, I'll shoot you on sight."

With a soundless prayer, Elyssa backed slowly toward the barn. She took care not to get between the open stall door and Gaylord Culpepper.

Gaylord swore and shifted in the saddle.

"Now, don't go to hurryin' off," he said. He looked at Elyssa with pale, predatory eyes. "We ain't done yet, not nearly."

"You're done," Hunter said.

"Where'd ya come from, son?" Gaylord asked.

"Hell."

"Huh. Well, it's plain as dirt ya don't know what's

needful for a man hopin' to breathe tomorrow's air.''

"Keep that hand clear of your six-gun or tomorrow won't ever come for you," Hunter said.

Gaylord looked at his right hand as though surprised to find it creeping up on his six-gun.

Slow? Dumb? Elyssa thought wildly. *Gaylord is dumb like a fox is dumb.*

And like a fox, there is something missing from his soul.

"Listen here, boy," Gaylord said. "You don't want no part of this. The Ladder S is as good as Culpepper land. We want it. We're takin' it, an' thet's all there is to it."

"Ride out or die," Hunter said.

The combination of calm and deadly promise in Hunter's voice made the hair at the nape of Elyssa's neck stir.

Gaylord reined his mule around and headed toward his men without another word. The four riders left as abruptly as they had come, leaving a wake of dust and barking dogs.

Elyssa wound her shaking fingers into Leopard's mane and held on tightly. Now that the crisis was past, her legs were trembling so that she was afraid they wouldn't hold her.

Rifle in hand, Hunter stalked out of the barn into the pouring sunlight. The barrel of Hunter's weapon was clean but not shiny. So was the stock. There was no silver, no gold, no fancy patterns carved in wood or etched in steel.

Without a word Hunter watched the raiders until they were no longer in sight. Then he pulled a bullet from the firing chamber, uncocked the rifle, and turned toward Elyssa.

The look on Hunter's face wasn't warm. He would be a long time forgetting how it felt when he realized that

Elyssa was dead center in the middle of whatever fight might break out.

She could be lying in the dirt right now, Hunter thought grimly, *her blood all red around her and her face pale as salt.*

The thought of Elyssa lying motionless on the ground disturbed Hunter in ways he could neither name nor understand. Death was no stranger to him, nor had he been worried about his own safety, yet fingers of fear were combing over his nerves.

For Elyssa.

The silence between them grew, unbroken but for the sound of the lazy breeze, Leopard's easy breathing, and the sporadic barking of dogs.

Then Elyssa sighed, pushed away from Leopard, and looked warily at Hunter.

Bleak gunmetal eyes looked back at her.

"You little fool," Hunter said through his teeth. "Why didn't you run to the barn? You had time. Or did you like standing there taunting Gaylord while he stripped you naked with his eyes?"

The aftermath of fear and a rush of fury proved too much for Elyssa's self-control. If she had a gun, she would have shot Hunter.

He knew it. He grabbed her wrist before she could decide to smack him silly instead of shooting him.

"All right. You didn't like it," Hunter said curtly. "Why didn't you run?"

"My legs were shaking too hard, that's why."

Surprise softened the lines of Hunter's face. For the first time he noticed how pale Elyssa was. A fine trembling was running through her. Had he not been standing close, holding her wrist, he wouldn't have noticed.

"You sure didn't look scared from where I was," he said.

"Only a fool shows fear to a predator, and despite your opinion, I'm not a fool."

Hunter barely heard the words. He was much too aware of the soft skin on the inside of Elyssa's wrist, of the intense blue-green of her eyes, and of the faint trembling of her lips.

"Next time you see a Culpepper," he said huskily, "run like hell in the opposite direction."

Elyssa nodded jerkily.

The quick movement of her head traveled down the length of her hair in a shimmering wave of light. Pale golden strands slid over her cheeks. A wisp caught on her trembling lower lip.

Hunter made a sound so deep it was barely audible. Rifle in one hand, tenderness in the other, Hunter stroked the hair away from Elyssa's face without thinking about what the action would reveal to her.

The softness of her hair sent tongues of fire licking over Hunter's skin. The quick leap of her breathing and the slow lowering of her eyelids told Hunter that she felt the sensual wildfire of their attraction as deeply as he did.

Hunter's breath came out in a whispering rush that was Elyssa's name. Very gently he smoothed the wisp of hair away from her lips, caught her face between rifle on one side and his palm on the other, and slowly lowered his head.

The slamming of the bunkhouse door cut the hushed tension between them like the crack of a rifle.

Hunter jerked as though he had been shot.

He yanked back his hands and spun away from Elyssa. Without a bit of hesitation he grabbed the top rail of the paddock fence and vaulted over with an easy, feline movement.

Mickey strode away from the bunkhouse toward the barn. There was no rifle in his hands. If he had noticed the raiders, he hadn't taken any precautions against their return.

Unless, Hunter thought sardonically, *Mickey was lying low in the bunkhouse because he was worried about his own dainty little hide.*

"Morning," Hunter said. "Little late getting to work, aren't you?"

"I cut my hand. Had to wrap it up."

Mickey waved his left hand in Hunter's face. There was a dirty bandanna wound around the palm.

"Unwrap it," Hunter said.

For an instant Mickey just stared.

Whatever he saw in Hunter's slate-gray eyes was persuasive. Without a word Mickey unwrapped his hand.

Hunter never looked away from Mickey's eyes. Only when the younger man's hand was naked did Hunter spare a quick glance at it. There was a shallow scratch across the palm.

"Hardly worth the trouble," Hunter said.

Mickey looked sullen.

"Didn't you hear the dogs barking?" Hunter asked softly.

"Damn dogs are always barking."

"Maybe that's because there are always raiders back in the bush, waiting for a chance to sneak up on the ranch."

"Nah," Mickey said. "Them Culpepper boys won't move openly so long as the army is mapping out this way."

"You can bet your life on that if you like, but don't bet Miss Sutton's."

"I wasn't—"

"Next time those dogs bark," Hunter interrupted coldly, "I better see your rifle poking out, looking for a target. Otherwise a man could be forgiven for wondering about the state of your backbone."

Mickey's mouth flattened, but he held his tongue.

"Where are Lefty and Gimp?" Hunter asked.

The younger man didn't respond right away, mainly because he was watching Elyssa walk hurriedly toward the ranch house.

"Counting cows, likely," Mickey muttered.

His eyes tracked Elyssa until she vanished beneath the shadows of the porch that ran along the front of the house.

"Where?" Hunter asked.

"Huh?"

"Look at me when I talk to you."

The knife edge of command in Hunter's voice got Mickey's attention. Uneasily he looked at Hunter.

"Where are Lefty and Gimp working?" Hunter repeated curtly.

"Down to Cave Creek and beyond, like you told them. They weren't none too happy about it. Ladder S riders have been shot at down that way."

"They're drawing double pay."

"Huh? I ain't!"

"Finish the water barrels. If you still want gunfighting pay, come to me and convince me that you're worth it. If you can."

For an instant Hunter thought Mickey would draw on him. Part of Hunter hoped he would. The thought of Mickey hiding out in the bunkhouse while Elyssa faced Gaylord Culpepper alone was enough to make Hunter's gun hand itchy.

He waited for Mickey to decide. Hunter didn't expect to kill Mickey, but he sure would teach the boy that a gunfight wasn't the only way to get hurt.

While Hunter was at it, he would teach Mickey a few manners. Not staring at Elyssa would be a good place to start.

With a muttered word, Mickey went back to winding the bandanna around his palm.

"I'll be hauling water soon," Hunter said. "Have those barrels ready."

Mickey grunted.

"What was that?" Hunter asked.

"Yes. *Sir.* Damn waste of time. That old crick may be little, but it ain't never run dry, and even if it did, the reservoir would be good for a week or two."

"Work on the water barrels and leave the strategy to someone who is trained for it."

Mickey knotted the loose end of the bandanna, jerked on the knot with his teeth, and headed for the barn.

Hunter stood for a time in the barnyard, listening carefully. The fitful wind carried no sound of gunfire. If Lefty and Gimp were in trouble, they were too far off for the sounds of battle to carry to the ranch house.

I need more men, Hunter thought. *Men I can trust.*

Or at least men who will take the pay and do the work without having me dogging their footsteps every hour of the day.

So much to be done.

So little time to do it.

Hunter stood without moving, thinking rapidly, planning the work as though it was a campaign against an entrenched enemy.

In many ways it was.

From what Hunter had been able to find out, at least one of the Culpeppers had been in Ruby Valley since before spring roundup. Gaylord, likely.

There were probably more Culpeppers around, brothers or cousins or both. As they all looked alike, it was hard to tell them apart at a distance.

And at a distance was the only way a smart man wanted to see a Culpepper.

There will be hell to pay combing those boys out of the mountains, Hunter thought, looking at the rugged thrust of mountain peaks. *Pure bloody hell.*

～7

$\mathcal{L}$eopard and Bugle Boy walked side by side along the wagon road leading off the Ladder S. Silently their riders scanned the countryside for signs of cattle or raiders, or both.

Dancer and Vixen ranged out a hundred yards on either side of the riders, checking the draws for cattle. Despite the dogs' keen noses, they had found only a handful of cattle so far, none of them steers.

All around the horses there was rustling, golden grass and the occasional deep green of piñons. The piñons thickened into a dwarf forest climbing up the steep slope of the mountains. Overhead, the sky arched like an empty, pure blue bowl.

It was noon. The autumn sun was hot enough to draw lines of sweat down the horses' necks and flanks.

Elyssa was no cooler, though her riding habit hid the results better. Discreetly she tugged at the high neckline, but got no relief from the noose of cloth and lace. Slowly she opened one button, then another, and then another.

Her fingers hesitated over the remaining buttons. Opening a fourth or fifth button might reveal the lace on her chemise. If she had been alone, she would have done it without a thought.

But she wasn't alone. She was with a man who had

been a breathless, aching moment from kissing her.

The look in Hunter's eyes had been tender and hungry and baffled all at once, as though the last thing he expected to find himself doing was bending down to kiss her in the middle of the sunlight and silence.

If he still wants to kiss me, Elyssa thought, *he is keeping the secret admirably.*

When Elyssa had showed up in the barn wearing her beautifully fitted riding habit, he barely looked at her. For all that he noticed, she might as well have worn nothing at all.

Oh, well, Elyssa consoled herself, freeing one more button from its hole. *At least he won't notice if I undo a button or two. It's too hot to be a proper lady.*

From the corner of his eyes Hunter had seen Elyssa's neckline deepen one button at a time. He watched her fingertips hover over the fourth button and wanted to groan when it finally, slowly, came undone. Her fingertips began rubbing where the stiff cloth and bunched lace had left marks on her creamy skin.

Hunter tried not to think how sweet it would be to lick off those marks like Cupid washing one of her kittens.

Don't think about it, Hunter told himself savagely. *Thinking about it is not only stupid, it's dangerous.*

Like kissing her when the dust from the raiders had barely settled.

Not that Hunter had kissed Elyssa, he reminded himself. He had just come so close that he could see the surprise and then the yielding in her eyes.

Hunter knew he should have been grateful to Mickey for coming out of the bunkhouse in time to prevent the kiss.

But he wasn't.

Hunter could have cheerfully skinned the boy with a dull knife and tacked his hide to the barn to dry.

Elyssa gave Hunter a wary sideways glance. She knew Hunter really didn't want her to go riding with him. Or with anyone else. The word "foolish" had come up several times while she saddled Leopard.

The only thing Elyssa had done that met with Hunter's approval was bring her hunting weapons from the house. The elegant gold and silver designs on the barrels of the carbine and shotgun had drawn a frown, but the clean state of the weapons—and their balance—had mollified Hunter.

"Have you ever had any trouble with the water supply?" Hunter asked.

The curt question startled Elyssa.

"For the cattle or for the house?" she asked.

"Both."

"The livestock aren't a problem. There are springs all along the base of the mountains. They run even in the driest years."

"What about House Creek?"

"It's never dried up that I know of, but . . ." Elyssa's voice died.

She really didn't want to list the series of mishaps and bad luck that had plagued the Ladder S since she had come back. She would sound like she was a whiner, a fact that Hunter would no doubt leap to point out.

"But?" Hunter prodded impatiently.

"There have been other problems," she admitted.

"Recently?"

Elyssa nodded.

"Spit it out," Hunter said curtly. "What happened?"

"Oh, little things. And then one of the longhorns got into the reservoir and drowned."

Hunter's eyes narrowed to slits.

"When?" he demanded.

"It was before the snow melted. By the time we

cleaned up everything and got it working again, we were late for roundup.''

"Any problems since then?"

"With the reservoir? No. The water has been clean."

For a few minutes there was silence.

It didn't bother Elyssa. She had learned quickly that Hunter was a man of long silences and few words.

Besides, the soft song of the wind through the grass, the rhythmic beat of the horses' hooves, and the calling of blackbirds from the marsh pleased Elyssa much more than pointless social chatter would have.

Vixen trotted up to within fifty feet and looked expectantly at the riders.

"Cattle?" Hunter asked.

"No. If there were, she would drive them toward us."

Elyssa whistled a single, brief note. Vixen spun and raced toward a new ravine farther ahead of the riders.

"Quite a dog," Hunter said.

"Mac and Mother trained all of them. Mac swore they were worth five men each when it came to combing cattle out of the draws and willow thickets and marsh."

As Elyssa thought of her mother and Mac, sadness replaced the pleasure of the ride.

Hunter saw, and wished he hadn't asked about the dogs. Then he became irritated at himself for caring.

It's not like she's a kid in pigtails, he reminded himself impatiently. *Anyway, I'm here to deal with Culpeppers, not sad-eyed orphans.*

I'd better start acting like the ramrod of the Ladder S and stop thinking about its owner.

"How many cattle did you find at spring roundup?" Hunter asked abruptly.

"Less than a hundred. The men started getting ambushed. Within a week, the Ladder S was down to Mac, Mickey, Lefty, and Gimp. Then Mac was killed."

"Has anyone tried to cut the water line leading to the ranch house?"

Elyssa looked startled. She began worrying her lower lip with her teeth.

"It broke several times before Mac died," she said slowly.

"Any sign of tracks?"

"He didn't say anything about finding tracks. He just fixed the breaks."

"Was Mac a good tracker?"

"The best. That's why he came west with Dad. He was a scout and a meat hunter. Then he lost an arm in a fight with Indians and took up ranching."

Hunter looked sideways at Elyssa.

"Mac," he said. "Is that his full name?"

"Macauley Johnstone."

"Macauley." Hunter smiled slightly. "My daddy mentioned a mountain man by that name. Opened up a few trails between here and Oregon."

"That's Mac. Oddly, he was good at ranching, much better than my father. Mac knew animals. He preferred them to people. Certainly to women."

"Understandable."

Elyssa shot Hunter a look.

He ignored it.

"Mac is the one who believed cattle could winter over anywhere buffalo or elk did," Elyssa said.

Hunter's black eyebrows rose beneath the dark brim of his hat.

"There was some talk of that down Texas way," he said. "Men wanted to drive cattle north not just for slaughter, but to turn loose in Montana and Wyoming, even the Dakotas."

"What happened?"

"Don't know. They were making up herds to drive to Kansas when I left after the war."

Hunter straightened in the saddle and looked around with slow, probing glances. The only thing he saw moving was an occasional flash of black and white as the dogs worked through the grass and into the piñons.

"If the longhorns could survive a Montana winter," Hunter said, "they sure wouldn't have any problem getting fat there in the summer. Be good cattle country."

"Our longhorns have done just fine."

"You don't have Montana winters."

"Not down in the valley where the house is. But up in some of those high canyons, it gets plenty cold and the snow is deep."

"Do you winter over cows in the high country?" Hunter asked, surprised.

"Not on purpose."

Discreetly Elyssa tugged at the neckline to her heavy riding habit, trying to get some air beneath the stifling cloth.

Hunter looked once, then looked away with a whispered curse. Her skin was as pale and perfect as an oriental pearl.

"But some of the wildest longhorns stay up there year-round," Elyssa said. "One of them is a mean old brindle bull whose horns are six feet wide between the tips."

"Year-round, huh?" Hunter asked, looking thoughtful.

Elyssa nodded.

"Be damned," he muttered.

She laughed, drawing a look from Hunter.

"That's what Mac called the bull," Elyssa explained. "Bedamned. He would have shot the bull more than once, but it was Father's favorite. He loved contrary, dangerous creatures."

"Sounds like Bedamned might be a good one to ship off to the army."

"The critter is just too much trouble. If you put Be-damned in a herd, you get a stampede. Leave him alone and he leaves you alone. In fact—"

Abruptly Elyssa stopped talking, silenced by a sharp gesture from Hunter. He had pulled Bugle Boy to a halt. She started to ask what was wrong, thought better of it, and waited.

Hunter was listening with the intense stillness Elyssa had noticed when she first saw him looming out of the darkness beyond her front porch. Then he turned his head slowly, cocking it slightly from one side to the other.

After a few minutes he shifted in the saddle and urged Bugle Boy ahead once more.

"What was it?" Elyssa asked.

Hunter shrugged.

"Thought I heard something," he said. "Must have been the wind in one of those narrow ravines off up there."

His gloved hand waved in the direction of the Rubies looming up to the left of the riders.

"Do you cut meadow hay for the winter?" Hunter asked.

"Usually. The Scots and English cows Mac favored aren't nearly as good at digging their food out of snow as the longhorns."

Elyssa flapped the divided skirt of her habit in the hope of getting some air against her legs. The cloth clung like a hot compress.

"But the tame cows carry much more meat," she continued. "The longhorns are skinny as deer and twice as wild."

Hunter smiled slightly and made an encouraging noise that said he was listening. While she talked, his eyes searched the surrounding land.

Elyssa described the merits of the few Herefords the

Ladder S owned. Then she talked about the more common holsteins, the edgy, aggressive longhorns, and the bulky oxen.

All of them were part of the Ladder S herd. The ragtag assortment of livestock had come west along immigrant trails until the places where grass or water or both ran out. There the livestock was abandoned. Some were eaten by Indians, some by vultures, some survived to go feral, and some were rounded up by the Ladder S.

The extent of Elyssa's knowledge about the good and bad points of each type of cattle surprised Hunter.

Even more surprising to him was her careful plan to upgrade the quality of the Ladder S herd. She wanted to introduce more of the meaty white-faced cattle while gradually culling the milk cows, oxen, and unruly longhorns from the herds. She even talked of fencing some of the land to keep out mustangs and feral cows.

Bemused and intrigued by turns, Hunter listened to Elyssa's dreams. At a time when few westerners even bothered to cut wild hay for winter feed, Elyssa wanted to introduce and raise a European hay known as alfalfa, which was much more nutritious than meadow grass. She also had ideas for irrigating more than the kitchen garden and small orchard that the Ladder S already had.

Horses were high on Elyssa's list of dreams for the future. She wanted to raise spotted cow horses that had the savvy, strength, and speed of Leopard. When the mustangs were rounded up to deliver to the army, she was going to look over the mares very carefully. The best she would keep and breed to Leopard.

"What about a stud like Bugle Boy?" Hunter asked.

"He has Thoroughbred in him, doesn't he? And Irish hunter?"

Hunter nodded.

"Clean limbs, deep chest, powerful, yet elegant in his movements," Elyssa said, looking at Hunter's horse.

And at Hunter himself.

"Steady eyes and enough room between them for a brain, if he ever uses it," Elyssa continued. "Gentle, too, underneath all that muscle and stubborn—"

Her teasing words ended in a cry of surprise. A huge longhorn was bursting like a brindle avalanche from a ravine a hundred feet away.

Horns lowered, hooves digging out chunks of dirt and grass with every running step, the longhorn charged at Leopard.

"Run!" Hunter shouted.

Elyssa reined Leopard hard to the left and dug her heels into his barrel even as she grabbed for the shotgun that lay in its saddle scabbard. The longhorn was so close that she could see the whites of its wildly rolling eyes and hear its sawing breath.

Too close, she thought in terror. *No time to lift the shotgun. God, that bull is quick!*

Frantically Elyssa spun Leopard on his hocks and yanked the shotgun free of the scabbard. Even as she tried to raise the gun, she knew it would be too late.

The bull had already turned to hook her. Horns gleamed wickedly.

Three rifle shots rang out, so closely spaced that they sounded like brief thunder.

The brindle longhorn lurched, took one more stride, slammed against Leopard, and fell. The big horse staggered before he gathered himself and started to run again.

Elyssa barely managed to hang on.

Rifle trained on the longhorn, using his knees to guide Bugle Boy, Hunter closed in on the fallen bull. Trained for the surprise and noise and blood of battle, Bugle Boy obeyed despite the nervous flicker of his ears and his edgy, stiff-legged strides.

The longhorn was quite dead. Two of the three bullets had gone through his heart.

Hunter looked up and saw Leopard not thirty feet away, approaching with mincing strides and rolling eyes. Elyssa was pale, but the barrel of the shotgun she was holding never moved from the fallen longhorn.

Hunter's eyes went over her like quick hands, searching for injuries. He saw none. His breath came out in a rush of relief.

I wouldn't have given a wooden nickel for her chances when that damned bull came charging at her.

Never had Hunter drawn and fired his rifle so quickly. He hoped he would never have to do it again.

He might not be that lucky twice.

"I told you to run," Hunter said harshly.

"I did."

"Not far enough. If I had missed—"

"You didn't," Elyssa interrupted. "Thank you."

Hunter let out another rough breath and looked back at the big longhorn.

"I was lucky," he said flatly.

"You're an excellent shot. If you hadn't been so quick, the bull would have hooked Leopard."

"Or you."

"Yes," she whispered. "Or me."

Elyssa closed her eyes, then opened them quickly. When she closed her eyes she saw the bull charging all over again, felt again the certainty of her own injury or death.

"Thank you," Elyssa said through trembling lips.

With a curt gesture, Hunter turned aside her thanks. He was angry with himself for feeling so protective of Elyssa and angry with her for making him notice how desirable she was with every breath she took.

The longer Hunter looked at her, the harder it was to keep his hands off of her.

Whatever happened to "once burned, twice shy"? he asked himself bitterly.

Why is it so damned hard to remember that Elyssa is a wide-eyed little flirt who is hell-bent on seducing every man in sight?

Remember Mickey. She's supposed to be as good as engaged to him, and she walked by him like a dirty shirt to flirt with me.

Why can't I remember that when I look at her and want her until I can't think for the wildfire in my blood?

There was no answer to Hunter's silent, savage questions.

Nor was there any relief from the fierce arousal that had come in the aftermath of his fear for Elyssa.

"Is this one of those high-country longhorns you were talking about?" Hunter asked.

The roughness of his voice was as much a warning to Elyssa as the bleak intensity of his eyes.

Hunter was furious.

She stared down at the dead longhorn. An old, blurred Ladder S brand was on the bull's hip. An even older, unreadable brand was just below that of the Ladder S.

"It *is* Bedamned," she said, surprised. "I wonder what brought him out of the high country."

Hunter levered another round into the firing chamber of his rifle. He looked toward the willow- and brush-choked ravine that had concealed Bedamned until it was almost too late.

"Follow me," Hunter said. "Stay behind me and keep real quiet so we can hear if something is sneaking around in the brush."

Hunter turned and fixed Elyssa with a level stare.

"I mean it," he said. *"Stay behind me.* Don't go galloping off on your own no matter what happens."

Numbly Elyssa nodded.

"Keep that shotgun handy," Hunter added as he

turned away. "It's better than a rifle in close quarters."

Again Elyssa nodded. She was grateful that she had the shotgun to hang on to. Her hands had developed an annoying tendency to tremble.

She gripped the gun even tighter so that Hunter wouldn't see how badly her fingers were shaking.

Elyssa needn't have bothered. Hunter wasn't looking at her. He was backtracking the bull at a trot, his rifle at the ready. The tracks weren't difficult to follow. The bull's hooves had dug deeply into the ground with the force of his charge.

Ears pricked, eyes nervous and wary, Leopard followed Bugle Boy toward the ravine.

Elyssa was as unsettled as Leopard. She watched the underbrush as though she expected it to explode at any moment with murderous longhorns.

After Hunter entered the ravine, the tracks were harder to read. The going was rough, often more stone than dirt, with occasional patches of slick moss where the sun rarely touched.

Yet there were enough tracks to puzzle Hunter.

Elyssa saw Hunter's expression, started to ask what had caught his eye, and remembered that she was supposed to be quiet. With a muffled sigh, she sat motionless and tried to coax her nerves into settling down.

Hunter was as motionless as Elyssa, but not because he needed to settle down. He was focused entirely on the tracks he could see and thinking about the ones he couldn't see.

Bedamned, either something was rousting you or you were one crazy son of a bitch, Hunter thought.

Most livestock simply wandered from feed to water and back, leaving meandering tracks. Bedamned had moved purposefully. When the bull stopped, he didn't graze. He simply pawed at the ground, digging out great clots of earth and leaving scars on stone surfaces.

Your tracks look like you were fighting something, but whatever got your dander up didn't leave any tracks of its own.

Were you crazed, or was something after you?

If so, what was it?

And is it still around?

Hunter sat without moving, letting the sounds of the land sink into him.

Wind rubbing and shaking willow branches.

A hawk's high whistle.

Magpies talking.

The bit jingling softly.

Bugle Boy swatting flies with his tail.

Nothing out of the ordinary. Nothing to tell Hunter why Bedamned had come helling out of the ravine right at Elyssa with murder on his mind.

It could have been bad luck, Hunter told himself. *Christ knows I saw enough of that during the war.*

Good man in the wrong place.

Good man dead.

No evil plot or subtle planning or higher meaning. Just plain bad luck and someone dies.

Hunter sat for a minute longer, listening to and sifting through the small sounds and immense silence of the Ruby Mountains.

Bad luck was one thing. It couldn't be helped.

Carelessness was another. A lot of what was called bad luck was just lack of care.

Hunter wasn't a careless man.

Finally he reined Bugle Boy around. Elyssa was watching him with clear blue-green eyes. Though her curiosity was as plain as the moonlight shine of her hair, she said not one word.

"Nothing to hang your hat on," Hunter said.

"What does that mean?"

"Lots of tracks, but the bull made all of them. Guess

he just turned killer in his dotage. It happens that way sometimes, especially with bulls.''

Elyssa let out a relieved breath.

"I was afraid we'd find one of the dogs trampled,'' she said. "If they had found Bedamned and tried to herd him toward us, the bull would have turned on them.''

Hunter's eyes narrowed. He swung down off Bugle Boy and went to a patch of damp earth. He looked at the nearby tracks with great care.

And saw nothing he could hang his hat on.

The next few patches of ground he looked at were the same. Bull tracks were easy to read. No other tracks were to be found in the chopped and churned earth.

"Well?'' Elyssa asked anxiously.

"Call in your dogs.''

Elyssa whistled shrilly through her teeth, three short blasts of sound.

Very quickly the dogs appeared. They stopped fifteen feet away and watched Elyssa alertly.

"Will they track?'' he asked.

"Cattle, yes.''

"Put them on the bull's back trail.''

A few minutes later the horses were pressing farther up the ravine, following the dogs. They moved at a brisk pace, for the trail was fresh.

Less than a quarter mile up the trail, horse tracks appeared along with the bull's. Quickly the horse tracks veered off to one side. It was impossible to tell which tracks had come first, the horse's or the bull's, because the tracks never crossed.

"Call the dogs off the trail,'' Hunter said.

Three quick whistles brought the dogs back on the run.

Hunter swung down and studied the horse tracks that came close to but never crossed those of the bull. The horse was shod. Its hooves had cut into the ground with the weight of rider and saddle. It was a rather small horse.

"Recognize the hoofprints?" Hunter asked.

"No. I'm not that much of a tracker. I can tell horse from cow or deer or elk, but that's about it."

"Not much call for tracking skills in fancy foreign drawing rooms."

"Just enough to find the door out," Elyssa retorted.

Hunter's smile was big enough to show a brief flash of teeth against his dark mustache. Though he had shaved that morning, beard stubble showed darkly beneath his tanned skin.

Silently Hunter sat on his heels and looked at the tracks. He noted and memorized each peculiarity—a notch where a shoe had been nicked by a rock, a blurring where the shoe had worn oddly, a mismatch in size among the hooves, a tendency to come down hard on the left foreleg.

When Hunter finally stood, he was sure he would recognize the tracks if he saw them again. He grabbed Bugle Boy's saddle horn and swung aboard with a quick, catlike motion.

"Well?" Elyssa asked eagerly.

"He could have been here any time since the last rain."

"Three days?"

"The tracks were probably made today," Hunter said. "The edges aren't dried out."

Hunter settled his hat more firmly on his head.

"But it's damp and shady in here," he added. "Hard to say how long ago they were made, much less who made them. Probably some drifter looking for a seep to water his horse."

"Then you think Bedamned just went loco?"

"Like I said, it happens."

Elyssa looked relieved.

"I was afraid . . ." she began, then let her words trail off.

"So was I."

Startled, she looked at Hunter.

"You were?" Elyssa asked. "You sure didn't look it."

"Neither did you. A miracle Leopard didn't dump you, the way he twisted and jumped sideways."

"If he hadn't jumped, Bedamned would have hooked us."

Hunter was silent. The thought had occurred to him with gut-chilling regularity ever since the longhorn had erupted from the underbrush.

"Well," Elyssa said, sighing. "Bedamned was the only rogue bull longhorn we had, so we won't have to worry about that happening again."

Though Hunter nodded, he didn't put his rifle back in the scabbard after he reloaded it.

Unease bloomed coolly within Elyssa once again. Obviously Hunter feared the same thing she did.

Bedamned could have been chased and chivvied down that ravine until he burst from it like a bullet from the barrel of a rifle.

And like a bullet, Bedamned could have killed her.

" $\mathscr{R}$ uddy beastly fly,'' Elyssa muttered.

She swiped her shoulder over her cheek to discourage the insect, but kept milking Cream without a pause. The fly buzzed around again, then flew off to annoy one of the horses.

Milk squirted into the bucket and foamed high. The cow known as Cream munched hay with bovine thoroughness while she was being milked.

Cupid purred insistently and watched each stream of milk with covetous yellow eyes.

"You'll get yours, cat," she said, "but first I have to get enough for pudding and gravy and butter and cheese."

Elyssa milked rhythmically, eyes closed, cheek against the cow's warm flank. Slowly she began humming her favorite waltz. As she did, she dreamed of what it would be like to dance with Hunter.

Maybe I'll get Penny to suggest a bit of waltzing. Hunter would turn himself inside out for her.

That thought took the curve out of Elyssa's mouth. In the eight days since Hunter had come to the Ladder S, she had spent many hours riding the land with him. Alone.

Not once had he been other than businesslike with her.

I must have dreamed the tenderness and hunger in his eyes the day Gaylord Culpepper came calling and Hunter almost kissed me.

Almost.

Lord, I didn't know I could ache so much for something I never had.

A dream, that's all.

Just a dream.

But Elyssa knew she hadn't dreamed the moment when she had looked up into Hunter's eyes. She had seen splinters of blue and green scattered through the quicksilver, and all of it was burning with concern and desire.

For her.

The memory haunted Elyssa as much as the restless heat of her own body. More than once she had awakened from dreams that made her blush when she remembered them. Never had she lain naked with a man like that.

Except in her dreams of Hunter.

Why won't he try to kiss me again? Surely he must know I wouldn't refuse him. I've done everything but trip him to get his attention.

Maybe I should try that next.

Elyssa sighed and turned her other cheek against Cream's warm flank, humming a waltz in counterpoint to her swirling thoughts. The violet silk of her dress shimmered and burned like purple flame with every motion of her body, every breath.

Hunter is brusque with me and sweetly teasing with Penny. But if I turn around quickly, it's not Penny he's watching.

It's me.

Yet he makes no effort to court me. Quite the opposite. He's a right bastard whenever I try to draw him into a bit of civilized conversation.

Maybe he hasn't gotten over losing his wife, even though it was more than two years ago.

Silently Elyssa wondered how much time a man would need before he was ready to love again.

She was afraid it was more time than Hunter had left on the Ladder S. All too soon the army deadline would be upon them. If the Ladder S met the deadline, Hunter would leave.

Elyssa sensed it as certainly as she had sensed the brutality that lay just beneath Gaylord Culpepper's slow talk and calculating eyes.

And if the Ladder S did not manage to meet the army deadline, Elyssa would have nothing left. Not even dreams.

Don't think about it, she told herself. *Thinking won't help. Only working will.*

And praying.

"Now, if you don't look pretty as a picture," Mickey said.

Elyssa started and glanced over her shoulder. A tendril of hair floated down over her nose. Impatiently she blew the hair aside and looked at the young ranch hand who appeared whenever she left the ranch house.

Mickey was leaning over the stall door. The look in his eyes might have pleased Elyssa if it had been Hunter doing the watching and hungering.

But it wasn't.

With barely veiled impatience, Elyssa turned back to her milking.

"What is it?" she asked. "Have you lost the whetstone again? Or is it the barrel staves you can't keep track of this time?"

"I'm through with those barrels. Done told him."

Elyssa didn't have to ask who "him" was. Mickey didn't like Hunter, but he was very careful around the older man.

"Told him he could hire me at gunfighter wages or I'd leave you flat."

Without breaking her silence, Elyssa turned and shot a squirt of milk at the cat. Cupid opened her mouth and caught the liquid with little fuss and less mess.

"What do you say to that?" Mickey challenged.

"What did Hunter say?"

"That he'd let me know before the week was out."

"Then that's what I say."

"Huh."

Ignoring Mickey, Elyssa kept working. When she thought she heard him move on down the aisle, she let out a silent breath of relief and went back to humming. Finally she stripped the last of the milk from Cream's teats.

When Elyssa stood up, she put her fists in the small of her back and arched. Slowly she stretched her back, straightening out the kinks of a week's hard riding over the Ladder S, hunting for cows.

"Damn, Sassy, but you make a man want to sit up and howl at the moon."

Startled, Elyssa spun around.

Mickey was still there, hanging over the stall door. He was looking at her breasts as though he owned them.

Angrily Elyssa turned her back on Mickey and adjusted the scarf she had put in the dress's low neckline. It had been pulled to one side during the milking, revealing the rising curves of her breasts.

"Aw, now, don't go and cover them up," Mickey complained. "If you hadn't wanted me to see them, you wouldn't have worn that dress, now would you?"

"You miserable—"

Hunter's voice cut across Elyssa's.

"Mickey, if you don't have anything better to do than lean on stall doors, you can check the irrigation ditches in the kitchen garden."

Mickey straightened so quickly he stumbled. Elyssa knew that he was as startled to find Hunter in the barn as she had been to find Mickey still hanging around.

"I'd hate to lose the garden harvest," Hunter said, "just because you're in a lather over a little flirt. Get going."

"Well, ain't you just a dog in the manger," Mickey complained. "You ain't getting any, so you don't want no one else to get none neither!"

A single look at Hunter's eyes made Elyssa feel chilled.

"Take care of the garden," Hunter said softly. "Now."

"What if I got on my horse instead?"

"Then I'd shoot you as a horse thief. Every head of stock around here is wearing a Ladder S brand."

"Not every head," Mickey said, smiling maliciously. "Lately I seen a lot wearing a Slash River brand. Ab Culpepper's brand. Covers the Ladder S like a blanket, don't it?"

"Are you going to work or get off the Ladder S?" Hunter asked.

Swearing like a sailor, Mickey walked out of the barn. On his way he grabbed a shovel.

"I told you about flirting with the men," Hunter said.

The contempt in his voice froze Elyssa.

Then it infuriated her.

"I was milking the ruddy cow," she snarled.

"Not when I saw you. You were arched up like a dancer or a lover, and your breasts—"

Abruptly Hunter changed the subject.

"Stop pushing me, Sassy. I guarantee you won't like what happens."

Hunter's use of her hated nickname infuriated Elyssa.

"Then stop looking at me," she said icily. "And you do look at me, Hunter. You know it as well as I do."

"You look right back."

"Yes. Why don't you do something about it?"

"Weren't you listening? You wouldn't like it."

"Try me."

Out beyond the barnyard, one of the dogs began barking. Sharp, high-pitched, urgent, the sound sent adrenaline racing through Elyssa. She barely managed not to knock over the bucket of milk as she leaped for the gun she had propped in a corner of the stall.

Hunter's hand shot out and wrapped around Elyssa's arm.

"What do you think you're doing?" he demanded.

"Seeing what set off the dog."

"Stay here. I'll take care of it."

Elyssa started to argue, then reconsidered.

Hunter nodded curtly, took her shotgun, and stalked to the entrance to the barn. Before he stepped out into the sunlight and autumn wind, he gave a careful look around.

"Well, it's about time," he said.

With that, Hunter walked easily into the sunshine. A moment later Mickey came racing in from the garden, rifle in hand. Hunter waved him off and continued across the yard.

Three small groups of men sat on horseback close to the ranch house. Their clothes were trail-worn and dusty. Like Hunter, some of the men wore remnants of Confederate uniforms. Others wore the blue trousers of the Union.

The rest wore the buckskin of plainsmen or the fitted leather pants and broad-rimmed hats of Mexican cowhands. Men who had come from the Texas thornbush country wore leather chaps.

Remainders of dusty blue and gray uniforms were mixed equally throughout the three groups, as were checkered shirts and buckskin, leather chaps and flannel and wool. No one lined up according to North or South or plains.

The former soldiers had left the war behind them in all but one way—they were well armed. Plainsmen, drifters, and soldiers alike wore their weapons as unself-consciously as they wore their boots.

The horses the men rode came in many sizes and all colors except one. White. A white horse made a man a target against every landscape, whether desert or grassland, thornbush or mountain meadow.

Four black-and-white dogs circled the men at a distance, barking wildly.

From behind Hunter came a staccato whistle. The dogs stopped barking as though shot. As one they turned and loped off to whatever livestock they had been tending before the ranch yard filled up with strangers.

Hunter looked back over his shoulder. As he had expected, Elyssa was following him.

At least she has that scarf tucked back in place, Hunter thought.

The memory of Elyssa's half-bare breasts rising from violet silk went through Hunter like lightning through a storm, tightening every nerve in his body.

I'm going to have to come down on her like a hard rain about her clothes. The men out here aren't used to seeing a woman like her running around loose.

Hunter was having a hard time getting used to it himself.

"I thought I told you to stay in the barn," Hunter said.

"Why? There's no danger."

"How do you know that?"

Elyssa shrugged. The motion loosened her scarf, revealing a kiss-sized patch of skin low on her neckline.

Hunter tried not to think what that soft skin would feel like beneath his lips, his tongue, his fingertips. He tried not to think how eagerly her nipples had risen at his accidental touch eight days ago.

He failed.

With a silent, searing curse, Hunter forced himself to look away from the tempting bit of skin.

"I could tell it was safe the instant you left the barn," Elyssa said.

"How?" he asked roughly.

"By the way you moved."

The words stopped Hunter like a wall. He hadn't realized that Elyssa had learned to read him so well.

Belinda was my wife for years, and she never figured out anything about me.

The insight made Hunter uneasy. The longer he was around Elyssa, the more ways he was discovering that she was different from Belinda.

Unlike Belinda, Elyssa knew and understood the work that went into a ranch.

Unlike Belinda, Elyssa truly cared about the horses and cattle, dogs and cats, that roamed the Ladder S.

Unlike Belinda, Elyssa was aware of the land itself, of its beauty and its dangers. She saw the ranch as more than simply a way to pay for a fancy carriage or drapes for a drawing room that was as out of place in the wilderness as Belinda herself.

Broodingly Hunter looked at the vital young woman who had left the safety and shelter of the barn in order to stand close to him in the sunlight and dust of the ranch yard.

You better remember that Belinda and Sassy are alike in the only way that matters, Hunter told himself harshly. *They're flirts right down to the sweet marrow of their bones.*

Next to that, no other difference matters.

"Cover yourself," he said.

The contempt in Hunter's voice was like a slap.

Elyssa's eyes narrowed in anger and a pain whose sharpness surprised her. She looked down at her neckline and saw a bit of skin no bigger than the ball of her thumb. The injustice of Hunter's reaction stung her.

"Good Lord above," she said, exasperated.

"Keep your voice down!" Hunter said.

"From your tone of voice," Elyssa said softly, "a body would think I was running around half-naked."

"You are."

"Rot. If you hadn't been looking so hard, you wouldn't have seen a ruddy thing!"

Hunter said something unpleasant beneath his breath. Elyssa ignored it.

"Who are those rough-looking men?" she asked. "Friends of yours?"

"They're riders looking to be hired at fighting wages."

Worriedly Elyssa counted the men. There were eleven.

"You said only seven," she protested.

"Some of them won't get fighting wages. They're not worth it."

"How am I supposed to be able to tell the difference?"

"You aren't. That's my job."

With that, Hunter turned on his heel and went up to the riders. They had been watching the byplay between Hunter and Elyssa with interest, amusement, boredom, or envy, depending on the man.

"Howdy, boys," Hunter said. "Good to see you, Morgan. Heard you were somewhere in Nevada."

"Thank you, suh. Good to see you again . . . on this side of the rifle barrel."

Hunter's smile was so quick that Elyssa almost missed it. She looked back at the rider who had spoken and saw that his hat, trousers, and gloves were all Union issue.

His smile was very white against the dark coffee color of his face.

Silently Hunter looked over the rest of the men.

"I assume you boys know what the Ladder S is up against," Hunter said.

Some of the men nodded. Others just waited.

"Miss Sutton will pay fighting wages," Hunter said. "No booze allowed."

"What?" asked two of the riders.

"Is she runnin' a church or a ranch?" demanded a rider who looked to be younger than Mickey.

"You don't like the rules, ride on," Hunter said.

One of the men grumbled, reached back into a saddlebag, and pulled out a pint bottle that had about half an inch of whiskey left in it. He poured the whiskey onto the ground.

Hunter looked at the boy who had wondered whether the Ladder S was a church or a ranch.

"What about you, son?" Hunter asked.

"What about me?" the boy retorted.

The kid had lank blond hair and eyes that were sullen, defiant, and oddly weary.

"Morgan," Hunter said.

He didn't say any more. He didn't have to.

Morgan reined his horse over to the boy's, reached into the saddlebag with his right hand, and pulled out a nearly full pint bottle of whiskey.

"What the hell ya think you're—" began the boy.

His words were chopped off by the sight of the six-gun that had appeared magically in Morgan's left hand.

"Morgan is Miss Sutton's first hire," Hunter said calmly. "He'll be my *segundo*. Any of you boys don't like taking orders from a colored man, ride out now and no hard feelings."

None of the riders moved to leave, including the boy

who was still staring at Morgan with a combination of dismay and awe.

"Johnny, Reed, Blackie," Hunter said, nodding to three men who wore remnants of southern uniforms, "you're hired. Put your gear in the bunkhouse and your horses in the corral back of the barn."

The three men nodded and reined their horses toward the corral.

"Johnny?" Hunter said.

The slender, chestnut-haired man looked over his shoulder. "Yes, sir?"

"Any chance that your brother Alex will show up?" Hunter asked.

"Comancheros got him last year. He was chasing some story about a redheaded child. He just couldn't believe Susannah died with the others."

"Damn," Hunter said softly. "Sorry to hear that. Alex was a fine man."

"That he was, for all the good it did him."

When Hunter turned back to the waiting men, his expression was bleak.

Curious, Elyssa looked between Johnny and Hunter. She sensed the deep currents of emotion running between them, emotions that neither man put into words. She wondered if they ever had.

Or could.

"All right," Hunter said curtly. "I don't know any of you, so I'll have to ask which of you boys favor the long gun."

Five of the remaining men spoke up.

A look passed between Morgan and Hunter. The black rider lifted his reins. His wiry pony loped out of the barnyard down toward the cottonwood trees.

When Morgan was about four hundred yards away, he reined in, stood on the saddle, and balanced the bottle of whiskey on a broad branch. Glass glittered in the sunlight.

"One shot each," Hunter said. "Notch the branch as close as you can without hitting the bottle. You on the left. Start now."

The man sighted and fired with an ease that spoke of long familiarity with rifles.

Bits of bark leaped, but only Morgan saw.

"Less than an inch!" hollered Morgan.

"Next," Hunter said.

The second man fired.

The top inch of the bottle exploded.

The rifleman said something beneath his breath and sheathed the weapon with a disgusted look on his face.

"Next," Hunter said.

The shooting continued until the fifth man was done. Two of the men notched the branch less than a finger's width from the bottle.

"If any of you boys fancy yourself with a six-gun, too," Hunter said, "go to the cottonwood."

Two of the riflemen left for the cottonwood tree, including the man who had shot the top off the bottle.

Silently Elyssa looked from Hunter to the men and back again, wondering what he would do next.

"I suppose if I walk off, you'll just follow me," Hunter said.

"Of course. The Ladder S is my ranch. I'll hire the men you choose, but at the very least I have the right to see how skilled they are."

"You'll get that fine silk all dirty."

Elyssa looked at Hunter in disbelief.

"The cow took care of this 'fine silk' with one swipe of her grimy tail," Elyssa retorted.

Hunter looked at the shotgun in his hands and fought not to smile. The graceful gold and silver tracings on the barrel reminded him that it was Elyssa's gun he carried, not his own.

Fancy gun for a fancy lady, Hunter thought acidly. *Silk and fire and the kind of body that haunts a man.*

Damn!

"Stay behind me," Hunter said, his voice rough. "Six-guns are chancy things, especially if a man is in a hurry."

Without looking at Elyssa again, Hunter walked to the cottonwood where the riders were gathering. Elyssa had to hike up her skirts and all but trot to keep up with him.

"All right, Morgan," Hunter said. "Let's see if your Arkansas toothpick still has a good edge."

Smiling, Morgan unsheathed a knife whose blade was as long as his forearm. With quick, hard strokes, he carved the Ladder S brand into the cottonwood's bark.

"Back up about forty feet," Hunter said to the men. "When I say so, draw and fire."

The men backed their horses, spread out slightly, and waited. Morgan went to stand beside Elyssa. He lifted his hat in silent greeting, but his eyes never left the horsemen.

"Fire!" Hunter said.

Shots shattered the quiet. The area between the two S-shapes of the Ladder S brand exploded into leaping bits of bark. Quite a few bullets ended up outside the brand as well.

"Cease firing!" Hunter commanded.

The men holstered their guns and turned toward Hunter. He signaled to Morgan.

"At the bottle. *Now,*" called Morgan.

One of the riders got off two shots before the other men recovered and began firing. The quickest man was the same one who had shot the neck off the bottle with a rifle.

"What's your name?" Hunter asked.

"Fox."

"Well, Fox, you're pure hell on bottles."

The other men smiled.

Hunter smiled in return, briefly.

"You're hired, Fox," Hunter said. "So are you two."

Hunter indicated the riders who had been almost as quick as Fox to get back into action with their six-guns.

"What about the rest of us?" asked the kid.

As he spoke, he reined his horse over until it was all but standing on Hunter's feet.

"Oh, Lordy," Morgan muttered. "That boy must have et a full plate of stupid for breakfast."

Elyssa looked at Morgan, who was slowly shaking his head. She started to ask what he meant, but Morgan was already talking.

"What's your name?" Morgan asked the kid.

"Sonny."

"Well, Sonny, you're buying a pig in a poke."

The kid stared at Morgan.

"What does that mean?" Sonny demanded.

Morgan shook his head.

"I'll take the shotgun, Colonel," Morgan said. "Hate to get such a pretty piece all dirty."

Without looking away from the kid, Hunter handed the shotgun back to Morgan.

If it hadn't been for the profound weariness in the boy's eyes, Hunter simply would have told him to ride on. But Hunter had seen too many like Sonny in the war, good boys who had been pushed too hard by life.

Some of the boys shattered like glass. Others pushed back savagely until they were too tired to care any longer. Then they either found relief or died.

"You're not gun-handy enough for fighting wages," Hunter said calmly to Sonny. "But we need cowhands. If you want a job, take it and welcome."

"No woman's fancy man is going to lord it over me," Sonny snarled, reaching for his gun.

Hunter moved so fast his hands were a blur. Before the kid knew what had happened, he was facedown in the dirt, gasping for the breath that had been driven from his lungs by Hunter's fist.

A long sigh of relief hissed out of Morgan. He knew what every other man there was just figuring out— Sonny had never been closer to dying than when he drew on the man called Hunter.

Hunter sat on his heels near the gasping boy and waited until Sonny's eyes focused on him.

"As I mentioned before," Hunter said, "you're not as gun-handy as you think you are."

Slowly understanding dawned on the boy. He had been laid out like a fish for filleting by a man whose hands moved so fast Sonny hadn't even seen them strike. If Hunter had chosen to use his six-gun rather than his fists, Sonny would be dead.

The boy went white and began to sweat.

"Well, at least he didn't eat second helpings of stupid," Morgan said.

Hunter's black mustache shifted to reveal a slow, thin smile.

"Guess not," Hunter said.

With deceptive ease he stood up, hauling Sonny with him. Then Hunter stepped back two paces.

"Kid, you've got two choices," Hunter said. "You can apologize to Miss Sutton or you can go for your gun again."

After a shaky breath, Sonny turned to Elyssa. Red climbed up his unbearded cheeks.

"I'm plumb sorry, ma'am. I was in the wrong. I had no call to speak about you like that."

Elyssa let out a shaky breath of her own. She was still stunned by Hunter's speed.

And by his restraint.

"It's all right," she said, smiling gently. "I know it won't happen again."

"No, ma'am. It sure won't."

The men who were within range of Elyssa's smile stared, entranced by the promise of feminine warmth and tenderness.

Elyssa didn't notice the men's reaction, for she was concerned only with defusing the situation.

But Hunter noticed the other men's response to the feminine promise in Elyssa's smile. His hand drifted down to the butt of his six-gun.

The motion drew every eye.

"Any man," Hunter said, "who passes remarks about Miss Sutton will answer to me or Nueces Morgan."

"Nueces?" the kid asked, shocked again. "From down Texas way?"

Morgan nodded.

"Suffering Jesus," the kid said in a low voice. Then, instantly, "Excuse me, ma'am. I was just plumb surprised to find myself standing this close to a famous gunfighter."

"Of course," she said absently.

In truth, Elyssa hardly noticed Sonny's apology. She was too busy registering the looks of surprise and calculation that were passing among the other men.

Though Morgan said not a word, his black eyes were alive with silent laughter.

"The boy's got promise," Morgan said to no one in particular.

For a moment Hunter didn't speak. He simply looked at the kid. Then he looked at Morgan.

"You want to take him on?" Hunter asked.

"Someone's got to. Enough boys already died dumb. Be nice to teach one how to live smart."

"You listening, Sonny?" Hunter asked.

The kid nodded.

"Morgan just offered to show you the ropes," Hunter said. "You interested?"

"Suffering Je—er, yessir!"

"You'll never find a man with more cow savvy than Morgan. Listen to him and you'll be a top hand."

"Cows?" Sonny asked unhappily.

"Cows."

"Cows," Sonny agreed, sighing. He turned to Morgan. "Well, I'll be pleased to learn whatever you want to teach me. It beats all heck out of being dead."

Elyssa laughed. It was a sound as contagious and feminine as her smile had been.

The men looked at her, then looked away quickly. None of them wanted the kind of trouble Hunter could deliver.

"The rest of you men can hire on here as cow punchers," Hunter said, "or try your luck with the Culpepper bunch, or ride on out of the Ruby Valley altogether."

The men nodded.

They understood what Hunter didn't say. If the men weren't working for the Ladder S and he saw them again, he would assume they had joined the Culpepper gang.

Enemies, in a word.

"If it comes to shooting, I'll see you get a bonus," Hunter said, "but it won't be the same as fighting wages."

One of the three Mexicans spoke up in a soft, Spanish-accented voice.

"We are the Herrera brothers, *señor*. We hear what happen to your family in Texas. It is the same with our own. We do not need gunfighter pay to kill *los diablos*."

For a moment Hunter was very still. Then he nodded.

"From the look of your rigs," Hunter said, "you're top hands. The Ladder S can use you."

"Gracias, señor."

"Pick out a bunk and feed your horses. We'll begin rounding up cattle and mustangs after lunch. You can draw straws to see who has the night watch."

As the men rode off to the corral, Hunter turned to Morgan and held out his hand. Morgan shook it and then thumped Hunter on the shoulder with the familiarity of an old friend.

"Sure glad Case got you out of that prison camp," Morgan said. "It was no place for man nor beast."

"Amen."

Hoping that the men would forget her presence and continue to talk about the past, Elyssa stood very quietly. She was intensely curious about what Hunter had done before he fought on the wrong side of the Civil War.

"Heard you were set up to trail one of the first herds from Texas to the Kansas railhead," Hunter said to Morgan.

"Yessuh. Good pay, but tiresome. Some of those boys are dumber than cows."

"You'd rather fight than ride drag, is that it?"

"That's a fact, Colonel."

"Just call me Hunter. Everyone else does . . . to my face. Only the devil knows what they'll call me in the bunkhouse."

Laughing, shaking his head, Morgan turned to Elyssa and tipped his hat.

"You're a fortunate girl to have Hunter Maxwell as your ramrod. He'll take care of that Culpepper trash, mark my words."

Elyssa watched as Morgan went to his horse, glided into the saddle, and trotted off to the corral. She turned to Hunter with a considering look.

"Hunter Maxwell," she said. "Of Texas."

He nodded curtly.

"Thank you, Hunter Maxwell."

"For what?"

"Defending my honor."

"I wasn't defending a flirt's honor," Hunter said bluntly. "I was defending discipline. Lack of respect like that can undermine an outfit faster than bad food."

Anger curled through Elyssa.

"Didn't like being called my fancy man, huh?" she asked with false sympathy.

The flat line of Hunter's mouth was all the answer a bright girl needed.

Elyssa ignored the warning.

"Ah, well," she said. "You'll get used to it, *fancy man,* just like I got used to being called Sassy."

With a sigh and a discreet knuckling of her tired back, Elyssa straightened from the kitchen sink. Baking for eleven extra men was hard work, especially after a day riding the rumpled, tawny grasslands and rugged piñon forests of the Ladder S.

The first day after the men arrived, Hunter ordered Gimp to take over the bunkhouse cooking. Wisely, Hunter continued to eat in the ranch house. Gimp was a decent camp cook, but the old man's skills didn't stretch to baking edible bread. That job fell to Penny and Elyssa.

Because Penny hadn't shaken off the lingering summer ague, the work of mixing and kneading the endless loaves had been taken over by Elyssa. She also had tried to do all the laundry and cleaning, but Penny refused, saying she had to be good for something.

"How are you feeling tonight?" Elyssa asked Penny as they finished cleaning up the kitchen.

"Better, thanks. That herb tonic you fixed for me seemed to help."

"Such a face you made when you drank it," Elyssa teased.

Penny smiled despite the queasiness that had plagued her for several weeks. She smoothed her hands over the

131

faded calico of her dress and looked at her work-scuffed boots.

"That tonic tasted like boot blacking," Penny said.

"Truly? Since when have you been sampling Hunter's army boots?"

Penny giggled and shook her head.

"Honestly, Sassy, you're as unsquelchable as a puppy."

"If Ah had been the squelching kind of child," Elyssa drawled, imitating the slow rhythms of Morgan's speech, "my sainted cousins would have squelched me so thin you could read newsprint through me."

"Watch out, or Hunter will do it for them," Penny said absently.

Elyssa shot the other woman a quick glance, but Penny didn't notice. The lines of strain around her mouth and eyes became more pronounced each day.

Waiting to be driven from your home by bankruptcy or raiders wore away at a person's soul.

"Oh, Hunter is more bark than bite," Elyssa said.

"Don't you believe it. That's one hard man."

"Maybe. Yet he smiles more now than when he first came here. Have you noticed?"

"No."

"Well, I have," Elyssa said.

Penny's hands smoothed over her skirt and apron again.

Frowning, Elyssa watched the haunted, grieving expression settle onto Penny's face once more.

"It's not the ague wearing you down," Elyssa said softly. "It's waiting for the Culpeppers to attack, isn't it?"

A shake of Penny's head was her only answer.

"Then it must be Bill," Elyssa said.

A sheen of tears appeared in Penny's soft brown eyes.

"He hasn't been here but once since you came

home," Penny said. "He took one look at you, saw Gloria, and could hardly bear to sit down and visit for more than two minutes."

"He wasn't seeing my mother," Elyssa said dryly. "He was seeing red. He was furious that I wouldn't sell him the Ladder S."

Penny said nothing.

"Hasn't Bill come here when I was out on the range?" Elyssa asked.

"No."

"Odd."

"Is it? There's nothing for him here."

The bitterness in Penny's voice scraped Elyssa's already too taut nerves.

"Bill had no right to expect me to sell my home, even to him," Elyssa said flatly.

A shake of Penny's head was her only answer. It wasn't so much disagreement with Elyssa's words as it was a gesture of hopelessness.

"Are you sure Bill hasn't been here while I'm gone?" Elyssa said.

Penny's hands clenched in her apron for the space of two heartbeats, then relaxed.

"I'm sure," Penny said tonelessly. "Why?"

"Nearly every time I go past Wind Gap, I see fresh tracks heading between Ladder S and B Bar land."

"You must be mistaken."

The tightness of Penny's voice and the slight trembling of her hands told Elyssa that the subject was painful for the older woman. Elyssa started to pursue it anyway, then sighed. No good would come of causing Penny more pain.

"Ah, well, it hardly matters," Elyssa said gently. "The kitchen is clean, the lamps are full of golden light, and I feel like dancing."

Elyssa held out her hands and smiled.

"Come on," she coaxed. "Dancing makes the world lighter, didn't you know?"

After a moment of hesitation, Penny smiled in return and took Elyssa's hands.

Elyssa curtsied amid a sigh of pale green silk and golden petticoats. Then she began singing a sprightly waltz. Soon both women were swirling around the kitchen, laughing, until Elyssa's pure contralto became husky and breathless. Penny became breathless, period.

"Enough," Penny gasped, laughing. "It's all I can do to stand upright!"

"Are you certain? Dancing alone isn't as much fun."

"I'm certain."

Shaking her head, laughing, Penny lowered herself into one of the wooden chairs that ran along the kitchen table where they ate every day. Then she looked beyond Elyssa and saw Hunter standing in the doorway, watching with no expression on his face and quicksilver eyes that burned.

"You might try Hunter," Penny said. "I doubt that he would get breathless after a few turns around the kitchen."

Elyssa spun around so quickly that her skirt lifted and fluttered like an exotic butterfly. Then she whirled completely around once, twice, and waltzed up to Hunter. She curtsied deeply, rose as gracefully as a dancer, and held out her hands to Hunter.

"No," he said.

"Why not?" she challenged. "Surely a man as co-ordinated as you are can't be intimidated by mere music."

"I lost the habit of dancing during the war."

Hunter looked past Elyssa to Penny.

"However, ma'am," he said to Penny, "if a waltz makes *you* smile like that, I'd be glad to attempt a turn or two around the kitchen with you."

The words went over Elyssa like ice water. Hunter's refusal cut her as the haughtiness of aristocrats never had.

In England she had become accustomed to being snubbed by men because her fortune was lacking. Or worse, she had been pursued because titled men thought the funny little Colonial would be an easy conquest.

Elyssa had hoped it would be different in America.

It wasn't.

"By all means dance with Hunter," Elyssa said softly to Penny. "I wouldn't want to interfere with your pleasure."

Before Penny could answer, Elyssa turned and went out through the back door into the autumn night. Cool air swirled as she shut the door behind her.

Penny gave Hunter a speculative look.

"Since you no more want to dance with me than with the milk cow," she said crisply, "why turn Elyssa against me?"

The surprise on Hunter's face told Penny that he hadn't thought of his actions in that way.

Hunter said something impatient under his breath and raked his fingers through his clean, collar-length hair.

"I'm trying to break Sassy of flirting," Hunter said after a moment.

"Why?"

Again, Hunter was surprised.

"You could do a lot worse than Elyssa," Penny said calmly. "She is the sole owner of the Ladder S, young, healthy, pretty, and obviously smitten with you."

Hunter's mouth turned down in a grim line.

"She's smitten with anything in pants," he said curtly.

"No. Men are smitten with *her*. It's hardly unexpected. She has her mother's looks."

"I married one pretty little flirt. It's a mistake I'll never make again."

Sighing, Penny closed her eyes. For a few moments she looked much older than her thirty years.

"Men," she said. "Why did God make them in the first place?"

"I could say the same about women."

"Yes, I suppose a man would."

Penny's eyes opened. There was a sorrow and disillusionment in them that made Hunter wince.

"What about Bill Moreland?" Hunter asked, changing the subject.

The shock on Penny's face was as clear as her wide, dark eyes.

"What do you mean?" she demanded.

"I heard you two talking about Bill. How he used to come here but doesn't anymore. How he wanted the Ladder S and Elyssa."

"He wanted Gloria."

"Maybe he did, once. From what you say, he's got Elyssa on his mind now."

Penny's fingers clenched in her skirt. Hearing Hunter speak her worst fear aloud was like having a knife turning in her soul.

"I know how it can be when a neighbor gets an itch for a girl," Hunter said flatly. "If she's a little flirt in the bargain, you can be damn certain that itch will get scratched no matter what it costs everyone else."

The dismay on Penny's face told Hunter that she was afraid he was right.

Well, Hunter told himself sardonically, *that explains the web of ghost paths between the Ladder S and the B Bar.*

Just like the paths between my ranch and my neighbor's back in Texas, paths made by two people meeting in secret.

The explanation for the web of trails through Wind Gap didn't make Hunter feel any better. The thought of Elyssa sneaking away to shiver and cry out with passion in another man's arms nettled Hunter in ways he didn't want even to think about.

Someone really ought to teach that little flirt a lesson. From the looks of those footpaths, she already has one lover—why the hell do some women have to seduce every man in sight?

There never had been an answer, no matter how many times Hunter had asked. To this day he didn't understand why Belinda had pursued men as relentlessly after marriage as she had pursued Hunter before.

"I'm sorry," Hunter said to Penny. "I didn't mean to upset you. I know you've been under the weather lately."

Penny smiled wanly.

"Don't worry," Hunter added in a gentle voice. "Morgan and I will fix those Culpepper boys for you. No one will take your home away."

Again Penny smiled, but the lines of strain on her mouth didn't ease.

"If you'll excuse me," Hunter said, "I'll be checking on the horses. Lord knows we're desperately short of mounts. If someone leaves a door or a paddock open, we'll all be afoot."

"Of course. Good night, Hunter."

"Good night, ma'am. Rest easy. Those Culpeppers won't make a move until all the work has been done for them."

"What?"

"They might snipe at the boys from time to time, but the Culpeppers are raiders, not ranchers. They don't know one end of a cow from the other."

"Then why do they want the Ladder S?"

"They're being hunted for what they did after the war."

Though Hunter's expression didn't change, there was a quality to his voice that made Penny glad her name wasn't Culpepper.

"They'll wait for us to round up all the cattle and break the horses," Hunter said.

"And then?"

Hunter smiled slowly. It wasn't a warm gesture.

"Then the Culpeppers will make a bad mistake," he said. "So sleep easy, ma'am. We're weeks from any shooting."

Hunter turned and went outside. He expected to find Elyssa in the barn, fussing over Leopard. In the time he had been on the Ladder S, he had discovered that she often went to the stallion when something upset her.

And Hunter had no doubt that Elyssa was upset. He had seen a turmoil in her eyes that belied the coolness of her words when she left the kitchen.

The barn was dark and empty but for Bugle Boy and Leopard. Hunter lit a lantern and walked down the wide center aisle. The stallions had their heads over the stall doors as though they were carrying on a silent equine conversation with each other.

Bugle Boy nickered at Hunter in greeting. Leopard lifted his head, sniffed audibly at the man's scent, and returned to hanging his head over the stall door.

Hunter talked to both horses for a few moments before he checked the feed and water in each stall. Though it wasn't necessary, he brought more fresh water, hay, and grain to both animals, for both had been worked hard in the past week.

Leopard accepted Hunter's presence in the stall without a fuss, even when Hunter ran his hand down the stallion's sleek, muscular neck.

"Maybe Sassy is right about you," Hunter said softly.

"Maybe you only fight if a fight is offered."

After a final pat to Leopard's spotted hide, Hunter blew out the lantern and left the barn. Though his voice had been gentle with the horses, his expression at the moment was savage.

Sassy must have run off to dance with her lover, Hunter thought bitterly.

A full moon poured light over the land, caressing the darkness with a thousand subtle shades of silver. The beauty of it squeezed Hunter's heart.

Once he had courted Belinda beneath a moon like this.

And many times she had betrayed him beneath the same ravishing light.

Which one of those faint paths did Sassy take? Hunter asked the night silently. *And where will he meet her? On B Bar land or on Ladder S?*

For a time Hunter stood motionless in the moonlight. In his mind he went over the faint web of paths that began out beyond the kitchen and herb gardens. Though no one path stood out, together they bound the Ladder S and the B Bar as surely as a spider's web.

A man sitting on the ridge above Wind Gap could look out over all of those vague trails. The full moon would offer plenty of light to a sharp-eyed watcher.

Won't she be surprised when she finds me waiting up on the ridge for her to come back?

Then I'll tear a strip off of her for risking everything just for some slap and tickle with her lover.

With long, impatient strides, Hunter walked the length of the barn. Once he was behind the barn, he skirted the large kitchen garden and headed down the row of fruit trees that shielded tender garden plants from the cold winds of spring. To his right House Creek seethed and foamed musically, a liquid counterpoint to the elegant silver light of the moon.

Hunter was so certain of his goal—and Elyssa's—that

he almost missed seeing her. She was walking away from him, down one of the long rows of the herb garden. She looked ethereal, a woman spun from moonlight and pale silk, a silver wraith that left no trace of her passage on the ground.

Reflexively Hunter froze, merging his outline into that of a big apple tree. Dark clothes, dark hair, dark beard stubble, sun-darkened skin . . . Hunter was invisible.

Then he turned his head. A bar of moonlight fell between apple branches and touched his face. His eyes gleamed like hammered silver.

This time she hasn't gone to her lover, Hunter thought with harsh satisfaction.

This time.

But that didn't explain away all the other times whose only evidence was the ghostly web of trails knitting together the two ranches.

Hunter watched as Elyssa slowly worked her way down a row of herbs, caressing a leaf here, a tiny flower there. Her fingers were like pale, delicate flames moving among the plants.

The stillness of the autumn night was so complete that Hunter could hear the glide of Elyssa's silk skirts over leaves and stems, the liquid sighs of the creek, and the musical whisper of a waltz breathed into the moonlight.

Pausing, Elyssa bent over one of the rosemary bushes that grew at the end of every row of herbs. Speaking words Hunter couldn't make out, she traced the bush's tallest branches with her fingertips.

When Elyssa moved away and walked down another row, her steps brought her within a few feet of the motionless Hunter. Her whimsical words slowly became understandable to him.

"Ah, Viscount Oregano," Elyssa murmured. "How well you look tonight in your green waistcoat."

Bending low, she cupped a stem of oregano in her

hand. When she released the stem, it swayed gently, as though dancing.

"Were it not for your gently rooted condition," she whispered, "I would gather you up in my arms and waltz away the night. Think of the scandal . . ."

Smiling, Elyssa moved on to another group of plants.

"Duchess Peppermint, I did not expect you to be here tonight," Elyssa murmured. "I am honored."

She curtsied deeply, rose, and cocked her head as though listening to someone speak. Then she smiled sadly and gently stroked the edges of the peppermint leaves. Plucking one, she tucked it into her mouth and chewed lazily.

"Such a tasty fringe you have on your dress," Elyssa said. "I must have the name of your seamstress. The same as Countess Spearmint's? Ah, I should have guessed."

Elyssa bent down to brush her cheek against the waist-high peppermint plant. Then she straightened and moved on once more.

From time to time she stopped and inhaled complex herbal fragrances as though they were costly French perfumes. Then she continued on, touching, tasting, immersing herself in the scented welcome of her garden.

She didn't notice Hunter in the dense moon shadow of the apple tree. Slowly she waltzed by him. Humming to herself, her eyes closed, she went down the garden row by touch alone, calling each plant by a common name and a fanciful title.

Snippets of conversation came back to Hunter, wounding him in ways he didn't understand.

Then he did understand, and wished he hadn't.

Little Em was like that. There were no playmates for her at home, so she named every rock and tree and bird.

And she sang to them.

Grief for his dead child raked Hunter with hooked

claws, bringing pain like black blood welling in the moonlight. Motionless, Hunter let the pain drench him as he had so many times before.

Slowly, heartbeat by heartbeat, agony drained away into the darkness of night.

At the end of the row, Elyssa turned and began walking back toward Hunter. Eyes still closed, she came up the outer row of the garden, keeping herself oriented by touching herbs on one side and the trunks of fruit trees on the other.

"Baronet Parsley, you grow more robust every day. Your seeds will overflow my hands this fall, and your children will overflow my garden next year."

The fluid murmuring of the creek was Elyssa's only answer. She needed none other.

"Ah, Princess Rosemary. What an unparalleled honor. Your presence graces my humble garden."

Elyssa stopped by the plant whose branches lifted like a hundred-armed candelabra toward the moon. The pale undersides of the narrow leaves glowed with ghostly radiance. It was as though tiny, spectral tongues of fire licked over the plant.

"What a magnificent dress," Elyssa murmured. "There is none to equal it. And your fragrance would make roses weep with envy."

Skillfully Elyssa picked a sprig of rosemary and rolled it between her palms, inhaling deeply of its scent. When she bent her head over her hands, her hair burned and shimmered as though silver flames were concealed within.

Hunter burned, too, consumed by the wildfire that had ignited when he rode up to the Ladder S and found Elyssa standing on the porch, bathed in lantern light.

He had never felt a hunger so deep, even when Belinda had teased and tormented him into marriage.

I should have turned around and ridden out, Hunter

thought. *Just like I should turn around and go back to the house.*

But he hadn't.

And he didn't.

Elyssa stole another sprig of rosemary, unbuttoned the center of her bodice, and tucked the rosemary between her breasts.

Hunter forgot to breathe.

He wondered if Elyssa had seen him and was teasing him with a glimpse of her pale, perfect breasts. The sight of her gliding across the kitchen, her arms held out to him, was burned into his memory. Watching her fingers gliding over supple, scented leaves made him want to howl his frustration like a wolf.

Elyssa was a silver wildfire consuming him.

Distantly Hunter realized why Elyssa's scent was always so pleasing to him. She wore rosemary and thyme rather than the heavy magnolia perfume favored by Belinda.

Without meaning to, Hunter took a step toward Elyssa, then another, like a wild animal lured unwillingly by a fire burning in the center of night.

On the third step a twig snapped beneath Hunter's boot.

∽10

$\mathcal{W}$ith a startled sound, Elyssa spun around. In the moonlight her eyes were wide, dark, as unreadable as the night itself.

When Elyssa realized that Hunter was near, she quickly turned her back. Her normally deft fingers fumbled with the tiny buttons on her bodice as she tried to fasten it up once more.

"What are you doing out here?" Elyssa asked, her back still turned to Hunter. "I thought you'd be waltzing with Penny."

"I wanted to see who you were meeting."

"Meeting? In the garden? At night?"

"Yes," Hunter said.

"Why on earth would I do that?"

"For a little . . . *conversation*."

The last stubborn button finally allowed itself to be pushed back through its hole.

Elyssa took a swift breath to collect herself. Then she turned and confronted the very man who had driven her to the solace of her garden in the first place.

"Clever of you to guess," she said.

Hunter's mouth flattened.

"A little civilized conversation is so hard to find

lately," Elyssa continued, her voice low and artificially sweet.

"Hoping to meet Mickey?" Hunter asked with false calm. "Or is it Bill you're pining for?"

"I was 'pining for' a bit of peace and quiet. People can be so trying."

"Women in particular," Hunter retorted.

"I was thinking of one man in particular. A man who is rude without reason. Abrupt. Impossible. *And dead wrong.* Surely you, of all people, understand my need?"

"Conversation," he said.

"Words," she agreed. "One after another. Pleasantries. Gallantries. Foreign to you, I'm certain, but not to my garden."

"You talk to your plants."

"Kindly."

Hunter struggled not to smile. He almost succeeded.

"I also weed, prune, mulch, fertilize, water, and generally pamper them to the best of my abilities," Elyssa said.

"I noticed."

"Remarkable."

Hunter ignored the barb.

"Whenever things upset you," he said slowly, "you come to the herb garden, don't you?"

"It's a habit I picked up in England. I spent so much time in the garden they called me a peasant, among other things."

Silence gathered while Hunter tried not to stare at the five buttons that had been undone so that a sprig of rosemary could lie in the velvet shadow between Elyssa's breasts.

When he spoke, it was without thinking.

"Who is Bill Moreland to you?" Hunter demanded.

"My father's stepbrother."

"No relationship?"

"As I said, my father's—"

"Stepbrother," Hunter finished curtly. "No *blood* relationship."

"In a word, none. I used to call Bill an uncle, but it was a courtesy title."

Hunter's eyes narrowed as he thought about the reasons why a girl might no longer call a man her uncle. Sex came to mind first.

"So Bill is a courtesy uncle?" Hunter asked.

"Yes."

"Too bad. With the Culpepper gang, you need something with more grit than a 'courtesy uncle' has to offer."

"Something such as you?" Elyssa asked acidly.

The corner of Hunter's mouth lifted in a smile as narrow as his eyes.

"No, Sassy. I'm a gentleman."

Elyssa laughed.

"A gentleman," she repeated sardonically. "How kind of you to point it out. Somehow I had managed to overlook it entirely."

The cool dismissal in Elyssa's tone rubbed Hunter's already raw nerves.

"Leash that tongue of yours," Hunter said, "or I'll take what you've been promising me."

"I never promised you anything but wages."

"Didn't you?" he taunted. "What about when you waltzed up to me in the kitchen and stood so close I couldn't breathe without taking your own breath inside me?"

"Do forgive me," she said recklessly. "I'll be certain never to ask you to dance again!"

"If I weren't a gentleman," Hunter said bluntly, "I would have taken the invitation in your smile and kissed you breathless."

"No man has ever made me breathless."

Hunter smiled.

Abruptly Elyssa realized that baiting Hunter was not like baiting her English cousins. They hadn't sent an elemental female awareness through her nerves.

Hunter did.

Especially when he stood as he was standing now, so close that his heat radiated through her clothing, sinking into her very flesh.

"Dance with me," he said softly.

"I thought you had lost the ability."

"So did I."

With that Hunter bowed and held out his hand as though they were on a polished dance floor with silken ladies and well-dressed men all around.

Automatically Elyssa put her hand in Hunter's. Without speaking he led her toward the stream, where cottonwood leaves whispered and trembled with each breath of wind. Beneath one huge old tree the ground was clear of everything but fallen leaves. They made a hushed carpet underfoot.

"I'll stumble," Elyssa said shakily.

"I'll catch you."

Hunter turned and faced her. Deliberately he took Elyssa's left hand and put it against his chest. Only then did he slide his right hand from the curve of her waist to the small of her back.

The intimacy of the act made Elyssa's mouth go dry. Other men had held her like this and she had been unmoved. Some had tried to hold her closer, which had only annoyed her.

None of those men had made her pulse race. None of them had made her dizzy with a touch, a glance. None of them had made her feel lighter than fire, more delicate, more mysterious.

Hunter did.

For Elyssa it was like being in one of her restless

dreams—darkness and moonlight, the scent of rosemary and the rippling murmur of water, Hunter's eyes watching her with a hunger that made her heart turn over.

"Sing for us," he whispered.

At first Elyssa's throat refused to cooperate. She swallowed and tried again.

The husky, hesitant strains of a waltz lifted into the night.

Hunter gathered Elyssa into his arms and began to dance as though in a ballroom suffused with laughter and lamplight. Gracefully she followed his lead, despite the uneven ground.

When Elyssa stumbled, she felt the power of Hunter's lean body. He lifted her without effort, breathed a word over her hair, and set her back on her feet once more in a swirl of silk.

"What did you say?" she whispered.

"Nothing."

"But you did."

Without warning Hunter turned in a full circle, then another, then a third, spinning Elyssa with him until she was breathless. She smiled, watching him with yearning in her eyes and a song on her lips.

"I dreamed of this," Elyssa said huskily.

"Of dancing?"

"Dancing. Moonlight. You."

She felt the subtle tightening of Hunter's body.

"I'm sorry," she said. "My cousins berated me for not being coy."

Hunter didn't want to talk about how Elyssa's loose conduct had shocked her proper English cousins. He didn't even want to think about it.

He just wanted to enjoy a bit of it himself before he called a halt and taught Elyssa that all men couldn't be controlled by the sleek, hot promise of a woman's body.

With an eagerness Hunter barely concealed, he allowed his arms to do what they had been wanting to do for a long time. Slowly he pulled Elyssa close, then closer still.

A subtle stiffening overtook her body as his thighs pressed against hers though layers of cloth.

"Why fight me?" Hunter whispered. "You sense the wildfire waiting for us as clearly as I do."

"What?"

"This."

Very carefully, Hunter fitted his mouth to Elyssa's.

The first smooth touch of her lips burned him so fiercely that it was all he could do not to groan aloud. The depth of his hunger shocked him.

Hunter wanted to thrust his tongue between Elyssa's lips and demand entrance to her mouth, but only a fool revealed the extent of his hunger to a flirt. Hunter wasn't a fool.

All he permitted himself was a chaste kiss . . . and a sweet nibbling along the line of Elyssa's mouth that was just short of a plea.

The catch and sigh of her minty breath over Hunter's lips was as heady as whiskey to his heightened senses. His arms tightened just a bit more, pulling Elyssa closer to the hungry contours of his body.

When she stiffened again, Hunter forced the coiled muscles in his arms to relax while his mouth sipped teasingly at hers. Elyssa shifted slightly in his embrace, finding a new balance.

Each brush of her body against his was fuel heaped on the sensual fire burning inside Hunter. His teeth closed with fierce restraint on the curve of Elyssa's lower lip. Holding the flesh gently captive, he traced it with the tip of his tongue. Passion and the taste of mint made him almost light-headed.

Hunter felt the trembling that went through Elyssa at the caress. He stroked her again with his tongue, hungry for another intimate taste of mint. Then he released her lower lip, tasting its warmth and satin underside as he did.

The mint-scented sigh that rushed over Hunter was an invitation he couldn't refuse. His tongue followed Elyssa's indrawn breath between her teeth, caressing her with an intimacy that drew a husky sound from the back of her throat.

Triumph and desire leaped equally in Hunter when he felt the telltale softening of Elyssa in his arms. Though he wanted to thrust into her, filling her with his heat and savor, he forced himself to continue the slow seduction of her mouth as though he were only casually involved in their mutual sensuality.

A civilized gentleman playing with elemental fire.

Hunter's teasing, restrained caresses both intrigued Elyssa and made her impatient for something she couldn't name. She knew it existed, though.

She had just discovered its fiery forerunners in the discreet, repeated glide of Hunter's tongue over hers.

Instinctively Elyssa knew she must get closer to Hunter. Where before she had stiffened when he pulled her against him, now it was her arms tightening, her body urging intimacy with his. Her hands shifted, her arms wound around his neck, and she leaned against his strength.

The luxurious, unexpected pleasure of matching her body with Hunter's drew another husky sound from Elyssa's throat. In the space of a hushed breath his arms hardened, shifted, tightened, dragging her so close that she couldn't breathe.

Elyssa didn't care. The taste of Hunter was more potent than wine, more complex, utterly untamed. She yielded her mouth to him and took his in turn. Her tongue returned the intimacy she had just learned from him, rubbing over his in a sensuous dance that took the world from beneath her feet.

The intensity of the kiss was like nothing Elyssa had ever experienced. Hunter was heat and lightning and hot caresses consuming her.

And she was fire.

Hunter said something dark against Elyssa's lips and was answered by the white flash of her teeth. Recklessly she caught his lower lip between her teeth. The exquisite, raking caress she gave Hunter drew a thick sound from his chest.

Instantly Elyssa released his lip.

"I didn't mean to—" she began.

She got no further. Hunter's mouth came down hard over hers, his tongue shot deep within, and he held her as though he wanted to sink through her flesh into her very bones.

At first Elyssa simply yielded to the hard luxury of Hunter's body. Then she fought for the embrace, struggling to get closer to him, closer, needing that closeness with an intensity that would have shaken her had she realized it.

Yet no matter how Elyssa twisted, no matter how she dragged her body over Hunter's, she couldn't get close enough to him to satisfy the passionate demands of her own flesh.

It was the same for Hunter. He was rigid with desire, his whole body flexed and hard, his mouth almost bruising in its search for a deeper joining. His hands swept from Elyssa's shoulders to her hips. His fingers sank into the taut, yielding flesh.

The sound of surprise and pleasure she made at the back of her throat nearly brought Hunter to his knees. He repeated the caress and was rewarded again by a throaty cry and a more complete softening of her body against his.

When Hunter's long fingers slid from Elyssa's hips to her ribs and then to her breasts, she stiffened in surprise.

Sudden pleasure drenched her, left her trembling, aching. She twisted hungrily, increasing the pressure of his hands on her breasts, for she sensed instinctively that he would soothe their aching.

Hunter said something dark and hungry. Never had a woman been like this for him, matching his sensuality, demanding his caresses, *needing* him.

Knowing he shouldn't, not willing to stop himself, Hunter began undoing the tiny buttons on Elyssa's bodice. While he worked over the buttons, his mouth joined with hers in an elemental intimacy that was as new to him as it was to her.

When the final button came undone, the fragrance of rosemary swirled up from her heated skin.

It was like breathing fire.

The sound Hunter made was of a man in torment. He wanted to kiss the nipples that had risen so swiftly at his touch, but he couldn't force himself to end the wild mating of his mouth with Elyssa's.

Distantly Elyssa understood that her dress was undone, her chemise was in disarray, and Hunter's hands were caressing her bare breasts.

She didn't care about her nakedness. All she wanted was to have the aching in her body be answered by Hunter's soothing, inciting, consuming caresses.

Hunter tore his mouth from Elyssa's and lifted her swiftly. The fragrance of rosemary was all around his face. He breathed it in, worshipped it, and suckled a soft breast whose nipple drew up hard against his tongue.

The coolness of moonlight and night against Elyssa's heated skin was like a benediction to her.

And Hunter's mouth was a sultry paradise.

Wildfire raced through Elyssa, shaking her, burning her. Every breath she took was a hungry sound, a sensuous whimper, a husky demand.

Hunter felt the night turning to fire around him. He

wanted nothing more in life than to release his restraint and sink into the heart of wildfire and beyond, into a burning land he had never known before, yet had hungered for all of his life.

He knew with utter certainty that such a world was here, finally, within reach. Within his arms. Burning.

For him.

And Hunter was on fire for her in a way far more dangerous than anything he had felt with Belinda.

The knowledge was like being dropped into ice water.

With a savage curse Hunter set Elyssa back on her feet. She stumbled and clung more tightly to him. He dragged her arms from around his neck and set her at arm's length.

"Hunter?"

Elyssa's dazed, husky voice undermined his determination. The sight of her creamy breasts and taut, hungry nipples nearly undid him.

The realization that he was so much within Elyssa's sensual grasp brought control to Hunter as nothing else could have.

"Damnation."

Self-discipline returned to Hunter in an icy rush. Along with it came scorn—at himself for his lack of self-control, at Elyssa for tempting him so mercilessly, and at his own body for being so easily and totally aroused by a little flirt.

When Hunter reached for Elyssa once more, she put her arms around his neck and lifted her face for one of the hot, drugging kisses she had just learned to lose herself in.

Hunter turned his face aside and removed Elyssa's arms from around his neck.

"That's enough," he said roughly.

Elyssa started to speak. No words came.

"Button up your dress before someone comes out of the bunkhouse," Hunter said.

Confused, off balance, uncertain, Elyssa just looked at Hunter. In the moonlight his eyes were as clear and cold as a winter sky.

"I don't understand," she whispered.

With an impatient curse, Hunter straightened Elyssa's chemise over her breasts. The brush of her taut nipples against his fingers made her breath break.

"H-Hunter?"

Elyssa's husky whisper tempted Hunter beyond endurance, as did her satin skin and hard-tipped breasts. With abrupt motions he began fastening her bodice.

"Fun's over," he said curtly. "I'm through fooling around in the moonlight with an experienced little flirt."

"I'm not a—"

"The hell you aren't," Hunter interrupted roughly. "You like getting all hot and bothered and having your breasts kissed. No innocent girl would have let me do that."

The flush that suffused Elyssa's cheeks was visible even in moonlight. She looked down at her bodice. The sight of Hunter's long fingers buttoning her back into her dress sent an odd weakness through her bones.

"I've never done this," Elyssa said huskily. "You're the first. Surely you know that!"

"Don't bother with all the lies about how I'm different from the others. I'm not a boy. I don't need lies to feel important."

Confusion, frustration, and flat-out irritation replaced desire in Elyssa. She put her hands on her hips.

"Why won't you listen to me?" she demanded.

"Keep your voice down unless you want to put on a show for the bunkhouse."

"You're acting like I'm the one who started all this," Elyssa whispered fiercely. "You did! I didn't have the least idea what you—what I—what we—*damn.*"

"Uh-huh," Hunter said, unimpressed.

He fastened the last button and stepped back, grateful to be finished. The feel of Elyssa's silky breasts was branded on his hands. His skin burned with the memory of her heat.

"I know it comes as a surprise to a flirt like you," Hunter said curtly, "but some men can't be brought to heel by a girl's soft body, no matter how experienced she is at love play."

"The only 'experience' I have is what you just gave me!"

"Are you saying," Hunter drawled sardonically, "that I'm so damned irresistible to you that you get all hot and bothered at a few kisses?"

Abruptly Elyssa remembered the lessons her English cousins had taught her. Her reckless temper cooled instantly.

"I'd be a fool to admit that, wouldn't I?" she whispered.

"Fool or a liar. Either one isn't guaranteed to attract a man."

"Really? Is that why you were all over me like a summer rash?"

Hunter's mouth tightened.

"You wanted me, Hunter." Elyssa looked pointedly at the fit of his trousers. "You still do."

The reminder of just how close he had come to losing control didn't help Hunter's mood one bit.

"Wanted *you?*" Hunter shrugged. "I wanted a woman, period. You were handy."

"I don't believe you."

"You should."

"Why? It's not true. You don't look at Penny the way you look at me, and she's a woman."

"Hell," Hunter snarled. "Give it up, Sassy."

"Give up what? The truth?"

"The truth is that a man no more cares who he eases his ache with than a stallion asks the pedigree of a mare before he mounts her."

Elyssa's breath came in hard. She fought not to give in to the emotions tearing her apart. Her only consolation was that Hunter, despite his denials, had been as involved in the passionate embrace as she was.

If all Hunter had in mind was lust, he would have kept on undressing me, Elyssa told herself. *God knows I wouldn't have stopped him.*

The realization of her own complex hunger for Hunter dismayed Elyssa. She had never been this vulnerable, even when she was a frightened fifteen-year-old thrown on the mercy of cousins who had no kindness in them.

How long is it going to take for Hunter to get over his wife and admit that he's falling in love with me? Elyssa asked herself fearfully. *He's so hardheaded.*

There was no answer to Elyssa's troubling question, unless it was Hunter's broad back as he headed toward the dense shadows of the barn.

Elyssa shivered and rubbed her arms to chase away a chill that had nothing to do with the night air. She watched Hunter until she couldn't separate him from the overwhelming darkness of the night itself.

With hesitant steps, Elyssa turned to her garden once more, taking what solace she could in the fragrant herbs.

For several days Hunter avoided being alone with Elyssa. She told herself it was a sign of victory.

Hers.

Hunter doesn't want to admit it, Elyssa assured herself, *but he has strong feelings toward me.*

And it's more than just lust.

Part of Elyssa believed what she was telling herself.

And part of her knew that she was whistling in the dark as she walked past a graveyard that she feared might hold her dreams.

Unhappily Elyssa shifted in the saddle. Her very bones ached from the constant riding. But at least there were no flapping skirts to deal with anymore.

She and Penny had ripped apart an old riding habit and thrown out the petticoats. The heavy black silk of the top still fit like a shadow, but she had narrowed the fullness around each leg until the skirt was little more than loose pants. One of Penny's old wool-lined buckskin jackets completed Elyssa's outfit.

With her hair tucked beneath her hat, Elyssa looked enough like a man from a distance that Hunter had quit complaining about dragging her all over the landscape like a fancy lure.

Elyssa reined Leopard around a fresh pile of rubble that had collected at the bottom of the gully. The stones and mud and brush had come down the steep slope of the ravine in a small avalanche during the last big rain.

It was a common problem during the monsoon months. The rain came in torrents, boiled down the mountain slopes, hurtled through ravines, and spilled into the marshland out at the edges of the ranch. Often, big chunks of the various ravines came down with the rains.

Elyssa stood in the stirrups, looking for any sign of cattle amid the brush and piñons. The dogs had come up this narrow, damp ravine and not come back.

She wasn't worried about the dogs. They were fully capable of working alone. Probably they had scrambled up out of the bottom of the ravine to search another of the thousand nameless gullies where cattle fed and sheltered.

As Elyssa settled into the saddle once more, her thoughts turned again to the moonlit garden. Though Hunter's embrace had lasted only a few moments, those moments had turned her world upside down.

No man with only lust on his mind would have kissed me so tenderly at first. And then so wildly.

And then stopped.

Just stopped.

A blush crept up Elyssa cheeks. Part of the color came from embarrassment at the memory of how wanton she had been in Hunter's arms. Part of the flush was anger at what Hunter had said while he buttoned her bodice.

And most of the heat in Elyssa's cheeks came from passion, pure and deep and potent.

Without warning Leopard's head came up hard. Ears pricked, he stood motionless for an instant.

With an odd, sighing grumble, a piece of the rim slumped away from the side of the ravine.

The stallion spun on his hocks, leaped, and lunged frantically up the steep slope on the side opposite from the avalanche. The abrupt, lurching movements unseated Elyssa. Without knowing it, she screamed. The scream was cut off when she hit the ground and tumbled head over heels.

Even before Elyssa stopped rolling, she sensed that she was safe from the avalanche. The stallion's catlike quickness had already taken her beyond the tangled rush of mud and stone that was sweeping down the ravine.

Elyssa's chilling scream brought Hunter at a dead gallop from the next gully to the north, spurring Bugle Boy every step of the way. What he saw when he entered the ravine was a tangle of debris, a spotted stud standing free of the mess, and an empty saddle.

"Elyssa!"

Nothing answered his cry.

A fear gripped Hunter that was like nothing he had ever felt. Heedless of the danger to himself, he sent Bugle Boy along the ragged, treacherous edge of the landslide.

Elyssa can't be buried underneath all that.

She can't be.

But she very well could, and Hunter knew it better than most men. The war had taught him how indifferent death was to human emotion.

"Sassy! Where are you?"

This time a faint groan answered Hunter's call. He reined Bugle Boy around with a fierce movement and sent him scrambling over to the far side of the ravine.

Elyssa lay on her back, tangled among willows. Her arms were flung out and her eyes were closed.

Before Bugle Boy could come to a lunging stop, Hunter kicked free of the stirrups and knelt by Elyssa's side. He could see that she was struggling for breath. At first it reassured him.

Then it frightened him.

"Sassy?" Hunter asked gently. "Honey? Where does it hurt?"

At first Elyssa thought she was in bed, dreaming.

Surely she couldn't be awake and hearing such tender concern in Hunter's voice.

She opened her eyes, prepared to be disappointed. The concern on Hunter's face was even greater than in his deep voice.

Shakily Elyssa caught his face between her hands and smiled despite the pallor of her lips. Knowing that Hunter cared about her was a warmth stealing through the chill in her bones.

"I'm—fine," she said raggedly.

As Elyssa spoke, she stroked Hunter's face. It was meant as a gesture of reassurance, but it quickly became something more.

She loved the masculine texture of the stubble that lay beneath his freshly shaved skin. Her pleasure showed in her lingering touch, in her face, in her blue-green eyes searching his.

Hunter took a breath that was almost as jerky as Elyssa's.

"You screamed," he said hoarsely.

"I—fell. Knocked—the wind—right out."

"You don't hurt anywhere?"

She shook her head. "Just—here."

Hunter followed the line of Elyssa's fingers to a point right below her breasts.

"Here?" he asked.

He brushed the back of his fingers over Elyssa's breastbone.

Her quickly indrawn breath owed nothing to pain and everything to the memory of Hunter's mouth caressing her breasts.

"Hunter," Elyssa whispered. "I—"

With a throttled sound, Hunter lowered his mouth and took her trembling lips in a kiss that he meant to be comforting.

And it would have been, if she hadn't moaned and shivered at the first touch of his lips. The kiss changed in an instant, becoming hard rather than gentle, demanding rather than comforting.

Elyssa didn't care. She put her arms around Hunter's neck and lifted herself into his embrace. The feel of his body against hers made her moan again. The adrenaline of fear flashed into another kind of response.

Wildfire raced through Elyssa, burning her until she moaned once more.

It was no different for Hunter, wildfire consuming him, making him forget all the reasons why he must control himself.

Wrong girl.

Wrong time.

Wrong everything.

Yet Hunter let himself be pulled down on top of Elyssa. Then he fitted himself to her until he lay between her legs. Every swift, hard movement of his hips told of his arousal, and every movement of his tongue was a blunt statement of his intent.

Hunter's hand swept up between Elyssa's legs until he held the hot center of her in his palm. His hand flexed and she gasped, arching up into the unexpected caress.

Even through layers of clothing, Elyssa's heat shocked Hunter, delighted him, made him shudder with raw need. He cursed as he searched for a way through her clothes.

And as he searched, he caressed.

"Hunter," Elyssa said brokenly. "Oh, Hunter, what are you doing to me?"

"What does it feel like?" he asked, his voice thick.

"Heaven."

Hunter shuddered as a bolt of desire went through him, a pleasure just short of pain.

Elyssa twisted slowly against Hunter's hand, increasing the sensuous pressure of his palm between her legs.

"Pure . . . wild . . . heaven," she said.

Hunter took Elyssa's mouth again, grinding against her, desperate for her. The ragged sounds of pleasure she made drove him like a whip.

Sanity returned in the form of three spaced rifle shots.

With an effort that left him shaken and furious with both of them, Hunter pushed away from Elyssa.

Blindly she reached for him. He grabbed her hands.

"Stop it!" he hissed.

At first Elyssa didn't understand.

"What?" she asked, dazed.

"Stop chasing after me," Hunter said in a raw voice.

"But—"

"Unless you want a roll in the hay," he said, ignoring Elyssa's attempt to speak.

"What?"

"This!"

Hunter slid Elyssa's hands down his own body until they caressed the rigid, hot flesh she so easily aroused in him.

Elyssa's eyes flew open.

"If you want a fast roll," Hunter said with deadly contempt, "I'm ready, willing, and by-God able to oblige. But that's all it will be, Sassy. Fast sex."

Hunter thrust Elyssa's hands away and went to Bugle Boy. He pulled his rifle from the scabbard. An instant later he fired three rounds into the air.

"Get up," Hunter said.

"What?"

"Get up! I'm warning you, Sassy. If you push me into touching you right now, I'll take you where you lie on the ground and to hell with whoever rides up."

Elyssa scrambled to her feet with more speed than grace. She was shaking with a combination of anger, hunger, and the aftermath of fear.

"You wanted me as much as I wanted you!" she snapped.

"Not quite. I stopped. You wouldn't have. Next time I won't, Sassy. I'll give you what you're begging for. Count on it."

"Fancy man, I wasn't begging for anything!"

"The hell you weren't. You were twisting and crying and—"

The sound of a horse galloping closer cut off Hunter's incautious words.

He was grateful. The memory of just how hot Elyssa had been was bad enough. Talking about it made him ache to his back teeth.

"Can you ride?" Hunter said through clenched teeth.

As an answer, Elyssa turned her back on him and walked to Leopard.

Hunter let out a quiet sound of relief when he saw that she didn't limp.

So help me God, next time I'll take what she's offering, Hunter vowed.

It's not like she's a virgin looking for a husband. She's an experienced little flirt who is no better than she has to be.

And in bed, she would be damned good.

"I'm going to check on something," Hunter said. "Mount up, but stay here."

Elyssa didn't respond.

"Morgan will be along in a few minutes," Hunter said. "Wait for him."

Silence.

"Do you need help mounting?" Hunter asked reluctantly.

Without a word Elyssa positioned Leopard on the downhill side of her. She got into the saddle with less than usual grace, but she got on alone.

"You better be over your sulk when I get back," Hunter said, swinging on board Bugle Boy. "I can't abide sulking."

"Fancy man, when I have something to say to you, you'll be the first to know."

Hunter's mouth flattened. He reined Bugle Boy around and headed up the far side of the ravine. Soon he was out of sight among the boulders and piñons.

He quickly found what he had hoped not to find—signs that another rider had waited at the lip of the ravine. After a quick reconnoiter to be certain the man was gone, Hunter went back to the place where the rider had waited.

Dismounting, Hunter sat on his heels as the other rider had. The boot tracks the man had left were quite plain, as were the tracks of the man's mount grazing aimlessly at the top of the ravine. Hunter had seen those horse tracks before, in the ravine where Bedamned had been before he burst out and tried to gore Elyssa.

There were marks along the rim of the ravine. The man had pried at a group of bounders on the unstable rim of the ravine. Then he had stood back and watched while boulders, brush, and earth hurtled down toward Elyssa.

That murderous son of a bitch, Hunter thought.

Rage ran through Hunter, a rage as great as the day when he learned how his children had died.

And why.

Grimly Hunter mounted and backtracked far enough to assure himself that the rider had left the scene in one hell of a hurry. Eyes narrowed, Hunter judged the direction the rider had taken.

Hunter wanted to follow, but he needed to be certain

Elyssa was safe. With a searing curse, he reined Bugle Boy back down the ravine.

Morgan came riding up the gully at a canter.

"Yo!" Hunter called.

"Got something to show you, suh," Morgan shouted. "Next ravine to the north."

"I'll meet you there."

With eyes that glittered like blue-green gems, Elyssa watched Hunter vanish back into the piñons. The man could set fire to her body—and her temper—with maddening ease.

But I'm getting to you, too, you stubborn son of a Missouri mule, Elyssa told herself with satisfaction. *You get on your high horse and get all insulting and then you ignore me, but I know better.*

I've felt how much you want me.

The memory of how Hunter had felt beneath her hands made Elyssa's breath shorten and her cheeks flame.

Morgan reined in beside Leopard.

"Is something wrong?" Elyssa asked him.

"Nothing you need to worry about, ma'am. Just a contrary critter."

"That's Hunter, all right."

A smile flashed on Morgan's face. He turned his horse around. With Leopard following, Morgan took the easy way out of the ravine.

"Have you found some cows?" Elyssa asked hopefully.

"None to speak of, Miss Elyssa."

"But these gullies are usually full of cattle."

"I can see the signs all around," Morgan said quietly. "But signs are all there are. No beeves. Just an old barren cow or two."

Elyssa tried not to show the cold that settled in the pit of her stomach at Morgan's words. Despite the lush

grass and clean seeps pooling in the gully, there were
few cattle around. Of those, none had been what the
cowboys called "beeves"—steers at least four years
old.

There should have been more. Many more.

Unhappily Elyssa looked around, probing shadows
and creases for cattle. She found nothing but the land
itself.

The meadows and flats near the marsh were dry, with
tall grass standing cured in the sun. Cattle could do very
well on the dried grass, but they preferred the tender
green variety.

Because of the small springs and seeps welling up
from the land, many of the ragged gullies were thick
with growing grass. Cattle came to those ravines like
chunks of iron to a big magnet.

Cattle had been here. Elyssa could see the hoofprints
and manure piles, the meandering trails and the muddy
seeps where hooves cut deeply.

Yet, despite the signs, there were no cattle now.

It was as though somebody had been here before the
Ladder S hands. Someone who knew all the creases and
grassy ravines where cows ruminated in the cool shade.

Someone who had rounded up all the cows before
their rightful owner could.

The chill in Elyssa's stomach increased. It was a feeling that had become more familiar each day . . . a growing fear whenever she thought about the future of the
Ladder S.

Don't think about it, she told herself. *Fretting until
your stomach churns won't help anything.*

Elyssa took a deep breath and let it out slowly. Then
another. Then one more.

Hunter is doing everything anyone could, she reminded herself.

She took another long breath, thinking of Hunter. He

was skilled, hardworking, intelligent, a born leader of men. Whatever could be done for the Ladder S, Hunter would do.

Hunter must have been a fine officer. The younger boys all but worship him, and the men respect him.

The few who don't respect anything are smart enough to fear Hunter.

Even Mickey.

A delicate shiver went through Elyssa as she remembered her dress caught on a nail and her breasts resting against Hunter's strong forearm.

Another memory cascaded through her in a glittering stream of sensation. Hunter's face in the moonlight, his lashes dark against his cheeks, his tongue hungry on her breast, his whole body hard with the intensity of his desire.

Then today, when she had measured the extent of his hunger with her own hands.

He can deny it until he's blue in the face, Elyssa told herself, *but he's as involved as I am.*

Another shiver overtook Elyssa. If she hadn't believed that Hunter was fighting an equally strong attraction to her, she would have been afraid.

Never had she been drawn to a man as she was to Hunter.

Her eyes followed him everywhere. She walked across the room to stand close to him. She asked him about the state of the land and the cattle and the men, anything to hear him talk, to be close enough to see the texture of his mustache and the movements of his lips.

I'll keep prying beneath his reserve, Elyssa promised herself. *I'll get to the gentleness and the laughter.*

And the passion.

Dear God, the passion.

The sound of a horse coming down the draw toward Elyssa made her breath catch. Bugle Boy was cantering toward her. Elyssa's face flushed and her heartbeat quickened.

Hunter didn't even look at her.

"Why did you fire the shots?" he asked Morgan.

"Found a branding fire."

"Show me."

Morgan kicked his tough little mustang into a canter. Hunter and Elyssa followed Morgan to the head of another draw. This one was part of a rumpled network of ravines and hillocks that unraveled into Wind Gap, which led to Bill's small ranch.

Hunter and Morgan dismounted. Hunter stalked along the tracks that went from Ladder S land to the Bar B. In addition to the tracks there were the scattered remains of a small fire.

The kind that was used for unofficial branding.

"If I was a sporting man," Morgan said, "I'd bet a Ladder S beef laid down here and got up as a Slash River beef."

"Too bad we weren't riding by here early this morning," Hunter said. "We could have cooked the rustler over his own fire."

Without another word both men mounted. Hunter shot Elyssa a hard glance.

"Where are the dogs?" he asked her.

"Don't glare at me. Last time I saw them, they were chasing steers for you."

Hunter started to whistle up the dogs, only to be stopped by a curt motion from Morgan.

Between the fitful gusts of wind came the clear sound of a horse running hard.

Hunter looked at Morgan.

"No, suh," Morgan said. "I sent the men off south looking for mustangs and Ladder S ponies, like you said they should."

"Get back into the ravine," Hunter said to Elyssa. "We'll be right on your heels. *Move.*"

She spun Leopard on his hocks and shot back into the mouth of the damp, brushy ravine. As Hunter had promised, they were crowding the spotted stallion's heels every step of the way. Very quickly the three horses were under cover.

Before Elyssa realized what Hunter was doing, he turned Bugle Boy in to Leopard. The motion pressed Leopard back even farther into the shelter of a tall willow thicket.

"Get off," Hunter said tersely. "You'll show above the brush."

While Hunter spoke, he kicked free of the stirrups and dropped to the ground. His repeating rifle was in his hands.

With no fuss at all Hunter went up the steep side of the ravine until he merged into the shadows of a piñon. The muted yet unmistakable sound of a shell being levered into the firing chamber came back down the ravine.

On an impulse Elyssa reached into Bugle Boy's saddlebag and pulled out the spyglass.

"Don't turn that in to the sun," Morgan warned in a low voice. "Glass can flash like a beacon. Give us away sure as sin."

She nodded, put the glass to her eye, and looked back down the ravine. The same willow, brush, and piñon that concealed the horses also kept her from seeing anything useful.

Elyssa turned and put the glass on Hunter. It brought him so close it was as though she was standing at arm's length. The midnight shine of his hair and mustache intrigued her, as did the shape of his lips and the winter glint of his eyes.

As she watched, Hunter's expression changed from alertness to a leashed savagery that chilled her. Smoothly he raised his rifle and sighted down the barrel.

Whoever the approaching rider was, he was known to Hunter.

And hated by him.

The sound of more horses approaching at a gallop came on the wind.

Slowly, reluctantly, Hunter lowered the rifle.

"Watch that stud, ma'am," Morgan said. "He catches scent of a lot of horses, he's likely to whinny."

Elyssa closed the spyglass, shoved it into Bugle Boy's saddlebag, and went to Leopard's head. She put one hand on the bit. The other settled on the horse's nose. She murmured to him in a low voice.

"What about Bugle Boy?" Elyssa asked quietly.

"He knows better. So does my pony."

Through the screen of willows Elyssa watched four horsemen ride by. They were perhaps three hundred feet away. They were joined by a fifth man, who was riding on a big sorrel mule.

Morgan took one look at the mule and began to speak so softly that Elyssa couldn't hear individual words. The expression on Morgan's face left no doubt that he was cursing.

Leopard's barrel swelled as he sucked in air, preparing to whinny a challenge to the intruders.

Elyssa's fingers clamped firmly down on the stud's flaring nostrils. He shook his head. Her fingers stayed in place. Leopard settled back into silence.

After a few moments the five men rode off in the direction of Wind Gap.

Not until the last faint sound of hoofbeats faded did Hunter leave his vantage point and return to the bottom of the ravine.

"Culpepper," Morgan said.

Hunter nodded curtly.

"Gaylord?" Morgan offered.

"No. Ab."

The quality of Hunter's voice chilled Elyssa.

"Ab," Morgan muttered. "The head devil hisself."

Hunter grunted.

"Well," Morgan said, smiling coldly, "we're getting close, then. A week, maybe two. Ab ain't a patient kind of man."

"Wonder where he's been," Hunter said.

Morgan shrugged. "Back and forth between here and the Spanish Trail, last I heard. Some of his kin was with him."

"Which ones?"

Morgan shrugged again. "Don't matter. You won't need to worry about them. They're chasing Spanish treasure. Digging for it, so I hear."

Hunter shook his head at such foolishness.

"Ab don't have much patience with anything like work," Morgan said, "so he comes north every few weeks. Beau and his bunch are on the way, too."

"Beau, Clim, Darcy, and Floyd won't be joining Ab," Hunter said with satisfaction.

"Heard something like that. Colorado, wasn't it?"

Hunter nodded.

"Lot of Yankee dollars on those boys' heads," Morgan said to no one in particular.

"The folks who earned the reward money didn't want it," Hunter said.

Morgan looked surprised.

"I sent the money back to Alex," Hunter said as he stepped into Bugle Boy's stirrup.

"Too late," Morgan said as he mounted.

Hunter nodded curtly and reined Bugle Boy around.

"Hope his mother gets it," Hunter said. "Her husband came back from the war with one arm and no legs."

Realizing that she was going to be left behind if she

didn't move quickly, Elyssa scrambled onto Leopard with the help of a handy boulder. She thanked Penny's scissors and thread every bit of the way into the saddle.

It was a lot easier to ride without a mass of cloth twisting around her legs every time she tried to mount or dismount.

"Are we going to track the men?" Elyssa asked.

Hunter shook his head.

"Why not?" Elyssa asked.

"They're five to our two."

"Three," she corrected. "I can shoot."

"Have you ever shot a man?" Hunter retorted.

"No, but I've been real tempted lately."

Morgan hid his smile.

"Want me to track them, ramrod?" Morgan asked blandly.

"All right," Hunter said. "But when you get on B Bar land, turn back."

"*If* you get there," Elyssa corrected instantly. "There's no guarantee that's where those men are going. They might just be passing through."

"Where to?" Hunter asked sarcastically.

"The other side," Elyssa shot back.

"*Adiós,*" Morgan said.

No one answered. Hunter and Elyssa were too busy glaring at one another to notice Morgan leave.

"Why is there bad blood between the Ladder S and the B Bar?" Hunter asked.

"What makes you think there is?" Elyssa countered.

"Two ranches cheek by jowl and no visiting between."

Elyssa thought of the last time she had seen Bill, when she had refused to sell him the Ladder S.

"At least, no *formal* visiting," Hunter added ironically, thinking of the web of ghost paths between the two ranches.

Elyssa's stomach clenched, for she thought Hunter was referring to the rustlers who came and went from both ranches. She didn't like to think about all the small bunches of cattle tracks she had seen heading through Wind Gap.

And no cow tracks returning.

Not even one.

Wind Gap led to Bill's ranch, and from there to one of the passes over the Rubies.

But despite all evidence, Elyssa simply couldn't believe that Bill was part and parcel of the naked rustling of Ladder S livestock.

He was like a father to me, she thought sadly.

He can't be destroying me. There must be another explanation.

"It's fall roundup," Elyssa said tightly. "No one has the time for social visits."

"Damned strange."

"Why?"

"Good old Bill hasn't even sent a rep to make sure we don't round up any of his cattle along with ours."

Hunter's voice was as sarcastic as the thin white curve of his smile beneath his mustache.

Elyssa closed her eyes.

"Bill knows we won't sell any cattle of his," she said.

"At this rate we won't be selling any Ladder S cows either," Hunter said bluntly.

"What?"

"They've all been driven onto B Bar land, and from there to market."

"No!"

"Hell," Hunter said in disgust. "You've got eyes, Sassy. Use them!"

"I did. The first week after I came home, I backtracked Ladder S cows from that damned whiskey peddler's Dugout Saloon."

Hunter became still. "What?"

"I knew from Mac that the peddler acted as an unofficial rendezvous point for people wanting to buy, sell, and swap animals," Elyssa explained, "so I—"

"You went into that thieves' den alone?" Hunter interrupted harshly.

"Not quite."

"Not. Quite." He bit off each word. "What in hell does that mean?"

"It means Mac told me to stay away from B Bar land. Period. He would handle whatever had to be done about stray cows."

"Thank God," Hunter muttered.

Elyssa ignored him.

"But I kept seeing cow tracks going through Wind Gap," she said. "So I went to the Dugout Saloon and backtracked a bunch of cows."

Hunter's black eyebrows shot up in surprise at Elyssa's ingenuity.

"Bet you tracked them right back to the B Bar," he said.

"Wrong. The tracks came from the marsh northeast of here. It's a dangerous maze of grassy hummocks surrounded by bogs and reeds."

Hunter was impressed despite himself that Elyssa had had the idea of backtracking rustled cattle.

The fact that she also had the nerve to carry through her idea chilled him.

Elyssa could easily have been killed. Rustlers and other felons were notoriously touchy about people dogging their trail.

"The B Bar is north of here," Hunter said.

"The tracks didn't come from B Bar land. They came from Ladder S land."

Hunter didn't look convinced.

"Besides," Elyssa said, "when our cows wander onto

B Bar land, Bill just hazes them back toward our land. Under all that gruffness and whiskey, he's a good man.''

The affection in Elyssa's voice when she spoke of Bill did nothing to improve Hunter's temper. She might respond to Hunter the way dry grass responds to a torch, but every time she spoke of Bill Moreland it was clear that she was besotted with him.

A man who was robbing her blind.

"Well, Sassy," Hunter drawled, "it sure seems that a whole lot of Ladder S cows have taken a notion to sift through the grasslands over onto B Bar land. And not one of those cows has wandered back."

"As Mac was so fond of saying, 'Cows and wimmen is plumb notional critters.' ''

The tone of Elyssa's voice plainly said that discussion of Bill Moreland and Ladder S cows was closed.

Hunter kept on talking.

"Bill was half-right," he said. "They're notional as all hell."

Elyssa didn't ask whether Hunter was talking about cows or women. She knew she wouldn't like the answer.

"Not cows, though," Hunter said. "Cows have more common sense than women."

"As women have more common sense than men, that means men—"

"Ha!" Hunter interrupted.

"Ha, yourself. Did you ever hear of cows going to war?"

"Hell, no."

"Or women?" Elyssa added sweetly.

For an instant she thought she saw Hunter smile. But she must have been wrong.

The silence that followed her retort wasn't broken all the way back to the Ladder S ranch house.

～12

$\mathcal{H}$unter woke up as he had so often during the war—in a wild, silent rush. Yet he neither sat up nor changed the pattern of his breathing. Instead, he lay motionless with his eyes slitted. To anyone prowling around close by, there would be no difference in Hunter's appearance.

After a few moments Hunter was certain that no one was in his room. Nor were the dogs barking out by the barn or the bunkhouse.

The night was absolutely quiet. Everything looked as peaceful as the moonlight pouring through the window at the side of his bedroom.

Yet Hunter was certain something was wrong.

With a single, feline movement, Hunter was out of bed. He yanked his pants on and then kicked into his boots while he was buckling the six-gun and holster around his hips. Ignoring his hat and shirt, he crossed the bedroom, stood to the side of the window, and looked out.

Nothing was moving anywhere along the road to the ranch. Nothing stirred in the yard. In the corral near the barn, horses stood three-legged, dozing in the moonlight that was pouring through a break between thunderstorms.

Water puddles gleamed in the yard. Water dripped from the house eaves and the cottonwoods. Spun silver clouds piled high and frothed across the sky. Lightning flickered on the shoulder of the mountains. Thunder muttered and rolled sleepily.

Hunter eased open the window. A faint sound came through the crack.

A horse snorting. Muffled hoofbeats.

Quickly Hunter's head turned toward the sound.

Leopard was pacing his paddock fence. His coat gleamed in the shifting silver light. The stud was snorting and tossing his head.

Suddenly the stallion stood stock-still, his neck stretched and ears pricked.

Leopard was watching the garden intently.

For an instant Hunter wondered if Elyssa had stolen off to her favorite haunt again. Then he dismissed the idea.

Hunter knew he would have awakened if Elyssa had tiptoed down the hall outside the room. He woke up every time she turned over in her bed, a bed that was less than two feet from his own, for all that there was a wall between them.

A glance at the angle of the moon told Hunter that it was too early for Gimp to be up and moving around, readying breakfast for the hands. Cooks got up well before dawn, but this was early by any standard.

Swiftly Hunter crossed to his bedside table. A flick of his thumbnail opened the big gold pocket watch that had been his father's.

Three o'clock.

Nothing but coyotes, wolves, and their human counterparts prowled at this hour.

Where the hell are the dogs? Hunter asked the night savagely. *God knows they bark fit for raising the dead when strangers are around.*

Maybe it's Elyssa out there after all.

Hunter went to the wall where the head of his bed was pushed snugly against the rough wood. Ear to the wall, he listened intently.

What came back to him was what haunted him every waking moment he lay in bed. Soft breathing, a sigh, and the intimate rustle of linen sheets as Elyssa turned over in bed.

Desire shot through Hunter.

He ignored it. He was getting very good at ignoring his body's insistent hunger for an unsuitable girl; he had had plenty of practice lately.

Too much practice. Beneath the denial, desire grew with every day, every minute, every breath.

With an impatient curse at his unruly sexuality, Hunter grabbed his rifle. He levered a round into the firing chamber on the way out of the bedroom. Moving quickly, lightly, Hunter ran down the hall to the stairs.

As always, the stairway creaked and popped with every step he took.

Elyssa was right about that, Hunter thought with faint humor. *Even a cat couldn't sneak up these stairs.*

Experience had taught Hunter that the front door didn't squeak when it was opened. The kitchen door did.

Hunter went out the front.

A cold wind was blowing fitfully. Hunter faded into the shadows beneath the eaves. He moved swiftly, silently, to the back side of the house.

Night air was chill against his bare chest. The wind tasted of rain. Hunter didn't notice the cold of the stormy autumn night. His attention was fixed on the kitchen garden.

The ground is too white, he thought. *Even moonlight shouldn't make it that pale.*

Within the whiteness a shadow moved.

A man.

If the dogs had been barking, Hunter simply would have raised the rifle and dropped the intruder where he stood. But the dogs hadn't sent up an alarm, which meant that Hunter couldn't be certain the man was an intruder.

The wind will cover any sound I make, Hunter thought, measuring the distance to the barn and from there to the garden.

But there's no cover between here and the barn. That moonlight is too bright for me to be running around in.

The hombre out there might not be as choosy about who he shoots as I am.

There was no way for Hunter to approach the garden without coming out of cover. Nor could he get close enough to identify the man unless he did.

Hunter waited for the space of five breaths, hoping that one of the boiling, windswept clouds would veil the nearly full moon.

The clear sky between the storms didn't change enough to make a difference. The huge autumn moon flooded light over everything.

Damn!

Shifting the rifle to his left hand, Hunter sprinted across the open yard, heading for the dense shadows along the barn. Every step of the way he expected to hear the distinctive metallic sound of a rifle or six-gun being cocked.

It didn't come.

Breathing lightly, soundlessly, Hunter vanished into the deep shadows along the side of the barn. He began easing to the back of the building. From there he might be able to see well enough to identify whoever was taking a predawn stroll through Elyssa's garden.

Something moved behind Hunter.

He spun, drawing his six-gun as he turned.

When he saw the black and white dog following him,

he holstered the gun with a swift movement.

Vixen. Why is she following me rather than whoever is out there?

The dog's tail waved in silent greeting. In the moonlight and wind, Vixen was almost invisible but for the gleam of her alert, watchful eyes.

The wind shifted, blowing from the garden toward the barn.

Hunter stared at Vixen. If the intruder was a stranger, the dog couldn't miss smelling him now.

Vixen looked expectantly at Hunter.

Whoever is out there isn't a stranger to the Ladder S, Hunter decided. *Why doesn't that make me feel better?*

Probably because Bill Moreland isn't a stranger.

A curt motion of Hunter's hand dismissed Vixen.

The dog looked disappointed at being deprived of a moonlight romp between storms.

Hunter gestured again.

Reluctantly Vixen turned and trotted off to the garden. The collie moved with the confidence of an animal that doesn't expect any nasty surprises to be waiting in the darkness.

Well, that ties it. Whoever is out there is known to the dogs.

Only one way to find out for sure who it is. And what the hell he's up to.

Just as Hunter started for the garden, he caught a pale flash of movement at the corner of his eye.

Someone was sprinting across the patch of moonlight between the house and the barn. It didn't take but an instant to see who it was. The feminine grace and cascade of pale hair could belong only to one person.

Hunter propped the rifle against the barn and waited. He didn't have to wait long. Elyssa was a fast runner.

With no warning Hunter's arms snaked out of the dense shadows and snatched Elyssa from the moonlight.

One of his hands clamped over her mouth, shutting off her instinctive cry. The other arm clamped around her body.

She was wearing silk. It was cold to his bare chest. Then the heat of her radiated through smooth cloth, sinking into him like a blow.

"Quiet," Hunter breathed fiercely into Elyssa's ear. "Not one sound. Understand?"

She nodded.

The motion sent the silvery softness of Elyssa's hair spilling over Hunter's bare hands. His breath came in with a barely audible hiss, as though he had been burned.

He felt like he had.

"Stay right here until I call for you," Hunter said in a voice that went no farther than Elyssa's ears.

She shook her head in disagreement.

"Yes," Hunter countered in a very low, very hard voice. "I don't want to shoot you by mistake."

Elyssa hesitated. Then, reluctantly, she nodded again.

Hunter lifted his hand from her mouth, bent to retrieve his rifle, and handed it to her.

"There's a round in the chamber," he murmured.

As before, his words were a mere thread of sound.

She nodded her understanding.

"Don't shoot me by mistake," Hunter said.

"How about on purpose?" Elyssa retorted.

But her voice was as soft as his.

Hunter's brief smile was as white as moonlight. He bent and gave Elyssa a swift, fierce kiss, surprising both of them equally.

Then he was gone.

Anxiously Elyssa stared into the cloud-tossed night. She knew that Hunter was out there, a shadow among racing cloud-shadows, but she couldn't see him.

Nor did she know why he was here. She knew only

that the sound of his footsteps going down the stairs had awakened her instantly.

That was hardly surprising. The sound of him shifting position in bed often awakened her . . . assuming she had been able to get to sleep in the first place. Being just scant feet from Hunter all night, every night, had an unsettling influence on her body.

Not to mention her dreams.

Hunter checked over his shoulder several times to see if Elyssa was keeping her promise to stay put. When he realized that she wasn't following him, he let out a soundless sigh of relief.

Unlike the herb garden, the kitchen garden was a thicket with many places for a man to hide. Pole beans, pea vines climbing on a big trellis, corn plants that stood higher than a man—there was a lot of cover for an intruder.

There was cover for Hunter as well.

Silently as moonlight itself, more quiet than the fat raindrops that had begun to fall, Hunter sifted between rows of corn. Without even being aware of it, he merged his outline with that of the tall plants around him as he moved.

Hunter had done the same thing so often during the War Between the States that it was second nature to him now. But during the war there had been an army of blue uniforms surrounding him.

Now there was only the night and a single man-shadow out there among the shades of darkness.

Motionless, Hunter stood and listened to the night and the ragged storm.

Nothing came back to him but the restless stirring of the wind and the spatter of raindrops against the garden plants.

Slowly Hunter crouched and ran his hand over the too

white ground. Sitting on his heels, he brought his fingertips to his mouth and licked lightly.

Salt.

You son of a whore, Hunter thought coldly. *Wait until I get my hands on you.*

The wind shifted like a woman turning over in bed. At the far end of the garden, pole beans rustled.

But it wasn't leaves stirred by the wind. It was a man drawing a bead with his six-gun on something pale that stood within the shadows of the barn.

Elyssa.

"Get down, Sassy!" Hunter yelled.

As he yelled, he drew his six-gun. He was off balance, trying only for speed and surprise. Before the shots ever left the six-gun, Hunter knew they would miss the target.

All he hoped was that the other man would miss, too.

Shots split the night, a man cried out, dogs erupted into barking, cowhands yelled from the bunkhouse, and Hunter cursed in the kind of words that could etch granite as he reloaded.

"Sassy! Are you all right?" Hunter yelled.

"Yes!"

"Stay there! Make sure none of the men shoot until they can see what the hell they're aiming at!"

Hunter didn't wait for Elyssa's answer. He just ran flat out between the cornstalks, chasing the shadow he had sensed disappearing down the garden rows.

Before Hunter reached the edge of the garden, he heard the sound of a horse running hard. The drumroll of hoofbeats faded rapidly into the wind and rain.

"Son of a *bitch*," Hunter snarled.

Barking wildly, Vixen burst from between hills of squash vines.

"Oh, shut up!" Hunter said in disgust. "The time for barking is long past."

Chagrined, Vixen fell silent.

"Colonel?" called Morgan. "You all right?"

The choppiness of the words made it clear that Morgan was running toward the garden.

"I'm fine," Hunter said. "Tell the men to swap their guns for shovels and lanterns."

Morgan broke through the last rows of corn, looking around hopefully.

"We having a burying?" Morgan asked.

"No," Hunter said in disgust. "The son of a bitch got the garden, damn his black soul."

"What?"

"Salt," Hunter said succinctly.

"Mother of God," Morgan said.

His eyes widened as he looked at the destruction of the garden written in trails of white running down the furrows. Cursing steadily, Morgan lit the lantern he was carrying and lifted it high.

White gleamed back at him from all directions.

Rain started to come down harder. Salt began dissolving before Hunter's eyes.

"Get those shovels over here now!" Hunter yelled.

A chorus of agreement came back through the gathering rain.

"Hunter?" Elyssa called. "Where are you?"

"Get back to the house," Hunter ordered. "You'll catch your death of cold in this rain."

A few moments later Elyssa appeared at the edge of the garden. She leaped from furrow to furrow with the grace of a deer, running toward the lantern light. She burst into the yellow circle around the lantern.

"Damn it, Sassy . . . !"

Elyssa ignored Hunter's protests.

"Are you certain you're all right?" she demanded

breathlessly. "There were so many shots."

Even as Elyssa asked, she looked Hunter over carefully. In the lantern glow, each ridge and swell of muscle was etched in golden light and emphasized by black velvet shadows. Hair as dark as night reflected fugitive sparks of light with every breath Hunter took.

Elyssa forgot to breathe. She had never thought to put the words "man" and "beauty" in the same sentence. But after looking at Hunter, she understood what had driven Michelangelo to create *David*.

Hunter looked like that. Intelligent. Powerful. Beautiful.

And very male.

The intense approval Hunter saw in Elyssa's eyes as she looked at his body made his breath shorten. Suddenly he was very much aware of the fact that he was half-naked, bathed in lantern light, his skin sleeked by rain.

And if she kept looking at him like that, he was going to embarrass himself in front of the men.

"I'm fine," Hunter said coldly.

"I heard shots," Elyssa said.

The huskiness of her voice set blood to beating visibly in Hunter's neck.

"He wasn't shooting at me," Hunter said.

"Who was he shooting at, then? Is everyone all right?"

Hunter didn't answer. He didn't like to think about the ice that had condensed in his gut when he realized that Elyssa was the intruder's target.

"Hunter?"

"Everyone's fine."

"Who was he shooting at?" Elyssa persisted.

"You," Hunter said roughly.

Elyssa's eyes widened. Her breath came in with a swift, broken sound.

"Maybe he thought she was one of the hands," Morgan offered.

Hunter looked at Elyssa. She was slender as an aspen, her pale hair was whipping in the wind, and she was wearing a long silk wrapper. The wrapper was tied around her waist, emphasizing the feminine curves of her body. Wind lifted the wrapper's hem, revealing and then concealing the creamy curve of Elyssa's calves.

Raindrops had made dark marks on the silk. Wet silk clung to her breasts. Her nipples were gathered against the cold and the rain.

"The shooter would have to be blind to mistake Sassy for a man," Hunter said huskily.

"Amen," Sonny said reverently from the darkness just beyond the reach of lantern light.

"I'll second that," said another voice.

"Same here," came a third voice.

"Me too."

"Yo."

"Amen, Lord. A-*men*."

Hunter's expression became fierce. Coldly he glared at the men who had gathered at the edge of the lantern light to agree with him that Elyssa looked very female indeed.

"Quit standing around with your bare faces flapping in the rain," Hunter snarled.

The men jumped.

"Mickey, get the manure cart," Hunter said. "The rest of you men start shoveling salt. Move!"

A chorus of yessirs and a flurry of shovels answered Hunter.

"I'll leave the lantern for you, suh," Morgan said.

Hunter nodded curtly.

Men dispersed into the darkness. Lanterns blossomed like exotic flowers throughout the garden. The cowhands, who under most circumstances despised all work that couldn't be done from horseback, shoveled dirt and salt without a single complaint.

No man was foolish enough to take on Hunter when he had that look in his eye.

Not even Mickey.

Belatedly Elyssa understood what Hunter had said.

"Salt?" she asked. "What salt?"

"The salt that son of a bitch left in the garden furrows," Hunter said.

Elyssa made a low sound, as though she had been struck. She tried to breathe, but couldn't. For the first time she looked away from Hunter to the ground.

Ragged lines of white looked back at Elyssa from furrows on both sides of the one where she stood.

"Salt?" she whispered.

Hunter nodded. Then, realizing that Elyssa hadn't seen the gesture, he spoke aloud.

"Yes," he said. "Salt."

"Are you c-certain?"

The trembling in Elyssa's voice went into Hunter like a knife. He looked at the fingers of his left hand, wishing that he had been wrong.

Tiny white crystals winked back at him in the lantern light. He lifted his hand, tasting again anyway. Just to be sure.

Salt.

"Yes," Hunter said. "I'm sure."

Unable to believe, Elyssa grabbed Hunter's hand and lifted it to her mouth. Her tongue flicked out. The taste of salt spread across her tongue.

There was no doubt.

Elyssa dropped Hunter's hand and turned her head away from his too knowing eyes. A tremor of suppressed emotion went through her.

My garden . . . my refuge, she thought wildly.

Oh, God, who would be so cruel?

Blindly Elyssa stared off into the darkness beyond the lantern light, fighting tears. Hunter already thought of her as a girl. She was damned if she would prove it by crying in front of him.

Emotions Elyssa refused to give way to made her throat ache. A sheen of moisture grew in her eyes.

The sound of dirt and salt being shoveled frantically came through the night. It was as though giant rats gnawed at the garden around the golden circles of light being cast by many lanterns.

While the men worked, the storm kept increasing. Before they could shovel up all of the salt, much of the garden would be ruined, and with it the very earth itself.

"Sassy?" Hunter asked after a time. "Are you all right?"

There was no answer.

Hunter wanted to take Elyssa in his arms. He wanted to give her what comfort he could.

But that was impossible. He couldn't trust himself to touch her in any way at all.

His fingertips felt as though they had been scorched by flames. With every heartbeat he could feel the sleek heat of her tongue on his skin as though it was happening all over again.

Hunter wanted Elyssa until he could barely stand up.

I shouldn't even be looking at her, he told himself bitterly. *That silk she's wearing looks like it's dissolving in the rain as fast as the salt.*

With every instant Elyssa stayed out in the storm, more of the creamy silk wrapper clung to her body.

Her nipples seemed to gather rain. Wet cloth shaped them. They stood proudly against the silk, as taut as though they had been loved by Hunter's mouth.

Judas Priest, Hunter thought, caught between anger and violent desire. *She's enough to make a bishop weep.*

"Go back to the house," Hunter ordered, his voice harsh.

Elyssa turned her face up to him. She looked bleak and vulnerable in the same instant.

"Was it a Culpepper?" she asked, her voice trembling.

"Sassy—"

"Was it?" she interrupted.

This time Elyssa's voice was as harsh as his.

Hunter drew a deep breath and thought fast. He didn't want to go into the identity of the intruder. He didn't like thinking about good old "Uncle" Bill, the man who was likely Elyssa's lover.

Almost certainly Bill was the man who had drawn his six-gun and sighted down its barrel at Elyssa.

But girls were notoriously blind about men they loved. That was the only explanation Hunter could think of for Elyssa's blindness about Bill.

"Well?" Elyssa asked impatiently.

"No," Hunter said. "It wasn't a Culpepper."

"How can you be so certain?"

"The dogs."

"I don't understand."

"The dogs didn't bark," Hunter said curtly.

"Maybe the wind was wrong for them to catch his scent."

"Vixen smelled the intruder when the wind shifted."

"And?" Elyssa asked.

"She didn't turn a hair."

"I can't—" Elyssa's voice broke.

Hunter waited, not knowing what to say. He didn't want to be in the position of pointing the finger at Elyssa's lover. If it came from him, she would reject it.

Let her figure it out, Hunter advised himself. *Shouldn't take her long.*

Rain came down harder now.

Elyssa swallowed and tried again to speak.

"You must—" she said huskily. She cleared her throat. "You must be mistaken."

"Did you hear the dogs barking?"

"No. But maybe it was one of the new hands. Someone who is working both sides of the street."

"He rode off on a horse."

"S-so?"

Hunter glared at Elyssa. The rain was coming down so hard now that there was more wet silk on her than dry.

"Morgan!" Hunter yelled.

"Yo!"

"Any hands missing?"

"No, suh!"

"How can he be sure?" Elyssa hissed. "He didn't even take time to count!"

"He didn't have to."

"Why?"

"Because I told him to keep track of the men we don't know," Hunter said in a clipped voice. "He's the last one asleep in the bunkhouse and the first one awake."

"But—"

"But nothing," Hunter interrupted impatiently. "Go back to the house. You're not dressed to be out here."

"And you are?" she retorted.

"Hell and damnation."

Out of patience, Hunter snatched Elyssa up like she was a child and set off through the rain toward the ranch house. Every step he took proved that she was no child. She fit against him the way only a woman could.

By the time Hunter reached the house, he was certain that an imprint of Elyssa's breasts was branded against his skin.

℘13

$\mathscr{F}$reshly picked vegetables were heaped in baskets, kettles, bins, and boxes all around the kitchen. Elyssa and Penny were all but dwarfed by the mounds of garden produce.

The day had dawned clear and hot, a return of summer in autumn. The sunstruck land radiated heat back up to the empty blue sky.

Inside the kitchen it was steamy from the canning that had been going on since well before dawn.

"At least the herb garden was spared," Penny said.

"Only because Hunter ran him off before he could finish," Elyssa said. "Morgan found bags of salt piled up, just waiting to be used."

"Funny that the dogs didn't bark."

Elyssa said nothing.

She had spent the night lying awake, alternating between wrestling with the identity of the intruder and the memory of how Hunter had looked bare to the waist.

Neither thought had made her sleepy.

Penny gave Elyssa a sideways look, wondering at her silence. Then Penny returned to studying the pumpkin's rich orange skin. Though she had a brush in her hand, she hadn't the wit or the will to use it at the moment.

The identity of the intruder was very much on Penny's mind.

"It must have been one of the new men," Penny said. "The dogs wouldn't bark at one of them."

"Hunter thinks not."

"Really? Why?"

"Morgan's job is to keep track of them."

"He might have slipped up," Penny said.

For an instant Elyssa closed her eyes. The thought that Bill was the man who had destroyed her beloved garden ate like acid at her soul.

Who else could it be? she asked herself silently, desperately.

Who both has reason to punish me and is known to the dogs?

No answer came but Bill, the one answer Elyssa couldn't accept.

"Perhaps Morgan was mistaken," Elyssa said.

But the tone of her voice said that she didn't think so.

"Or the dogs might have missed the scent," Penny said firmly. "The wind was blowing the wrong way. He was downwind of the dogs."

Elyssa said nothing.

"Well, that explains it," Penny said. "The dogs just didn't catch his scent."

"Vixen did. She trotted off toward him."

Abruptly Penny stopped scrubbing the small pumpkin. She had been mostly pretending anyway. When she looked up, her dark brown eyes were angry and haunted.

"You think it was Bill," Penny said accusingly.

"Did I say that?"

"You don't have to! He's the only man the dogs know who wasn't at the ranch last night."

Silence was Elyssa's only answer.

"You're wrong!" Penny said, her voice rising. "He

wouldn't do a low thing like that! He's not—''

The kitchen door slammed behind Hunter, cutting off Penny's defense. Hunter's arms were full to overflowing with burlap bags of carrots, onions, potatoes, and apples. Some would be canned. Most were destined for the cellar beneath the house.

"Who's wrong about what?" Hunter asked mildly.

"Elyssa is implying that Bill salted the garden," Penny said. "She's wrong. He's a kind and decent man.''

Hunter didn't say a word.

"Well, he is!" Penny said.

Spots of color flared on her otherwise pale face when no one agreed with her.

"I know him better than anyone alive," Penny said, "and I say he wouldn't do anything like that!"

"Whiskey changes a man," Hunter said finally.

"No," Penny said flatly. "Bill wouldn't do a vicious thing like that no matter how much he drank!"

"Don't take on so," Elyssa said, sighing. "The garden was a delight, but not really necessary for our survival.''

Hunter remembered the sheen of tears he had seen in Elyssa's eyes when she looked at the garden. He knew she was telling only half of the truth.

The garden had been a rare source of peace and pleasure for Elyssa, a gentle place in a land that could be very harsh on women.

Knowing that he hadn't been able to protect it angered Hunter unreasonably.

But then, Hunter reminded himself sardonically, *her murderous lover has an edge in that department that I don't. He knows the ranch—and its mistress—a hell of a lot more intimately than I do.*

Penny looked at Elyssa for a long, tense moment. Then Penny bit her lip hard enough to leave marks and went to check on the glass jars that were boiling merrily, supported by the wire canning rack. The sands in the little hourglass had just run through.

"Let me get that," Elyssa said quickly. "You're distracted and haven't felt well and the rack is heavy. I don't want you to burn yourself."

Before Penny could object, Elyssa brushed past her. The pot holders in her hands were big, thick, and stained with long use. The contrast with Elyssa's orchid silk afternoon dress couldn't have been greater.

Hunter reached around Elyssa from behind and snatched the pot holders from her hands. The rosemary scent of her hit him like a blow.

The scarf holding back Elyssa's hair was a confection of gauzy silk whose purple depths heightened the silvery gold paleness of her hair. The smooth, fine-grained skin of her nape made a sensual contrast to the scarf, which had been tied peasant style at the back of her head.

I wish I could break her of wearing silk and satin around the ranch, Hunter thought savagely. *It's pure hell on a man.*

"I'll take care of the jars," Hunter said.

Caged between the heat of the stove and the power of Hunter's body, Elyssa froze.

"You don't have to," she said. "I can—"

"Don't be foolish," Hunter interrupted, his voice curt. "Where do you want the jars?"

"On the table. Thank you."

Hunter lifted a rack from each huge pot and put it on the long, scarred wooden table. Glass steamed and dried instantly.

Quickly Penny and Elyssa filled the jars with green beans, added salt and water, and screwed down the lids. Normally Elyssa would have added onion or garlic or herbs to the beans, but there was nothing normal about this canning session.

Today they were canning everything they could, no matter if it wasn't at the peak of ripeness.

Once the dissolved salt in the garden reached the plant roots, there would be no ripening. The garden would die. Then vegetables would rot, unless they were picked quickly and canned immediately.

While Elyssa and Penny went to work on the canning jars, Hunter surprised both women by calmly beginning to scrub the smallest potatoes, preparing them for canning. The larger potatoes would go in the root cellar, along with the bigger onions, carrots, turnips, and the like.

Elyssa screwed down the last lid and lifted one of the racks of jars. Before she had it more than an inch off the table, Hunter's arms shot around her and took the weight. She made a startled sound that went no farther than Hunter's ears.

"I'll take that," he said. "You chop up some more beans."

Elyssa wanted to be as matter-of-fact as Hunter was, but her voice wouldn't cooperate. The feel of Hunter's arms around her was literally breathtaking, despite the fact that he was simply being helpful.

Then Elyssa looked over her shoulder and saw Hunter's quicksilver eyes. The desire in them was as naked as the power of his arms caging her.

"I—I can't," Elyssa whispered.

"Can't what?"

"Cut up green beans."

"Why not?"

"We just did the last batch."

"What about peas?" Hunter asked.

Elyssa licked her lips nervously.

The sudden narrowing of Hunter's eyes as he watched her tongue was as clear as the too rapid beating of the pulse in Elyssa's neck.

"Then maybe you better duck under my arm and shell peas," Hunter suggested softly.

"Peas?"

"Little round green things. They come tucked close together in little green pods. Remember them?"

At the moment Elyssa was lucky to remember her own name. All she could think of was how Hunter's mouth had felt against hers, how he had tasted, how sweet his breath had been.

"If you tease me by licking your lips again," Hunter said low and hard, "I swear I'll back you up against the table and give you exactly what you're begging for."

A flush climbed Elyssa's cheeks. She ducked beneath Hunter's arm and went to the sink.

Blindly she began cleaning out a pumpkin. Great handfuls of the sticky center plopped heavily into a colander that stood in the sink. The pulp hit the colander so hard it rattled on its three metal legs.

"Do you want to save those pumpkin seeds for planting?" Penny asked Elyssa.

"What?"

"The pumpkins seeds."

"Oh. Them."

Elyssa looked at the pumpkin seeds as though they had just grown in the sink. The creamy, slightly pointed ovals were plump, obviously ripe.

"Save them for next year's garden," Elyssa said.

If there is one.

For a moment Elyssa was afraid she had spoken her doubts aloud. When no cool retort came from Hunter, she let out a silent breath of relief.

Behind Elyssa, Hunter set one rack of full jars in a huge kettle, then put the other in a similar kettle. He added more wood to the stove. Afterward he went back to scrubbing potatoes as though he had never breathed Elyssa's scent and felt pure fire in his veins.

Sonny came up to the kitchen door. Leafy stalks of dill overflowed his arms. Beets dangled from his fingers, which were clenched around the red-streaked green of the tops.

"Miss Elyssa?" he called out.

She sighed and stretched her back subtly. But she was smiling when she turned toward Sonny.

"Come in," Elyssa said. "Set the dill on the table and the beets in the sink."

Sonny approached her slowly. He was so busy looking at the orchid silk of her dress and the tendrils of flaxen hair that had escaped her chignon that he ran right into Hunter.

"Uh, sorry, sir."

Hunter gave Sonny a look that was both impatient and sardonically amused.

"That's all right," Hunter said, "but I'd take it as a personal favor if you would stand on your own feet from now on. Mine have their work cut out as it is."

Sonny looked down, saw that he was indeed standing on one of Hunter's big feet, and backed off hastily.

"Uh, sorry. Truly am," Sonny said.

Hunter sighed.

Hurriedly Sonny put the beets in the sink and the herbs on the table. He stumbled several times because he was looking at Elyssa when he should have been watching where he was going.

"How are the cucumbers coming?" Elyssa asked.

"Three bushels so far," Sonny said eagerly. "Maybe four in all. Little fellers, all of 'em."

"Good," Elyssa said. She smiled wearily as she thought of the long hours stretching ahead. "Everyone likes pickles."

Sonny smiled as though he had been given a month's pay. Then he just stood and watched Elyssa, who had turned back to gutting pumpkins.

"Sonny," Hunter said.

It was all he had to say. Sonny jumped and left the kitchen as though his heels were on fire.

Elyssa cleaned pumpkins and scooped out pulp and tried not to think of Hunter. She was fairly successful until Hunter came and stood alongside her at the sink. With swift, strong motions he worked the pump. Water gushed out over the mound of pumpkin fiber and seeds in the sink.

From the corner of her eye, Elyssa watched while Hunter separated seeds and pulp with surprising deftness.

"You're good at that," she said.

"You sound surprised."

Wisely, Elyssa changed the subject.

"We already have more than enough seeds for next year," she said. "You don't need to bother with the rest."

"Why let the ripe ones go to waste?" Hunter asked. "They're good eating."

Elyssa blinked.

"I beg your pardon?" Penny asked, turning to Hunter.

"I learned to eat *pepitos* when I was in Texas," he said.

"What's that?" Elyssa asked.

"Roasted, salted pumpkin seeds," Hunter said. "My vaqueros loved them."

Elyssa looked at the mess in the sink with new interest.

"Truly?" she asked.

Hunter nodded. Then he smiled.

"Of course," he added, "they put enough chili powder in with the salt to set fire to the baking tin."

"We have chiles," Elyssa said.

"Saw them."

"You didn't pick any."

"You don't like chiles?" Penny asked.

"Love 'em."

Elyssa looked at Hunter, lured by the laughter buried in his voice.

He was still smiling. It gentled the lines of his face, making Hunter so handsome to Elyssa that she couldn't help staring at him.

"Then why didn't you pick the peppers?" Penny asked.

"Only have one set of gloves," he said succinctly.

"Oh. The juices," Elyssa said, frowning. "They burn."

"Hotter than the devil's breath," Hunter agreed. "Darned shame that Mickey drove off your vaqueros and the Hereras are too busy to garden."

"I have quite a few gloves," Elyssa said. "I'll pick them."

"No need," Hunter said easily.

"I don't want them to go to waste."

"They won't. Mickey is harvesting the little devils."

Elyssa tried not to smile.

It didn't work. She knew that Hunter was punishing Mickey for his treatment of the vaqueros.

"Did you tell him not to rub his eyes?" Elyssa asked.

"Twice. Once when I put him to work. Again when he started bleating that his eyes hurt."

"Maybe next time he'll listen," Elyssa said.

Hunter shrugged. "Doubt it. That boy makes a stump look real bright."

The mound of cleaned pumpkins grew.

"Dear me," Penny said after a time. "Do we have enough spices to make pie filling of all that?"

"I'm thinking about pumpkin chutney, pumpkin relish, and dried pumpkins," Elyssa muttered. "Soup, too."

"Chutney." Penny smiled despite the sadness that came to her face along with the memories. "Gloria loved chutney."

"So do I. I've never made it with pumpkin, but . . ." Elyssa shrugged.

"It should work," Hunter said.

"Do you think so?" Elyssa asked, surprised.

"Sure. Most recipes were invented when a cook had too much of one thing and not enough of another. Pumpkin chutney shouldn't be any different."

"It shouldn't?"

"No."

Elyssa looked bemused. "I do believe you're right."

Hunter shot her a sideways look.

"I think he is, too," Penny said. "Gloria always told me that food customs began with what was at hand."

"Good food is like beauty," Hunter said, looking away from Elyssa. "A matter of taste."

"Ha," Penny said.

She chopped a pumpkin in half with one swipe of her big knife.

"There's one 'taste' that men the world over share," Penny added, her voice hard.

"Really?" Elyssa asked. "What?"

"Blondes," Penny said succinctly.

"Not all men," Hunter said.

"Name one," Penny challenged.

"Me. I prefer a good, steady woman with a smile that lights up a room. Like yours."

Penny looked surprised. Then she smiled, and proved Hunter's words about lighting up a room.

"Like food," Hunter said without looking at Elyssa, "beauty is a matter of working with what you have rather than worrying about what you don't have."

This time it was Elyssa who went through a pumpkin with a single slashing cut.

"You're a good woman," Hunter continued, looking at Penny. "You should take one of the marriage offers you've gotten from the men around here."

Again, Penny was surprised.

"How did you know?" she asked.

Hunter shot a look at Elyssa and said, "All men aren't blinded by sunlight shining on pale hair."

Penny's smile faded.

"The right one was," Penny said. "And he's the only one that matters."

That afternoon everyone but Penny, who still wasn't feeling well, abandoned the kitchen and garden to go back out on the range. Lefty had come in on the run, full of news about a big band of mustangs to the south, down by the marsh. It was an opportunity too good to ignore.

The shortage of mounts was more critical than the need to can vegetables. The hands had only one or two extra mounts apiece. They needed at least six for the brutal work of combing cattle out of the Ladder S's rugged highlands. On hot days like today, they would have gone through eight horses each, if they had them.

Morgan rode with Hunter and Elyssa in search of the mustangs. When Hunter had anything to say, he said it to Morgan. Otherwise, silence reigned while the three of them combed the hot, rumpled land along the edge of the marsh for any sign of mustangs.

Elyssa was just as happy to be ignored. The sharp side of Hunter's tongue was no pleasure, and the sharp side was all she had felt since last night.

The land dipped down once again, leading to the bottom of yet another ravine. The mouth of the ravine was the marsh itself. Without a word Hunter dismounted and looked around for tracks. Very quickly he vanished in the tall grasses that flourished above the rich, damp earth.

Morgan drew his shotgun and urged his horse to stand close to Elyssa's.

Elyssa couldn't help wishing that it was Hunter guarding her and Morgan doing the tracking.

The horses waited with their heads low, dozing on three legs, as though struck dumb by the sun. Their stillness underlined the relentless labor of the past weeks. The animals wasted no time grabbing whatever rest was available.

Though Elyssa would never admit it to Hunter, she wished for a break herself. She had left Leopard in his paddock, giving him a rest from the grueling schedule of dawn-to-dark work. The big, rawboned mare she was riding now was rough-gaited, but wise in the ways of mustangs.

Bugle Boy grazed calmly just a few feet away. From time to time he raised his head and looked around. Then he went back to grazing.

Overhead, hawks turned lazy circles in the deep autumn sky.

Elyssa looked across the gully where Hunter was working his way up to the top of the ravine on foot. With an intensity she wasn't aware of, she watched his every move. She enjoyed his unique combination of masculine strength and grace.

At the moment Hunter was moving very carefully. He had no desire to give away their position to mustangs or hostile men. A small spyglass was in his hand.

The horses Lefty had seen near the gully weren't wholly wild. A Ladder S brand had been put on most of the animals.

But the horses were nonetheless spooky.

"Hope Lefty was right about those brands," Morgan said softly to Elyssa. "We need more horses the way guns need bullets. Green-broke mustangs aren't good enough, especially if it comes to shooting.''

"Lefty knows Ladder S horses," Elyssa said in a low voice. "If he says they're ours, they're ours."

"What if they're wearing the Slash River brand?"

"Then the brand will be so new the flesh won't have healed," Elyssa said bluntly. "And a Ladder S brand will lay just beneath."

"Likely," he agreed. "You plan on killing one and skinning it out to be sure?"

Elyssa grimaced. The customary way to prove that an old brand had been altered was to kill the animal and peel off the part of the hide that had been branded. From the inside, the first brand usually showed clearly, no matter what changes had been made to the outer hide.

"I'll take Lefty's word for it," she said.

"Them Culpeppers won't."

"The Culpeppers are keeping low to the ground since the shooting odds have changed," Elyssa said dryly.

"Like Hunter says, it's the nature of snakes to be low to the ground. Don't mean there's no poison in their fangs."

Elyssa's eyes narrowed against the wind that was gusting over the land. To her immediate left lay the nearly dry marsh. Tawny reeds bent and rattled and bowed beneath the weight of the wind. To her right the grassland rumpled up to the base of the Ruby Mountains. Storm clouds were gathering over the peaks, concealing their jagged outlines.

The wind rushing down from the heights had the taste and feel of winter in it.

"Then you think Hunter is right, that the Culpeppers are just waiting for us to do all the work of roundup before they attack?" Elyssa asked.

"First thing you learn about Hunter," Morgan drawled, "is that he's usually right."

"Not always."

Morgan's smile flashed.

"No, ma'am, not always. He chose the wrong side in the war, and that's gospel."

Shifting in the saddle and shading his eyes against the brilliant, relentless sun, Morgan looked behind them. Unlike his soft, easygoing voice, his eyes were swift, probing, and hard.

"Of course," Morgan said, "joining up with the South was mostly Case's doing, and Belinda's. Young hotheads, believing all that moonshine about nobility and cotton."

"Belinda?"

"His wife, God rest her soul." Then, under his breath, Morgan added, "More likely the devil is closer to her resting place."

Elyssa didn't hear. Knowing the name of Hunter's dead wife made her all too real.

Hunter had loved a woman. He had married her. She had died.

And now his heart was buried with her.

"Case?" Elyssa asked quickly. "Who is he?"

"Hunter's younger brother."

"Did he die, too?"

"No, ma'am, though more than one Union boy did his best."

"Including you?"

Morgan shook his head.

"I owed the Maxwell brothers my life," he said simply. "When the time came, I helped them the same way they had helped me."

"How?"

"I helped Case get into the prison where Hunter was being held. Case did the rest."

Elyssa flinched at the thought of Hunter being im-

prisoned. Military prisons had been infamous for the
pain they inflicted on their inmates.

"Case might have been a hothead before the war,"
Morgan continued, "but he got cured of it all the way
to the bone. He's a hard man, now. Real hard."

"And before the war?" Elyssa asked. "Is that when
Hunter helped you?"

Morgan nodded.

"What happened?" Elyssa asked.

Sighing, Morgan shifted in the saddle and reined his
horse to the right so that he could watch a fresh section
of marsh.

"Long before the war," Morgan said softly, "some
white trash down Texas way thought they'd hang this
colored boy from a tree, just to see how long I'd kick."

Horrified, Elyssa turned and stared at Morgan. He was
watching the ridgeline and the marsh in turn.

And he was smiling like a man enjoying a memory.

"Hunter rode up and started talking to them boys,"
Morgan said. "He was real quiet like. Didn't take him
a minute to figure out I hadn't done anything to earn a
hanging."

Elyssa watched Morgan, appalled.

"Hunter made some sign and Case came out of cover
behind those boys," Morgan continued.

"So they let you go," Elyssa said.

"No, ma'am. All six of them went for their guns."

"Six?" Elyssa asked faintly.

Morgan nodded.

"Case is as quick with his hands as his big brother,"
Morgan said. "When the shooting stopped, two Culpeppers were dead and the other men were bleeding and
looking for ways to be somewheres else. Pronto."

"Culpeppers? The same ones who are here?"

"Same clan, different branch. I was Hunter's *segundo*
from that day on. And from that day on was the begin-

ning of Hunter's problems with the Culpeppers. Those problems will finally end here, mark my words.''

''What do you mean? Did Hunter come here because he knew Culpeppers were—''

Morgan held up his hand, silencing Elyssa. She followed his glance to the top of the ravine, where Hunter lay nearly concealed in the sun-cured grass and rabbit brush.

A faint drumroll of hooves came down the ravine.

''Hellfire and damnation,'' Morgan said. ''Something spooked the mustangs.''

With that he grabbed Bugle Boy's reins and kicked his horse into a run.

Hunter met Morgan partway down the ravine. He swung onto Bugle Boy as though he always mounted on the gallop.

''Cut toward the mountains!'' Hunter said. ''We'll run the horses toward the ranch.''

Morgan waved in response.

''Watch out for Culpeppers,'' Hunter warned. ''Something spooked those horses.''

The smile Morgan gave Hunter was wolfish. Plainly Morgan was looking forward to meeting up with a Culpepper or two. He spurred his horse forward.

Hunter turned to Elyssa.

''Stay close,'' he said curtly.

He spurred Bugle Boy forward before she had a chance to respond.

14

As the rangy mare thundered across the landscape, Elyssa was less concerned about Culpeppers than she was with staying right side up in the saddle. Her mount was having a tough time keeping up with Bugle Boy, but at least the mare was surefooted.

At the moment, agility counted for more than speed. Racing along the edges of the marsh was a dangerous game. The footing went from hard to soft and back again without warning. A tangle of grasses could conceal a muddy depression or a hillock or even an outcropping of rock.

Any of the three could bring down a horse and send its rider flying.

The sunstruck ground whipped beneath the mare's feet with dizzying speed. Elyssa ducked her head, squinted against the wind tears in her eyes, and rode the mare with a skill she had honed while foxhunting at her cousins' English estates.

Despite the rush of air around them, the hard-running horses soon raised a sweat. The horses' coats darkened, then began to show white lines of lather. The marsh, with its memory of water and clouds of birds, seemed like a tawny mirage conjured out of the heat of the dry land.

Abruptly Bugle Boy cut hard toward the mountains. Then the big horse really flattened out, neck stretched and tail streaming in the wind. Heedless of the danger, Elyssa's mare thundered down the side of the shallow wash, turned, and followed Bugle Boy up the wash at a reckless pace.

Hunter glanced quickly over his shoulder. The raw-boned mare was fifty yards behind him, running hard. Elyssa was bent low over her horse's neck. She clung like a burr to the mare's long, black mane.

Abruptly the mare staggered, thrown off stride by a hidden obstacle beneath one foot. Elyssa stood in the stirrups and hauled up on the reins to pull her mount back into balance. After a heart-stopping few seconds, the mare collected herself.

Elyssa's brush with disaster chilled Hunter. He faced to the front again and wished futilely that there had been a way to avoid this.

I should have made her stay at the ranch, Hunter thought savagely. *She has no business risking her neck out here!*

Yet Hunter had no way of enforcing such an order, short of tying Elyssa hand and foot to the bed.

And if he got her anywhere near a bed, it wouldn't be to tie her up and leave her.

With a searing curse, Hunter reined Bugle Boy to his right. The horse lunged up and over the lip of the shallow wash. All around Bugle Boy's flying hooves the grasslands unfolded in sunny, tawny glory.

On Hunter's right, less than a mile away, lay the vast stretch of the dried-up marsh. It rippled beneath the wind in shades of gold and brown.

About a quarter mile ahead, a large band of mustangs thundered flat out across the land, pursued by Ladder S riders and their straining mounts.

Hunter and Elyssa joined the chase. As they closed

the gap between themselves and the mustangs, they were careful to stay between the wild horses and the marsh.

Any mustang that thought to run off into the tawny maze of the marsh would be turned back by one of the Ladder S riders. Other riders took up positions that kept the mustangs running toward the old brush corral that had been built years before for the annual wild horse roundups.

By the time the mustangs reached the wide end of the brushy funnel that led to the corral, the horses were lathered and blowing hard. They swept down the funnel in a sea of whipping manes and tails, and flashing, driving hooves.

Behind them riders leaned low in the saddle and dragged the concealed gate close. Before the mustangs understood what had happened, they were caught.

Elyssa pulled her hard-breathing mare to a walk, wiped sweat from her own eyes, and tucked stray ribbons of hair back behind her ears. Eagerly she circled the big brush corral, trying to count horses.

Inside the corral, mustangs milled in seething circles, looking for a way out. Countless sharp hooves churned through grass to dirt. Dust rose like smoke into the sky.

It was impossible to count the mustangs, but Elyssa was grinning just the same after she finished her circuit of the corral. She had seen many Ladder S brands on the horses' hips, which meant that a lot of the horses had already been broken. They would quickly get used to men again.

Hunter rode up alongside Elyssa's rawboned mare. Though he wouldn't have admitted it, he wanted to reassure himself that she was all right after the dangerous ride.

A single look told Hunter that Elyssa was excited and exhilarated rather than hurt. Her cheeks were pink, her blue-green eyes were as vivid as gemstones, and her smile was radiant.

Hunter couldn't help smiling in return.

"How many do you think we caught?" Elyssa asked jubilantly.

With an effort, Hunter forced himself to look away from red lips to the churning sea of mustangs that had been dammed behind brush fences.

"Maybe two hundred," Hunter said slowly. "At a guess, I'd say about half of them are fit to ride."

Then he smiled rather coldly, thinking of the army officer who had wanted Elyssa along with the horses.

"But then, the army didn't say the horses had to be good, did they?" Hunter asked softly. "Just green-broke."

Elyssa laughed. Like her smile, her laughter was vibrant with pleasure. Possessively she looked at the mustangs.

For the first time she began to believe the ranch might truly be saved. With that many fresh, vigorous horses, surely the men would be able to find more cattle.

"A lot of the horses have Ladder S brands," Elyssa said.

"Some have Slash River brands."

Elyssa frowned. Impatiently she pulled a stray ribbon of silver-gold hair from her eyes and tucked it up beneath her hat.

"Ab Culpepper's brand," Hunter added.

"Fresh, no doubt," she said sarcastically. "Real fresh."

Hunter shrugged. "Ab hasn't been here long enough to have old brands."

"How many of ours do you think he has branded?" Elyssa asked.

"We'll know tomorrow or the next day, after the mustangs settle down long enough for us to do a real tally."

As Elyssa watched, a familiar-looking mare galloped by just inside the brush corral. A Slash River brand was dark and fresh on her hip.

Yet the mare was one of the Ladder S's best brood-mares, and a fine cow pony as well.

"Damn him!" Elyssa burst out.

"On that we agree."

Hunter stood in the stirrups and whistled shrilly.

Morgan emerged from the dust cloud surrounding the corral. His tough little pony was streaked with sweat and breathing deeply, but still game for whatever its rider wanted. The horse trotted over to Hunter and Elyssa with its head high.

The air tasted of dust and shimmered with the intense autumn sun.

"Tell the boys they did a good job," Hunter said to Morgan. "Then pick two of them to sleep out here and make sure none get away."

"Yes, suh."

"The dogs could do that," Elyssa said.

"Not if whoever was in the garden decides to punch a hole in the corral," Hunter said bluntly.

Elyssa's mouth turned down, but she didn't disagree.

Hunter was right. The dogs could no longer be trusted with any kind of guard duty.

"Send for Mickey and a wagonload of those water barrels," Hunter said to Morgan.

"Yes, suh!"

"A horse with a gut full of water doesn't buck nearly as hard as a thirsty one," Hunter added dryly.

Morgan gave a shout of laughter, saluted, and trotted off toward the barn, which was barely a quarter mile away.

The Ladder S hands who were particularly good with a rope went into the corral. Bandannas pulled up over their noses against the dust, the men rode among the milling mustangs, picking out targets.

With as little fuss as possible, men began roping horses that wore a brand of any kind. Those were the animals that went from wild to mostly tame the instant a loop settled around their necks. They offered no fight while they were led out of the brush corral, trotted across the grassland, and put into the home corral close to the barn.

By the time Morgan returned, the brush corral was down to perhaps seventy horses. Few of them wore brands. All of them were wary and wild as deer.

Mickey drove up with a buckboard loaded with full water barrels. It was pulled by six broad-shouldered oxen. Morgan and his pony walked alongside to encourage the oxen.

The sight of the water barrels reminded Elyssa of just how much she would have liked a bath. The surprising heat of the sun, the exertion of the work, and the endless dust felt like a blanket wrapped around her dark riding habit.

Elyssa had long since unbuttoned her jacket, but that was no longer enough. She stripped off the jacket and tied it behind her saddle. Then, surreptitiously, she unbuttoned a few buttons on her high-necked muslin blouse. Air flowed through the opening to the thin cotton chemise, and from there to the hot skin beneath.

She made a murmurous sound of pleasure that went into Hunter like a knife.

"Mickey! Sonny! Reed!" Hunter barked. "Help Morgan with those barrels!"

Hunter dismounted and went to add his own strength to the task.

"Mickey, roll them down those planks one at a time," Hunter said. "Careful, boy! If one of those ran over a man, he'd be flatter than a shadow."

One by one the men rolled barrels down two stout planks from the wagon bed to the hot ground. Then each barrel was rolled and shoved over to the trough at one edge of the corral.

Morgan knocked out the stopper on the first barrel. With a grunt of effort, Hunter tipped the barrel up onto the edge of the trough. Silver water gushed and danced into the dusty trough.

The scent of fresh water brought the milling mustangs to a halt. Heads turned, ears pricked. The animals all but licked their lips in anticipation as they eyed the trough.

Elyssa knew just how the mustangs felt. She would have given a great deal to be able to stand beneath the gurgling, leaping water and get wet all the way through to her skin.

"Mickey," Hunter called. "Bring the next one."

Elyssa barely noticed Mickey's bulging muscles as he wrestled a barrel into place. She was too busy noticing that Hunter had undone a few buttons of his own. Black hair gleamed through the opening in Hunter's pale blue shirt.

Without thinking, Elyssa dismounted and walked closer.

"Watch out, Miss Elyssa!" Sonny called.

Elyssa looked up, saw that a barrel had gotten away from Sonny, and leaped nimbly aside. The barrel bounced from the top of the planks and fell apart when it hit the ground.

Water exploded, drenching everything within reach, Elyssa included.

Her startled shriek drew every man's eyes, but it was the sudden feminine laughter that held them.

Hunter vaulted the corral gate and ran toward Sonny with mayhem in his eyes.

"Oh, gosh, Miss Elyssa," Sonny said. "I'm plumb sorry. That durned barrel just had a mind of its own."

Laughing, plucking at the blouse that was plastered to her skin, Elyssa turned aside Sonny's apologies.

"That's all right," she said. "I was just wishing for a bath, and then I had one."

Hunter gave Sonny a look that made the younger man long for a place to hide.

"Did anything but water hit you?" Hunter asked Elyssa roughly.

"No."

"You sure?"

"Uh-huh. And even if it had, it would have been worth it." Elyssa threw back her head and laughed at the sky. "Lord but that water feels good!"

Hunter didn't answer. Desire held him in a cruel vise. He couldn't breathe for the violence of the blood beating in his veins.

Every curve, every softness, everything feminine about Elyssa stood out clearly against her drenched clothes. Her nipples were drawn into hard peaks that fairly begged for a man's eyes, for his hands, and most of all, for his mouth.

Then Elyssa looked at Hunter and her eyes changed, dilating in an instant, answering the sweet violence of his own desire.

With swift, savage motions Hunter went to Elyssa's horse and got her jacket.

"Put it on before you get a chill," Hunter said, holding the jacket out to her.

"A chill? Today? If you haven't noticed, it's hot and—"

"You're making a spectacle of yourself," he said icily, "but you already know that, don't you? *Put it on.*"

Elyssa opened her mouth to argue, noticed that all the men were staring, and shut her mouth fast. Angrily she took the jacket and began jamming her wet arms into the narrow sleeves. The motion made her breasts sway against the clinging fabric.

Hunter wanted to howl with frustration. With a pungent curse he turned away from the endless temptation that was Elyssa Sutton.

The first thing Hunter noticed was that all the ranch hands were still watching her.

"Show's over," Hunter snarled, looking at each man in turn. "Get back to work!"

"Miss Elyssa, are you sure you should be out here alone?" Sonny asked anxiously.

"I'm not alone. You and Morgan are with me."

Elyssa's tone was abrupt. Since the incident of the water barrel yesterday, she had stayed away from the men.

But she was heartily tired of canning, pureeing, pickling, chopping, peeling, and otherwise dealing with the produce of her ruined garden.

Besides, the day was too beautiful to stay indoors all the time. The slanting, buttery light of late afternoon had lured her out to look at the mustangs they had captured. Her hopes for the future of the Ladder S were pinned on their glossy backs.

"Yes, but—" Sonny began.

"But nothing," Elyssa interrupted. "I'm the owner of the Ladder S, not Hunter. It's a fact everyone should keep in mind."

"Especially Hunter?" Morgan drawled behind Elyssa.

Warily she turned around. The humor and understanding in Morgan's black eyes disarmed her.

"Especially Hunter," she agreed with a wry laugh.

"He's just protecting you from the men," Morgan said quietly.

"Really? Then why do I feel that he's protecting the men from *me?*"

Sighing, Morgan lifted his hat and resettled it on his thick, tightly curled black hair.

"Well, if you had known his wife, you would understand," Morgan said finally. "She was a pretty young thing like you. She came to grief because of it. So did he."

"What happened?" Elyssa asked, hungry for knowledge of Hunter's past.

"Not my story to tell. Excuse me, miss. I'd better be getting back to those mustangs."

"But—"

"Now, don't you wander out from the buildings without an escort," Morgan cautioned. "That intruder was here before dawn again."

"What? Hunter didn't say anything about it to me."

"Nothing to say. He slipped past the bunkhouse and opened the corral gate. There was hell to pay rounding up those new horses in the dark."

"Were any missing?" Elyssa asked sharply.

"Hard to say," Morgan admitted. "The horses are all strangers to us."

"What does the tally show?"

"Twelve missing."

"Only the branded horses that were in the home corral are gone?" Elyssa asked.

"Yes, ma'am. The mustangs are too wild to be worth the trouble of stealing. Once they're green broke, though . . ." Morgan shrugged.

"Only horses with Ladder S brands were taken?"

"Yes, ma'am. It looks that way."

"Bloody hell," she said angrily.

"Yes, ma'am. It's all of that."

Elyssa climbed the corral for a better view of the remaining horses. Ignoring the dusty rails, which left broad marks on her rust-colored riding habit, she sat on the top rail and examined the brands of the horses.

Less than half of the remaining horses wore the Ladder S brand. Except for a scattering of B Bar brands, the animals wore the Slash River sign.

Elyssa's temper flashed. Angrily she leaped down and went to the barn. She saddled and bridled Leopard, jammed the shotgun in its saddle sheath, and mounted in a flurry of dark cloth.

The weight of the divided skirts hampered every move she made. Muttering under her breath, vowing to rip apart this riding habit as she had the other, Elyssa headed for the boundary between the Ladder S and the B Bar.

Before Elyssa was beyond the ranch yard, Morgan reappeared. He was mounted on a bay gelding that had been running with mustangs just a few days ago.

"I'll be going with you, ma'am."

"I'm not going far," she said.

"Yes, ma'am."

"But you're going with me anyway, is that it?"

"Yes, ma'am."

"I'm carrying a shotgun," she said tartly.

"Yes, ma'am."

"I'm a good shot."

"Yes, ma'am."

"You have more important work to do."

"No, ma'am."

With a muttered word, Elyssa reined Leopard toward the web of ghost trails that led to Wind Gap—and the B Bar.

Morgan followed.

As the bay turned alongside Elyssa, she saw that the Ladder S brand on the horse's hip had been changed to read Slash River. It was a simple alteration, a matter of filling in the space between the original S-S and adding a diagonal bar across the middle.

"What if some Culpepper objects to your riding his so-called horse?" Elyssa asked acidly.

"Then I'll know for certain that God is kind."

Morgan's wolfish smile said more than his words. He was plainly yearning to meet an angry Culpepper.

Elyssa tried not to smile. It was impossible.

She liked Morgan. Besides, it was Hunter's orders that had turned Morgan into her personal, armed escort, rather than any inclination on Morgan's part.

"Stay behind me," Elyssa said, giving in. "I don't want any more horse tracks than are already out there."

"Yes, ma'am."

Elyssa lifted the reins and sent Leopard into a canter. She headed straight for the web of ghost trails that joined the B Bar and the Ladder S.

It didn't take much of a tracker to see what had happened. A small group of unshod horses had wandered—or been driven—from Ladder S to B Bar land during the night.

There were no tracks coming back to the Ladder S.

Damn it, Bill, Elyssa thought bitterly. *Why are you giving Culpeppers free rein on your land?*

Are you doing it to ruin me because I wouldn't sell you the ranch?

The idea simply didn't fit with what Elyssa knew of Bill. He was a hard man at times, but no more than the wild land required.

And he had always been gentle with her, even when he was angry that she wouldn't sell him the Ladder S and stay in England for the rest of her life.

Is it because Bill is just one man against the Culpepper clan? Did he decide that it's better to lose a ranch than his life?

Elyssa hoped that was the case. She could understand discretion being the better part of valor.

She couldn't understand naked thievery.

Having met Gaylord Culpepper, Elyssa knew that it would take a very strong, very brave, very determined man to take on the Culpeppers alone. She couldn't blame Bill for figuring it just wasn't worth the grief.

Elyssa urged Leopard forward, following the tracks of the horses that had been stolen from the Ladder S's home corral. The tracks headed for B Bar land, then veered off to one side in a line that went straight down into a particularly thick section of the marsh.

Mac had once told her that there were trails and by-ways and islands of solid land hidden among the tall, tall reeds. At least, that's what the Indians had said to him.

A man could hide a lot of livestock in the marsh . . . if he knew how to get from bog to dry land in a maze of reeds, mud, and drying waterways.

Elyssa stood in the stirrups and shaded her eyes as she stared down the gentle incline to the marsh. There could be hundreds of cattle and horses scattered through the reeds and grassy tussocks.

Or there could be none.

It could be simply a tawny ambush baited with horse tracks and lined with Culpepper rifles.

"Ma'am?" Morgan said. "You wouldn't be thinking of sashaying on down to that there swamp, would you?" Elyssa didn't answer.

Morgan cleared his throat apologetically.

"I wouldn't do that if I was you, ma'am. In fact, I would be right firm about seeing that you don't."

A glance at Morgan's face told Elyssa there was nothing tentative or apologetic about his expression. He meant exactly what he had said.

"Hunter's orders?" she asked.

"Common sense," Morgan said bluntly. "Unless you're half swamp rat, you're going to get lost out there."

"Or ambushed."

Morgan blew out a breath and resettled his hat on his head.

"Yes, ma'am. The thought has occurred to this cowboy ever since I first saw them tracks heading off into that choice slice of hell."

The longer Elyssa stared at the tracks, the more certain she became that they were false, dangerous, or both.

This isn't Bill's way of doing things.

Bill asked outright for the sale of the Ladder S to him, and then told me how rock-stupid I was for not doing it.

Face-to-face.

Yelling.

Not sneaking around in the small hours of night, playing cruel pranks.

After a final look at the marsh, Elyssa sat back in the saddle and turned to Morgan.

"Where is Hunter?" she asked crisply.

"Bustin' broncs."

Elyssa reined Leopard around and headed for the brush corral at a gallop.

Morgan followed. His eyes watched the marsh until they were well beyond rifle range.

When Elyssa and Morgan arrived at the brush corral, Reed had a mustang by the ears and was hanging on for all he was worth. Hunter grabbed the bridle right at the bit, pulled the bronc's head around nearly to the left stirrup, and vaulted into the saddle.

"Let 'er rip," Hunter said, releasing his hold on the bit.

Reed let go of the bronc's ears and dove for the other side of the corral gate.

Smiling, Morgan sat back in his saddle to enjoy the show.

The mustang was a wiry little stud with springs in his feet. He swapped ends, crow-hopped, and twisted his hindquarters like a fish in an effort to unseat his rider.

Hunter rode him like a cat, never moving more than necessary, never showing daylight between himself and the saddle. He used the spurs not as a punishment, but to make certain the stud was doing his best.

After a few minutes the mustang stopped bucking, snorted hard, and turned around to look at the strange growth on his back.

Speaking in a low, calm voice, Hunter stroked the horse's neck. Then he dismounted with a peculiar, flowing movement that never left him off balance in the stirrup.

Hunter's boots barely touched the ground before he took hold of the bridle, held the stud's head up, and got back into the saddle once more.

The stud snorted, sidestepped, bucked halfheartedly, and then stood still.

For the first time Elyssa noticed that the mustang sported a new Ladder S brand on his hip. It was the same for every other mustang in the corral.

Hunter dismounted.

The stud simply looked at him.

"Tally this one and get the next," Hunter called to Reed.

The horse was officially green-broke, which meant that a good rider could mount him in reasonable safety without the help of another man.

"Damn, but that man's a sight to behold with a bronc," Morgan said, grinning. "Only seen one better than him."

"Better? I doubt that," Elyssa said.

"Ask Hunter. He'll agree that his brother has a finer hand with broncs."

Holding his lasso ready, Reed rode slowly toward the mustangs milling at the far end of the corral. There was a flurry of shying, snorting, and lunging to the side, but to no avail. A loop shot out and settled around the neck of another bay.

Reed wound his end of the rope around the saddle horn and dragged the reluctant bronc to the snubbing post to be saddled.

Without looking at Elyssa or even acknowledging that she was there, Hunter stripped the bridle and saddle from the first mustang and headed toward the snubbing post.

"Hunter," Elyssa called. "I have to talk to you."

He stopped and looked at her over his shoulder.

"Later," Hunter said curtly. "I'm busy."

"It's about the missing horses."

"That's why I'm busy. I'm breaking new ones to replace the others."

"It will just take a few minutes."

"That's worth one bronc, Sassy."

With that, Hunter resumed walking toward the snubbing post at the far end of the corral.

Elyssa aimed Leopard at the gate.

Before Hunter realized what was happening, Leopard had jumped the gate and pivoted to a stop dead across Hunter's path.

Damn her recklessness, he thought savagely. *She's going to take that stud over the wrong fence someday and both of them will end up in a tangle in the dust.*

But that wasn't what was really bothering Hunter, and he knew it.

He wanted Elyssa so much, and hated wanting her at all, that it angered him even to look at her. The memory of her laughter after being drenched with cold water haunted him.

The memory of her nipples showing clearly through the thin, wet blouse set him afire.

"It's about Bill," Elyssa said. "I'm worried."

Hearing Elyssa's voice soften on Bill's name, and seeing the concern in her eyes, put the finishing touches on Hunter's already raw temper.

"Just what is it about that cow-rustling, horse-thieving, Culpepper-loving son of a bitch that worries you?" Hunter drawled.

"We can't prove that Bill is stealing livestock."

"What kind of proof do you need, little girl? A confession? A track-by-track demonstration of how he did it? *A shot in the back from ambush?*"

"Bill would never hurt me," Elyssa said urgently. "You don't know him like I do. I'm—"

"That's gospel," Hunter said in a savage voice. "I've always preferred women."

The insinuation didn't even register on Elyssa. She just kept talking right over Hunter.

"—afraid that he's being held hostage by the Culpeppers," she finished.

"Hostage. Judas H. Priest."

"It's the only explanation that makes any sense."

"You can't see the truth when it stands on your feet and spits in your eye, can you? Dear old Bill is stealing you blind!"

"No! He needs our help!"

"He needs a bullet."

Elyssa looked at Hunter's bleak eyes and remembered the tangible hatred he had for everything associated with the Culpeppers.

Cow-rustling, horse-thieving, Culpepper-loving son of a bitch.

"No," she said in a raw voice. "I won't let you hurt Bill. Do you hear me? Don't hurt him!"

Hunter gave her a raking, contemptuous glance.

Then he wondered why pretty flirts like Elyssa and Belinda ended up losing their heads over two-bit cheaters twice their age who happened to be neighbors.

Swiftly Hunter stepped closer to Leopard. When he spoke, only Elyssa heard him.

"Quit dogging my tracks and wearing silk," Hunter said in a low, icy voice. "If I wanted what you're flaunting, I'd be the one guarding you, not Morgan."

"I'm not—"

"The hell you aren't," he interrupted. "The boys laugh about it in the bunkhouse, all the hip swinging and lip licking and come-hither looks you give me."

"I do no such thing!"

"That will come as news to me and the boys," Hunter retorted. "Go away, Sassy. When I feel like taking what you're shoving in my face, I'll let you know."

Elyssa flushed with a combination of anger and embarrassment that her interest in Hunter was a subject of jokes in the bunkhouse.

"Morgan," Hunter barked. "Open the gate."

The gate squealed and creaked behind Hunter.

"Now, get that spotted stud out of my way," Hunter said. "I have better things to do than talk to a flirt."

Elyssa looked at Hunter for a long, tight moment. There was no give in him, no hint that he would relent and act on her fears for Bill.

Fine, she told herself fiercely. *I'll do it myself.*

Ignoring the open gate, Elyssa reined Leopard toward the wide brush fence of the corral. The stud took it like a spotted deer, leaving Hunter swearing in the dust.

~15

*H*olding her breath, Elyssa crept down the staircase. She prayed every step of the way that Hunter was so exhausted by breaking broncs that he wouldn't awaken.

Or if he did, that he would mistake the creak and pop of the stairs for more complaints of the house as the damp ground fog settled into the wood.

The thought of facing Hunter after the way he had stripped her pride raw in the brush corral made Elyssa feel hot and cold at once.

Don't think about Hunter and the hands laughing at you. Next to what's happening on the Ladder S, all of the rest is just chicken feed.

But Elyssa still didn't want to face Hunter. She didn't know whether she would ignore him or lift the shotgun and watch him sweat.

The latter thought had great appeal.

Don't think about Hunter.

Only when the door to the kitchen closed behind her did Elyssa relax and let out a sigh of relief. She had gotten away from her sharp-tongued watchdog.

She hurried across the open area between house and barn. A pumpkin-colored moon hung big and low in the sky. There were a few high clouds, remainders of an evening storm. Despite the moon's size, it cast little light. What illumination reached the earth was sucked up by a ground fog that clung to every dip, hollow, and crease.

Something cold nudged Elyssa's fingers. She muffled a startled shriek and looked down.

Vixen looked up at her, wagging her tail hopefully.

"No," Elyssa whispered. "Go back to guarding the barn."

Vixen cocked her head, hesitated, and then trotted off to the barn.

Elyssa looked toward the bunkhouse. Streamers of ground fog danced like silver flames in a faint wind. Not a bit of light shone from the bunkhouse. She was up even before Gimp.

Quickly Elyssa went to the barn, saddled Leopard, and headed for Wind Gap. With her black riding habit, a dark stockman's coat, and a black scarf tied around her hair, she was very hard to see even in the gaps between the fog.

In the fog itself, she was invisible.

The ride to Bill's ranch had never taken Elyssa longer. In addition to the fog, she used every bit of available cover to conceal her passage through the night.

There was no way of knowing if the Culpeppers had anyone watching Wind Gap.

As Elyssa had hoped, once she was through Wind Gap, the fog became thicker. But experience told her that the fog wouldn't last much beyond daybreak. By then, she had to be back at the ranch.

And Bill Moreland had to be with her.

Elyssa feared what would happen if Hunter met Bill over a rifle.

What is it about that cow-rustling, horse-thieving, Culpepper-loving son of a bitch that worries you?

Elyssa shivered at the memory of what she had seen

in Hunter's eyes when he had drawn a bead on Ab Culpepper a few days ago.

Hatred.

He needs a bullet.

Elyssa was afraid that Hunter would shoot Bill on sight, the same as he would four-legged vermin stalking a calf.

I can't let that happen, Elyssa thought starkly. *Just because Bill hasn't lifted a finger to help me, that doesn't mean he deserves to die.*

He was so good to me all those years before I went to England.

With determination in every line of her body, Elyssa guided Leopard through the fading darkness. If any Culpeppers were guarding the approach to Bill's cabin, they didn't raise a cry when Leopard ghosted past.

Tautly Elyssa watched ahead for any sign of light. There was none. She dismounted and tied Leopard to a bush. With great care she crept as close to the cabin's privy as she dared.

There was a thicket of brush only ten feet from the back of the privy. Crouching, Elyssa merged her outline with the shrubs as Bill had taught her to do when they hunted together.

Elyssa licked her lips, pursed them, and whistled softly. A clear, lilting nightingale call lifted into the fading night. Bill had taught her the whistling notes years ago, when she was a girl and her mother's silver laughter rang through the house.

No light came on in the cabin in response to Elyssa's whistle.

No one called through the night to her.

Nervously Elyssa looked at the sky. The stars were already gone. A faint peach color glowed in the east.

She sent the lilting call through the silence again.

Nothing happened.

Maybe Bill drank too much and is sleeping too hard to hear me, she thought anxiously.

Licking lips that felt as dry as flannel, she pursed again and whistled. A false nightingale sang to the black cabin for a third time.

No lantern flickered to life.

Dawn condensed across the eastern sky in a pale wash of pink.

Elyssa waited.

And waited.

Just as she was going to give up, the front door of the cabin creaked. A man came out and headed for the privy.

Bill.

Relief coursed through Elyssa.

Bill walked to the privy with the hesitating steps of a man who was hung over or half-blind in the predawn gloom. Somehow his ragged stride led him past the privy to the thicket.

"Over here," Elyssa whispered. "It's me."

"Christ, Sassy," Bill hissed. "I told you when you got back never to come here! Go home!"

Elyssa tried to make out Bill's expression. What she saw of his eyes in the rising light didn't comfort her.

Bloodshot.

Angry.

And most of all, afraid.

"Just like your mother," Bill whispered, furious. "Reckless to the bone! Get out of here!"

"Come back with me," Elyssa whispered coaxingly. "I need you."

"Go home."

Though Bill's voice was soft, the expression on his face wasn't.

"Bill—"

"Go!"

"No," Elyssa said in a low, hard voice. She stood up

in a rush. "Too many Ladder S cows have been stolen. Too many horses are missing. The tracks all lead to—"

"Well, well," said a stranger's voice from behind Elyssa, "would you lookee here. Someone brung Ab a prime piece of woman-flesh."

Bill stumbled and fell into Elyssa. She found herself propelled away from the stranger.

"*Run,*" Bill whispered fiercely.

This time Elyssa didn't argue. She turned and ran.

Within three steps she was brought up short by the iron band of a man's fingers wrapped around her upper arm. She gasped in pain as she was spun roughly toward Ab Culpepper. He was tall, rawboned, and had pale eyes that glittered in the gloomy light. The look in those eyes made Elyssa's stomach turn over.

"Really prime," Ab said.

Elyssa jerked her arm. "Let go of me!"

"Not so fast, gal. Just because ol' Bill here is too gone with drink to entertain a lady don't mean you have to leave all disappointed like."

"Let me go," Elyssa said between her teeth.

"No gal never said Ab Culpepper can't rise to the occasion," Ab drawled.

Instinctively Elyssa looked at Bill, knowing that she couldn't defeat Ab alone.

Bill's hands were nowhere near the six-gun he wore on his hip.

Cold seeped into Elyssa's soul. Bill wasn't going to help her now any more than he had helped her in the past two months.

Then Elyssa realized that Bill was looking past her, as though she were no longer important. The bleak, helpless rage on Bill's face told her more than words could have.

She turned to follow Bill's glance.

Culpeppers materialized out of the dawn as Elyssa

looked. First one. Then another. Then Gaylord. They were no more than ten feet away from Bill. Tall, rawhide-lean, pale blue eyes; the Culpeppers were alike as peas in a pod.

Or devils in hell.

"Say howdy to the boys," Ab urged Elyssa.

"Release me," she said distinctly.

Ab smiled.

Elyssa's stomach lurched again. The cruelty in Ab was frighteningly clear.

Gaylord Culpepper might have been missing a piece of his humanity, but Ab was missing his entire soul.

"Just ignore ol' Bill," Ab advised. "He's been right testy for a time. Comes of not having a gal to poke."

Not a word passed Elyssa's bloodless lips. Her eyes had told her that words would do no good. The Culpeppers had Bill dead where he stood.

All they had to do was pull the trigger.

Ab saw the direction of Elyssa's glance and smiled. The pressure of his fingers on her arm eased a bit.

There was nowhere for Elyssa to run. Even if there had been, the fog was vanishing as she watched. The last pale wisps were barely knee-high.

No cover.

No place to hide.

Ab pulled off Elyssa's hat with a fast swipe of his hand. Flaxen hair glowed in the light.

"Thought so," Ab said with satisfaction. "You be that Sassy bitch."

"My name is Elyssa."

The look on Ab's face said he didn't care what her name was.

"Let's go to the cabin," Ab said, smiling. "We got business to take care of."

Bill gave Ab a quick, savage glance.

Ab didn't even notice. All he cared about at the moment was the girl with the flaxen hair and stubborn blue-green eyes.

"We have no business together," Elyssa said distinctly.

"Now, don't be so hasty, gal. You might like my business," Ab said slyly.

"I'm late. I'm expected back at my ranch."

"That's what we'll be talkin' about."

"What?"

"You gettin' shuck of the Ladder S," Ab said impatiently. "All nice and legal like. Nothin' for them blue-bellied Yankees to cry over."

"No."

"Thirty Yankee dollars," Ab said. "That's my first and last offer."

Elyssa looked at him as though he was mad. Thirty dollars couldn't buy a Ladder S corral, much less the whole ranch.

Just as quickly as Elyssa had glanced at Ab, she looked away. Looking into Ab's eyes was terrifying.

"No," she said hoarsely.

A fourth man materialized out of the rising dawn, rifle in one hand and six-gun in the other. He was standing well away from the Culpeppers. Gun drawn, he waited.

There was no eagerness in his stance. Nor was there any of the feral lust that possessed the Culpeppers. The calm readiness of the man's body was more dangerous than the weapons he held.

With great clarity Elyssa sensed that the fourth man was more deadly than the rest of the Culpeppers put together. She was as certain of it as she was of her own too rapid heartbeat.

My God, what have I done? she asked herself in dismay. *Bill is little better than a prisoner of these raiders. And now I am, too.*

The thought of being at the mercy of the likes of Ab

Culpepper made Elyssa's stomach twist. Without stopping to think, she jerked her arm and stepped back out of his reach.

The motion was so swift it caught Ab by surprise. He grabbed for Elyssa, but a word from Gaylord stopped him cold.

Ab glanced over his shoulder. He said something vicious. Then his hand fell to his side once more.

Elyssa turned to Bill even as she retreated toward Leopard.

"Come back with me," she coaxed. "Penny is worried about you. We need you."

Bill shook his head curtly.

"Leave and don't come back," he said. *"Go."*

Elyssa didn't argue. She scrambled on Leopard, reined him around, and kicked him into a canter.

Just as she was congratulating herself on having brazened out her escape, Elyssa noticed what the Culpeppers obviously had already seen.

A bit ahead and to her right, there was a rifle poking out from the cover of boulders and brush.

As Elyssa galloped by, the barrel didn't waver from tracking each breath Ab took. Clearly whoever was on the other end of the weapon wasn't a friend of the Culpeppers.

Hunter, Elyssa thought. *He heard me going down the stairs after all.*

Part of her was very grateful.

Another part of her wanted nothing more than to get beyond the reach of the scorching lecture she was certain to get from Hunter. She leaned low over Leopard's neck, urging him into a faster gait.

Despite Elyssa's desire to flee, she kept the big stallion well below the pace she wanted. She might have been reckless, as Bill had accused, but she was far from suicidal.

The same couldn't have been said of Hunter at the moment. He caught up with Elyssa before she crossed onto Ladder S land.

The bleak fury in Hunter's eyes made Elyssa want to hide.

The fact that he didn't say a word until they were within sight of the ranch building only made it worse.

Abruptly he urged Bugle Boy across Leopard's trail, forcing the spotted stud to stop.

"Pull up," Hunter said coldly to her.

With visible reluctance, Elyssa reined in.

"I thought if I talked to Bill—" she began.

"Talk? Is that what girls like you call it?" Hunter interrupted sarcastically. "Well, that puts my mind considerably at ease."

"—he would realize how desperate it was on the Ladder S," Elyssa continued in a rush, "and then he would help or at least not hurt. I didn't know that—"

"You didn't know one damned thing but that you had an itch and he was the man to scratch it," Hunter interrupted.

"What are you talking about?"

"Hell," Hunter said in disgust. "I'm talking about a young girl and a neighbor man who's old enough to know better."

"It's not Bill's fault he can't take on the Culpeppers single-handed," she retorted. "My God, you won't even take them on with *seven* hands!"

Elyssa's defense of Bill infuriated Hunter. It reminded him too much of Belinda's tirades whenever things didn't go her way. He could still hear his dead wife blaming her husband, blaming the war, blaming Texas, blaming the kids, blaming everything on earth but herself for whatever made her unhappy.

"You're just like Belinda," Hunter snarled. "You don't give a damn about the people who depend on you.

You don't give a damn about your responsibilities. All you care about is a female itch that has to be scratched and to hell with what's right.''

Elyssa blinked, startled by the unexpected turn in the conversation.

"So you go running off to the neighbor," Hunter continued, "risking everything, including your own foolish life. But will you listen to common sense?"

"I—"

"Hell, no," Hunter said savagely. "You'll go sneaking off to meet the neighbor halfway, and while you're rolling around in the grass, your kids are being defiled by Culpeppers and then sold into slavery with the Comancheros.''

When Elyssa realized what Hunter was saying, a wave of sickness went through her.

"Hunter—'' she said hoarsely.

He didn't even hear. He was living in the hell of the past, a hell that haunted him every waking day of his life.

"The Culpeppers got around to Belinda, finally," Hunter said. "Before they were finished, I imagine she was glad enough to die. Ted and little Em probably would have been glad to die, too. They weren't as lucky as their mother. It took days. When I think of how those Culpeppers dragged little Em—"

"Hunter. Stop."

Hunter closed his eyes. Silently he struggled to control the rage inside his soul.

When he opened his eyes, he found himself in the present rather than the ruined past. He looked down at Elyssa's fingers. They were wrapped around his wrist in a painful grip.

"Torturing yourself won't help," Elyssa said urgently. "It's over, Hunter. They're dead and you're alive. Tormenting yourself won't help them one bit."

Slowly Hunter's eyes focused on Elyssa.

"I wasn't there when they needed me," Hunter said in a raw voice. "My kids died and I wasn't even there."

"I'm sorry," Elyssa whispered. "Oh, Hunter, I'm so sorry."

And she was. For his children. For his dead wife. For Hunter.

For herself.

Elyssa finally understood why Hunter refused to let himself love her. It wasn't that he had loved his first wife so much.

It was that he had been betrayed by her.

Hunter jerked his wrist from Elyssa's grasp, as though her touch was distasteful to him.

"Stop sneaking off to see Bill," Hunter said harshly. "After I bury those damned Culpeppers, you can move in with Bill for all I care. But not until."

"I'm not like Belinda. I love Bill, but not in that way."

Hunter's upper lip curled in silent disbelief.

"I saw four Culpeppers," he said. "Were there any more?"

Elyssa wanted to argue about the differences between herself and Belinda, but a look at Hunter's eyes convinced her that now was the wrong time.

Maybe tomorrow.

Or the day after.

Maybe by then Hunter would be more reasonable.

Maybe by then his eyes wouldn't look like clear black slices of hell.

"I didn't see any other Culpeppers," Elyssa said. "There was another man, though."

Hunter watched her with unnerving intensity.

"I think he was the most dangerous of all," she said.

"You recognized him?"

"No. Not by name."

"Then how do you know he's dangerous?"

Elyssa blew out a soft breath. Some of the deadly chill was leaving Hunter's voice.

"By the way he didn't move," she said simply.

"What does that mean?"

"Most men fidget or shift their weight or fiddle with their mustache or their cartridge belt or something."

Hunter waited, motionless. His very stillness reminded Elyssa of the other man.

"This man didn't move except to breathe," Elyssa said. "He wasn't keyed up or frightened or bloodthirsty or anything at all. He was just . . . ready."

"For what?"

"Whatever came. He would take it, whatever it was, without flinching. As though nothing could touch him but death, and death held no terrors for him. Like you were when you first came to the ranch."

Bugle Boy snorted and pulled against the bit.

Hunter ignored the horse. The realization that he had missed one of the men surrounding Elyssa made him deeply uneasy.

"I didn't see him," Hunter said.

"He was standing apart from the Culpeppers."

"What did he look like?"

"He was . . ."

Elyssa's voice faded. She looked at Hunter.

"He was rather like you in height and build," she said finally. "Or maybe it was just that he was wearing bits of an old Confederate uniform that made me think of you."

"Left- or right-handed?"

"Six-gun in one hand and a repeating rifle in the other."

Hunter smiled thinly. "No wonder he wasn't worried."

"And moccasins," Elyssa said.

"Moccasins?" Hunter asked, his voice sharp.

"Yes. He was wearing knee-high moccasins. Fringed. Like Apache moccasins."

Elyssa tilted her head to one side as a thought occurred to her.

"I don't think," she said, "that anyone else saw him. He just sort of appeared at the edge of a willow thicket when the mist cleared."

"Fringed moccasins," Hunter repeated softly. "Be damned."

Elyssa stared. There was a blending of emotions in Hunter's voice that intrigued her. Affection was one emotion. Respect was another. Anticipation was a third.

But it was compassion that gave Hunter's voice a gentleness that was startling.

"Do you know him?" she asked.

"Maybe. A lot of men wear moccasins."

"Not all that many, surely."

Hunter smiled. "I've been known to myself, when I was on the stalk."

"Who is he?"

"If he's who I think he is, you're right. That boy wasn't the least bit worried about what would happen next."

ᥫ16

That night, long after everyone was asleep, a stair creaked softly under Hunter's weight.

Damnation, he thought fiercely.

He waited, breath held, for sounds that would tell him Elyssa was awake and moving around in her room.

Nothing came to Hunter's ears but the rhythm of his own heart and the gusting of the cold autumn wind around the eaves.

Carefully Hunter resumed sneaking down the stairs. Making no noise, he went out the kitchen door and walked quickly across the ground to the barn.

Though clouds were piled heavily over the mountains, bright moonlight poured over him every step of the way.

I could read brands at thirty feet by this light.

Hell.

Wish that storm would stop grumbling and get on with covering the sky.

But there was no time to wait for the storm to consume the moonlight. After what Elyssa had said about the man in knee-high moccasins who had appeared at Bill's ranch today, Hunter had decided to try for a meeting tonight, whether moonlight or storm accompanied him.

Cautiously, swiftly, Hunter went on foot into the

night. His moccasins made no noise on the earth. He took the first ghost trail he found.

And as he did, he wondered how many times Elyssa's soft little feet had trod on the same path. The thought didn't make him feel more kindly toward Bill Moreland.

Hunter was still on Ladder S land when a low voice spoke behind him.

"Hell of a night for a walk."

Hunter froze. Then he spun around, smiling.

"Hello, Case," Hunter said. "I was beginning to wonder if you got lost."

"That will be the day."

Hunter smiled, thumped Case on the shoulder, and got thumped in turn. Case didn't smile in return, but Hunter knew there was no lack of welcome in his younger brother.

Hunter hadn't seen Case smile since the war.

"Follow me," Case said in a low voice. "You keep running around in the moonlight like some damned fairy and you'll get yourself killed."

With a soft laugh, Hunter followed his brother.

A few minutes later Hunter and Case were in a shallow, dry watercourse. It was edged by willows and arched over by big cottonwood trees. Moonlight gave way to dense shadows.

Over the mountains, lightning ripped through the sky. Thunder grumbled raggedly. Wind swirled in the cottonwoods, stripping off frost-killed leaves and whirling them into the night.

"When did you get here?" Hunter asked in a low voice.

"Three days ago. Morgan's message caught me down toward the Spanish Bottoms."

"Did you find Culpeppers there?"

"What's down there will keep. Ab's up here."

Hunter heard all that Case didn't say. It was Ab Culpepper who had led the bloody, cruel raid on Hunter's ranch in Texas.

It was Ab Culpepper the brothers had sworn would be brought to justice, no matter what.

"So I saw," Hunter said. "Twice."

"I wondered about that. I'm surprised you didn't just drop him."

There was no question in Case's voice, but Hunter answered anyhow.

"The first time I saw him, Elyssa was along. I was getting ready to drop him anyway, but he met up with four other men."

Case's eyebrows rose. "So?"

"So I didn't want to put her in danger. The second time was this morning. Ab was standing too close to her. If I missed . . ." Hunter shrugged.

"Not much chance that you would miss a man-sized target at that range."

"I didn't want to risk it, no matter how small the chance."

Case's hazel eyes gave Hunter a considering look. Though Case said nothing, he was still surprised that Hunter hadn't just dropped Ab where he stood.

There were enough Wanted, Dead or Alive, posters out on Ab to make it perfectly legal. Besides, Ab had earned whatever death came his way, however it came. So had his kin, whether they were cousins, brothers, or half brothers.

Or, in some cases, two of the three. Pappy Culpepper hadn't much worried about blood relation when he felt randy.

"How many men does Ab have?" Hunter asked.

"About twenty."

"How many Culpeppers?"

"Five, including Ab," Case said. "He got here just before I did."

"I've seen Gaylord. Who are the other three?"

"Erasmus, Horace, and Kester."

Hunter ran through his mental list of Culpeppers. Norbert and Orville had been killed by Texans just before the rest of the Culpepper clan ran amok.

Sedgewick and Tilden had been foolish enough to stick around Texas, raiding banks, mule trains, and settlers until Case and Hunter returned from the war. The two Culpeppers drowned in the Rio Grande trying to escape to Mexico. As the river was only knee-high at the time, the boys would have lived if they hadn't been too drunk to lift their faces out of the water.

That left five of the Culpeppers who had been involved in the Texas massacre unaccounted for.

"What happened to Ichabod and Jeremiah, and Parnel, Quincy, and Reginald?" Hunter asked.

"Ichabod and Jeremiah drew cards in the wrong game down toward Spanish Forks."

Hunter's black eyebrows rose.

"The other three are still looking for Spanish treasure," Case said.

"Jeremiah was supposed to be greased lightning with his six-gun," Hunter said neutrally.

"So I hear," Case said. "Ichabod was faster, though. He damn near got me."

Hunter whistled softly through his teeth.

"Watch out, brother," Hunter said. "You'll get yourself a reputation as a gunslick. Then every kid with a six-gun and a yen to swagger will hunt you."

"Nobody knew me when I walked into that whiskey emporium. Nobody knew me when I walked out."

"Where was Ab?" Hunter asked.

"Already headed for the Rubies."

For a moment Hunter studied the ragged patches of moonlight that made their way through the cottonwoods.

"Ab, Erasmus, Gaylord, Horace, and Kester," Hunter

said finally. "Any other raiders worth mentioning?"

Case shrugged. "The rest of the men are all gun handy, when they're sober, but nothing to keep a man awake nights worrying."

Hunter snorted. He couldn't imagine anything that would keep Case awake nights worrying.

"How many men do you have?" Case asked.

"Seven, plus some cowhands. Eight, counting you."

"Almost four to one."

"That's the way I figure it," Hunter said.

"Well," Case drawled, "don't count out Bill Moreland. He may look drunk, but that old boy is shrewd as a hungry bear."

"That son of a bitch has tried to kill Elyssa at least three times that I know of."

One of Case's dark eyebrows rose. He whistled very softly through his teeth. Then he shook his head.

"No," Case said quietly.

"What does that mean?"

"Bill wouldn't hurt his Sassy."

"The hell he wouldn't. I saw him draw a bead on her with a gun!"

"When?" Case asked.

"Three nights ago."

"Then it wasn't Bill."

"How can you be so damned certain?" Hunter asked angrily.

"I played cards with him from sundown to dawn."

"But . . ."

Case waited for Hunter to finish.

"Damn!" Hunter said.

"Something wrong?"

"If it wasn't Bill Moreland—"

"It wasn't," Case interrupted.

"— then there's a traitor on the Ladder S payroll."

"That's what I'm figuring," Case said.

"What makes you say that?"

"There's a man out there somewhere who keeps bringing information to Ab and Gaylord."

"What kind of information?" Hunter asked.

"How many hands the Ladder S has. How many of them are gunmen."

Hunter muttered something unpleasant.

"How many cows you've collected," Case continued neutrally, "what kind, and where they're being held. How many mustangs."

A hissed word was Hunter's only response.

"How many branded horses," Case said. "How many green-broke broncs. That kind of thing."

"The kind of thing you used to do during the war. Information."

Case nodded.

"Damn!" Hunter muttered. "We've got enough going against us without having a spy in the bunkhouse."

"Was I you, I'd start dropping Culpeppers where I found them."

"Too dangerous. If we don't get all of them at once, it will be Texas all over again. The survivors will kill every man within reach of their guns, rape and kill the women, poison the land, and set fire to anything that burns."

Case didn't deny it. The Culpeppers had fully earned their reputation as ruthless, brutal raiders.

"Then you'd better find your traitor and hang him," Case said bluntly. "He knows too much."

Hunter didn't say a word. He was thinking fast and hard.

None of his thoughts brought comfort.

Case waited for his brother to talk again. There was no impatience in Case as he stood there. Impatience meant that a person had a weakness—he was looking forward to something.

After a few years of war, Case had looked forward

only to going home to Texas. Then he had gone home and discovered that his beloved niece and nephew had been sold to Comancheros.

After Case found what was left of Ted and little Em, he had stopped looking forward to anything at all.

Even vengeance.

To Case, bringing Culpeppers to justice was something that had to be done, like slaughtering pigs or digging a new hole for the privy. No man enjoyed the duty, but no man worth the name shirked it.

"Well, that ties it," Hunter said savagely. "What does the man look like?"

"I don't know. I can't get close to him."

"I didn't think there was anything you couldn't sneak up on."

"Neither did I. Live and learn. He knows that marsh the way a hawk knows the sky."

"Is he big?" Hunter asked, thinking of Mickey.

"I don't know. He's real careful not to leave tracks."

"Figures. Who does he talk to?"

"Gaylord or Ab," Case said.

"When?"

"Whenever he feels like it. As I said, he knows the territory real well."

"And the dogs know him," Hunter said, disgusted.

"I wondered about that. I keep hearing how he comes and goes from the Ladder S any time he pleases."

"It must be Mickey, Lefty, or Gimp. No one else has been here long enough to know the land as well as this damned ghost does."

"I don't think a man with a limp could have shaken me off," Case said. "That marsh gets real rough, real quick."

"That leaves Mickey or Lefty," Hunter said. "Frankly, I'm thinking it's neither."

"Why?"

"Mickey is mean enough," Hunter said, "but I doubt that he knows the land well enough to shake you off his trail. Lefty knows the land, but he isn't mean enough."

"Someone sure to God is."

"Are you certain it isn't Bill?" Hunter asked. "He's mean enough and he knows the land."

"He's mean," Case agreed, "but not mean enough to kill his own daughter."

"His *daughter?*"

Case made a small, swift motion that demanded silence. He drew his gun with frightening ease and started toward the underbrush.

Hunter breathed in fast. The scent of rosemary came to him on the wind. His hand shot out, holding Case back. Hunter shook his head slightly.

"Sassy," Hunter said.

His voice was too low for anyone but Case to hear.

Hunter had halfway expected to find that Elyssa had followed him. Part of him even had hoped that she would come to him in the night.

The thought of walking Elyssa back in the darkness made his body tighten and his blood sing.

Without a word Case holstered his gun.

"What makes you think Bill and Sassy are related by blood?" Hunter asked.

"Bill got drunk and talked about a woman called Gloria," Case said bluntly. "Said he loved her. Said he was her lover."

"No wonder Sassy wants to protect Bill," Hunter muttered. "He's her father."

"She doesn't know. At least, that's what Bill said."

Hunter turned toward the willows.

"Well, Sassy," he said, raising his voice just enough to carry to Elyssa. "Is Bill right?"

For a few moments there was nothing but silence and the wind.

"Come on out," Hunter said in a low, impatient voice. "You might as well meet my brother Case."

The willows shivered and parted. Elyssa walked out into the shadows at the base of the big cottonwoods. She didn't even look at Case. She looked only at Hunter.

There was enough shifting moonlight to show the shock on Elyssa's face. Her expression told the men she was trying to get used to the idea that Bill Moreland claimed to be her father.

"I didn't know," she whispered. "But it explains . . ."

Elyssa's voice died.

"Explains what?" Hunter asked softly.

"What went wrong between my father and Bill," Elyssa said simply. "And why Bill was like a father to me whenever my own father was gone. Which was most of the time. Father was a prospector."

Hunter's eyes narrowed. He, too, had been gone a lot during his marriage. He had been soldiering rather than hunting gold, yet the result was the same.

Belinda had been left alone long enough to get into trouble with the neighbor man. And, if rumor was to be believed, others as well.

"But still," Elyssa whispered, "it's hard to believe that my mother and Bill were that . . . close. "

"It happens," Case said calmly.

"A faithless flirt of a woman," Hunter said, his voice rough. "Like Belinda."

Elyssa flinched. "Mother wasn't . . ."

Again her voice faded to silence. Given what Bill had said, she could hardly argue that her mother had been faithful to her father.

"She wasn't a flirt," Elyssa said. "She must have loved Bill very much. Yet she loved her husband, too."

"At least you have a friend in the Culpepper camp," Case said.

For the first time Elyssa really saw Case. She looked from his fringed moccasins to Hunter, who also wore moccasins. The resemblance between the brothers didn't end there. The men were the same size, the same build, and they walked alike.

The difference between them was subtle, but very real to Elyssa. Case was a dark, brooding, motionless presence. Even in sunlight, Elyssa doubted that laughter would light his eyes. Hunter had been like that when he first arrived at the Ladder S.

But no longer.

Now Hunter smiled. Sometimes his eyes even gleamed with laughter. Often they smoldered with passion.

Elyssa had made a difference in Hunter. He could deny it, he could rage at her, he could call her a flirt, *but she had gotten past his guard.*

The realization made Elyssa almost dizzy with relief. Only then did she understand just how much of her heart belonged to Hunter. She had been so afraid that he wouldn't be able to love her in return.

Elyssa looked away from Hunter, afraid that her new knowledge somehow would be revealed in her eyes. Then Hunter would find an excuse to push her away.

She couldn't take that right now.

She was too raw over discovering who her real father was, and wasn't.

"Case," Elyssa said. "You're with the Culpeppers."

"They think so," Case said.

"I see."

She took in a deep breath and let it out.

"What are our chances?" Elyssa asked Case bluntly.

"They'll be a sight better as soon as I figure out where your cattle are being held."

"They haven't been sold?" Hunter and Elyssa asked as one.

"No. The breeding stock are being held in one place and the steers in another."

Hunter's teeth gleamed in the moonlight.

"That's good news," he said.

Case grunted. "Maybe. Depends on who owns the Slash River brand."

"Ab Culpepper," Hunter said.

"Not according to what passes for a brand register in Nevada."

"What?" Hunter said.

"Some man by the name of J. M. Johnstone registered the brand," Case said.

Hunter looked at Elyssa. "Do you recognize the name?"

"No. The only Johnstone I know around here is Mac, and he's dead."

"When did he die?" Case asked.

"About three months ago."

"Could be the same one. The brand was registered in 1863."

Elyssa frowned.

"That was the year my parents died," she said.

"Of what?" Case asked.

"Lung fever took Mother. My father walked out into a storm and never came back. He's buried with my mother."

Hunter gave Case a swift look.

"Did Mac ever mention having his own brand?" Hunter asked.

There was silence while Elyssa tried to remember the few conversations she had had with the late, laconic foreman of the Ladder S.

"Mac never said anything about it to me," she said after a few moments.

"Did your father let Mac run his own cattle and horses on Ladder S land?" Case asked.

"I don't know."

"Did you give permission?" Hunter asked Elyssa.

"The question never arose. Mac was a difficult man for a woman to talk to."

Case and Hunter looked at one another again. Both were thinking the same thing.

Mac might have been branding Ladder S mavericks with his own brand. It wasn't unheard-of, although most ranch owners understandably saw the practice as little better than outright rustling.

"Sounds like Gaylord came along," Case said, "saw a good thing, and decided to cut himself in on it."

"You think the Culpeppers deliberately killed Mac because he had registered a brand they wanted to use?" Elyssa asked.

"A brand, and a bunch of mavericks handy to use it on."

"You think Mac was stealing from the Ladder S?"

"It wouldn't have been the first time a foreman branded a few calves on the side," Case said calmly.

"It's not theft, in some eyes," Hunter said. "Back in Texas, there was so much livestock on the loose after the war that men killed cattle for their hides and let the meat rot."

"I see," Elyssa said slowly. "Well, I suppose Mac might have seen the Ladder S as his own after my parents died. I was in England, and Bill wanted me to stay there."

Hunter turned to Case.

"Have the Culpeppers said why they settled on taking over the Ladder S?" Hunter asked.

"About what you'd think," Case said. "They're tired of running from us. They're hunting a hole, and the Ladder S is a well-built, well-watered ranch."

Elyssa swallowed hard.

"Running from you?" she asked tightly.

"Hunter and I have been dogging their tracks since Texas, two years ago," Case said.

"I see."

She gave Hunter a swift look.

"No wonder you didn't ask about pay," Elyssa said to Hunter. "You would have hunted Culpeppers for free."

"If you don't think I'm earning my pay as ramrod—"

"I didn't say that," she interrupted quickly.

"What are you saying, then?"

"You're the best ramrod the Ladder S has ever had," Elyssa said. "But you have no interest in the ranch beyond the fact that the Culpeppers want it."

Hunter started to say something, looked at Case, and shut his mouth.

"Looks like I'll need a new ramrod after the Culpeppers are taken care of," Elyssa said, her voice strained.

"No point in crossing a bridge before you get to it," Case said. "We could all be dead before we ever get to the river."

Elyssa closed her eyes.

"Yes," she said softly. "We could die. All of us."

"Let's not start hanging crepe," Hunter said. "Once we figure out who the spy is, we'll be all right."

"Maybe," Case said. "But I have a bad feeling."

Hunter's attention switched instantly from Elyssa to Case.

"What is it?" Hunter demanded.

"Those boys are getting impatient," Case said.

"They were born impatient and lazy," Hunter said coldly. "That's why they're raiders."

Case nodded. "That means the Culpeppers might not wait until you have everything rounded up and green-broke for them."

"I've thought about that," Hunter said.

"I figured you had. What preparations have you made?"

"Enough water and food to withstand a siege," Hunter said. "Gimp is filling burlap bags to soak up stray bullets."

"What if they burn you out?" Case asked.

Elyssa's breath came in with an audible rush. She hadn't thought of that.

"They wouldn't," she said.

"They would," Case countered matter-of-factly. "They've done it before."

"Are they planning to?" Hunter asked.

"They haven't said anything to the men about it either way."

"I've set up a place to retreat to, if it comes to that," Hunter said.

"Where?" Case asked.

"A cave in the foothills about half a mile from the house. There's a spring. I've laid in supplies."

"Who else knows about it?" Case asked.

"You, me, Elyssa."

"Keep it that way," Case said bluntly.

"I don't think we'll need it," Elyssa said.

Case looked at her.

"Why?" Hunter asked.

"Gaylord said he was tired of being hunted, remember?" she asked.

Hunter nodded.

"They're lazy," Elyssa said. "They want the ranch intact, ready for them to move in. Ab even tried to buy the Ladder S from me this morning."

Surprise showed clearly on Hunter's face.

"Buy it?" he asked in disbelief.

"Yes," Elyssa said. "All nice and legal, Ab said. Nothing for the blue bellies to get upset about."

"I'll be damned," Hunter said.

"Why didn't you take it?" Case asked Elyssa.

"The Ladder S is worth more than thirty Yankee dollars," she said succinctly.

"Yes, ma'am," Case agreed. "It sure is. But it's probably all the cash money that sorry swine has."

"The point is," Elyssa said, "that the Culpeppers are looking for a nice, legal way to settle down."

"Guess they found out raiding isn't all it was cracked up to be," Hunter said dryly.

"More likely they're going to go at it the Comanchero way," Case said. "Settle the clan in a stronghold and raid a few days' ride away."

"The only raids those boys might make in the future will be in hell," Hunter said.

Elyssa shivered. It would have been easier to take if Hunter had said the words hotly, with anger vibrant in his voice.

But he spoke the words calmly, with no emotion at all.

Like Case.

"Do they trust you?" Hunter asked Case.

"As much as they trust anyone who isn't a Culpepper."

"I hope that's enough."

"I'll give you all the warning I can," Case said simply.

The wind swirled again, making Elyssa shiver. There was a bite to the air that spoke of winter.

"We better get you home," Case said. "I'll follow you as far as the barn."

"You might be seen," Hunter said.

"I'll be careful, but I want to meet those dogs. No sense in having them set up a howl if I have to come to the ranch."

"All right." Hunter turned to Elyssa. "Wait here for a bit. I want to talk with Case. Don't wander off."

"Where on earth would I go?" she asked tartly.

"Wherever you went when you made all these ghost trails in the first place," Hunter retorted.

With that, Hunter drew Case to one side and began talking in a voice too low for Elyssa to overhear.

"I'm going to set a—" Hunter began.

"Don't you trust her?" Case interrupted, his voice equally low.

"Oh, I trust her as well as I trust any flirt."

Case lifted his left eyebrow and said nothing.

"Point is," Hunter said, "that someone made all these ghost trails between the B Bar and the Ladder S."

Case waited, saying nothing.

"Since Elyssa wasn't going off for a bit of slap and tickle with Bill, who in hell *was* she meeting?" Hunter asked.

The shrug Case gave said that he didn't care who Elyssa might be seeing or not seeing, and he didn't understand why it should matter to Hunter either way.

"What does that have to do with catching Culpeppers?" Case asked mildly.

"Probably nothing, directly," Hunter admitted.

"Uh-huh," Case said.

Speculatively Case glanced from Elyssa to his brother.

"You wouldn't be interested in Bill's Sassy, would you?" Case asked neutrally.

"I married one flirt. Once was enough to cure me."

Case started to speak, shrugged, and looked at Hunter.

"What's your plan?" Case asked.

"First objective is to set a trap for our spy," Hunter said.

Case nodded.

"If you hear in the next day or two that I'm registering a Twin River Connected brand," Hunter said, "we'll know that Mickey is our man."

"Twin River Connected," Case said. Then he nodded

approval. "Good. Should cover a Slash River or Ladder S brand like a bad reputation."

Hunter smiled without humor.

"The idea will make those boys real nervous," Hunter agreed.

"What if I don't hear anything?" Case asked.

"Then I'll tell Lefty the same thing."

"And if that doesn't work?"

"Then we'll raid the Culpeppers before they can raid us," Hunter said.

"Now you're talking."

17

"**H**unter doesn't trust me," Elyssa said starkly.

Surprised, Penny looked up from the beans she was putting on to boil for supper later that day. She and Elyssa had just finished clearing away the breakfast dishes.

"Whatever makes you say that?" Penny asked as she bent to check on the stove fire.

"I went to see Bill early this morning—" Elyssa began.

"What!" Penny interrupted. Then, quickly, she asked, "Is he all right?"

"He looked a little red around the eyes and hadn't shaved for days, but otherwise he seemed fine. Or as fine as any man can be when he's all but a prisoner on his own ranch."

"What do you mean?" Penny demanded.

"The Culpeppers have moved in on him."

"Dear God," Penny whispered. "Maybe that's why he . . ."

Penny's voice faded.

"That's why he what?" Elyssa asked.

Shaking her head, Penny bent over once more to check on the progress of the fire.

"Penny? What did you mean?"

Penny closed the firebox door with a clang and turned to face Elyssa.

"You shouldn't be surprised that Hunter doesn't trust you," Penny said bluntly.

Elyssa stopped chopping onions and turned toward Penny.

"What are you talking about?" Elyssa demanded. "I've done nothing to earn Hunter's distrust."

"No?" Penny asked coolly.

"No!"

"Maybe he doesn't like the fact that you're sneaking off for a little slap and tickle with Bill."

Shocked, Elyssa simply stared at Penny.

Penny stared right back.

"What in God's name are you talking about?" Elyssa asked finally.

"Oh, don't bother to deny it. Bill loved Gloria, and he took one look at you when you came back from England in satins and silk and shining flaxen hair and he saw Gloria all over again."

"Penny—" Elyssa began.

"He hasn't so much as looked at me since you came home," Penny interrupted raggedly. "Not once!"

Penny turned away, but not quickly enough to hide the tears that were streaming down her face.

Stunned, Elyssa simply stood motionless. But her mind was running at top speed, remembering what Hunter had said about men and pale hair.

All men aren't blinded by sunlight shining on pale hair.

And what Penny had said in return.

The right one was, and he's the only one that matters.

For Penny, the right one had been—and still was—Bill Moreland.

"You made all those footpaths to the B Bar," Elyssa said.

Shoulders straight, spine rigid, Penny kept her back turned to Elyssa.

Elyssa went to the other woman and hugged her.

"How long have you loved Bill?" Elyssa said.

For a time it seemed that Penny wouldn't answer. Then her whole body trembled as she gave way to the grief she had tried for so long to hide.

"Since I was b-barely fifteen," Penny said in a strained voice. "But he couldn't see p-past Gloria to me."

Elyssa hugged Penny harder.

"Then Gloria died," Penny whispered, "and after a time it s-seemed that Bill was finally s-seeing me."

Silently Elyssa held Penny, stroking her back soothingly, wishing she could do more to comfort the older woman.

"Then you c-came home," Penny said starkly. "Bill stopped looking at me at all."

"It's not like that between us," Elyssa said, her voice gentle.

"The hell it isn't!" Penny retorted. "He n-never comes to the rise by Wind Gap anymore. I g-go out there and I wait and I wait and I—"

Penny's voice broke.

"It's not because of me," Elyssa said. "He's probably afraid the Culpeppers will follow him."

"It's you he wants now," Penny said wearily. "That's why he doesn't come to me anymore."

"Penny," Elyssa said gently. "It's not what you think. Truly."

"It is!"

"I'm Bill's daughter."

Penny went absolutely still. For the first time she looked Elyssa in the eye.

"His *daughter*?" Penny said.

"That's what he told—"

Abruptly Elyssa changed her mind. She wouldn't talk about Hunter's brother, a spy in the Culpeppers' camp.

Someone might overhear.

"—me," Elyssa finished.

"When?"

"Does it matter?" Elyssa asked calmly. "The fact is, I'm Bill's daughter, not his paramour."

A long, shaky breath came out of Penny.

"Truly?" Penny asked.

"Yes."

Penny let out a long sigh and hugged Elyssa hard.

"You don't seemed surprised that I'm Bill's daughter," Elyssa said after a moment.

"I'm not, now that I think about it."

"Why?"

"About two years before you were born, word came that your father—that is, John Sutton—had died hunting gold in Colorado Territory."

Elyssa thought of her mother alone and waiting for her husband's return. Waiting while the absence grew longer and longer, waiting and hoping and fearing. Then word of John Sutton's death arrived.

It took no great wit to guess what had come next.

"It took Bill more than a year," Penny said tightly, "but he finally won Gloria."

Elyssa closed her eyes but never stopped stroking Penny, trying to soothe away the tremors that ran through the other woman's body in long waves.

"Then one day your father—John—rode up," Penny said. "Gloria was hysterical. John and Bill had a terrible fight. Bill left and started the B Bar. Nine months later you were born."

"Then I could be just what I thought I was. John's daughter, not Bill's."

"I don't think so."

"Why?"

"I don't think your father could get a woman pregnant," Penny said simply. "He stayed home for five years after you were born, but Gloria never was pregnant again."

"There's no guarantee that Bill could, either."

"Yes, there is."

"What do you mean?"

"I'm pregnant," Penny said simply.

Elyssa couldn't hide her surprise.

"That's why you've been feeling so puny," Elyssa said after a moment. "Morning sickness, not the ague."

Numbly Penny nodded.

"Does Bill know?" Elyssa asked.

"No," Penny whispered.

"We'll have to tell—"

"No!" the other woman interrupted fiercely. "If he cared, he would ask."

"But the Culpeppers—"

"Didn't stop him from talking to you," Penny interrupted again.

"By going there I nearly got Bill killed and myself hauled off to be a Culpepper whore," Elyssa said bluntly.

Penny's eyes widened in shock.

"If Hunter hadn't followed me," Elyssa said, "only the devil knows what would have happened."

"Dear God," Penny said. Then, hesitantly, "If Bill isn't your lover and you didn't know he was your father, why did you risk so much to see him?"

"Because I was tired of seeing Ladder S livestock go through Wind Gap and never come back."

"Bill wouldn't—" began Penny hotly.

"I know," Elyssa interrupted. "But drink changes a man, as Hunter pointed out."

"Bill wouldn't steal Ladder S livestock."

"Unfortunately, he can't keep the Culpeppers from stealing it, though," Elyssa said. "The Ladder S is just about picked clean."

Penny closed her eyes and made a low sound.

"What are we going to do?" Penny whispered.

"Hunter will think of something," Elyssa said.

He has to. But she kept that thought to herself.

"Are you feeling better now?" Elyssa asked after a moment. "Maybe you should lie down for a time."

"No need. Working takes my mind off . . . everything."

Elyssa smiled sadly.

"Are you happy about the baby?" Elyssa asked, her voice soft.

"Oh, yes," Penny said, smiling for the first time. "I've wanted a baby ever since I can remember."

"All right. We'll take care of the Culpeppers and then make arrangements for raising a baby on the Ladder S."

"You don't think less of me for letting Bill . . . for being his woman even though we aren't married?"

Elyssa thought of how hot passion ran in her when she was in Hunter's arms. If he had wanted to put a baby in her, she would have helped him every bit of the way and not counted the cost until it was far too late.

Pregnant.

Unmarried.

Utterly alone.

"No," Elyssa said. "I think it's very, very hard not to give yourself to the man you love. If he wants you."

Penny smiled again despite the tears still shining on her cheeks.

"I was afraid you would throw me off the ranch," Penny admitted.

"Never."

"Many women would, and even more men."

"I won't."

The certainty in Elyssa's voice gave Penny more ease than she had known since she had discovered that she was pregnant.

"Thank you," Penny said simply.

"Don't be foolish. You and your baby are all that I have in the world, except for . . ." Elyssa hesitated.

"Hunter?" Penny asked.

"I was thinking of Bill. Hunter doesn't want to love me. He doesn't even want to like me."

"But he watches you the way Bill used to watch Gloria."

Hope raced through Elyssa.

"Really?" she asked breathlessly.

Penny nodded.

"You watch him, too," Penny added.

"I can't help it," Elyssa whispered. *"I love him."*

From the direction of the corral came the squeal of a frightened horse followed by a man's raw shout of anger.

Without hesitating Elyssa grabbed the shotgun that was never far from her reach these days and went to the back door.

One of the green-broke broncs had just unloaded Mickey into the dust. He got up, grabbed the bridle close to the bit, and began whipping the bronc with a quirt.

The terrified animal screamed again and threw its head up, trying to escape the whip. Mickey hung on to the bit and kept whipping the animal.

Shotgun still in hand, Elyssa headed toward the corral at a run.

Hunter was faster. He came out of the barn, saw what was happening, and yelled at Mickey to stop.

Mickey ignored him.

An instant later Hunter hit Mickey like a falling mountain. Mickey slammed into the corral bars with a force that made the poles rattle and groan. Staggering back, he shook his head, saw Hunter, and made another bad mistake. He charged Hunter with all the finesse of an angry bull.

Hunter stepped aside, stuck out his boot, and let Mickey's own weight do the rest. The big cowhand went end over end. He landed in a sprawl of awkward limbs and dust.

A few moments later Mickey made his third mistake. He went for his gun.

Hunter kicked Mickey's hand with enough force to send the gun flying in a broad arc. Then Hunter stood just out of Mickey's reach and waited to see how stupid the other man was.

The younger man shook his head, rolled over onto his hands and knees, and came to his feet. He swayed and cradled his right hand. Though he looked angry enough to kill something, he didn't reach for the second gun he wore.

Hunter nodded.

"Take your temper out on digging post holes," Hunter said flatly.

"It's nothing but a damned flea-bitten bronc!" Mickey shouted.

"It was good enough to throw you."

Mickey's face reddened with rage.

"No man worthy of the name beats a horse just for throwing him," Hunter said. "Dig post holes or get out."

Sullenly Mickey went to his hat, picked it up, and walked on to where his gun lay in the dust. He bent down.

Hunter's stance changed in a way that was unmistakable. If Mickey wanted to make a fourth mistake by trying to use the gun, Hunter would draw on him.

Without checking to see how dirty the weapon might

be, Mickey jammed it into his holster and stalked off toward the barn.

Hunter watched Mickey go by. The sullen cowhand didn't even look his way. Hunter wished that he could simply fire Mickey and be done with his brutal presence. Unfortunately the Ladder S was too short-handed to let anyone go for any act short of drunkenness or cold-blooded murder.

Besides, Mickey could be the Culpeppers' spy. If so, there were much better uses for him than digging post holes.

The sound of a shotgun being uncocked startled Hunter. He spun toward the sound.

As he turned, he drew his six-gun.

Elyssa's breath came in sharply. One instant Hunter's hands were empty. In the next instant he was holding a six-gun that was cocked and ready to fire.

"Planning to use that on me?" Hunter asked.

"I could ask you the same question."

With a smooth motion Hunter uncocked the six-gun and returned the weapon to its holster.

"Glad to see that the shotgun isn't cocked," Hunter said. "You look like you're planning to shoot me rather than Mickey."

"I'm thinking about it."

"Any reason in particular?"

"I'm remembering when Mickey grabbed me hard enough to leave bruises, treated me like a prostitute, and all you did was tell him to quit wasting time and get to work."

Hunter waited, looking at Elyssa's stormy eyes and her hands ready to cock the shotgun all over again.

And shoot him.

"But when Mickey takes a quirt to a bronc," Elyssa said through her teeth, "you knock him into next week."

"The horse wasn't doing anything wrong."

"And I was?" she demanded.

Hunter's bleak, dark eyes raked over Elyssa. As always, she was dressed in silk or satin. Sexy cloth that shivered and sighed and caught a man's eye with every breath she took.

"Yes," he said coolly. "You were in the wrong."

"*What?*"

"Men come to a point whenever you walk by. You know it, but you keep on walking by."

"What am I supposed to do? Stay locked inside behind curtains and veils?"

"Yes."

Elyssa's eyes widened.

"You're serious," she said in disbelief.

"Damned straight."

Rage whipped through Elyssa.

"Tough luck, fancy man," she said recklessly. "I'm not staying in jail just because I was born a woman instead of a man."

"I figured you would take it that way. Some females just don't know they're alive unless some man is admiring them."

The naked contempt in Hunter's voice was like a slap.

"I'm not like that," Elyssa said. "I never have been."

"That's what they all say."

"Damn it, I'm not like your wife was!"

"Yell a little louder," he drawled. "I'm sure the boys are hanging on every word."

With that Hunter turned his back and walked toward the barn.

"Hunter!"

There was no hesitation in Hunter's stride. He just kept on walking.

Elyssa was on the edge of yelling at him again when

she became aware of Lefty and Gimp. The two old hands were standing just outside the barn, listening.

With a combination of resentment and embarrassment, Elyssa turned on her heel and went back to the kitchen.

This can't go on, Elyssa promised herself. *I have to make Hunter understand.*

Perhaps if I talk to him when there's no one to overhear . . .

The more Elyssa thought about it, the more the idea appealed to her. She needed privacy to discuss such personal things with Hunter.

Obviously the memory of his unfaithful wife still hurt him deeply. Hunter didn't want to risk his heart again.

Once burned, twice shy.

Somehow Elyssa had to make Hunter understand that it was all right to trust his heart to her care. She would cherish the gift of his love and have her own love cherished in return.

If only she could make Hunter understand.

Tonight, after Penny is asleep. I'll talk to him then. I'll make him understand.

The door to Elyssa's bedroom creaked slightly when she opened it. She froze in place, but heard no stirring downstairs or in the next room.

Letting out a slow breath, Elyssa eased the door shut behind her. With trembling fingers she tied her pale blue satin wrapper more tightly around her waist.

Fingers crossed for luck, Elyssa tiptoed down the short stretch of hallway that separated her bedroom door from Hunter's. The floor felt cool through the thin satin slippers she wore, but not as cold as her hands. She was nervous about the coming conversation.

Hunter's door was closed.

For a long minute Elyssa stood in front of the door,

her hand resting on the doorknob and her heart pounding. Just before her courage faltered entirely, she opened the door a few inches.

"Hunter?" she whispered.

The distinct sound of a revolver being uncocked seemed as loud as a cry in the silence.

"What the hell do you think you're doing?" Hunter asked softly, furiously.

Elyssa jumped. The question had come from a point not six inches to her left.

"We have to talk," she whispered.

"It can wait until morning."

The door started to close in Elyssa's face.

She stuck her satin slipper through the crack and leaned hard on the door with both hands.

"No," she countered. "It has to be now, when there's no one to overhear."

"Keep your voice down!" Hunter demanded very softly.

"Then let me in."

Hunter hesitated, trying to cool the hot racing of his blood that had begun when he realized Elyssa was standing outside his doorway late at night.

He took in a swift breath. The air Hunter breathed in was suffused with Elyssa's unique scent, a garden spiced with rosemary and moonlight.

The heat in Hunter redoubled.

"This isn't a good idea, Sassy."

"It is."

"No."

"Yes!" she hissed. "I know what I'm doing, Hunter."

He didn't doubt it.

The thought made him even hotter.

Why not? Hunter asked himself savagely. *God knows we both want it bad enough to taste it.*

It isn't like she's a virgin, after all. Mickey made that clear enough with his brags in the Dugout Saloon.

And Sassy confirmed it when she talked about shocking her proper cousins with her behavior.

Without warning the bedroom door opened wide.

Elyssa all but tumbled into Hunter's arms. Automatically he reached out to steady her. The heat of her body through the satin wrapper was like fire.

And like fire, it burned him.

Because Hunter wanted so much to strip Elyssa and take her with all the furious passion she aroused in him, he forced himself to release her. Letting a flirt control him was something Hunter had sworn he would never do again.

Instead of pulling Elyssa close, Hunter reached past her and shut the door. The faint click of the latch drew a quick, whispering sound from Elyssa, as though she had just taken a swift breath.

"All right," Hunter said in a low, husky voice. "What's so all-fired urgent that it couldn't wait until morning?"

18

*E*lyssa opened her lips to speak, only to discover that her mouth had gone completely dry. Hunter's naked chest gleamed in the moonlight flooding through the window.

The male beauty of muscle and sinew and midnight hair riveted her.

The intimacy of being alone with Hunter in his bedroom broke over Elyssa in a long, seething wave of emotion.

"Sassy?"

"Um."

Elyssa swallowed and licked her lips. She wanted to ask Hunter to put on a shirt, but didn't. He already thought her girlish as it was.

"I just wanted to . . ." Elyssa's voice dried up.

Hunter waited.

His stillness irritated her.

Here I am hardly able to draw a breath for being this close to him, Elyssa thought angrily, *and he's looking at me like it's nothing at all for him to be half-naked with a woman in his bedroom.*

Realization hit Elyssa with a force that shook her.

Of course, nitwit, she told herself. *Hunter was mar-*

268

ried. It's nothing for him to have a woman in his bedroom.

Or his bed.

Elyssa swallowed hard. Then she squared her shoulders and quelled her nerves. She was determined not to appear juvenile in front of this irritating man.

"I'm not flirting with Mickey," Elyssa said.

"Keep your voice down!"

"All right," she whispered angrily. "Did you hear me?"

"Hell, half the hands on the Ladder S probably heard you."

"Listen to me. I'm not flirting with Mickey or Bill or any other man on the face of this earth."

"Do tell."

"I just did!"

"Then what do you call it when you cut sideways glances at me and lick your lips like you can't wait to find out if I taste as good as I look?"

Elyssa hoped her blush didn't show in the moonlight. She felt like sinking between the cracks in the floorboards. She hadn't thought that her actions were so transparent.

"Only with you, Hunter," Elyssa whispered painfully. "I only look at you."

"Uh-huh."

The sound should have meant agreement, but Elyssa knew it didn't.

"Hunter Maxwell," she said in a soft, incensed voice, "you have less manners and intelligence than a mule. I am not like your wife was!"

Hunter felt like laughing out loud. Here Elyssa was standing in front of him and insisting upon her innocence, yet she had come to his room in the middle of the night dressed in the kind of boudoir clothing that set fire to a man's body.

But then, she always dressed that way, setting fire to the men around her.

"You're something, Sassy," Hunter said in a low voice. "Really something."

Wisely, Hunter didn't say what that something was. He didn't want her outrage to wake up every living person on the Ladder S.

"You've got to believe me," she whispered.

"Why?"

Elyssa blinked.

"Because it's important," she said, frustrated.

"Why?"

"Dear God, are all men this dense or are you a special case?" Elyssa retorted in a low, seething voice.

Hunter smiled slightly. It was intriguing to watch Elyssa maintain her innocence with a force that set her breasts to swaying seductively beneath her satin wrapper.

"Hunter?"

"I'm listening."

"You're the most mulish man," she whispered in exasperation. "Sometimes I feel like shaking you until your teeth rattle."

"Then why did you come to my bedroom in the middle of the night?" Hunter murmured.

"Because either one of us could die tomorrow and I . . ."

Elyssa's voice died. She couldn't say *I love you* to a man who was watching her with such wary, faintly predatory patience.

Damn his wife, Elyssa thought bleakly. *She ruined Hunter for anyone else.*

"Well?" Hunter asked.

"I . . ."

Elyssa made a small, helpless gesture with her hands and looked mutely at Hunter.

"You want me," he said in a low voice. "Any girl bold enough to come to a man's room like this shouldn't shy from the words."

"Hunter," Elyssa whispered.

"Say it."

She drew a shaky breath.

"Say that you want me," Hunter said.

Elyssa opened her mouth. No words came out.

Hunter took a single step. It brought him so close to Elyssa that he could feel the heat of her body radiating through the sleek wrapper.

"It's not a secret," Hunter coaxed in a low voice. "Your eyes give you away every time you look at me."

"I . . ."

Elyssa's voice died. Hunter's sheer closeness was overwhelming. She hadn't felt like this since the night in the garden, when they had danced and kissed and more, much more.

"Your eyes," Hunter whispered, "tell me that you're remembering what it felt like when I kissed your breasts and you moaned."

A faint shivering went through Elyssa, echo of the wild passion she had felt when his mouth caressed her.

"You want to feel that way again," Hunter whispered. "Don't you?"

Elyssa swallowed as heat bloomed softly in her body. The sweet, unexpected fire made her tremble.

He's right, she realized. *I want to feel that way again.*

Shivering, Elyssa closed her eyes.

"I . . . want you," she whispered.

"Was the truth so hard?"

Hunter's words were breathed against Elyssa's forehead, the hollow of her cheek, the corner of her mouth.

The tremor that went through Elyssa was felt by both of them. Hunter took a swift breath and allowed himself to remember what it was like to set fire to her with a few caresses. No woman had been like that for him.

Ever.

Her response haunted him.

"Hunter," Elyssa whispered, "would you kiss me? Hard. Very hard. The way it was in the garden."

The words dragged a low groan from Hunter. His arms went around Elyssa and his head bent down to her. When his mouth touched hers, he found it open, hungry. His tongue shot between her teeth as he gave her what she had asked for.

Hard. Very hard.

The mating of Elyssa's tongue with Hunter's was neither coy nor hesitant. She remembered what it was like to be caressed and consumed by his kiss. She had dreamed of it, longed for it, hungered for it with an intensity she was only now realizing.

With a husky moan, Elyssa wrapped her arms around Hunter's neck and lifted herself against him. She wanted to be close to him, even closer than she was.

She had to be closer.

Elyssa's abandoned response and the feel of her satin covered breasts twisting against his chest made Hunter forget all the reasons he was a fool for even kissing her. The taste of her was like wine running in his blood, flooding him with hunger and fire.

He wanted so much more than a hot kiss and the feel of her breasts on his skin.

And he was going to have it.

Without warning Elyssa felt herself lifted off her feet. The power of Hunter's arms was a lure and a promise and a memory combined. She gave herself to it recklessly.

Then the fire of Hunter's kiss burned everything else from Elyssa's thoughts. Distantly she realized that the pressure beneath her back came from bedcovers that were bunched under her, but it had no meaning other than to drive her closer to Hunter's body.

With a passionate whimper Elyssa drew her hands over the flexed power of Hunter's back. The shudder of excitement that went through him was as heady to her as straight whiskey.

She repeated the caress, kneading and testing his strength with her hands. Her tongue tasted him as deeply as he was tasting her. Hesitantly, then heedlessly, her nails caressed the long muscles on either side of his spine.

The low sound Hunter made in response was intoxicating. A delicious kind of heat coiled through Elyssa's body, drawing it tight and then tighter still. She twisted against him, trying to ease the ache in her breasts.

"I want—" she began raggedly.

Hunter's hand came down hard over Elyssa's mouth.

"Quiet," he whispered roughly against her ear. "I know what you want."

His other hand moved swiftly, opening Elyssa's satin wrapper. He bent his head and found one of her breasts with his mouth. Heedless of the fine silk of her nightgown, he drew the tip of her breast into his mouth.

Fire raced through Elyssa. She arched up to the caress, wanting more.

Hunter gave it to her with teeth and tongue and the wild, changing pressure of his mouth.

Excitement coiled harder and harder within Elyssa's body, drawing her so taut that she moaned. Then excitement burst, drenching her in liquid fire. She made a broken sound and trembled and softly pleaded for more.

Hunter laughed low in his chest and repeated the caress on her other nipple.

Elyssa arched up into Hunter's mouth. She didn't fight the masculine hand muffling her incautious cries. She didn't even notice it. Her whole being was focused in the exquisite burning of her flesh.

Hunter's free hand swept down and buried itself between Elyssa's thighs. She stiffened in surprise, but he didn't notice. Her heat and drenching response swept all thoughts from him but one. His hand curved around her softness. Long fingers tightened in a probing caress.

Fierce pleasure shot up Elyssa's body. The startled cry she gave went no farther than the hard palm across her mouth.

Then Hunter's hand moved sharply between her legs and excitement stabbed through her again. This time the sound she made came from passion rather than surprise.

"Damn," Hunter said beneath his breath. "We're going to have to find a more private place the next time. I want to hear every sound I drag out of you."

His hand clenched, pressing deeply into Elyssa's softness. Her body arched like a tightly drawn bow. He barely muffled his own groan when her liquid heat spread over him.

"Open your legs," Hunter said against her ear.

Elyssa hardly understood the words. Her legs were moving restlessly, seeking more of the wild, stabbing pleasure she had just known.

But Hunter's hand was no longer between her legs, caressing her with pure fire. She shook her head and tried to speak, wanting to tell him that she wanted more, not less, of his touch.

"Hush, Sassy. I'm just as eager as you are."

Elyssa sensed Hunter moving, settling between her knees, forcing her thighs apart. Then hard fingers moved again, with no cloth to dim the heated contact.

Pleasure washed through her. Instinctively she lifted her hips, wanting more of the wild caress.

His thumb moved again and once more her body was drenched in pleasure.

"God," Hunter said hoarsely.

His body tightened, his hips drove hard, and he was buried inside her.

All that kept Elyssa's cry of surprise and pain from ringing through the house was the strength of Hunter's hand over her mouth. She twisted and shoved at his shoulders, trying to dislodge the burning weight of him between her legs.

Hunter gave a low, husky groan and drove into Elyssa again. Then his body became rigid, he shuddered from head to heels, and abruptly went slack against her.

Dazed, Elyssa turned her head aside, escaping Hunter's hand. This time when she shoved at his shoulders, he rolled aside.

Without a word, Hunter withdrew from Elyssa, turned his back, and rearranged his clothing.

She waited for him to speak, to say something.

Anything.

Silence expanded with every heartbeat until Elyssa thought she would suffocate beneath its weight. Just when she had lost hope, Hunter spoke in a low, emotionless voice.

"Go back to your bedroom, Sassy. It will be another long day tomorrow."

At first Elyssa couldn't believe that was all Hunter had to say to her.

"Wh-what?" she whispered.

"Fun's over for tonight. Go back to your room."

Elyssa closed her eyes as the truth broke over her in a black, icy wave.

Well, now I know, she thought bleakly. *It wasn't love for me that Hunter was fighting. It was lust.*

And we both lost.

The pain of it was shocking.

Instinctively Elyssa knew she couldn't let it overcome her. Not yet. Not here.

Not in Hunter's bed.

I won't cry.

It's my own fault. Lord knows that Hunter warned me often enough. I just didn't believe him.

Fool.

I won't cry.

"Sassy?"

Without a word Elyssa shot off Hunter's bed. She moved so quickly that her wrapper lifted and fluttered behind her like ruined wings.

The bedroom door opened and shut without a sound.

Hunter grimaced and cursed beneath his breath. He had been too quick, too hard. He had tried to slow down, but the liquid silk of Elyssa's response had stripped away his control. He had never wanted a woman the way he wanted her.

"Hell," Hunter muttered, disgusted with himself.

He suspected that Elyssa had been waiting for some soft words and gentle petting. He had been sorely tempted to do just that.

But he hadn't let himself.

Hunter was damned if he was going to dance at the end of puppet strings for Elyssa just because he had taken what she offered.

Even so, next time will be different, Hunter promised himself. *Next time I won't let her sweet little claws and her body twisting beneath mine push me right over the edge.*

The thought of taking Elyssa again sent a hot thrill through Hunter's body.

There was no doubt in his mind that there would be a next time.

Any girl as passionate as Sassy will get hungry again real soon. She'll come knocking on my door in the middle of the night again.

I'll be waiting for her.

It won't be long.

Smiling slightly, Hunter lit a candle and went to the washbasin. He stripped out of his trousers and underwear and reached for a washcloth.

The sight of blood on his slowly softening flesh stopped him cold.

What the hell!

I wasn't rough enough to draw blood. I was quick, but she was ready.

Hunter had no doubt of that. It was the sleek, liquid welcome of Elyssa's body that had shattered his control.

It must have been her time of the month.

Soft, muffled sounds came from the next room.

Hunter went still, cocked his head, and listened. After a few moments he decided that Elyssa must be crying.

Uneasily Hunter washed himself. The subdued, broken sounds continued from the next room.

Still naked, he went to the wall between their bedrooms and listened intently. The sounds weren't coming from Elyssa's bed. She wasn't doing what Belinda had done, lying in bed and sobbing noisily until she got what she wanted from him.

In fact, it sounded like Elyssa was doing everything she could to make no noise at all.

I must have hurt her.

Damn! I can't believe I was harder on her than a rambunctious lout like Mickey.

Sickened and angered by his own lack of control, Hunter dressed quickly and went to Elyssa's room.

When he opened the door, the sound of crying became more distinct. An acrid scent struck his nostrils, as though someone was burning cloth.

Hunter closed the bedroom door behind him. A quick look told him that Elyssa was in bed now. Something was smoldering sullenly on the small hearth.

"Sassy?" Hunter asked softly.

The sounds of crying stopped as though cut off by a knife.

Making no noise, Hunter went to the bed and sat on its edge.

When Elyssa felt the mattress give way under Hunter's weight, she wanted to flee. But she was stark naked. The stained remains of her nightdress and wrapper were smoldering in the hearth.

Like a trapped animal Elyssa lay utterly still, silently willing Hunter to go away. To be caught crying by him was just one more in a long list of the night's humiliations. She didn't think she could bear any more.

Elyssa flinched when Hunter's hand stroked her hair. He felt the betraying motion and swore.

"I'm sorry," he said simply. "I didn't mean to be rough."

The next time Hunter stroked her hair, Elyssa forced herself not to acknowledge it in any way. Yet she couldn't prevent the tremors that lashed through her body, her nerves stretched to the point of breaking.

"You were smaller than I expected," Hunter said in a low voice. "It had been a long time for me and you were ready and I wanted you like hell on fire."

Elyssa said nothing, did nothing. She simply lay and shivered beneath Hunter's gentle, unwanted touch.

The stark trembling of Elyssa's body was salt rubbed into the fresh wound of Hunter's self-esteem.

"Take it easy," he murmured. "I'll be gentle as sunlight with you from now on. Next time you'll enjoy it more. There's so much passion in you, Sassy girl. In that, at least, we're well matched."

Sassy.

The hated nickname destroyed Elyssa's self-control. With an inarticulate cry she struck out at Hunter like the cornered animal she was. Fingers hooked like claws reached for his face.

Reflexively Hunter caught her wrists.

"Take it easy, Sassy. Aren't you listening? I said I'll never hurt you again."

"I hate you," Elyssa said in a low, savage voice. "Get out before I scream down the house."

"For God's sake, settle down and stop acting like an outraged virgin."

"Why shouldn't I? It's what I am! Or rather, *was*."

"What are you talking about? My wife never bled, not even the first time."

"Fancy man," Elyssa snarled, "I'll bet this ranch that you weren't anywhere near your wife her first time!"

Realization swept through Hunter, staggering him.

It had been a virgin's pain, not a flirt's practiced passion, that had caused Elyssa to stiffen and thrash harshly beneath him.

And he had held his hand over her mouth the whole time.

"Sweet Jesus," Hunter whispered, appalled. "Why didn't you stop me?"

"I tried!"

Rage swept through him at the implications of what Elyssa was saying.

"Damn you, Sassy," he said in a low, dangerous voice, "I didn't rape you and you know it! You were with me every step of the way, right up to the instant I—"

Hunter's words cut off as he realized where they were leading. Elyssa had been with him right up to the instant he ripped through her maidenhead.

For a time Hunter's searing blasphemies hung in the air like the acrid smoke from Elyssa's ruined nightclothes. She listened to his words and bared her teeth in feral response, coldly gratified to know that in this, at least, she had finally reached through Hunter's barriers.

Hunter saw Elyssa's travesty of a smile and knew that her rage was as deep as his own.

"You could have fought me," he said. "Why didn't you until it was too late?"

"I thought I loved you," Elyssa said, her voice as low and vicious as Hunter's. "I thought you loved me. I thought you were just reluctant to show it because of your first wife."

Shocked silence was Hunter's only answer.

Then, softly, he said, "You little fool."

"For once we are in complete agreement."

"Weren't you listening to me?" Hunter demanded. "Did I ever talk about anything but lust between us?"

Humiliation and rage fought for possession of Elyssa's tongue. Both won.

"No and no. But I'm listening now, fancy man. I'm all bloody ears."

"Too damned late," he snarled.

Elyssa didn't argue with that, either.

Silence claimed the room.

"What is that stink?" Hunter finally asked irritably.

"Whatever I was wearing when I left your room."

The cool precision of Elyssa's voice and the continuous, rippling shine of tears on her face told Hunter how precariously she was in control of herself.

Not that he blamed Elyssa. At the moment, he was feeling a little precarious about control himself.

"God, what a tangle," he whispered.

Elyssa ignored Hunter, concentrating instead on controlling herself.

It had never been more difficult.

"Well, there's no help for it," Hunter said in a low voice. "I'll have to marry you."

Elyssa's head whipped toward him in disbelief.

Hunter didn't notice. He was too caught in the tangle

he had made of what should have been a simple, straightforward affair.

"Tomorrow we'll tell everyone we're engaged," Hunter said. "As soon as this mess with the Culpeppers is cleared up, I'll find a preacher and we'll get married."

Elyssa stared at Hunter as if he had gone mad.

Then Hunter turned and pinned her with a bleak glare. When he spoke, his voice was equally bleak, like a whip of ice.

"But with God as my witness, Elyssa Sutton, if you don't grow up and be a good mother to my children, you will rue the day you teased me into marrying you."

"No," she said savagely.

"What?"

"No. I won't marry you."

"Don't be foolish," Hunter said, his voice impatient. "It's what you wanted all along."

"But then, we've already agreed I was a fool. Unlike you, Hunter, I do learn from my mistakes. I won't marry you."

"Why?"

"If we get married, you have the right to do that to me whenever you want."

"You'll want it, too. I'll see to it. I just never thought you could be a virgin. Not the way you responded to me, like setting a match to straw."

Hunter smiled at the memory.

The smile caught Elyssa on the raw, completing her humiliation.

"Listen to me, you smug son of a bitch," she snarled. "Right now there's no law telling me I have to suffer a man's rutting ever again. I'm going to see that it stays that way."

Hunter grimaced. "I told you, next time you'll enjoy it."

"My God, you must really think I'm stupid. 'Next

time you'll enjoy it,' " she mimicked savagely. "What rot!"

"Calm down and use your head instead of your sharp little tongue. If marriage was so bad, do you think women would put up with it?"

"Once the marital knot is tied around a woman's stupid neck, she doesn't have much choice, does she?" Elyssa said in a scathing voice. "No wonder churches and townships make sure girls are virgins before they marry. They would never suffer it otherwise."

Hunter bit back a searing remark and tried sweet reason on his unreasonable lover.

"What if you're pregnant?" he asked.

"What if I'm not?"

"What if you are?" Hunter insisted.

Elyssa looked at him with wild, glittering eyes, feeling control slipping away with every breath.

"Get out, Hunter. I don't want you anymore. Ever. In any way."

"Damn it, Sassy, you can't just—"

"Get. Out."

Abruptly Hunter stood and stalked toward the door.

"We'll talk again in the morning," he said, "when you're not in a snit."

He closed the bedroom door behind him and stood in the hallway, listening.

Not one sound came back through the door to him.

Not even tears.

Elyssa's silence made a cold knot form in Hunter's stomach. She wasn't acting the way Belinda always had. Belinda had used tears and words and the swing of her hips to flay a man's pride until he had none left. With Belinda, sex had been a savage little game.

But Elyssa wasn't like Belinda. With Elyssa, sex wasn't a game at all.

I don't want you anymore. Ever. In any way.

Hunter told himself that Elyssa would feel differently in the morning. Beneath the feminine outrage she was too intelligent not to understand that marriage was necessary now.

He had taken her virginity.

The fact that he hadn't understood she was a virgin didn't matter. He had torn her maidenhood, spent himself completely inside her, and they must marry.

She'll come around once her nerves settle, Hunter reassured himself.

The absolute silence from the other side of the door told Hunter that he was as wrong in this assumption as he had been in his others about Elyssa Sutton.

Elyssa wasn't Belinda.

The implications of that simple truth kept breaking over Hunter through the long, sleepless night.

19

With outward composure Elyssa pulled on work clothing she hadn't worn since she had been sent to England years ago. The pants were a soft, navy blue wool gabardine that once had fitted her very loosely. Now they were snug across the hips. The pants were too short, but her boots would cover up that problem.

The blouse was a more difficult affair. The checked flannel shirts that Elyssa once had worn with the pants strained across her bust. At fifteen, she had been considerably less curvy than she was today.

Nor would any of her mother's old clothes fit. Elyssa was bigger than her mother had been.

I'll just have to find something else to wear on top, Elyssa told herself grimly.

Anything else.

There was no chance that Elyssa would wear her English dresses. Hunter's scathing comments about her clothes were branded on her mind.

Some girls just don't know they're alive unless some fool boy is admiring them.

Men come to a point whenever you walk by. You know it, but you keep on walking by.

Elyssa refused to stay locked in the house like a harem

girl, but she could do her best to disguise everything feminine about herself.

Sharply she tugged at the flannel shirt, trying to give her breasts more room. It was futile. There simply wasn't enough space beneath the flannel.

But if she wore her silks and satins, Hunter would give her a look with his bleak, knowing eyes.

If you want a fast roll, I'm ready, willing, and by-God able to oblige. But that's all it will be, Sassy. Fast sex.

Hunter was a man of his word. Fast sex was just what it had been.

Tears of shame and anger pricked behind Elyssa's eyes, an echo of the sad, savage moment when she had learned just how little Hunter thought of her.

With God as my witness, Elyssa Sutton, if you don't grow up and be a good mother to my children, you will rue the day you teased me into marrying you.

Hunter's words hurt Elyssa far more than the tearing of her maidenhead had. His words told her that she had given her love to a man who had neither respect nor affection for her.

Just lust.

Damn him.

And damn me for being a fool.

Dry-eyed, Elyssa rummaged around in dusty chests until she found one of her father's buckskin shirts carefully wrapped up and laid away. The shirt was still soft and pliable.

She pulled it over her head, rolled up the sleeves, and let the straight-cut hem cover her hips. The fringe hung and swayed from her breasts in an annoying fashion, but otherwise hid her curves quite well.

A quick check in the mirror told Elyssa that her cream-colored chemise showed through the laces of the buckskin shirt. Impatiently she pulled the laces tighter. Then she found one of her father's large bandannas and knotted it at the back of her neck. The faded red cloth hung down over the laces, concealing everything.

Though Elyssa hated wearing her hair braided and knotted up and skewered against her skull, she braided the long, silky mass, wound it up tight, pinned it harshly against her head, and pulled her hat down until not one pale bit of hair showed.

Another check in the mirror satisfied Elyssa that even the most narrow-minded, mean-spirited, thick-skulled ex-rebel colonel couldn't accuse her of trying to catch a man's eye with a flashy way of dressing.

Elyssa went down the stairs to the kitchen, certain that she wouldn't have to confront Hunter right away. She had heard him leave the house earlier.

Not early, mind you. He had gone downstairs nearly a full hour later than usual.

Exhausted by all that lust, no doubt, Elyssa thought bitterly.

There was a grim set to her mouth when she walked into the kitchen.

"Good heavens," Penny said. "What happened to you?"

"I beg your pardon?" Elyssa said, wondering if Penny somehow knew about last night.

"Your, er, clothes."

"Oh." Elyssa shrugged. "I'm tired of the English clothes."

"Sassy, you can't—"

"Don't call me Sassy."

The anger buried in Elyssa's voice startled Penny.

"I'm sorry," Penny said. "I didn't realize you disliked Bill's nickname for you."

Elyssa shrugged and gathered her fraying self-control.

"You can't wear those clothes out of the house," Penny said.

"Why not?"

"They're men's clothes!"

"I'm doing a man's work. Why should I be trussed up in silk and satin?"

"You sound just like your mother," Penny muttered.

Saying nothing, Elyssa pulled on rough leather work gloves and lifted the shotgun from its pegs over the kitchen door.

"Aren't you going to eat breakfast?" Penny asked.

"I'm not hungry."

"Let me pack a lunch for you."

"If I want something, I'll come back and get it."

"You and Hunter," Penny said, exasperated. "Must be some kind of autumn fever going around."

Elyssa spun back to the other woman.

"What's this about Hunter?" Elyssa demanded.

"He wasn't hungry either."

Good, Elyssa thought. *I hope his conscience grinds on him until he's a shadow.*

The worried look on Penny's face told Elyssa she should get a better grip on her feelings.

Again.

"What about you?" Elyssa asked calmly. "Are you feeling better?"

"Yes. I guess I'm about through the morning sickness."

A shock wave went through Elyssa.

I might be pregnant.

"Don't worry about anything," Elyssa said to Penny. "We'll do just fine without men."

Penny smiled wanly.

Elyssa gave her a quick hug, then set off for the barn with a determined stride. The movements made her wince slightly.

The memory of Hunter lying between her thighs speared through Elyssa like lightning. Memories of the pleasure that had come before the pain expanded through her body in shimmering waves.

In the dark pauses between pleasure, shame bloomed.

Fool.

Bloody idiot.

But no matter what names Elyssa called herself, the embers of a very sweet fire smoldered beneath her anger. Hunter might have hurt her when he took her maidenhead, but he had also brought her a shocking pleasure up to that point.

If marriage was so bad, do you think women would put up with it?

Hunter's question had both mocked and lured Elyssa, telling her that there was more to sex than what she had just experienced.

Last night she had been too angry to respond to Hunter's confidence with anything but greater fury. Now the echoes of his sensual confidence went through her, unsettling her.

You'll want it, too. I'll see to it.

Elyssa shivered as Hunter's words rang through her mind, through her body.

"I said, 'Morning, Miss Elyssa. You must be feeling better.' "

Elyssa blinked and focused on Gimp.

"Hunter said you were feeling poorly," Gimp explained, "and wouldn't be riding today."

Bright spots of color burned on Elyssa's cheeks. She was indeed a bit tender in unexpected places. Realizing that Hunter knew she would be was embarrassing.

And infuriating.

"Hunter is wrong," Elyssa said crisply. "But then, he's wrong about me a lot. I'll be riding Leopard."

"Uh . . ."

"What is it?"

"Hunter doesn't want you riding alone."

"Hunter can go to hell."

Leaving a shocked Gimp in her wake, Elyssa went to Leopard's stall. A few minutes later she rode the stallion out of the barn and right over the paddock fence.

"They're working the north marsh," Gimp called after her.

Elyssa waved.

"Watch out for Injuns! Morgan said he saw some!"

She waved again.

Leopard's long legs stretched into a lope that ate distance quickly. After a while Elyssa's thighs quit protesting and settled into the familiar rhythms of riding.

The land flew by in the tawny shades of autumn. The windswept sky and brilliant sunlight had a soothing effect on her spirits.

All too soon Elyssa found herself at the edge of the marsh, no longer alone. Two armed men cantered briskly toward her, cutting off her advance.

"This is Ladder S land," Reed called out curtly. "We don't take to strangers."

"No, we certainly don't," Elyssa said evenly as the men rode up. "Good morning, Blackie, Reed."

Reed stared, half-swallowed a profane remark, and uncocked his shotgun.

Blackie did the same.

"It's you, Miss Sutton," Reed said. "I, uh, I didn't recognize you underneath all that, uh . . . gear."

"Didn't you recognize Leopard?" she asked tartly.

"No, ma'am. Some of the Culpepper raiders ride spotted ponies."

"Have you found any cattle?" Elyssa asked Reed.

"A few head. Breeding stock, mostly."

Elyssa grimaced. "Well, better that than nothing."

"Yes, ma'am," both men mumbled.

They kept sneaking sideways glances at Elyssa, as though assuring themselves that the sweet, husky female voice was actually coming from the mound of men's clothing atop Leopard.

"Where do you need another rider most?" Elyssa asked.

"Uh, well, uh . . ." Reed said.

Elyssa waited. She suspected what would be coming next.

"I better ask Hunter," Reed said.

"Hunter," Blackie confirmed, relief clear in his voice.

Might as well get it over with, Elyssa told herself bracingly. *The longer I wait to face him, the harder it will be.*

"Get him," she ordered in crisp tones. "Until then, I'll be working along some of the marsh trails I know."

"Yes, ma'am," Blackie said.

He reined around and put his heels into his wiry little pony. With frank envy Reed watched his partner leave.

"Go with him," Elyssa said. "You'll only be in my way. The trails I know are quite narrow."

"But Hunter said you weren't ever supposed to be alone," Reed objected.

"Hunter isn't the owner of the Ladder S. I am. Do keep it in mind."

"Uh." Reed swallowed. "Yes, ma'am."

Unhappily he reined his tough little pony around and headed after Blackie.

Elyssa turned Leopard north and trotted along the edge of the marsh. As she rode, she searched for signs that cattle had been entering and leaving the tall reeds.

Although there weren't many trails into the marsh, the cattle knew each one. The marsh was a cool place to retreat when the summer sun became too hot, and a moist place long after the grasslands had cured to hay beneath the autumn sun.

The sky overhead was hung with a few bright clouds and alive with wind. All around Elyssa was the rustle,

sway, and gentle whisper of tall grass and taller reeds.
From hidden places came the call of horned larks startled
by Leopard's big hooves.

As always, riding out beneath the vast, radiant sky
brought peace to Elyssa. Slowly the pain of the previous
night ebbed, allowing her to take a deep breath for the
first time since she had walked into Hunter's bedroom.

Don't think about Hunter, Elyssa told herself. *Think
about cows. They're your future.*

Hunter isn't.

Leopard's ears swiveled this way and that, checking
out each sound. His flaring nostrils drew in air as he
sampled the wind for scents. The knotted reins lay
loosely against his mane. Whatever guidance he needed
was provided by his rider's knees as often as the reins.

At all times Elyssa was aware of the stallion's response to the land. She knew that the horse's senses
were much keener than hers. If anyone or anything was
in the marsh, Leopard would notice it long before she
did.

Just as Elyssa spotted what looked like freshly broken
reeds, Leopard stopped and whipped his head around,
looking in the opposite direction. Ears pricked, head
high, the stallion stared off toward the mountains.

Wind carried the sound of shots and shouting to
Elyssa. Shading her eyes, she stood in the stirrups and
looked toward the Ruby Mountains.

After a moment Elyssa made out the shape of
someone running on foot down a long swell of land
toward the marsh, about half a mile from her. A few
more moments told Elyssa that it was an Indian girl who
was running so. She carried what looked like a bundle
of clothing in her arms.

Well behind the running figure, four riders trotted
along after the girl. They were whooping and hollering
like drunken men at a turkey shoot. Obviously they

weren't worried about catching the girl before she reached whatever safety might lie ahead in the marsh.

Elyssa stiffened and narrowed her eyes, hoping against hope that she was mistaken.

She wasn't. Two of the men were riding big sorrel mules.

Culpeppers, Elyssa thought with dread, yanking out her carbine. *That poor girl doesn't have a chance. They're just playing with her, enjoying her fear.*

Elyssa fired three quick shots in the air to warn the Ladder S riders who were working the margins of the marsh. Then she jammed the carbine back in the saddle scabbard and slammed her heels into Leopard's sleek hide.

The stud went from a standing start to a gallop in a few furious strides. Elyssa bent low over his neck and urged him to an even faster pace, heedless of the dangerous, uneven ground whipping by beneath his hooves.

Elyssa could tell the instant she was spotted. One of the riders yelled and whipped his mule, sending it out in front of the others. The remaining men pulled their rifles and began firing at the fleeing Indian girl.

The shots rang out in a ragged volley. At the same instant, Elyssa realized that the girl wasn't carrying a bundle of clothes after all.

It was a baby.

Elyssa kicked Leopard again and shouted for more speed. The big horse stretched out and ran like thunder over the wild land.

Wind clawed at Elyssa with invisible talons. The force of it yanked off her hat. Her braids tore free of their pins. In moments the braids were unraveled. Her hair streamed out like a flaxen flag, whipping in the wind behind her.

Elyssa clung to Leopard's neck, riding with all her

skill. She never took her eyes from the narrowing gap between the Indian girl and Leopard.

And the Culpeppers.

Lord, but those mules are fast! Elyssa thought in dismay.

She had only instants to decide whether to cut the Culpeppers off from the girl and pray that the Ladder S men would arrive before the Culpeppers grabbed her.

Or Elyssa could grab the girl and race headlong into the cover of the marsh.

The Indian girl finally heard the pounding of Leopard's hooves over the harshness of her own breathing. She veered away from the big stallion.

"No!" Elyssa screamed. "Friend! I'm a friend!"

Either the girl believed that safety lay with the flaxen-haired stranger, or she was simply too tired to run a longer path to the marsh. The Indian girl veered back, bent her head, and clung to the bundle of clothing that swaddled the baby. Her bare feet flew over the earth.

Elyssa was close enough now to recognize a Culpepper as the closest man. Gaylord Culpepper wasn't far behind. They were gaining at a terrifying pace.

And the first Culpepper was aiming his rifle at the fleeing girl.

Elyssa didn't know she had drawn and fired her carbine until it kicked against her shoulder. She kept levering in rounds, firing as fast as she could while Leopard thundered closer and closer to the hard-running riders.

Abruptly the Culpepper shouted, threw up his hands, and fell beneath the hooves of his mule. Gaylord barely pulled his own mule around before he trampled his kin underfoot.

Relief and sickness roiled equally within Elyssa. She ignored both.

As she drew alongside the running girl, Elyssa jammed the carbine back into its sheath. Still running, the Indian girl held out her baby in mute plea that it be saved even though it was too late for her own life to be spared.

The remaining men would be on them in moments.

Elyssa grabbed the baby and cradled it against her side with her left arm. Simultaneously she kicked free of her right stirrup and held out her right hand to the straining girl.

"Come on!" Elyssa shouted. "Take my hand! You can't outrun them!"

The gesture meant more than any words. The Indian girl sprang like a cat at the stirrup.

Somehow Elyssa managed to hang on to the girl long enough for her to gain a foothold in the stirrup. She crouched with one foot in the stirrup and clung to the saddle horn with both hands.

Elyssa turned Leopard and sent him toward the marsh at a dead run.

Shots peppered the ground around them. It was only a matter of time until the raiders brought down the fleeing stallion.

With one arm Elyssa supported the Indian girl as she clung precariously to the saddle. Elyssa's other arm cradled the bundle of rags protectively against her body, shielding the helpless baby from bullets in the only way she could.

"Hang on!" Elyssa said fiercely. "No matter what, hang on!"

If the Indian girl understood, she said nothing. Her eyes were dazed, exhausted. Her face was livid with bruises.

Leopard thundered toward the marsh without slowing down, no matter how rough the going. A quick glance back told Elyssa that Gaylord Culpepper was no more than three hundred feet away. He was riding easy in the saddle, taking his time as he sighted down the barrel of his rifle.

From the corner of her eye Elyssa saw Ladder S riders burst from the marsh almost a mile away. Bugle Boy was in the lead, running as though fleeing hell, narrowing the distance between Hunter and the raiders with gigantic strides.

Hunter's rifle was in his hands. He rode like a centaur, firing as he came.

The range was too great for accuracy from the back of a racing horse. Elyssa knew it, just as she knew it was all Hunter could do until he got closer.

And by then, Gaylord would have picked off the two women with the ease of a man shooting fish in a barrel.

A shot came from the marsh just ahead and to the right of Elyssa. A split second later, a shot from behind her whipped by so close that she saw dust leap from the ground just to the left of Leopard's flying hooves.

Suddenly Leopard was into the marsh's tawny embrace. Catlike, the stud hurtled down a narrow, mud-caked trail. Elyssa dragged the horse to a jolting stop just as the other girl's strength gave out. The girl fell to the ground in a tattered heap of clothing.

The sounds of firing erupted behind Elyssa in ragged volleys. Leopard stood calmly, breathing hard. Elyssa kicked free of the stirrups and slid off, holding the baby in one arm and her carbine in the other.

The Indian girl made a ragged noise and held out her hands. Elyssa bent and handed the baby to its mother. Then a noise from deeper in the marsh made Elyssa spin around, carbine leveled and ready to fire.

The Indian girl made a sharp sound and tried to rise, but her strength was gone.

"Easy, Sassy," said a voice from the reeds. "It's Case."

Elyssa felt as though the world had been lifted from

her shoulders. She made a hoarse sound of relief and pointed the carbine barrel at the sky.

Case emerged from the marsh carrying a rifle.

The Indian girl seemed to recognize him. Slowly she relaxed and began crooning softly to the baby, who had not made one sound during all the flight. A small fist emerged from the rags. Tiny fingers patted at the girl's face. The smile she gave her baby was as radiant as the sky.

"Are you hurt?" Case asked Elyssa.

Elyssa's mouth was far too dry to attempt speech. She simply shook her head.

"Wait here," Case said. "I'll give the call of a horned lark when I return. You hear anything else, get ready to shoot."

She nodded.

Case gave her an intent, searching look.

"Hang on, Sassy. I won't be long."

Numbly Elyssa nodded again.

Sporadic shots sounded from beyond the marsh. Hooves made a distant drumroll that faded into the rustling of the dry, wind-fretted reeds.

It seemed like an hour, but really was only minutes, before the call of a horned lark came softly through the reeds.

"All clear," Case said. "They're running away like the coyotes they are."

Elyssa made a low sound as relief swept through her. On its heels came nausea and weakness. She swayed, shaking.

What's wrong with me? I wasn't the one running for miles over the land like this poor girl.

The answer came to Elyssa as she saw again the instant when the Culpepper threw up his hands and fell beneath the hooves of his racing mule.

Grimly Elyssa swallowed and then swallowed again,

trying to quell the rebellion of her stomach.

As soon as Case emerged from the reeds again, Elyssa turned to the Indian girl. When she bent down to check on the baby, a wave of nausea hit her. Blindly she went to her knees and crawled away from the girl and the baby.

Spasm after spasm of sickness convulsed Elyssa. She retched until she was too weak to hold up her head. Vaguely she realized she didn't have to. Someone was doing it for her.

Strong arms lifted Elyssa, turned her, cradled her. Gentle hands wiped her face with a cool, damp bandanna. She lay against a man's chest and shuddered.

"Hunter?" she whispered hoarsely.

"Not yet," Case said. "He'll be along real quick, though."

"No," she said, struggling to sit up.

Case caged Elyssa against his chest with equal parts strength and gentleness.

"Easy, little one," Case said. "Rinse your mouth out with this. You'll feel better."

"The girl—" Elyssa began.

"I checked her. She didn't catch a bullet. Neither did the baby. She's nursing him right now. Or trying to. Poor thing had a hard time of it with those Culpeppers."

With a shuddering sigh, Elyssa took a sip of water.

The sound of men approaching made her push weakly at Case's arms.

"Let me up, please," she pleaded.

"You're still shaking. Give your nerves time to settle."

"No!" Elyssa said hoarsely. "I don't want him to know what a weakling and coward I am."

"Coward?"

Case looked at Elyssa in disbelief. Ignoring her small struggles, he resumed washing her face as though she was a child. The gentleness of his touch was at odds with the bleakness of his pale green eyes.

"You're neither weak nor a coward," Case said calmly. "A lot of men break and run at their first taste of gunfire and death."

Elyssa made a muffled sound.

"I know," Case said. "You don't like remembering that you might have killed a man, even though that Culpepper needed killing as much as any man ever born."

The cool, damp bandanna smoothed over Elyssa's forehead and eyes.

"But you did what had to be done," Case said. "You stood your ground and saved lives at the risk of your own. No soldier could have been braver."

Elyssa looked at Case's eyes and understood all that he wasn't saying.

"It happened to you, too, didn't it?" she whispered. "The—the shooting and the sickness."

"I got over it," Case said matter-of-factly. "You will, too. You're a strong woman, Sassy. A lot stronger than a man would guess from looking at you."

Reeds crackled as something brushed them aside. With shocking speed a six-gun appeared in Case's hand.

"It's me," said Hunter.

"Whistle next time or it could be your last."

Hunter shoved aside the reeds and wondered what Case would say if he knew his brother's mouth was too dry to whistle.

It had been like that since Hunter had seen a rifle pointing at Elyssa and known with terrible finality that there was nothing he could do to stop a bullet from reaching her.

"Thank you," Hunter said in a low voice to Case. "I owe you. Again."

"I wasn't the one who saved her."

"Who was?"

"I'll let you know when I find out," Case said dryly.

Hunter barely heard. He knelt next to Elyssa and pushed a cascade of silver-gold hair away from her face.

"Are you all right, Sassy?" Hunter asked.

With a small sound Elyssa buried her face against Case's chest, shutting out Hunter.

"She's not hurt," Case said.

"Then why are you holding her as tenderly as a Christmas kitten?" Hunter retorted.

What Hunter didn't say was that he wanted to be the one holding Elyssa. Unfortunately, she was making it clear that the feeling only went one way.

"She likely killed a Culpepper," Case said.

The shock on Hunter's face would have made any man but Case smile.

"It's not sitting easily on her stomach," Case added.

Elyssa gave a small groan of humiliation and tried to vanish into Case's gray flannel shirt. Case simply held her and gently stroked her hair.

"What happened?" Hunter demanded.

Eyes tightly closed, Elyssa shook her head, her humiliation complete.

"Bill and I untied the girl while everyone was asleep. Then I started tracking that damned ghost," Case said.

"The spy?" Hunter demanded.

Case nodded.

"He came to Bill's place just before dawn," Case said. "There was some kind of argument. He left. I've been playing tag with him ever since. He led me here."

"He's in the marsh somewhere?"

"Yes."

"Then he didn't come from the Ladder S," Hunter said. "All our men are accounted for."

Case grunted. "When I heard gunfire, I sifted out to the edge of the marsh and looked around. The Indian girl was making for the marsh as fast as she could run. Four of the raiders were chasing her.''

Hunter glanced at the girl.

Sensing his interest, she looked up from her baby. The bruises on her young face—combined with the fear and calculation in her eyes—told Hunter everything. He had seen women with that look during the war, after they had been hard-used by strangers and had no reason to trust any man.

Hunter held his left hand in front of his body, palm up. He touched the center of the palm with his right index finger.

The girl understood. Reassured, she went back to caring for her baby as best she could.

''Go on,'' Hunter said in a low voice to Case.

''Sassy was on that big spotted stud. They were coming across the grassland like hell on fire.''

Hunter said something under his breath.

''When the first Culpepper spotted her,'' Case said, ''she didn't even pull up from a dead run. She just dropped the reins, yanked out her carbine, and started firing.''

Hunter's expression became even more grim. He looked at the cascade of pale blond hair that concealed Elyssa's face from him.

''Damn it, Sassy,'' Hunter hissed. ''You never should have been here in the first place. You could have been killed!''

Elyssa ignored him.

''Instead, she dropped a Culpepper,'' Case said matter-of-factly. ''A good day's work, if you ask me.''

''I didn't,'' Hunter snarled.

Big hands reached out and plucked Elyssa from Case's arms. Hunter turned Elyssa's face against his chest and began stroking her hair even more tenderly than Case had.

Elyssa struggled for a moment before she gave in. Hunter's gentleness was too beguiling to fight against. She hungered for it, for some sign that she hadn't misread him totally. A man with only lust on his mind wouldn't bother to care tenderly for a queasy girl.

"Then Elyssa reined her stud up alongside the Indian," Case continued, "took the baby in one arm, grabbed the girl with the other, and hauled her up to the stirrup."

Hunter's breath stopped. "What about the other raiders?"

"They were coming down on her fit to scare a stone statue," Case said.

"Jesus."

Hunter's hand contracted in Elyssa's hair.

"Gaylord was drawing a bead on her scalp," Case said, "when a bullet came out of the marsh. Knocked him right out of the saddle. He was dead before he hit the ground."

"The ghost saved Sassy's life?" Hunter asked skeptically. "That makes no sense. He has tried to kill Sassy himself."

Case shrugged. "Maybe he just wanted to scare her into pulling up stakes and leaving the ranch behind."

"Maybe." Hunter's tone said he doubted it.

The sound of men approaching the marsh came clearly through the air. Case stood and faded back among the reeds.

Frowning, thinking hard, Hunter continued to stroke Elyssa's hair and back. Slowly the tremors were leaving her body.

"Feeling better now?" Hunter asked gently.

She nodded.

One of Hunter's hands fitted itself beneath Elyssa's chin. He tilted her face up so that she couldn't avoid his eyes.

Elyssa's body stiffened. Despite Hunter's tender care, he was furious with her.

"If you ever pull a damfool stunt like that again," Hunter said in icy, precise tones, "I will peel you like a grape. You had no business leaving the house alone and you know it!"

Using the last of her strength, Elyssa started to push herself away from Hunter.

For an instant Hunter's arms closed more tightly around her. Then, reluctantly, he let her go.

"What I do is my business, not yours," Elyssa said.

The declaration was ruined by the hoarseness in her voice.

"Not after last night," Hunter countered, his voice low and furious.

Elyssa blushed scarlet and stumbled to her feet.

"Last night gives you no rights over me," she said through her teeth.

"The hell it doesn't."

Hunter came to his feet with a strength and grace that made Elyssa want to shoot him where he stood.

"You could be pregnant," he said. "Remember?"

"A gentleman wouldn't—"

"Hunter!" Morgan called from beyond the reeds, interrupting Elyssa's low, angry words. "Where are you?"

Hunter's whistled shrilly.

"I'm not a gentleman," Hunter said softly. "I proved that last night when I hurt you. I'm sorry about that, Sassy."

Sassy.

"I hate that name," she said.

"Why? It suits you."

"Just like 'fancy man' suits you. *Now.*"

Hunter's mouth flattened.

Elyssa went to Leopard. She tried to mount, but her

body betrayed her. Her legs were like string.

With easy strength Hunter picked up Elyssa and dumped her in Leopard's saddle.

A moment later Bugle Boy pushed into the small clearing among the reeds, summoned by Hunter's whistle.

Hunter went to the Indian girl and began making signs. She watched intently, hesitated, and made the sign for yes.

Very gently he picked up the girl and her baby and placed them in Bugle Boy's saddle. Then he swung up behind her, took the reins, and headed out of the marsh.

When Hunter looked over his shoulder, Elyssa was gathering her reins with fingers that were visibly uncertain. Hunter wanted to go to her, to pull her in his arms and hold her, simply hold her, reassuring both of them that she was still alive.

But Hunter had seen the shame and defiance in Elyssa's blue-green eyes. He knew that she would go for his face like a cat if he tried to touch her.

Well, soldier, you got what you wanted, Hunter told himself bitterly. *She no longer looks at you with admiration and desire. And she sure as hell isn't building dreams around one Hunter Maxwell anymore.*

That's what I wanted, isn't it?

Isn't it?

The question echoed in Hunter's mind through the ride back to the ranch.

It's better this way, Hunter told himself many times. *We're all wrong for each other. She's too young.*

The image of Elyssa racing at breakneck speed to save the Indian girl and her baby lanced through Hunter's mind, reminding him that age had little to do with bravery. During the war, he had seen boys do what had to be done at a time when seasoned soldiers turned pale and shook.

Too bad Belinda didn't have as much courage in her whole body as Sassy has in her little finger, Hunter thought painfully. *Ted and Em might be alive today.*

The thought was like a knife twisting in Hunter's soul. He had let lust choose his wife, and his children had paid.

It still wouldn't work, Hunter told himself fiercely. *Brave or not, Sassy is still too young to know her own mind. When the babies started coming along, she would be like Belinda, always hungering for the butterfly life she left behind.*

It's better this way.

It has to be.

There's no going back.

Yet the pain Hunter had caused Elyssa gnawed on his soul as mercilessly as his hunger for her. The shock waves of a single, shattering truth kept shaking him.

Elyssa had been a virgin when she came to his bed.

And an angry, humiliated woman when she left it.

20

$\mathcal{B}$roodingly Hunter stood in the doorway and watched while Elyssa cared for the Indian girl and her baby. Even three days after the skirmish with the Culpeppers, Hunter still went cold when he thought how close Elyssa had come to dying.

Every time he closed his eyes, he relived again the horrible moment when he realized that he would be too late to save Elyssa from the murderous Culpeppers.

Nor had Case found out who did save her.

That ghost is going to be the death of us, Hunter thought grimly.

"That's the way," Elyssa encouraged the girl. "The baking soda will ease his rash."

The Indian girl gave her a brief, shy smile and resumed washing her baby in the shallow basin.

Penny bent over the little scrap of humanity and made cooing noises. The baby watched her with curious black eyes.

"How old do you think he is?" Penny asked.

"Barely two weeks," Hunter said.

Elyssa's hands jerked. She hadn't realized that Hunter was in the kitchen.

Lately it seemed that every time she turned around, Hunter was there, watching her with stormy gray eyes.

"What about her family?" Penny asked.

"Ute, as Sassy suspected. Right, Sassy?"

The tone of Hunter's voice told Elyssa that he was using the nickname to get under her skin.

The more she avoided him, the more he dug at her.

"Right," Elyssa said tersely.

She shook out a fresh diaper with a vigor that made the cloth snap. In front of other people she couldn't ignore Hunter as she wanted to. He took advantage of that, forcing her to speak to him when she plainly didn't want to.

"Sassy thinks the girl is related to a chief," Hunter continued, "because of all the beads and shells on her clothes."

"So I heard," Penny said.

Elyssa finished folding the diaper and reached for another. Not once did she look at Hunter.

"I'll do that," he said, reaching past Elyssa. "I've folded more diapers in my time than you have."

"It's not necessary," she said tightly.

Elyssa flinched when Hunter's hand brushed over hers.

"It's very necessary," he said in a low voice.

Before Elyssa could retreat, Hunter deliberately repeated the small, tender caress. Shocked, she looked up at Hunter.

Angry words died on her lips when she saw the bleak memories in his eyes. She knew he was thinking of his own dead children.

The realization stripped away Elyssa's anger at Hunter, leaving only her raw hurt and vulnerability.

I was truly a fool to think that my love would make a difference to Hunter, Elyssa thought sadly. *His heart is buried with his children.*

I've been a fool about him from the very first, seeing

what I wanted to see instead of what was right in front of my face.

"I'll work on supper," Elyssa said, turning away.

"I'll do that, Sas—er, Elyssa," Penny said, correcting herself quickly. "The girl is more comfortable when you're around."

Elyssa started to object, but it was too late. Penny was already on her way to the kitchen. Elyssa and Hunter were alone but for the Indian girl, who knew no English.

Or admitted to knowing none.

Hunter shook out a piece of soft cloth and folded it deftly.

"You're better at it than I am," Elyssa said, determined to keep the conversation impersonal.

"I've had more practice than you," Hunter said. "Belinda didn't have a whole lot to do with babies."

"Just one more way I'm like your late, unlamented wife," Elyssa said bitterly before she could think better of it. "That must comfort you no end."

Hunter shot Elyssa a narrow, sideways glance.

"Does that mean you're finally ready to stop running and talk to me about the night we—" he began.

"Did Case find out any more about the girl?" Elyssa asked quickly, talking right over Hunter.

The last thing Elyssa wanted to do was talk about the unsettling night when Hunter had taken her virginity in a storm of lust.

I offered, she reminded herself harshly. *Much as I'd like to heap all the blame on him like a hail of stones, I can't.*

"The Culpeppers happened on a small Ute hunting camp," Hunter said. "Most of the warriors were off fighting the army. Damned hotheads should have been home protecting their own women and kids."

Elyssa looked at the Indian girl. If she understood what was being said, she didn't show it.

"The Culpeppers shot up a few boys," Hunter said, "grabbed the girl, and ran off before the hunters could return."

"Did Case learn her name?"

"The Culpeppers never asked it," Hunter said.

"Not surprising. Men with lust on their mind don't much care about the name of the girl who—"

Elyssa's words stopped on a sharply indrawn breath. Hunter's fingers were clamped around her wrist with a force just short of pain.

"Don't you dare compare what happened between us to what the Culpeppers did to that poor girl," Hunter said in a soft, deadly voice.

"Let go of me."

The pressure on Elyssa's wrist didn't lessen.

"You bathed her," Hunter said. "You tended her fever. You saw what those animals had done to her."

His eyes were brilliant slits of gray. They were radiant with a rage and frustration that was almost tangible.

For days Hunter hadn't been able to get close enough to Elyssa to talk to her, much less to touch her. Whenever he appeared, she faded like a ghost into the shadows.

Hunter felt like he had spent his life looking at Elyssa's back as she retreated from him.

"If you hadn't been a virgin, you never would have felt a bit of pain and you damn well know it," Hunter said savagely.

"Do I?" Pointedly Elyssa looked at her wrist. "You're hurting me now."

"No, I'm holding you, and you know that too. Say it, Sassy. Say that you know I never meant to hurt you."

"My name is *Elyssa*."

The grip on her wrist changed subtly. She was still caged by Hunter's strength, but it was different now. Almost caressing.

And then it was frankly caressing.

His fingertips traced the veins on the soft inside of Elyssa's wrist with the delicacy of a kiss. Once, twice, three times, until her heart was beating so rapidly she was certain he could feel it racing.

"Hunter . . ." Elyssa whispered. "Don't."

She felt the shudder that went through Hunter when she spoke his name. Slowly he lifted her wrist and put his lips where his fingertips had been. The tip of his tongue traced the veins with aching restraint.

Elyssa made a small sound and shivered very much as Hunter had.

"Stop running from me," Hunter whispered against Elyssa's soft skin. "I'll make it so good for you. I swear it, honey."

The hungry response of her own body to Hunter's caresses both shocked and infuriated Elyssa. She snatched back her wrist.

"Thank you for your generous offer," she said with cool sarcasm, "but pain is an excellent teacher. I have nothing new to learn from you."

"You have *everything* to learn from me."

"Then I'll go through life as ignorant as an egg."

"Are you pregnant?"

The question hit Elyssa like a bucket of ice water.

"Are you?" he asked softly.

"Go to hell, Hunter Maxwell."

"I have a right to—"

"How many mustangs are green-broke now?" Elyssa cut in. "Are we going to meet the army contract with the horses, at least?"

Hunter looked at Elyssa's glittering blue-green eyes and clenched his jaw in frustration.

It had been the same for the past three days. If he cornered her into talking to him, she refused to talk about anything but business. He was fed up with it.

Hunter also was unsettled by his own relentless hunger for Elyssa. He had sworn never to let a woman have that kind of hold over him again, but Elyssa had made a mockery of his defenses.

Touching her right now had been a mistake. A bad one. The scent and softness of her skin had hardened his body in a rush of blood so fierce it made him lightheaded.

It also made him angry with himself, with her, with everything.

"The Herrera brothers are breaking the last of the mustangs now," Hunter said tightly.

Elyssa sensed the anger seething just beneath Hunter's control. She gave him a wary glance. Between worrying about the ranch and worrying about facing him every minute of every day, she felt as tightly strung as a dance fiddle.

But at least Elyssa felt more certain of herself when ranch business was the topic of discussion.

You have everything to learn from me.

Hunter's flat statement echoed in Elyssa's mind, unsettling her as much as the tender, incandescent caress of his tongue on her inner wrist.

"What about beeves?" Elyssa asked.

"We're short."

"Any chance of making it up?"

"We're working on it," Hunter said laconically.

"I'm aware of that. Will we make the contract?"

"One way or another."

"What does that mean?"

Pointedly Hunter looked at the Indian girl and said no more.

Elyssa's eyes widened slightly. Apparently Hunter, too, wondered just how much English the girl understood.

"The boys are combing the marsh in all the places

you showed them,'' Hunter said. "Morgan and Johnny have the dogs working the high canyons.''

"I see.''

"You will,'' Hunter vowed under his breath. "One way or another, if it's the last thing I do on this blessed earth.''

A pink flush appeared on Elyssa's cheeks. She suspected that Hunter wasn't talking about cattle at all.

"If anything changes,'' she said in a remote voice, "please advise me at once.''

"You'll be the first to know. I guarantee it.''

That was one promise Hunter was looking forward to keeping.

But first he had to figure out a way to get Elyssa alone. He had to do it quickly, for his time on the Ladder S was running out. If Ab's raiders didn't attack soon, Hunter would have to go after them.

Then he and Case would go back to the Spanish Bottoms. The sooner they got there, the sooner the last of the Culpeppers who had raided in Texas would be brought to justice.

Standing just beneath the ridge overlooking Wind Gap, Hunter merged into the piñons and waited. All around him the night seethed with wind and the promise of rain.

A lark's call sifted between the piñon boughs. Hunter returned the call as softly as it had come to him.

Case appeared in front of his brother.

"You keep riding your men so hard, you're going to lose them,'' Case said quietly.

"What does that mean?''

"Even Morgan is tiptoeing around you, and God knows he is a tough son.''

"How do you know what's going on at the Ladder S?'' Hunter retorted.

"Same way I know what it's like in the Culpepper camp," Case said sardonically.

"I've got a lot on my mind."

"Yeah. Her name is Sassy. What went wrong with you and that little gal of yours?"

"She's not mine," Hunter said curtly.

"The hell she isn't. She's yours whether you've ever had her or not."

Even in the uncertain moonlight, Case saw the change in Hunter's expression.

"So that's the way of it," Case said quietly. "Is she pregnant?"

"It's none of your damned business," Hunter snarled.

"The last time you said that to me, I was telling you what a common piece of trash Belinda was."

The frustration and anger in Hunter leaped without warning. He went after Case in an undisciplined rush. There was a short, sharp skirmish, but the advantage was all Case's. He was in control of himself.

Hunter wasn't.

Rather quickly Hunter found himself facedown on the ground, breathing hard, trying to buck Case off his back.

"Give it up," Case said, increasing the pressure on Hunter's neck and arm. "You're the one who taught me this hold. You can't break it without breaking your own stubborn neck."

Hunter kept struggling.

"Damn it!" Case said. "Stop acting like a green kid. You weren't the first man Belinda fooled, or the last."

Abruptly, self-control returned to Hunter.

"Let me up," Hunter said through his teeth.

"Not just yet," Case said calmly. "First I want to know if I'm going to be an uncle any time soon."

Tension snaked through Hunter's body again, but he made no effort to throw off Case.

"I don't know," Hunter said.

"Ask Sassy."

"I did."

"And?"

"She told me to go to hell."

Case muttered an indistinct word. An instant later he released Hunter. Simultaneously Case stood up in a lithe rush.

Warily he watched Hunter come to his feet. When Hunter showed no inclination to jump him again, Case let out a long breath.

"Sorry," Case said quietly. "I thought you were just being pigheaded about Sassy, the way you were when you wanted Belinda."

"And you told me she was a shallow little flirt."

"She was."

"I know. Now." Hunter's voice was both weary and bitter. "What a goddam shame it cost the lives of two fine children for me to find out what I had married."

"Their dying wasn't your fault."

"That's what I tell myself fifty times a day."

"Do you believe it?"

"No." Hunter hesitated, then said simply, "Thinking of them scared and hurting and crying for their daddy . . . It eats me alive."

"So you're going to spend the rest of your life punishing yourself, is that it?"

Hunter shrugged.

"You think that will make it right?" Case asked.

"I don't know what I think. All I know is . . ." Hunter's voice died.

"I'll tell you what I know," Case said. "You come to a point like a bird dog whenever Sassy is in sight."

A hissing curse was Hunter's only answer.

"Why don't you marry her?" Case asked calmly. "The world needs more decent people. The two of you would have good kids."

The sound Hunter made could hardly be called a laugh.

"Not Elyssa," Hunter said bluntly. "Not with me."

"Why?"

"She didn't like it one bit. When I tried to make it right, she went for my eyes like a cat."

Case's expression shifted very slightly, as close to a smile as he ever came since the war.

"Seems to me," Case drawled, "that a girl with that much passion in her would be worth the trouble of gentling."

"First I have to catch her. She's as hard to get close to as that ghost you keep chasing."

"Interesting thing about that ghost," Case said.

"Did you find out who he is?" Hunter asked quickly.

"No. I haven't seen hide nor hair of that critter since Gaylord was killed. Nobody is giving information to Ab now, either."

"How do you know?"

"That's what I'm supposed to be doing now," Case said ironically. "Spying on the Ladder S for Ab."

"Interesting."

"I thought so."

"Does Ab trust you?" Hunter asked, thinking fast.

"Ab doesn't trust anyone."

Hunter grunted.

"Like you and women," Case continued. "Ever since you let that faithless bitch lead you around by your dumb handle, you haven't had a good word to say about women."

Hunter gave Case a long, measuring kind of look. Quietly Case waited to see if his brother would lose his temper again.

In the moonlight Case's pale green eyes looked the same as Hunter's—like hammered silver.

"You're riding me pretty hard," Hunter said. "Why?"

"You're riding Sassy harder."

"If you're that steamed about it, marry her yourself."

"I've thought of it," Case said easily.

"What?"

"Keep it down unless you want visitors."

"What's this about you and Elyssa?" Hunter demanded in a low, seething voice.

"Nothing but a few facts."

"Such as?"

"Sassy is a woman alone in a country where women have a hell of a hard time alone," Case said. "She has a fine ranch and a desire to make it work. If she didn't believe in such a damn fool thing as love, I'd have a ring on her finger so fast it would make your head spin."

"No."

"Why not? Are you planning to marry her?"

"It's the only decent thing for me to do," Hunter said simply. "But she's not having any part of it."

Case grunted. "She was a virgin, then. I wondered."

It wasn't a question, but Hunter answered anyway.

"Yes," he said distinctly. "Elyssa was a virgin."

"At least you know who she's been with," Case said. "Girl like Belinda, you never could tell how many neighbors were looking at her and remembering what it was like to climb into her saddle."

Hunter grimaced but didn't disagree.

For a few minutes the men stood and listened to the sounds of the night. Then Case turned his attention to his brother once more.

"Ab is going from bad to worse," Case said. "Gaylord was a favorite of his."

"Ain't that just too damned bad."

"You getting ready to go after Ab?"

"I don't have much choice," Hunter said. "The army

will be wanting their livestock in less than two weeks.''

"How many head of cattle do you have for them?''

"Beeves? Less than fifty. Maybe another hundred in breeding stock.''

"The Ladder S won't last long without breeding stock,'' Case said.

Hunter didn't answer.

"But that's not our problem, is it?'' Case continued. "Culpeppers are.''

"Have you found where the stolen cattle are being held?'' Hunter asked curtly.

"Funny thing about that. Lately I've noticed some prime Ladder S strays on B Bar land.''

"Strays?'' Hunter asked sharply.

Case nodded. "It's as though some of the cattle are drifting out of wherever they've been held.''

"Backtrack them.''

"I did. They seem to be coming from the willow bottoms north of the B Bar.''

Hunter grunted. "That's a rough stretch of land from what I've heard.''

"You heard right. Lots of ravines reaching back up into the Rubies. A man could hide a lot of cattle up that way.''

"Not good enough. I have to know where the cattle are before I risk a raid.''

"I'm getting close,'' Case said.

"You've got three days.''

Case nodded.

"If you find out about the cattle before then, don't wait for dark to tell me,'' Hunter said. "Just get over here quick. We'll need you at the ranch more than at the raiders' camp.''

"What if I can't find the cattle?''

"At dawn on the fourth day, I'll raid the B Bar and let the devil take the hindmost.''

"Where do you want me?" Case asked.

"Wherever you won't get shot by my men."

Case nodded. Then he slid his gun from its holster, spun the cylinder to check the load, and returned the gun to its place with an easy motion.

"Watch yourself on the way back," Case said.

"What about you?"

"I'm not distracted by a girl I want who's mad as a dunked hen at me."

"I'm not a fool."

"Most of the time," Case agreed sardonically. "What's really bothering you? That you can't have Sassy?"

Case shook his head.

"It's the ranch I want," Case said. "The ranch is something to build on when the last Culpepper is dead. Something that can't be brutalized and dumped like broken whiskey bottles by the side of the trail."

Hunter was too shocked to speak. He sensed that Case was talking about how Em and Ted had died. It was a subject Case had refused to discuss, ever.

Until now.

"I'll never speak of it again," Case said. "I just wanted you to know that you're the only living thing I'm able to care about since I found those kids. If Sassy can give you any ease with yourself and the past, I'll be as happy for you as I can be for anything."

Hunter closed his eyes as a wave of grief went over him for all that had been lost to the cruel past.

And part of what Hunter mourned was Case's laughter. In some ways Case was dead as surely as Hunter's own children.

"Case . . ."

There was no answer.

Case had gone into the darkness as silently as he had come.

have to show you some-thing,'' Hunter said.

Elyssa gasped and spun around so quickly she almost dropped her mug of breakfast coffee.

She had been certain Hunter was gone. From her bed-room window she had seen him ride out on Bugle Boy just after dawn. Then, after she could no longer see Hun-ter silhouetted against the rising light, Elyssa had drawn a long breath.

It had been her first deep breath since yesterday, when the delicate touch of Hunter's tongue had sent heat splin-tering through her body.

The darkness in his eyes haunted her.

"I thought you left," she said.

Hunter gave Elyssa a hooded look. She was wearing the muffling men's clothes again. He acknowledged that they were more sensible for range work, but he missed the shimmer and sigh of silk swirling around her legs.

"I did leave," Hunter said neutrally. "Then I came across something you have to see."

"What?"

He shook his head.

"If I tell you, it will prejudice you," Hunter said. "I

need your first impression. How soon can you be ready to ride?''

Puzzled, Elyssa set aside her coffee. As she faced Hunter, she told herself that her heart was beating faster because she was startled. It couldn't be racing simply because she was about to ride out over the land with Hunter once more.

Alone.

''Where are we going?'' she asked.

''Not far.''

Within minutes Elyssa and Hunter were mounted and riding away from the ranch house. Hunter rode with the rifle across his saddle and his eyes ceaselessly searching the land.

Elyssa rode the same way. The only difference was that her eyes kept straying back to Hunter. When she realized it, she was angry with herself.

It made no difference. Hunter drew her glance the way flame drew a moth. The shattering tenderness of yesterday's caress still burned against her wrist.

Asleep, she dreamed of him.

Awake, his words echoed seductively in her mind, undermining her anger.

You have everything to learn from me.

Silently Elyssa followed Hunter across the land. The storms had taken a toll of the tawny grasses. Most were beaten flat by wind and rain. For the lowlands, autumn was a time of turmoil and defeat.

But high on the shoulders of the mountains, aspens were coming into their full autumn glory. Leaves on some groves had turned as yellow as the summer sun. Other aspen groves were an orange so vivid it looked like tongues of fire licking up the deep canyons and long, shallow ravines.

Broodingly Elyssa's eyes returned to Hunter, her

autumn lover, a man as complex and compelling to her as the land itself.

Hunter was aware of Elyssa's quiet glances. That, and the emptiness of the land, eased some of the tension that had been riding him.

No matter how hard Hunter searched the wide land, he saw no sign of other people. He and Elyssa could have been alone on the face of the earth. Despite that, he kept to the lengthy, meandering route he had chosen.

Finally Hunter brought Elyssa to a place where mountains and the long, wide valley merged at the edges in a series of rumpled ridges and canyons. At the head of a small, steep canyon there was a cave mouth shielded by a riot of shrubbery. Clear, sweet water flowed between the willow thickets crowding the banks of a small stream.

Elyssa recognized the place. She had been to Hidden Creek before, but not for many years. And never by such a circuitous route.

Without dismounting, Hunter rode Bugle Boy through a thicket and into the creek itself. As he turned the horse upstream, Leopard followed. Limber willow branches bent away from the horses, then sprang back into place with little to mark the fact that horses had passed through.

When Hunter reached the cave mouth, he reined aside. A gesture of his hand urged Elyssa to ride in front of him into the cave itself. After Leopard walked past, Hunter bent low on Bugle Boy's neck and followed. Calmly both horses walked beneath an overhang of rock and into the mouth of a cave.

Just beyond the smaller opening, the cave was perhaps a hundred feet wide and three times that deep. Because it was autumn, there was a wide margin of dry, sandy bank around the pool that was concealed within the cave.

The pool itself was like a black mirror reflecting daylight from the entrance. Any disturbance to the water left ghostly, quicksilver traces on the surface. At the back of the pool was a long, narrow crack in the mountain.

In spring, water would gush from the crack with a sound like thunder. Today water welled up silently, filling the pool as quickly as the small creek drained it.

Hunter dismounted and grabbed a loose screen of freshly cut brush. He pulled it into place across the lower part of the opening, concealing the mouth of the cave.

With the brush screen in place, the light filtering into the cave became as mysterious as the quicksilver motions of the pool itself. Bugle Boy went to the water and drank. Silver circles shimmered outward from his muzzle.

"Can you see?" Hunter asked.

Elyssa started. Hunter was standing at Leopard's shoulder. His left hand was on the stallion's bit.

"All I can see is that we've ridden four miles and we're only a half mile from the house," Elyssa said. "Why?"

"Get down. It's over here."

Hunter stepped aside as though he knew that his closeness was making Elyssa nervous. Retreating a few steps, he waited for her to dismount. When she did, he turned immediately toward the stream.

"This way," he said.

After a moment of hesitation, Elyssa followed Hunter. He went to the point where the pool overflowed to create Hidden Creek. There he waited until she came to stand by him.

"Where is it?" Elyssa asked.

"Other side."

Elyssa peered into the oddly luminous darkness on the other side of the creek. She could just make out blurred shapes of boxes or bedrolls or both.

"Can you see it?" Hunter asked.

The subtle, leashed anticipation in his voice made Elyssa curious.

"No," she admitted. "I'm afraid I can't see much at all."

"Hang on."

With that, Hunter lifted Elyssa off her feet, carrying her across his chest like a child. He was splashing through the creek before she realized what had happened.

"Hunter!"

The word echoed around the cave, Elyssa's voice doubled and redoubled, calling his name.

Hunter cocked his head, listened, and smiled.

The tenderness and sensuality in his smile made Elyssa forget to breathe.

"Hunter?" she whispered.

"I'm right here."

He walked out of the stream onto the sandy bank and kept on going.

"Put me . . . down," Elyssa said, swallowing.

"In a minute. We're almost there."

As Hunter walked, sand whispered and slid away from his boots with a silky sound.

Elyssa started to speak, then closed her mouth. She was afraid her voice would give away the turmoil of her mind and body.

Hunter was too close. Too powerful.

Too gentle.

He carried her as though she was made of a crystal so fragile that a breath would set it to shivering and singing. It made her feel just that fragile, just that shivery.

The tremors that went through Elyssa were felt by Hunter as well. He looked down into her face. All he saw was the flash of her half-closed eyes, the tightness of her lips, and the pallor of her smooth skin.

Hunter's mouth flattened. Elyssa looked like a woman who was afraid of something. When he thought about what had happened the last time he was this close to her, he had a good idea of what she feared.

I told you, next time you'll enjoy it.

My God, you must really think I'm stupid. "Next time you'll enjoy it." What rot!

Suddenly last night's foolproof plan looked like purest folly in the light of day.

I hate you.

I don't want you anymore. Ever. In any way.

Nothing had changed since Elyssa had made those searing declarations.

Tension drew Hunter's body so tight he had to fight to breathe. Slowly he lowered Elyssa's feet to the sand until she was standing next to the bedroll he had so carefully prepared.

When Hunter spoke, his voice was much more harsh than he intended.

"Don't be frightened of me," he said. "I swear before God I never meant to hurt you."

Elyssa didn't trust herself to speak. She simply closed her eyes and turned her face away from Hunter.

"Do you really hate me so much?" he whispered.

Her eyes flew open.

"Do you?" he asked in a raw voice.

Silently Elyssa shook her head.

"Then why are you trembling and turning away as though you can't bear the sight of me?" Hunter asked. "My God, you won't even speak to me."

"I—" Elyssa's voice broke.

She turned her back on Hunter and swallowed again, fighting for control of herself.

"It—it would be easier to hate you," she whispered.

"But I can't. So I hate myself instead. I was such a fool."

Hunter's eyelids flinched at the pain in Elyssa's husky voice. He turned her until she was facing him again.

Facing him, but not looking at him.

"Marry me," Hunter said starkly.

Elyssa shook her head. Though she said nothing, her past words hung between them in an echo of feminine outrage.

No wonder churches and townships make sure girls are virgins before they marry. They never would suffer it otherwise.

With aching tenderness Hunter's fingertips brushed over Elyssa's eyebrows, her cheeks. Tears were caught in her eyelashes like warm rain.

"Don't cry, honey," Hunter whispered. "I'd rather be horsewhipped than make you cry again."

Elyssa didn't answer.

She couldn't. Hunter's lips were touching her tenderly, brushing butterfly kisses against her temples, her cheeks, her eyelashes. In hushed, trembling silence, he stole her tears before they could fall.

Breath caught in Elyssa's throat. Her heartbeat speeded in a wild rush. Tremors she couldn't control rippled through her. Her fingers curled into her palms until her nails left marks.

He doesn't love me.

I can't stop loving him.

Elyssa felt as though she was being torn apart. She wanted to flee. She wanted to stay in Hunter's arms. She wanted to push him away from her.

But most of all she wanted to bathe in the healing, intoxicating fire of Hunter's gentleness.

"Don't be frightened," Hunter whispered against her lips. "I just want . . ."

Hunter's voice died. What he wanted would send Elyssa running right out of the cave.

He closed his eyes and called himself fifty kinds of fool. Then he hugged Elyssa very gently against his chest, rocking slowly, stroking her back with one big hand.

"It's all right," he said huskily. "I won't hurt you. Please, honey. Don't cry."

With each word came a tender kiss, a tear sipped from her eyelashes, another kiss.

The trembling in Elyssa increased.

"It's all right, little one," Hunter whispered against her lips. "You're safe. I'll let you go as soon as you stop trembling. If that's what you want . . ."

Though Hunter didn't mean to, the tip of his tongue traced the outline of Elyssa's mouth in a silence that trembled with possibilities.

"Is that what you want?" he whispered.

Hunter's breath was warm and sweet against Elyssa's skin. She made a small sound.

"Is that yes or no?" Hunter asked. "Let you go or keep you close?"

The smooth heat of his lips against her eyelids both reassured Elyssa and increased the trembling of her body.

When Hunter felt the tremors raking through her, he ached with an emotion more complex than desire.

"Elyssa?" Hunter whispered helplessly against her lips. "Let me kiss you. Just one kiss, honey. Then I'll let you go, if that's what you want. I can't stop thinking how it felt just to kiss you. You liked that much of my lovemaking, at least."

Before Elyssa could think of all the reasons to refuse, her face lifted to him. The taut jerk of Hunter's body at her acceptance of his kiss brought more tears to her eyes.

He didn't love her, yet he wanted her with a force

that made him tremble. But despite the depth of passion
in him, he was fully in control, fully restrained.

This time.

He cares for me that much, at least, Elyssa thought
helplessly. *He is gentle with me.*

Elyssa whispered Hunter's name as his lips moved
tenderly over hers.

Another bolt of emotion tore through Hunter. With
light touches of his hands, he gathered Elyssa closer
against his chest. Softly he kissed the edges of Elyssa's
mouth until she shivered and opened her lips for him.
Only then did he allow himself to deepen the kiss as he
had longed to do.

The first taste of Elyssa was sweeter and at the same
time more arousing than anything Hunter had ever
known. Holding her carefully, he tasted her again and
again, slowly immersing himself in the dark, heated
wine of her kiss.

The restrained, sensual joining of mouths unraveled
Elyssa's caution. With each gentle glide of Hunter's
tongue, she gave more of herself to the kiss.

And to him.

Her hands crept up the front of his jacket, lifted, hesitated. Finally they rested, trembling, on his freshly
shaved cheeks.

Another tremor jerked through Hunter, telling Elyssa
that her caress moved him. Tears burned in her eyes and
overflowed again.

It's only desire that Hunter feels for me, Elyssa reminded herself.

And she was trembling with much more than desire.

But it was very sweet for Elyssa to be able to touch
Hunter in any way at all. To be touched by him with
such tenderness made the world begin to dissolve and
swirl slowly around her.

The tiny, passionate sound Elyssa made at the back

of her throat sent pure fire through Hunter's veins. The kiss became deeper, more hungry, yet his strength remained tightly leashed. He held her like a rainbow arched and shimmering in his arms.

Elyssa's fingers slid from Hunter's cheeks to his thick, black hair. His hat tumbled unnoticed to the ground. The heat of his scalp drew another small sound from her throat. Her hands tightened in his hair with sensuous urgency.

Catlike, Hunter's head moved against the caress, heightening the pressure of her fingers against his scalp. The frank sensuality of the movement sent ripples of heat through Elyssa.

Recklessly she drew her fingers down Hunter's scalp to his bare nape. The lightning stroke of desire that arced through him in response was echoed in her own body.

Elyssa's hands were hungry to caress more than the narrow strip of skin between Hunter's hairline and his jacket collar. Her palms remembered what it was to rub unhindered over his chest, to feel the masculine bunch and swell of muscle, to savor the soft abrasion of his hair curling against her skin.

Belatedly Elyssa realized that her hands were pushing Hunter's jacket away from his chest. Shocked by her own unruly hunger, she froze.

Hunter knew only that Elyssa no longer was returning his hungry kiss. Instead, her hands were pushing against his shoulders. Reluctantly he lifted his mouth, as he had promised he would.

Just one kiss.

"It's all right," Hunter said huskily. "You don't have to fight me. I'll let you go."

Yet even as he spoke the words, he couldn't force himself to release Elyssa entirely. Delicately his fingertips stroked her hands where they pressed against his chest.

The tiny, yearning caresses made Elyssa ache for all that she would never know of Hunter's heart. But she could know the elemental power of his desire. She could be the center of his world.

For a time.

Elyssa hesitated, shivering. Her body was certain that this time there would be more than pain waiting for her in Hunter's arms. The promise he had made was as much a lure to her as the male power of his body lying coiled and waiting against her palms.

You'll want it, too. I'll see to it. Like setting a match to straw.

Taking a ragged breath, Elyssa gathered her courage.

"I wasn't fighting," she whispered.

"You were pushing me away."

"Not you. Just your jacket."

When Hunter understood, desire stabbed violently through his body. For a moment he couldn't speak. He couldn't even breathe.

With a sinuous twist Hunter stripped off his jacket and tossed it aside.

"It's gone," he said in a deep voice. "Now what?"

"I . . ."

The twilight of the cave couldn't hide the flush that came to Elyssa's face.

Abruptly Hunter remembered. For all Elyssa's reckless response to him, she was just a brief step removed from innocence. She had taken that step with him, but only after he had dragged a confession of desire from her.

I . . . want you.

And then he had mocked her for having difficulty with the words.

Was the truth so hard?

"I . . ." Elyssa began again.

Hunter touched her lips with his thumb, sealing them.

He couldn't take back what had happened the first time Elyssa trusted her body to him. He could only try to make her understand that the shame was his, not hers.

"Hush," Hunter said gently. "I didn't mean to tease you that way. I want you until I can't breathe, but I don't want to frighten you and I'm no damned good at reading your mind. That's why I asked what you wanted next."

Smiling despite the tears gathering in her eyes, Elyssa kissed Hunter's thumb.

The simple caress sent a surge of emotion through Hunter. His eyes closed and his world shrank to the warmth of Elyssa's breath flowing between his fingers.

"Let me show you how it should have been the first time," Hunter said, opening his eyes. "Let me show you . . . everything."

The only thing Elyssa could say was Hunter's name. All her doubts and hesitations vibrated through her voice.

So did her passion.

Finally Elyssa nodded because her throat was too tight for her to speak again.

"This time," Hunter said in a low voice, "I won't cover that sweet mouth of yours. I'll hear each sound you make, every word you say. Even if the word is *no*."

Elyssa's breath rushed over Hunter's hand again. He tested the fullness of her lower lip with the ball of his thumb.

The simple intimacy of the caress made Elyssa tremble.

"Do you understand?" Hunter asked softly. "If I go too fast, just tell me. I'll slow down. I'll even stop, if that's what you want."

Again, Elyssa nodded.

"Are you sure?" Hunter asked.

The tip of her tongue touched his thumb.

Breath hissed out from between Hunter's teeth.

"Tell me in words," he said hoarsely. "Just this once. I won't ask again. But I have to be sure, this time."

Elyssa looked at Hunter's clear, burning eyes and knew that he needed the words.

"I want what I had with you before you . . . before . . ." Elyssa took an uneven breath. "If that means taking the pain along with the pleasure, well, it wasn't that bad. Just . . . unexpected . . . after all the pleasure."

Hunter closed his eyes. The thought that he had prevented Elyssa even from crying out when he hurt her was acid eating at his soul.

"I'll give you just the pleasure," he said. "I'll keep the pain to myself."

"I don't understand."

"I know. But I do."

"But—"

Hunter smiled sadly and skimmed Elyssa's lips with the ball of his thumb.

"Wouldn't you rather kiss me than ask me questions?" he whispered.

⌒22

$\mathcal{E}$lyssa wished she could still the shakiness in her body and voice, but she couldn't. So instead of trying to speak, she just braced herself against Hunter's strength and stood on tiptoe to reach his mouth.

He met her halfway, then lifted her the rest of the way. She made an odd sound as she felt the length of her body resting on his.

Hunter heard and started to lower Elyssa to the ground again. Instinctively she locked her arms tightly around his neck. The movement kept her body pressed against his.

"I didn't mean to frighten you," Hunter said against Elyssa's ear.

"You didn't."

"You cried out and trembled."

"It felt so good," she whispered.

"To be lifted?"

"To feel you from my forehead to my knees."

The passionate tightening of Hunter's body at Elyssa's words couldn't be concealed, especially when she was pressed so closely against him. He made a ragged sound and fought to subdue his wild hunger for her.

Elyssa tipped her head back until she could see Hunter's face.

"Are you frightened?" she asked, her voice shaky and teasing at the same time.

"Me?" Hunter asked in disbelief.

"You cried out and trembled."

Hunter's smile was as slow and hot as the kiss he gave Elyssa's neck.

"Sassy to the core," he murmured. "I like that."

"You do?" she asked, surprised.

"Mmm."

The purring sound Hunter made vibrated against Elyssa's neck in another kind of caress.

"It's part of the passion in you," he said.

Hunter's head turned. He brushed his lips over Elyssa's. The tip of her tongue darted out, tracing his smile. What began as teasing quickly became a kiss of drugging intimacy.

For a time Elyssa forgot where she was, who she was, what she was doing. She knew only Hunter's complex taste, his heat, the full, rhythmic penetration of his tongue . . . and the fire of her body rising to meet his.

One kiss became another and another and then another, until Elyssa was dizzy and breathing raggedly, and every breath came out with a small whimper.

For Hunter each tiny sound was a separate flame licking over his hungry body. He held Elyssa closer, harder, and was held just as fiercely in return.

Before the final kiss ended Elyssa was trembling and straining to be even closer to Hunter. Her body twisted against his with each urgent breath she took.

Hunter dragged his mouth away from Elyssa's and struggled to subdue a passion more intense than he had ever known. The broken, pleading sound of his name on Elyssa's lips nearly snapped what remained of Hunter's control.

Slowly he sank to the bedroll, taking Elyssa with him.

He hadn't planned to do it. His knees simply refused to hold any longer.

"Hunter?"

"It's all right. I won't hurt you. I just—" He took a swift, ragged breath. "You take the ground from beneath my feet."

Elyssa looked at Hunter's dilated, smoky eyes and felt an answering fire lance through her.

"That's only fair," she said.

"How so?"

"You do the same to me. You always have. I just didn't know why."

"And now you do?"

"No one can stand upright on fire," Elyssa whispered. "All you can do is sink into it . . . and let it burn."

Distantly Hunter wondered how much more he could take before he lost control.

He didn't know.

But he knew he was going to find out.

"Hunter?" Elyssa whispered. "Is something wrong? You look so fierce."

He smiled. Like his expression, Hunter's smile was rather uncivilized.

"Nothing is wrong," he said. "In fact, something is very, very right."

"It is?"

"You don't need your boots right now, do you?" Hunter asked, removing his own as he spoke.

Elyssa blinked, startled by the change of subject.

"Er, no," she said. "I don't often wear them in bed."

Hunter gave a crack of laughter and shook his head. His fingers never hesitated as he nimbly removed boots and bright red socks from Elyssa's feet.

"Bill named you right," Hunter said, smiling. "Sassy."

The caressing quality of Hunter's voice took all the sting out of the nickname.

Elyssa smiled up at Hunter despite the race of her heart and her unsettled breathing. He was caressing her feet, her ankles, the curve of her calves beneath her loose trousers.

The sensations were indescribable, delicious. She wanted to twist and turn against the caresses like a cat.

"Such enticing little cries," Hunter said huskily. "They tempt me to pull off these men's clothes and find all the soft woman hidden beneath."

As Hunter spoke, his hands shifted to the waistband of Elyssa's trousers. The buttons started coming undone at a rapid rate.

Elyssa's eyes widened at the thought of being absolutely naked in front of Hunter. She stared at the male hands that were even now urging the thick fabric of the trousers down toward her hips.

"But we didn't—" she began. "Before, I wasn't—"

"Naked?" Hunter offered.

Hesitantly Elyssa nodded.

"My fault," he said in a low voice. "You should have been as naked as a flower. And I should have been all over you like warm, gentle rain."

A shiver went through Elyssa.

Hunter stopped trying to pull the trousers down over her hips. Though the last thing he wanted to do at the moment was lift his hands away from her clothes, Hunter did just that.

"Too shy?" he asked.

"I never thought of myself as shy," Elyssa whispered. "But—"

"Would this help?"

Hunter took a thin cotton blanket from the end of the bedroll. He shook the blanket out over Elyssa.

"Is that better?" Hunter asked.

She clutched the blanket and nodded.

"May I continue?" he asked.

Elyssa looked away from Hunter's intent, dark eyes, but she nodded agreement.

"Tell me if you change your mind," he said.

Hunter bent and kissed Elyssa slowly, thoroughly. Before he lifted his head, she was breathing in soft bursts, as though she had been running.

The heat of Elyssa's response was addictive to Hunter. He wanted more of the hungry, sensuous kisses, but he was uncertain of his own control. Her combination of shyness and abandon aroused him as nothing ever had.

Instead of searching beneath the blanket for the waistband of Elyssa's trousers, Hunter began unlacing her hunting shirt. After a few moments his fingers slid into the opening he had created. He stroked one of her smooth, warm breasts. The tip hardened instantly at his touch.

Hunter clenched his teeth against a husky sound of need as his own flesh leaped in response. He removed his fingers so slowly that it was a long caress rather than a withdrawal.

"I'll need your help now," Hunter said in a low voice.

"How?" Elyssa whispered.

"I want to take off your shirt, but the way you're clutching that blanket . . ."

Hunter waited.

Letting out a tightly held breath, Elyssa dropped the blanket into her lap, grabbed the hem of the buckskin, and began pulling off the shirt.

Hunter's long, strong fingers slid beneath the buckskin. At first he helped Elyssa move the shirt upward. Then he simply caressed her, enveloping her breasts in his warm hands.

A husky cry came from beneath the buckskin tangled around Elyssa's head. She didn't even know she had made the sound. She knew only that Hunter's hands sent the sweetest kind of fire cascading from her breastbone to her thighs.

The buckskin shirt landed unnoticed beyond the bedroll. Elyssa didn't realize that she had dragged off her chemise with her shirt until she felt the untamed heat of Hunter's mouth where his fingers had been moments before.

Elyssa's back arched in abandoned response. Her fingers speared into his thick black hair. Twisting slowly against his mouth, she held Hunter close. Small cries rippled out of her, echoes of the hot pleasure cascading through her and pooling in the secret places of her body.

Fierce response stabbed through Hunter, making him shudder with need. He gave Elyssa's breasts nibbling kisses and listened to the broken, urgent breathing of her response.

"May I finish undressing you now?" Hunter asked in a low voice.

The feel of his tongue tracing first one hard nipple, then the other, made a coherent response impossible for Elyssa. Instead, she simply began tugging at the loose trousers.

Hunter lifted Elyssa's hand to his mouth. He kissed her palm, bit the pad of flesh at the base of her thumb, and smiled at the jerk of response that traveled visibly through her body.

"Let me undress you," Hunter whispered.

"Yes. Yes, please."

Yet when Elyssa felt her trousers sliding down her legs, she instinctively made a grab for the drawstring waist of her soft linen drawers. The trousers vanished, leaving her wearing only the sheer, loose leggings of the drawers.

A moment later Hunter's long fingers tangled with Elyssa's at the waistband. Slowly he drew his fingertips down the open front of her drawers.

Elyssa jerked as though touched by lightning.

Her eyes grew wide as she realized that her underwear would give Hunter free access to the moist, sensitive flesh between her legs. The drawers were sewn together only at the waistband and down both sides of the legs. The crotch remained completely open.

Elyssa didn't know if that fact tantalized or terrified her. It was the same for Hunter's hand hovering so very close to discovering her most private places—desire and fear intertwined in her.

Hunter stopped just short of the pale, thick curls he knew lay beneath the fine linen of Elyssa's drawers. Slowly, repeatedly, he drew his fingertip over her abdomen.

"I love touching your skin," he said. "So smooth. So warm. Makes me wonder what it tastes like. Cream, I'll bet. Spiced with cinnamon."

An odd sound came from Elyssa's throat when Hunter kissed the skin just below her navel.

"Fear or pleasure?" Hunter asked against her skin.

Elyssa couldn't answer. The feel of his fingers sliding down the central opening of her drawers took her breath away.

When Hunter skimmed the heated petals of her desire, Elyssa's response spilled softly onto his fingertips.

"Pleasure," he said huskily, relief and passion combined. "Pure, wild pleasure."

Hunter repeated the gentle touch and again was rewarded by Elyssa's hot, helpless response. Each slow movement of his hand brought more heat, more pleasure, more freedom between her legs for his caresses. Finally he parted the soft, slick petals and found the sensitive nub concealed within.

Elyssa's eyes closed as a wave of wild pleasure swept through her, lifting her against Hunter's hand. Another wave lifted her, then another and another until she was crying huskily with each breath, each caress.

Slowly Hunter's fingertips skimmed, circled, then gently probed the deep well of her response. The slick heat of her made his whole body clench with need. With great care he pressed inside her, first one finger, then two.

And every bit of the way he wished that he was truly, deeply joined with her rather than merely teasing her and tormenting himself.

The increasing pressure inside Elyssa's body returned sanity to her in a rush. Memories of the first time returned. First the exquisite pleasure. Then pressure.

Then pain.

"Hunter, I—"

Elyssa's words ended in a hoarse sound of pleasure as Hunter's thumb rubbed over the slick, shimmering knot of passion he had teased into life.

"It's all right," Hunter said gently. "You're tight, but I was expecting it this time. I won't hurt you. Remember my promise? All of the pleasure and none of the pain."

Elyssa made a ragged sound as pleasure coiled and burst inside her.

Through lowered eyelids, Hunter memorized the picture Elyssa made as she lay undressed but for the fine drawers that served to emphasize rather than to conceal the swollen petals of her desire. The trust implicit in her abandon humbled him.

The hunger in his own body raged at him.

Deliberately Hunter moved his hand, measuring and pleasuring Elyssa in the same smooth motions. Pressing, sliding, caressing, stretching the snug, incredible softness of her body. With each movement he gently seduced the very flesh he had once taken in a storm of ignorance and desire.

When Hunter could press no deeper he bent down to the passionate nub that now lay exposed. The tip of his tongue circled the knot of flesh, stroked it . . . and then he sucked hungrily.

Surprise and violent pleasure shot through Elyssa.

"Hunter."

His hands and mouth moved in slow, caressing response.

Husky cries rippled from Elyssa's throat as she lay helpless, open, a willing captive of the man whose unexpected loving burned her to her core.

Hunter heard, felt, tasted her response; and forced himself to remember all the reasons why he shouldn't open his pants and plunge into the very fire that was burning both of them alive.

Without warning ecstasy transfixed Elyssa, held her arched and quivering, wholly abandoned to Hunter. Like the hot, hidden convulsions of her body, the wild song of her pleasure was a bittersweet torment to him.

Finally, reluctantly, Hunter withdrew from Elyssa's body. Only after he pulled the thin cotton blanket over her did he trust himself to gather her into his arms. He held her in his lap and rocked gently, trying to calm both of them.

Slowly ecstasy eased its fierce grip on Elyssa's mind and body. With a deep, shattered breath, she opened her eyes and looked at Hunter.

He smiled almost sadly at the wonder in her blue-green eyes.

"Good," he said. "That's what it should have been the first time."

"I . . ."

A delicious echo of ecstasy shivered through her, stealing her ability to talk.

"I have no words," Elyssa said after a moment.

She lifted herself to brush a kiss across Hunter's lips.

The gentle caress twisted his guts into an even tighter knot. Hunter closed his eyes and battled with the savage clamor of his body.

When he could trust himself to look at Elyssa again, she was watching him with troubled eyes.

"What's wrong?" he asked.

"You."

"What about me?"

"The first time I had the pain and you had the pleasure," Elyssa said. "The second time I had the pleasure and you had the pain. Is it always that way, one hurting and the other helpless with pleasure?"

"I'm not hurting the way you did."

"You don't look it," Elyssa said unhappily. "You look . . . drawn."

"I'll get over it."

Elyssa shifted her position to get a better look at Hunter. The motion made her hip move against his abdomen. His breath hissed in between his clenched teeth.

"You *are* hurting," she said quickly. "Is there anything I can do?"

"Don't tempt me," Hunter said under his breath.

But Elyssa heard him.

"Tempt you?" she asked quickly. "How?"

Hunter closed his eyes and tried not to think of all the ways a girl with Elyssa's passion could tempt him.

And then satisfy him all the way to the soles of his feet.

A threadlike groan was dragged from Hunter's throat. He fought not to give in to the hunger pulsing through his body. He had done what he had promised himself he would do. He had pleasured Elyssa thoroughly, making up in the only way he could for his haste and misjudgment the first time.

"Hunter?" Elyssa whispered.

He couldn't answer. All he could do was remember how she had looked lying open to him, abandoned, shivering with the ecstasy he had brought her.

Elyssa gave Hunter's face quick, tiny kisses, whispering his name between each caress. Her arms wound around his chest as she pulled herself even closer, trying to comfort him.

The blanket fell unnoticed to her hips.

Hunter's body jerked. His arms shifted to push Elyssa away. Then he felt her breasts against him. Without meaning to, he caressed her nipples with his fingers. Tight crowns rose to his touch.

The shudder of response that went through Elyssa surprised Hunter. He hadn't expected her to enjoy being touched so soon after she had found her satisfaction.

Belinda certainly hadn't like being petted. After they were married, she lost interest in sex, other than to tease him mercilessly whenever she wanted a new dress or better curtains for the drawing room.

Hunter looked down at Elyssa's soft breasts resting against his hands. Even in the cave's twilight, he could see the deep, pouting rose color of the nipples and the creamy contrast of her skin. She looked fragile against the strength of his hands, but the shivers that went through Elyssa didn't come from fear.

"You feel so good," Hunter whispered against her hair. "I could get drunk just touching you."

"May I . . . touch you?"

Hunter's hands hesitated. The thought of Elyssa's fingers stroking him made his body clench with need.

"I don't think it would be a good idea," Hunter said roughly.

"Don't you like being touched?"

"I would love to have your hands all over me. Too damned much."

Elyssa understood only that Hunter wanted her caresses. In a hush whose tension grew with each breath, she began unbuttoning his shirt.

"I've been wanting to do this ever since I saw you half-naked in the garden," Elyssa confessed.

"It's not a good idea."

"Why?"

"I didn't want to take you this time," Hunter said bluntly. "I just wanted to teach you the pleasures of your own body. To make up for hurting you."

"By hurting yourself?"

"Like I said. I'll get over it."

"I'll help you."

"Elyssa—"

Hunter's breath caught hard in his throat and stayed that way. His shirt was open. Her naked breasts swayed and pressed against his chest as she pulled shirttails free of his pants.

With a murmur of discovery and approval, Elyssa ran her hands over the masculine territory she had just uncovered.

Hunter watched Elyssa through half-opened eyes. He knew he should stop her.

And he knew he would not.

He had just made a discovery himself. It was a wild, hot pleasure to have a woman pet him with admiration rather than calculation in her eyes.

The longer Hunter was with Elyssa, the more he realized what a cold, manipulating female Belinda had been. Elyssa might be reckless and maddening at times, but no one could accuse her of lacking passion.

Hunter's hands tightened on Elyssa's breasts, his thumbs circled her nipples, and he smiled to hear the throaty sound of her response.

"Hunter?" Elyssa asked huskily.

He made a rumbling sound deep in his chest.

"May I kiss you too?" she asked.

Hunter bent to take Elyssa's mouth, only to find that she had another kind of kiss in mind. Her lips and tongue and teeth made hot forays across his chest while her fingers kneaded muscles with open delight.

The resilience of the hair on Hunter's chest seemed to particularly intrigue Elyssa. She tugged sensually on the cushion of hair, buried her fingers in it, and probed with her tongue to taste the flesh beneath.

Soon she discovered the small, smooth disk of a male nipple. She repeatedly teased the tight little nailhead in the center with her tongue.

The caresses dragged a groan from Hunter.

Instantly the curious, oddly hungry strokes of her tongue stopped. Elyssa's head lifted.

"Did that hurt?" she asked huskily.

"Does this?"

Hunter's fingertips closed on her hard nipples and tugged.

Elyssa's breath caught on a ragged moan. Then she understood that her question had been answered.

She smiled slowly.

The reckless curiosity and sensual anticipation in Elyssa's smile made fire pulse through Hunter.

"How about this?" she asked.

Her hands slid down Hunter's body. He sucked in his breath hard when he felt her fingers working over the buttons on his trousers, then his underwear.

Very quickly Elyssa uncovered a thin strip of Hunter's skin between folds of cloth. Delicate fingertips traced the skin, found the thatch of hair growing below, and brushed lightly.

Hunter bit back a curse and a prayer.

"Does that hurt?" Elyssa asked, only half teasing.

"No more than this."

Hunter's long index finger skimmed the opening in

her drawers, parted thick curls, and probed sensuously.

The reflexive jerk of Elyssa's body made Hunter smile. He watched her face while he felt her hand slide inside his clothes, searching, finding, caressing.

Hunter closed his eyes and shuddered with raw need.

"Hunter?"

"Dangerous," he said through clenched teeth. "Damned dangerous."

"Why?"

Hunter's fingers slid into Elyssa, found her even hotter than his memories.

"Because I want this," he said bluntly.

"Then it's yours," she whispered.

The slow, deliberate movement of Elyssa's softness against his hand, and the liquid silk of her response, snapped Hunter's control. He stretched out suddenly, taking her down to the pallet with him. As he did, he freed his aroused flesh from the confinement of his clothes.

Before Elyssa could draw a breath, Hunter was between her legs, opening them. The pressure of his caresses tore a cry of passionate surprise from her.

Abruptly Hunter realized what he had done, pushing Elyssa onto her back, forcing her legs apart, giving her no chance to protest or to push him away.

Again.

Hunter forced himself to stop just short of taking Elyssa. She was so close to his erect flesh that he could feel the heat of her reaching out to him, licking over him, promising him fiery oblivion.

His body vibrated with the sexual tension that was tearing him apart.

"Damn," Hunter groaned thickly. "I'm sorry, honey. I didn't mean to—again."

He kissed Elyssa's eyelids, her cheeks, her lips, her

throat, and with every kiss he whispered words of raw need that made her shiver.

The heat of Hunter's body against Elyssa's hands was like a wild fever. The tension vibrating through his flesh made her desperate to ease him.

"Show me what you need," Elyssa said. "Show me!"

"You're so small, and I—"

"But I'm not fragile," she interrupted quickly.

Hunter shuddered. He had never been harder, more ready. Yet he knew very well the slick resilience of Elyssa's body. If he was careful, she would take him like a sleek satin glove.

He groaned.

"Hunter," Elyssa pleaded. "Do whatever you must. It's all right."

For a moment she thought he hadn't heard. Then she felt the probing, intimate caress of his fingers between her legs. The delicious stretching sensation came again.

A wave of pleasure curled down from Elyssa's breast-bone to her thighs. The wave broke and spilled hotly between them. The sensuous, caressing pressure increased, sliding deeper.

"Hunter," she protested raggedly, "I'm supposed to be pleasuring you, not the other way around."

He tried to answer, but couldn't. The hot, snug ease of Elyssa's acceptance took his breath. His hips bunched as he pressed more deeply into her.

Another wave gathered and swept through Elyssa. Her abandoned, silken response made the world begin to slide away from Hunter, spinning him into a place where only fire existed.

Elyssa called Hunter's name as her body arched, drawn taut by forerunners of ecstasy. Her head turned from side to side as she felt the wildfire biting into her body, a fire conjured by his caresses, a heedless blaze that increased with every motion of his body between her legs. He was burning her alive.

And she loved every sweet sting of the flames.

"This isn't fair," Elyssa said raggedly. "You're giving me—everything—and taking nothing—for yourself."

Hunter had no words to answer Elyssa. Her body was taking him so hotly, so perfectly. He pushed deeper into her and then deeper still, drawing her legs up beside his, opening her even more.

Liquid fire answered him, urging him to press harder, deeper, quicker.

"Hunter," Elyssa whispered. "I—"

Her breath was unraveled by sharp, golden claws of ecstasy. Small cries were torn from the back of her throat.

Hunter caught Elyssa's mouth beneath his. Then he sank into her, kissing her until their mouths were as intimately joined as their bodies.

When Hunter could go no deeper into Elyssa, he began to move. With each motion of his hips, she cried out. She clung to him, moving with him, sharing the sharp, shocking pulses of sensation that lanced through her. With each shared motion, fire burned more intensely, biting deep into her flesh.

Abruptly Hunter's hips locked hard against her. His head lifted and his whole body shuddered wildly, repeatedly. Her name was ripped from him in a ragged cry of ecstasy.

The sound of her name breaking on Hunter's lips consumed Elyssa. Crying, holding him with fierce strength, she gave herself to the fire of their joined bodies.

And to him.

It was a long time before Hunter was able to gather himself enough to look down at Elyssa, to see if his wild ardor had hurt her.

Eyes closed, she lay quietly beneath him, utterly relaxed but for the random echoes of ecstasy that shivered through her without warning.

He hadn't hurt her at all.

Gently Hunter eased from Elyssa's warmth, gathered her in his arms, and rolled to the side. He held her, stroking her slowly, enjoying the weight of her body against his. He had never felt like this with a woman, both at peace and as powerful as a god.

I could get used to this, Hunter thought. *Except for the belt buckle digging into my thigh . . .*

He laughed silently, both amused and amazed by the passion he and Elyssa ignited so effortlessly in one another.

"My sweet, sassy girl," Hunter said, kissing Elyssa's hair gently. "Next time I really will have to slow down long enough to get properly undressed."

Elyssa smiled and nuzzled against Hunter's chest.

"Maybe after we're married," he added lazily.

A chill went through Elyssa as she remembered the first time Hunter had discussed marriage.

With God as my witness, Elyssa Sutton, if you don't grow up and be a good mother to my children, you will rue the day you teased me into marrying you.

"It's not necessary," Elyssa said with a calm she didn't feel.

"What?" Hunter asked, shocked.

"I'm not a virgin. Just because we're . . ."

Elyssa's voice died. She didn't know how to describe what they were to each other.

"We're just lovers," she said after a moment. "No promises are necessary. We don't have to marry."

Hunter didn't believe what he was hearing.

And not hearing.

Abruptly Hunter realized that for all the sweet cries he had dragged from Elyssa, her love for him had not been spoken aloud. In the heat of passion he hadn't noticed.

He was noticing now.

"Don't be a fool," Hunter said roughly.

"Exactly," she retorted. "I'm glad we agree."

"I'll send for a preacher as soon as—"

"What for?" Elyssa asked in a tight voice. "If you're missing a formal sermon on Sundays, go to Camp Halleck."

"Damn it, Sassy, what we just had is too good to walk away from!"

"Yes, but it's not enough for a life sentence."

"Of all the damn fool—"

"You want a woman for a wife, not a sassy girl," Elyssa interrupted tonelessly. "You want a woman you respect, someone you can trust to raise your children. That's not me, is it?"

For an instant Hunter hesitated as memories rose in a black wave. The last time he had let desire choose his wife, his children had paid with their lives.

Hunter's hesitation was all the answer Elyssa needed. Quietly she closed her eyes and fought not to cry.

He made love to me so carefully this time, I had hoped . . . she thought. Then, painfully, *Hunter's right.*

I'm a fool.

Hunter felt the change in Elyssa's body, tension replacing relaxation, distance replacing trust. When she tried to sit up, he held her against his body.

"I was thinking of the past just now, not of you," Hunter said.

Elyssa shook her head.

"Damn it, honey. It's not how you took it."

Elyssa looked at Hunter. In the mysterious twilight of the cave, her eyes were as darkly gleaming as the pool.

"If I were a widow," she said, "would you be pressing marriage now?"

Hunter stared at Elyssa, not able to believe that she could calmly get up from their shared bed and act as though nothing special had happened.

We're just lovers.

No breathless promises of love.

Just lovers.

Anger replaced the contentment that had stolen through Hunter.

"You aren't a widow," Hunter retorted. "You're a hot-blooded, reckless girl who doesn't know her own mind from one minute to the next."

Hunter heard his own words and realized that his temper was digging a hole deep enough to bury him. He bit off a savage curse and tried again to reason with Elyssa.

Just lovers.

"You're a young woman," Hunter said with great care, "and I'm a man old enough to know better. I'm prepared to do what is right."

Anger flicked through Elyssa's veins.

"I'm not," she said.

"Damnation, Sassy! A few days ago you said you loved me!"

Hunter's words went into Elyssa like knives. Her breath sucked in on a wave of pain.

"Did I?" she asked in a brittle voice.

"You damn well did and you know it."

"Well, what do you expect from a *hot-blooded, reckless girl* but girlish declarations of love?"

Hunter winced at hearing his own words. Tenderly he stroked Elyssa's long, tangled hair and tried to gather her closer. The stiff resistance of her body didn't change.

"Honey," Hunter said gently, nuzzling her ear, "I didn't mean that as an insult to you. I love your reckless passion."

A sensuous shiver went through Elyssa at Hunter's caress. Even angry and hurt, she couldn't help responding to him. It didn't even surprise her anymore.

Elyssa had never known anything close to the incandescent pleasure Hunter gave her. Just the thought of sharing his body again made her breath shorten.

"In bed, yes, you love my reckless passion," Elyssa said. "But there's more to marriage than sex."

"Will you listen to reason?" he asked tightly.

"I always do. But you're not always reasonable."

Before Hunter could answer, Elyssa was speaking again. The sad acceptance in her voice should have come from a woman much older.

"Don't let your conscience grind on you," Elyssa said against Hunter's neck.

Hunter's fingertips caressed her hair and the downward curve of her mouth. He didn't know what to say. Every word he spoke only seemed to make it worse.

"I know I'm not the love of your life," Elyssa said. "But like marriage, love isn't necessary for pleasure, is it?"

"Sassy, that's—"

"We just proved it," she interrupted. "Didn't we?"

Elyssa's teeth closed not quite gently on Hunter's neck. If all she could have of Hunter was his body, she would take it. Deliberately her hands smoothed down Hunter's torso until she found the place where he was most different from her.

Hunter's eyes narrowed against the sudden, impossible leap of his flesh. Her fingertips caressed him like living flames, tracing each sensitive ridge of flesh, every changing texture, learning his growing strength in a silence that burned.

Then Elyssa's hot, hungry mouth slid down Hunter's body, tasting all that she had discovered, memorizing him in a way that left him shaken and wild.

"Now I know why they're called fancy men," Elyssa breathed against Hunter's aroused, painfully sensitive flesh. "I'm so plain compared to you."

With a hoarse sound Hunter dragged Elyssa up his body, rolled over and buried himself in her, ending one sweet torment and beginning another. He moved heavily inside her, sparing her nothing of his potency. Her cries and the hot scoring of her nails told Hunter that Elyssa liked his power.

The third time Hunter held Elyssa arched and shivering with ecstasy, he let go of control. The endless, pulsing release left him too spent to raise his head.

Only later, much later, did Hunter realize that no more had been said about duty or conscience or marriage.

Or love.

～23

$\mathcal{B}$y the time Hunter and Elyssa finally left the twilight intimacy of the cave, it was mid-afternoon. Silently they rode toward the ranch.

Neither spoke, for neither wanted to argue about what their future should be. For the time being it was enough simply to ride close to each other, near enough to give a gentle touch and receive the flash of a smile in response.

When Hunter and Elyssa were still a mile from the ranch house, Morgan came at a gallop toward them.

"Did you see her?" Morgan asked them.

"Who?" Hunter asked. "Penny?"

"The Indian girl."

"No," Hunter and Elyssa said together.

"Well, she's gone."

"What happened?" Hunter demanded.

"No one knows," Morgan said. "When Penny found out the girl was gone, she rang the dinner bell."

"When was this?" Elyssa asked.

"Morning."

As Morgan spoke, his glance went from Elyssa to Hunter. Morgan's shrewd brown eyes didn't miss the telltale red of her cheeks. The color could have come from rouge, except that Elyssa didn't wear makeup. It could have been sun or windburn, but Morgan suspected the color came from something closer to hand.

Hunter's beard stubble, to be precise. A girl with skin as tender and fair as Elyssa's showed each loving abrasion of a man's cheek.

"She can't get far on foot," Elyssa said.

"She isn't on foot," Morgan answered. "She took that big bay mare we caught running wild last week, the one with the fresh Slash River brand on her hip."

Elyssa bit back a curse. "That mare was one of my mother's favorites. Thoroughbred and Arab. I had hopes for her as a broodmare."

"No one ever accused Utes of lacking an eye for good horseflesh," Hunter said sardonically.

Elyssa thought of the battered, bloodied Indian girl who had suffered so much at the Culpeppers' hands. Elyssa couldn't blame the girl for taking a Ladder S horse and running back to her own people at the first opportunity.

"One horse more or less won't break us," Elyssa said after a few moments. "Let her go and worry about the cattle."

Hunter and Morgan exchanged a glance. Hunter nodded minutely.

"Yes, ma'am," Morgan said. "I've got a bunch in mind."

He spun his pony and cantered off toward the marsh.

"What are you two planning?" Elyssa asked.

Hunter's head snapped toward her.

"What do you mean?" he asked.

"Just what I said."

For a moment Hunter considered lying to Elyssa. Then he saw the clear, measuring intelligence in her blue-green eyes and knew it wouldn't work.

"Nothing you need to worry about," Hunter said.

"Rot."

Despite Elyssa's waiting silence, he didn't speak again.

The look in her eyes changed. Bleak acceptance replaced the memories of intimacy.

"You don't trust me at all, do you?" she said neutrally. "Not even a little bit."

Hunter's hand closed over Leopard's reins just before Elyssa could turn the stallion away.

"I didn't want to worry you," Hunter said.

"Of course."

The polite agreement in Elyssa's voice nudged Hunter's uncertain temper.

"Damn it, Sassy. What good would it do for you to fret about the Ladder S raiding the Culpeppers?"

"None at all, from your point of view."

"To hell with me. I'm worried about you! There's too much on your plate already, what with the Culpeppers and Penny still sick and finding out Bill is your father and the missing livestock and the battle over that Indian girl and . . ."

Hunter's voice trailed into silence.

"Taking my first lover?" Elyssa finished.

Curtly Hunter nodded.

She gave him a haunting, bittersweet smile.

"Fancy man," Elyssa said caressingly, "you are by far the best part of what is on my plate."

Hunter winced at the nickname but didn't protest it. Since he had felt Elyssa's wild, sweet mouth all over him, he couldn't react with real anger when she called him "fancy man."

"I wish we were back at the cave," Hunter said in a low voice, "and I was bathing you again, tasting you again. Cinnamon and cream and fire, a kind of fire I'd only dreamed of until you."

Elyssa's hand went to Hunter's mouth, stilling his words. The trembling of her fingers against his lips told

Hunter that she remembered as clearly as he did.

His tongue slid between her fingers.

"Hunter," she said shakily. "Don't."

"Why? We both like it."

"But we can't do anything about it!"

"You'd be surprised what two can do on horseback," he said, his voice teasing.

Inviting.

Elyssa bit back a groan.

"You're used to this kind of thing," she said. "I'm not."

"Used to it?" Hunter shook his head emphatically. "Weren't you listening, Sassy? I've never wanted a woman more after I've had her than before I did. Never."

Elyssa's eyes widened. "But that's the way I feel with you. Each time more. Isn't that, er, customary?"

"Not for me," Hunter said. "It's damned addictive, though. Like you."

Ruefully he shifted in the saddle, trying to accommodate his sudden, surging arousal.

"I think," Hunter said carefully, "we'd better change the subject. Unless, of course, you'd like to climb up in the saddle with me right now."

The thought of it made Elyssa smile.

"Don't tempt me," she said, repeating Hunter's earlier words to her.

He gave a crack of laughter. Then he touched her mouth with breathtaking tenderness.

"When the men ride out tonight," Hunter said in a low voice, "don't follow. Promise me."

Elyssa paled. "Tonight?"

"Yes."

"That's why you took me to the cave today," she said starkly. "You were afraid you wouldn't come back."

"I couldn't leave you with the memory of pain and humiliation. The thought of it . . . tore at me."

"Let me go with you," she said urgently.

"No."

The word was like Hunter's expression, hard and inflexible.

"But—" she began.

"No. Promise me."

"But—"

"Do you want me to die looking over my shoulder for you?"

"That isn't fair!"

"Do you?" Hunter asked again.

It was the very softness of his voice that told Elyssa she had lost.

"Of course not," she said in a defeated voice.

"Then stay home."

Methodically Hunter went through the ranch house and closed all the shutters. Because John Sutton had been a plainsman, an Indian fighter, and a cautious man, he had built heavy wooden shutters on the inside of the house rather than the outside. The shutters were meant to keep out bullets and arrows, not wind and rain.

Elyssa moved alongside Hunter, followed by the dogs. She had called them into the house to avoid any possibility that they would give away the men's presence to the raiders.

As Hunter closed shutters, she opened the gun slits that ran in a vertical line down each shutter. There were slits in the heavy log walls, as well.

Penny tended to those openings before she took the dogs into her room and shut them up out of the way.

"Don't show any light," Hunter said.

Elyssa nodded.

"Someone will come to you after dawn," Hunter continued. "Sonny, probably. Morgan has done wonders with that boy."

"Why can't I wait for you on the ridge at Wind Gap and—"

"No," Hunter interrupted curtly. "You've plenty of food and water. Even if a few of the raiders get away from us, you'll be safe here while we drive the cattle to Camp Halleck."

Elyssa closed her eyes and turned away, struggling not to show her fear to Hunter. The terror wasn't for her own safety.

It was for his.

"Elyssa?" Hunter said urgently.

"I'll stay. Will you . . ." Her voice frayed.

"What?"

"After you sell the cattle, will you . . ."

Come back to me?

But Elyssa couldn't say the words aloud. Those were the words of a sweetheart or a wife, a woman who had some claim to a man's respect, his trust, his esteem.

Her only claim was to Hunter's body.

"Never mind," Elyssa whispered. "It doesn't matter."

"Tell me, honey."

Closing her eyes, Elyssa shook her head wearily. Tears slipped from beneath her lashes.

Hunter wanted very much to take her in his arms and kiss away her anxiety, but he knew it would be futile. Elyssa was too intelligent not to understand the danger of this raid to everyone involved.

What haunted Hunter was that the danger might be even greater to those who stayed behind. His greatest fear was that Ab Culpepper had been waiting to be raided all along.

It was what Hunter would have done in Ab's place.

Pick your killing ground and wait for the enemy to

come to you, Hunter thought in bleak silence. *Spring the trap. Pin them down in a cross fire and cut them to ribbons.*

That was just one kind of trap Hunter easily could imagine. Another would be to have a few men engage the enemy . . . while the rest of your men stole away to wreak havoc elsewhere.

The Ladder S, for instance.

The thought was like a lump of ice in Hunter's gut. It was why he had put off raiding the Culpeppers until time had run out and there was no other choice.

He was cutting it very fine as it was. There would barely be enough time to drive the cattle to Camp Halleck before the first day of winter.

Maybe Ab is just lazy rather than wise.

Maybe.

Grimly Hunter wished that he had more men to leave behind at the ranch. The Herrera brothers had insisted on going with Hunter, which meant only Lefty and Gimp remained to guard the Ladder S. The old hands were game, but were still only two against however many raiders Ab might throw at them.

Elyssa and Penny were both good shots, but the idea of them going up against the Culpepper raiders left the brassy taste of fear in Hunter's mouth.

The thought of what would happen if Ab got his hands on Elyssa was unbearable.

"Elyssa."

Hunter's hoarse whisper reached Elyssa the instant before his mouth closed over hers. The kiss was as hard as his thoughts, but Elyssa made no complaint. She simply wrapped her arms around Hunter and gave back the kiss with all of the leashed wildness inside her.

"Promise me," Hunter said urgently.

"Yes," Elyssa whispered.

An instant later the kitchen door closed behind Hunter. He paused long enough to hear the bar thumping into place. Then he set off for the barn.

Hunter and Morgan rode out of the ranch yard first. They sat warily, repeating rifles drawn and laid across the saddle, their eyes quartering the darkness for any sign of movement.

They saw only wind blowing through trees stripped of all but a few pale leaves. Clouds raced overhead, veiling and unveiling the stars. The moon gave enough illumination to reveal movement.

A hunter's moon.

Reed and Fox left the Ladder S a few minutes afterward. Their destination was the same as that of the first two men, but their route was slightly different. They had another part of the Ladder S to ride over, hoping to find raiders.

Or be found by them.

Live bait for a trap that could swing shut on them without warning.

By twos, the remaining men slipped into the darkness. Each took a different trail to the same place.

Hunter and Morgan rode to the rendezvous point and waited, listening intently to the small noises of the night.

No sound of shots came. No alarm was raised.

Two by two, men began materializing out of darkness at the rendezvous. Soon all but the final pair of men had arrived.

Hunter sat off to the side on Bugle Boy, glancing at his watch.

Case, damn it, where are you? Hunter thought impatiently. *The longer we wait here, the more likely we are to be discovered.*

Two more minutes. Then the last vaqueros will be here.

I can't wait any longer than that.

Seconds ticked into the moonlight like fleeing ghosts.

Silently Hunter prayed that Case wasn't lying wounded or dead in some nameless ravine. And as Hunter prayed, he couldn't help remembering the time he had queried Case on how secure his position was with the raiders.

Do they trust you?

As much as they trust anyone who isn't a Culpepper.

Two men rode up quietly. Their wide-brimmed hats were silhouetted against the moonlight.

Morgan rode to Hunter's side, saw the watch in his hand, and waited.

The last second fled.

The watch clicked shut with a final sound.

"No sign of Case, suh," Morgan said softly.

"We'll have to go in without him."

"Yes, suh." Then, unhappily, "It's not like him."

"No," Hunter whispered. "It isn't."

"I'll pray for him."

"Pray for all of us."

Hunter urged Bugle Boy forward. Morgan came up alongside. The other men fell in behind, two by two.

They had gone less than a quarter mile when they heard the sound of a horse running hard, destroying the silence of the night.

The horse was coming toward them.

Hunter signaled everyone into cover. Then he spurred Bugle Boy down a steep ridge, racing toward whatever was coming at him out of the night. The big stallion plunged forward in wild leaps, then sat on his hocks and slid the rest of the way down.

"Damn," Sonny said under his breath. "That man sure can ride."

"He shoots better," Morgan said.

The men watched from cover as Bugle Boy hit the flats and raced recklessly over the moonlit land.

After several hundred yards a horse burst from a ravine and ran toward Hunter. The horse's rider was crouched low over the animal's neck, barely a shadow against the flying mane. A rifle barrel gleamed dully in the moonlight. There was no bulk of a saddle on the horse's hard-running body.

"Bareback," muttered Fox.

"Injun," Mickey said, lifting his rifle.

Morgan knocked it aside.

"What the hell!" Mickey said. "I had him dead to rights!"

"Be glad you didn't pull the trigger," Morgan said curtly. "That's Hunter's brother out there."

"His brother?" Mickey said. "I didn't know he had one."

"You do now. Keep it in mind. Case is as hard a man as you'll find on the right side of the law."

Morgan watched the two riders below. Within seconds, his worst fears were confirmed.

Case didn't bother stopping to talk to Hunter. He simply shouted something and swept past at a dead run.

He was heading for the Ladder S.

Fully dressed, Elyssa paced her bedroom like a caged animal. Back and forth. Back and forth. She looked through first one gun slit, then the other. Then she paced.

Back and forth. Back and forth.

Peer through gun slits toward the B Bar.

Back and forth. Back and forth.

Stare out the other window, two more gun slits.

Listen for the sound of shots.

"Where are you, Hunter?" Elyssa whispered. "You and Morgan and all of the men. Are you all right? Have you found the cattle? Have the Culpeppers found you?"

Only silence answered Elyssa's questions. The ranch yard was empty. The dogs were quiet. Penny was in her room, trying to sleep. Lefty and Gimp were downstairs drinking coffee in the kitchen, trying not to sleep.

Elyssa looked at her watch. More than an hour had gone by since the men had ridden out by twos into the darkness.

Like a restless ghost she went from window to window. Back and forth. Back and forth.

Stare out the gun slits.

Dawn was coming on in a shimmer of pale orange and red and yellow. The peaks were already glowing. Soon daylight would slide down the rugged mountains and fill the Ruby Valley with light.

Elyssa barely noticed the beauty of the gathering dawn. She simply paced back and forth.

Three equally spaced shots shattered the night's silence.

Danger.

Carbine in hand, Elyssa turned and ran downstairs, calling to the others every step of the way. When she reached the first floor, Penny was standing in her bedroom doorway. She was carrying Elyssa's shotgun.

"What is it?" Penny asked quickly.

"I don't know. Just three shots."

Suddenly the dogs erupted into a frenzy of barking.

Elyssa ran to the shutter and peered through a slit. She saw a racing shadow in the darkness that preceded dawn. Moments later she made out the shape of a horse galloping flat out toward the ranch house from the direction of Wind Gap.

Elyssa's heart soared in the instant before she realized that big, broad-shouldered rider who was crouched low on the horse's neck wasn't Hunter.

"Don't shoot!" she yelled to Lefty and Gimp.

"Sassy, you know we don't *never* shoot at what we can't personally i-den-ti-fy!"

Ignoring the indignant reply, Elyssa stared into the darkness where hoofbeats made a rolling thunder.

The horse galloped past the garden and right up to the front porch of the house.

"Open up!" Case yelled.

Elyssa was already yanking the bar out of its supports before she heard Case's command. He dove through the doorway just as gunfire broke out beyond the barn.

"Don't shoot!" Case commanded. "Hunter and the rest are coming in behind me!"

"Front or back?" Elyssa asked.

"Any damned way they can. The Culpeppers will be all over them like a rash in about two minutes. Close that door, but don't bar it yet."

Elyssa slammed the door shut behind Case. He went from rifle slit to rifle slit, peering into the fading darkness.

The sound of galloping horses came from the distance like a mutter of drums.

"Lefty!" Elyssa called out.

"Yo!"

"Come in here and cover me when I open the door. Penny, Gimp will cover you at the kitchen door. If you men see any strangers coming in, shoot."

"Hunter won't like having you anywhere near the doors," Case said bluntly. "A lot of bullets could be coming through with the men."

Elyssa said only, "How good are you with that rifle?"

"Tolerable," Case said dryly.

"The approach to the back door can be covered from the nursery upstairs. The front approach can be covered from the first bedroom on the left."

Case was running for the stairs before Elyssa finished speaking. He went up them with the speed and coordination of a cougar. She could barely stand to watch. Case was so like Hunter in his size, his build, his way of moving.

Gunfire erupted through the night in a deadly staccato

hail, drowning out the growing rumble of horses' hooves.

Hunter, Elyssa thought. *Oh, God. Hunter!*

Lefty came to stand beside Elyssa at the front door. The sound of glass shattering upstairs told her that Case was breaking out a windowpane to make room for his rifle barrel.

The pounding of horses' hooves became a rolling thunder sweeping toward the house.

"Our men are coming in the back way!" Case called from upstairs. "Get ready!"

Elyssa forced herself not to run toward the darkened kitchen. Her job was at the front of the house, not the back.

Rifle fire erupted from the upstairs.

"Some are coming to the front!" Case called. "Get ready! The Culpeppers are right on their tails!"

Lefty moved to a rifle slit by a window, broke out the glass pane, levered a round into the chamber, and waited. Even though the old hand had refused to sign on for gunfighting wages, he was calm and efficient in his movements.

"Open the kitchen door!" Case yelled.

Abruptly the sound of horses and gunfire became louder, telling Elyssa that the kitchen door was open. She didn't turn away from the front door even when she heard shouts and curses and Ladder S men calling out their own names as they fought their way into the kitchen.

"Front door!" Case yelled.

Elyssa threw it open and then ran to the nearest rifle slit, carbine in hand. She peered out and saw nothing but a turmoil of shadows lunging out of the darkness that preceded dawn.

Bullets thudded into the thick wood of the house as Elyssa lifted her carbine to break out the glass. Before the steel barrel met windowpane, glass exploded. She flinched and gave a startled cry. Then she realized that the raiders had done her a favor—now she wouldn't have to break the glass herself.

On the other side of the door, Lefty fired several times at a muzzle flash in the cottonwoods along the stream.

Men hurtled through the open doorway. Lefty yanked his rifle out of the gun slit and turned toward the men, listening and watching. They were calling out their own names as they lunged into the room.

"Fox!"

"Reed and Blackie!"

Dimly Elyssa realized that Reed was supporting the other man. Blood gleamed like wet paint on Blackie's pant leg above the low top of his boot.

"Hunter set up a dispensary in the root cellar," Elyssa said tightly. "No light will show from there. Penny! We have an injured man!"

"I'll take the kitchen door, ma'am," said Fox.

There was a pause, then two more men raced through the front doorway.

"Sonny here," said the first man. "Morgan is right on my ass."

A dark shadow leaped through the door after Sonny and dove to one side.

"Morgan," said the shadow. Then he raised his voice and shouted, "Close and bar the kitchen door!"

"Yo!" Gimp answered from the back of the house.

Elyssa held her breath, waiting, waiting.

No other men hurtled through the open front doorway.

"Hunter," Elyssa cried. *"Hunter."*

She didn't know she had gone to the opening to call out his name until Morgan yanked her out of the doorway. Bullets whined and screamed through the dark room.

Morgan slammed and barred the door. Bullets thudded into the triple-thick planks.

"Ammunition!" Case yelled from upstairs.

"Ma'am?" Sonny asked.

"In the root cellar," Elyssa said numbly. "There's plenty. Hunter saw to it."

"Two boxes for everyone," Morgan said.

"Follow me," she said.

As Sonny followed Elyssa down an indoor stairway and into the basement, the young man's eyes widened in appreciation of Hunter's preparations.

Lantern light glowed up from a corner of the large, dirt-walled room at the bottom of the stairway, illuminating the cellar. In addition to the usual sacks of onions and carrots, potatoes and apples, there were ranks of barrels, stacks of ammunition boxes, and seven cots with blankets. Other boxes and full gunnysacks of supplies were stacked neatly about, waiting to be used.

Blackie was on one of the cots. One of his boots was off. Penny was working over his leg.

"By God," Sonny said, taking it all in. "Morgan wasn't fooling, was he? Our ramrod must have been some kind of Johnny Reb soldier boy."

"Yes," Elyssa said. "He was."

She turned away. The thought of Hunter outside in the danger and darkness was too painful for her to bear.

"The ammunition is over there," Elyssa said tautly. "As soon as you get some to Case, distribute boxes to the other men."

"Yes, ma'am," Sonny said.

While he grabbed cartridge boxes, Elyssa asked the question that had been gnawing at her.

"Hunter? Did you see him?"

"No, ma'am. He was back up on the ridge, covering our retreat. That man can shoot like hell on *fire*. Without him, we wouldn't have made it through Wind Gap without being cut to doll rags."

Sonny straightened and trotted past Elyssa on his way to the stairs.

"Excuse me, ma'am. They'll be needing these cartridges."

Sonny ran up the stairway.

"How is he?" Elyssa asked, turning to Penny.

Blackie answered before Penny could.

"It's just my calf," he said, disgusted. "Soon as Miss Penny wraps it up, I'll be ready to fight."

"That's not necessary," Elyssa said.

"The hell it ain't," he retorted. Then, "Excuse me, ma'am, but there's more than forty raiders out there. We need every hand."

"Hold still," Penny said. "I'm going to wash the wound."

"Hell, ma'am, just pour some whiskey through it and get me out of here."

"As you wish."

Liquid gurgled out of a bottle. Blackie hissed a string of words that both women pretended not to hear. Penny began wrapping the wound. She had barely knotted the bandage before Blackie swung his legs off the cot, crammed his foot back in his boot, and picked up his rifle.

When Blackie's injured leg took his weight, he grimaced, paled, swore . . . and walked unevenly to the stairway, using the butt of the rifle as a crutch.

Elyssa turned to follow him.

"Wait," Penny said to her. "You're bleeding."

"What?"

"Your face," Penny said simply.

Elyssa held her hand up to her face. Her fingers came away red and sticky. She stared at them, shocked. Only then did she realize that her forehead and right cheek stung as though on fire.

"Come here," Penny said.

She wrung out a cloth in warm water and started cleaning Elyssa's face with gentle touches.

"What happened?" Penny asked.

"It must have been the glass," Elyssa said, remembering. "It exploded before I could knock it out of the rifle slit."

Penny smiled wryly.

"John warned Gloria that would happen, but she wouldn't hear it," Penny said. "She insisted that a proper home needed proper panes of glass, not thick shutters with gun slits in them. So they compromised. Glass and shutters both."

Gunfire came sporadically from inside and outside the house.

Elyssa closed her eyes and tried not to think of Hunter out there in the night, unprotected.

Hunter wounded, bleeding, alone.

Dying.

"Are you all right?" Penny asked, concerned.

Elyssa nodded.

"You turned white as salt," Penny said.

"Hunter."

"What?"

"Hunter covered the men's retreat. He's still out there."

Penny made a small sound, then hugged Elyssa.

Belatedly Elyssa realized that Bill also was out there in the dangerous dawn.

Somewhere.

"Rider coming in! Hold your fire!"

Elyssa recognized Case's voice. She turned and ran up the basement stairs and then up the stairway to the second floor.

Case was standing at a rifle slit. Despite his shouted order, he was sighting down the barrel of his rifle, tracking the rider.

"Is it Hunter?" Elyssa asked urgently.

"Likely."

In the silence Elyssa could hear the sound of hoofbeats approaching rapidly.

"Why aren't the Culpeppers firing at him?" she asked.

"It's a goddam riderless mule!" Fox yelled from downstairs.

"Hold your fire!" Morgan commanded harshly.

Elyssa looked toward Case. He was tracking the mule over the rifle barrel with a single-minded intensity that was chilling.

"Unbar the kitchen door!" Case yelled without looking away. "Morgan, stand by with your pistol!"

"Yo!"

Elyssa turned and ran downstairs. As she reached the kitchen, she heard Case yell for them to open the door and get the hell out of the way. She froze in place.

No one noticed her. Every eye was on the kitchen door.

Revolver cocked and drawn, Morgan stood to one side of the door as it swung open.

A man dove through the door a bare instant before the mule careened into the side of the house. The force of the impact made the building shudder.

The kitchen door slammed shut before the man stopped rolling.

Morgan tracked every motion the man made. Then Morgan's smile flashed and he holstered the pistol.

"Welcome home, suh," Morgan said.

"Glad to be here," Hunter said, coming to his feet fast. "What's the situation?"

The easy power of Hunter's movements told Elyssa

that he was unhurt. The relief she felt was so great that it made her dizzy.

"Blackie is shot through the leg," Morgan said. "Mano Herrera took a crease along his shoulder. Penny is patching him up now. Blackie's already back on the job."

"Elyssa?" Hunter asked.

"I'm here," she said in a low voice. "I was—worried —about you."

Hunter let out a long breath.

"So was I," he said. "I was lucky. Damned lucky. All of us were."

"Yes, suh," Morgan said. His smile flashed again. "We'll all be churchgoing, Bible-thumping sons of God from now on."

Hunter's smile was rather grim.

"You were the luckiest of all," Elyssa said to Hunter. "I'm surprised those raiders let you through."

"They couldn't see enough of me to shoot at. I was hanging on the side of a mule."

What Hunter didn't say was that there had been no need for the Culpeppers to waste a good mule in order to kill him. They had the ranch surrounded, all ways out blocked, and all the time in the world.

They could kill Hunter—and everyone else on the Ladder S—at their leisure.

"Those Culpepper boys value their mules too much to kill one just to get at Hunter," Morgan said. "If you were riding Bugle Boy, though . . ."

"That's what I thought," Hunter said. "Bugle Boy is too good a stud to kill on a stunt like that, so I just stripped off his tack and turned him loose."

"How did you get a mule?" Elyssa asked.

Hunter's smile was as cold as a knife coming out of its sheath.

"They were beating the brush for me," he explained.

A chill went over Elyssa as she thought of Hunter being pursued like an animal.

"I came up out of cover," Hunter said, "pulled off the mule's rider, and sifted into the shadows. By the time the raiders figured out what had happened, it was too late to stop me."

"What now, suh?" Morgan asked.

"Divide the men up. You know the drill."

"Yes, suh. I sure do."

24

"Jsee fire," Case yelled.

Then, moments later, Case called out the bad news.

"Hunter, they're going to burn us out! I'm going up on the roof!"

"Mickey," Hunter yelled. "Start opening water barrels. The rest of you, stop the men carrying torches!"

The men moved to carry out Hunter's orders, but not as quickly as he wished. Three days of battling the raiders had worn the Ladder S men down to the bone. Half of the raiders could sleep while half fired at the ranch house.

It took every Ladder S man to defend the place.

In the cellar dispensary, Elyssa went down the row of sleeping men, quickly waking the ones who were fit to fight.

"Upstairs," Elyssa said in a low, urgent voice. "The raiders are coming with torches."

The men rolled off the cots fully dressed. They grabbed the weapons they had stacked by the stairway and ran up the steps.

Penny sat up on the last cot in the row. Her eyes were dazed with exhaustion.

"What is it?" Penny asked.

"Raiders."

"Again?"

"Get into those pants I brought you," Elyssa said. "We may have to leave. A skirt will just be in the way."

"Leave? But—"

Penny was talking to empty air. Elyssa had turned and was running up the stairs, her carbine in her hand.

When Elyssa stepped out into the first floor, she didn't notice the crack of rifle fire and the sound of brass casings hitting the floor. The sounds of battle had become so familiar to her that they no longer registered.

The first man Elyssa saw was Hunter. She ignored the kick of her heart and the shivery sensation in the pit of her stomach that came at seeing him. She had been very careful not to make any special claims on Hunter's time and attention just because they were lovers.

Hunter had slept little since the first attack. He barely sat down to eat. He spent most of his time on his feet, walking from man to man, checking on their needs. If he stopped to talk, it was about angles of fire and rationing ammunition and shifting watches to accommodate men whose stamina had given out.

Elyssa knew that the demands on Hunter were so great he barely had time to breathe, much less to soothe the fears of a girl whose only claim was on his sexuality.

A carefully shielded lantern provided the sole illumination in the kitchen, which had become Hunter's command post. The red light gave a hellish tint to everything.

In a single yearning look, Elyssa memorized Hunter's face. His black hair was disheveled, as though he had just run his fingers through it. His skin was drawn tautly over his cheekbones and forehead. His jaw had a black shadow of beard. He had dark smudges beneath his eyes, yet the clarity of his glance was unchanged. He gave orders in a quick, calm tone.

"Ma'am?" Sonny said. "Shouldn't you be downstairs?"

"I can shoot as well as most men here and considerably better than the men who are still downstairs."

Sonny started to argue. A curt order from Hunter sent the young man running to his post.

"Go downstairs," Hunter said to Elyssa.

"I'm more use up here."

Hunter hesitated. He wanted Elyssa down in the cellar, where it was safer. But he needed more riflemen, especially now.

If the house caught fire, everyone in it would die.

"Morgan," Hunter said.

"Yo."

"Take Case's post upstairs. Elyssa will take yours."

Morgan grabbed his rifle and extra ammunition, tipped his hat to Elyssa, and went past her to the stairway.

Without a word to Hunter, Elyssa went to Morgan's post and looked out.

The mountains loomed over everything, blacker than night itself. Elyssa was surprised to see that it was still dark. Time had lost all meaning down in the cellar, where night and day were the same.

Overhead came the sound of rifle fire as Case spotted a torch. Elyssa saw it too. The raider must have been coming at a gallop toward the ranch house. The torch bobbed and jerked at each lunging stride.

Abruptly the torch flipped end over end, fell to the ground, and lay there burning sullenly.

Rifle fire came from all sides now as other men rushed toward the house with torches. Elyssa fired at the raider who was nearest. So did the men on either side of her. She didn't know who hit the raider. She only knew that the torch came no closer.

It was the first of many attacks. Sometimes the raiders

were merely feinting to draw fire or to cover a more earnest attempt from another quarter. Some of the raiders came at a gallop. Some came at a trot.

The smartest crawled forward on their bellies with unlighted torches. Only after they were next to the house did they set the torches ablaze. That was when the cry for buckets would go out inside the house.

Methodically Elyssa fired, reloaded, fired, and thought of nothing else. When she ran out of ammunition, she called for more like the other men.

It was Penny who brought the ammunition. Every other able-bodied person was either hauling water or firing at the raiders.

By the time dawn came, Elyssa was so tired she was leaning against the shutter just to stay upright. Her arm muscles were locked and trembling from the strain of keeping the carbine leveled and ready to shoot at any instant.

Tongues of fire licked downwind from the ranch. The house itself was scorched in places, but intact. The same couldn't be said of the grasslands and some of the piñon uplands. They were burned blacker than night. The rising wind stirred ashes and lifted smoke to the sky.

In the end, it was the wind that had saved the Ladder S from the raiders. At dawn the wind had shifted, driving the fire from fallen torches back at the raiders.

Numbly Elyssa wondered who the wind would favor tomorrow night.

"Elyssa."

She turned her head toward the voice. As she did, she realized that it wasn't the first time her name had been called. It was merely the first time she had noticed.

Hunter's breath came in hard when Elyssa turned toward him. Her eyes had the blank stare of exhaustion that he had seen before, when men were pushed too hard, too long. He wondered when she had last eaten. Or slept.

Belatedly Hunter realized that he had kept track of the men under his command, but hadn't thought to do the same with Elyssa. He hadn't thought it would be necessary, because she wasn't standing watches.

So, like Hunter, Elyssa had ended up sleeping and eating less than the men around her.

Gently he lifted the carbine from her hands.

"It's over for now," Hunter said gently. "Go get something to eat."

"The men . . . cellar."

"Gimp is seeing to them."

"Penny?" Elyssa whispered.

"She's asleep. You should be, too."

Elyssa looked at Hunter, but her eyes didn't focus. She closed them, leaned her forehead against the shutter, and wondered how she would have the strength to walk down the stairs.

Same way the men do, Elyssa told herself wearily. *One step at a time.*

She pushed away from the shutter and started taking one step at a time. But it was toward the cellar she walked, not toward her bedroom.

Hunter reached out to stop Elyssa. At the last minute he withdrew his hand. The wounded men needed tending after the long night. Someone had to do it. Elyssa had the skill.

Cursing silently, Hunter headed for the upstairs.

Case looked up as his brother walked quietly into the nursery. The men no longer noticed the stark contrast made by mounds of spent rifle shells stacked in a cradle and butterflies dancing over the walls.

"Let me start going out at night," Case said without preamble. "I can guarantee there will be less raiders before dawn."

"Not yet."

"When."

It wasn't a question. It was a blunt demand.

"When there's no other chance left and not a moment before," Hunter said just as bluntly.

"Just what chance are you seeing that I'm missing? We damn near burned to the ground last night."

There was no anger in Case's voice, no hope of a miracle, no real curiosity as to his own fate. He simply wanted to know what he had overlooked that Hunter hadn't.

"The army could get interested after three days of gunfire and columns of smoke coming from Ladder S lands," Hunter said tersely. "Even a drunk has to have noticed."

Case made a sound of disgust.

"The army is on the far side of the Rubies, chasing Indians and making maps," Case pointed out. "The handful of men left at Camp Halleck doesn't give a tinker's damn about the Ladder S."

Hunter didn't argue.

Nor could he bring himself to send Case out to his death alone.

"When you go," Hunter said. "I'm going with you."

"No. You're needed here."

"Morgan can—"

"*No.*"

Case's interruption was soft and final.

"The only way you can stop me," Hunter pointed out calmly, "is to kill me."

"What about Elyssa?" Case asked. "Have you thought about her?"

Hunter's eyelids flinched. Between battles with the raiders, he had found some time to think about Elyssa.

Not one of his thoughts had been comforting.

During the long days and nights of the siege, Elyssa

hadn't spoken to Hunter of love. She made no special effort to come and stand near him, to talk to him, to touch him, to take comfort from his presence or to give him comfort in turn.

Elyssa hadn't even rushed into his arms after he had outrun raiders by riding a mule right to the kitchen door. She simply had said she was "worried" about him.

Nor had Elyssa turned to Hunter this morning, when she was so tired she could barely stand up. She had walked by him as though he was a stranger.

No wonder she didn't want to marry me after we made love in the cave, Hunter thought bleakly. *She had already figured out that she didn't really love me.*

But she wanted me. God, I've never been wanted like that by a woman.

Brave, passionate, reckless . . . and too damned young to know her own mind. I knew that from the first time I laid eyes on her, but I couldn't stop wanting her.

It's just as well she stopped thinking she loved me. Sure as hell I would have married her.

Sure as hell we both would have regretted it.

Too young. Elyssa and Belinda are alike in that, if in no other way.

Sin in haste and repent forever.

"Well?" Case pressed. "What about Elyssa?"

"She's young," Hunter said neutrally. "Whether I live or die, she'll be over me before Christmas."

Case's left eyebrow rose in a black arc.

"You haven't slept worth mentioning for three days," Case said. "You're not thinking straight."

"I've gotten as much sleep as you."

"Is that what Elyssa said?" Case persisted. "That she doesn't love you?"

Hunter's eyes darkened as he heard again Elyssa's denial of her previous declaration of love.

We're just lovers.

He didn't know why Elyssa's statement should cut him so deeply. He only knew that it did.

"Yes," Hunter said distinctly. "That's what Elyssa said."

Case started to speak, then shook his head. He made no claim to understanding women, but Elyssa had seemed different, at least where Hunter was concerned.

"She fooled me," Case said finally.

In silence he looked from rifle slit to rifle slit. The openings were a vivid contrast to the dark shutters. The light coming into the room was blue-white, intense, pure; burning fragments of the brilliant autumn morning.

"When it's full dark," Case said, "I'm going out. I've an idea where I might find Ab."

Hunter closed his eyes for an instant, then nodded.

"We'll go at full dark," he agreed bleakly, knowing it would be the last thing he ever did.

When Hunter looked around the dispensary that afternoon, six of the seven cots were occupied. Some of the men were merely sleeping. Others were injured. Fox was one of them. He had taken a bullet in his side and was in the grip of pain and fever.

Despite that, Hunter expected Fox to be on his feet in a day or two. The war had taught Hunter that a few days generally told the story with wounds. Heal or die.

Penny walked by each cot, checking the men. Her quiet competence was as comforting to the gunfighters as the gentle touch of her fingers on fevered skin.

"Where is Elyssa?" Hunter asked in a low voice.

"I made her go to bed hours ago. She hadn't slept for nearly two days."

"What about you?" he asked.

"I've had more sleep than anybody."

Hunter looked around the dispensary again. No one needed him here.

He needed no one here.

"Hunter?"

He turned back to Penny.

"We aren't going to make it, are we?" Penny asked quietly.

"Case and I are going to change the odds."

"How?"

"You don't want to know."

Penny looked at Hunter's eyes. Quickly she looked away.

"When?" she whispered.

"Tonight."

She bit her lip and nodded. Then she looked up at him with beseeching eyes.

"If you find Bill out there," she whispered painfully, "remember that . . ."

Penny's voice died.

"I don't expect to find Bill," Hunter said carefully. "He wouldn't help the Culpeppers rape and murder his own daughter."

Tears ran down Penny's cheeks.

"You think he's dead, don't you?" she whispered. "You think they killed him."

"I don't know. Neither do you. Bill knows this land better than anyone else alive. If he's half-smart, he went to ground as soon as he was sure the Culpeppers were going to attack."

Blindly Penny nodded. Tremors ran through her, telling of the strain she was under.

"Penny?"

"I'm all right," she whispered.

Hunter drew Penny into a gentle hug.

At first she resisted. Then she put her face against Hunter's chest and wept for all that had never been . . . and likely never would be.

After a time Penny stirred, blotted her cheeks with her

palms, and gave Hunter a watery smile. Then she pushed away from him and began walking slowly up the row of sleeping men again, checking them for signs of fever.

Restlessly Hunter went upstairs. He paced through the first floor of the ranch house. Everything was in order. It was the same on the second floor. Sonny was watching out one side of the house, Case the other. Neither man had seen anything but sunlight and a slow gathering of clouds as the afternoon wore on.

The door to Elyssa's bedroom was shut. Hunter stood there, listening intently.

Small, ragged sounds came from inside the room.

Softly Hunter tried the door, wondering if Elyssa had bolted it from inside.

The door opened without any restraint.

Hunter told himself he would only look in and check that Elyssa was all right.

She was turning restlessly on the bed. A bar of light from a rifle slit fell across her face. Tears shone on her cheeks.

Though Elyssa seemed to be asleep, she was crying.

In one stride Hunter was through the doorway. The door clicked shut behind him. The bolt slipped into place without a sound. Making no noise, he went to stand by the bed.

A quick look told Hunter that Elyssa wasn't awake. She didn't even know she was crying. Whimpering softly, she was held within the uneasy coils of nightmare.

A loaded pistol lay on the bedside table. Hunter knew without being told that it was Elyssa's way to insure that she didn't fall into Ab Culpepper's hands alive.

Why didn't you come to me for comfort? Hunter asked silently.

The answer came with cruel finality.

We're just lovers.

Just lovers.

Swiftly, recklessly, no longer caring what the men might think of Elyssa or of him, Hunter stripped off his boots and got into bed with her. As he slid beneath the bedcovers, the scent of gun smoke and rosemary and a woman's warmth lifted to his nostrils.

Desire and something else spread through Hunter's body, something very much like grief. He didn't understand the vise of sorrow gripping him, but he had no such problem with the passion.

A single glance when Hunter slid into bed had told him Elyssa was fully clothed except for shoes. The buckskin had been traded for a soft flannel shirt that once had been red. Now it was so faded it was barely pink.

Hunter's hands trembled at the thought of unbuttoning the cloth and finding taut, creamy flesh beneath. He didn't want to wake Elyssa, yet he needed her in a way he didn't understand.

With a tenderness that was sorrow and passion combined, Hunter stroked Elyssa's pale, tangled hair. More asleep than awake, she turned toward him and murmured his name.

"Don't wake up," Hunter whispered, drawing Elyssa into his arms. "I just want to hold you while you sleep."

It was a lie. Hunter wanted much more. If all he could be to Elyssa was her lover, then he wanted to be that one last time; for after tonight, there would be no more time for him.

Sighing, Elyssa burrowed into Hunter's arms. His body leaped at the feel of the womanly warmth resting against him. Fierce arousal stretched him on a rack of need. He closed his eyes and bit back a groan, not wanting to awaken her.

When Hunter finally could breathe around the savage ache in his groin, he opened his eyes. Elyssa was watching him. The passion and grief in her eyes matched his.

"Don't worry, honey," Hunter said softly. "Ab Culpepper will be dead before the sun comes up. Tomorrow night you won't have to fall asleep with a loaded pistol beside your bed again, wondering if you'll have to kill . . . someone."

A shudder worked through Elyssa's body. Saying nothing, she wrapped her arms around Hunter and held him.

The baffling grief moved through Hunter again, both easing and increasing his hunger. He kissed her hair very gently.

"It will be all right," Hunter whispered. "Case and I are going out at dark."

"*No.*"

The hoarse whisper was torn from Elyssa's throat.

Hunter didn't try to argue with her. He knew what was necessary. When she thought about it, she would too.

"It's the only way," Hunter said. "If we're lucky, we'll get Ab and his kin."

"No!"

"Even if we can't get to Ab, he doesn't have any hold over his raiders but greed. If some of them start turning up with their throats slit in the morning, the rest might well bolt."

"You'll be killed."

Again, Hunter didn't argue.

If he had thought sneaking past Ab's guards would be easy, he would have taken the women and run for the safety of Camp Halleck days ago.

But sneaking through the raiders would take every bit of skill he and Case had, and the devil's own luck in the bargain.

If the situation hadn't been desperate, Hunter wouldn't even have considered it.

Hunter bent his head slightly to kiss Elyssa. He meant

the kiss to be gentle, to soothe her fears and his own, but the first touch of her lips went through him like torch fire through straw.

With a hoarse sound Hunter caught Elyssa's mouth beneath his and twisted hard, opening her for the kiss. His tongue shot into her mouth with an urgency that was little short of desperation.

The fierce kiss arched Elyssa's neck over Hunter's forearm and forced her head back into the pillows. She didn't even notice. Her fingers were clenched in his hair and she was straining to get closer to him with every bit of her strength.

Hunter's blood caught fire at Elyssa's headlong answer to his need. Even as he deepened the kiss, he began undressing her with quick, impatient motions of his hands.

She fought to help him. Together they stripped off her trousers and kicked them aside.

"I didn't mean to—" Hunter began.

Elyssa took his mouth again, desperate to be close to him in the only way she could. She pulled one of his hands to the aching heat between her thighs.

Hunter forgot what he had been trying to say. Elyssa was hot, soft, and she wept for him at his first touch. The liquid fire of her burned away every thought of control. He jerked open his pants and rolled over onto her, wild to be inside her.

A quick thrust of his hips buried Hunter in Elyssa's heat. She jerked and a keening cry broke from her throat. Shuddering with stark pleasure, Hunter pulled back, trying to spare her.

Instantly Elyssa wrapped her legs around Hunter's thighs and pushed upward with her hips, forcing him even deeper into her.

The proof that she wanted him as desperately as he wanted her took all restraint from Hunter. He drove into her repeatedly, powerfully, as though he must experience all of her or die in his next heartbeat.

Elyssa arched up to Hunter, meeting his driving need with her own fierce demands. He gave her everything she asked for, and more. Without warning ecstasy poured through her in a cataract of fire, transfixing her.

The feel of Elyssa's shivering climax hurled Hunter over the edge. Just enough sanity remained for him to take her mouth in a deep kiss, muffling the sounds that came from both of them as he spent himself deeply within her.

They fell asleep that way, interlocked, knowing only each other and the ecstasy that still shuddered through them.

An hour later Hunter and Elyssa were awakened by Case's knock on her bedroom door.

The Ladder S was under attack again.

$\mathcal{E}$lyssa stood near the rifle slit, peering out into the slanting light of late afternoon with eyes that burned. Hunter stood just behind her, his body curving over hers almost protectively. He looked past her pale hair to the shimmering golden light and blackened ground that lay beyond the rifle slit.

Involuntarily, Hunter took a deep breath. He was close enough to Elyssa to smell the mingled scents of rosemary and gun smoke. The vital warmth of her body reached up to him.

Just lovers.

"I don't see anything," Elyssa said, sighing.

She straightened, only to find herself held between the shutter and the coiled power of Hunter's body. Sensations cascaded through her, a glittering network of heat coupled with a yearning that had nothing to do with desire.

"Do you— see anything?" she asked huskily.

To Hunter the catch in Elyssa's voice was like a caress. It took him a moment to answer, for he didn't trust his own voice not to reveal his elemental response to her.

"I guess," Hunter said carefully, "they were just making sure we didn't get any rest. But unless Case and

I stop them, the raiders will come at us again with torches in the hours before dawn.''

Fear tightened Elyssa's body at the thought of Hunter out beyond the walls, feeling around bare-handed in the dark for rattlesnakes.

And finding them.

"Don't go," she said in a low voice.

Hunter's only answer was Elyssa's name breathed into her hair.

"I'd rather die with you," she whispered. "Please, Hunter. Don't go."

"It's our only chance. And . . ." Hunter touched Elyssa's hair with his lips. "I can't let my brother go against Ab Culpepper alone."

Elyssa closed her eyes for an instant.

What did I expect? she asked herself ruthlessly. *Hunter loves his brother.*

In bleak silence Elyssa opened her eyes and watched the burned land for signs of the raiders.

"Elyssa?" Hunter whispered, bothered by her unnatural stillness.

"No one."

"What?"

"No one is coming."

"That's not what I—"

Whatever Hunter had meant to say was lost in simultaneous cries from Morgan and Case, who had the upstairs watch.

"Gunfire! North and east!"

"West and south sides, look alert!"

"Get ready, men," Hunter called. "Don't shoot unless you're sure of your target. We're damned low on ammunition."

Elyssa bent to pick up her carbine.

Hunter turned and headed for the stairs at a run, rifle in hand. The sound of rifle fire came from all directions, telling him that the attack wasn't merely a feint to keep them stirred up. But there was something odd about the shooting.

By the time Hunter raced upstairs, he figured out what was bothering him. The shots weren't coming any closer.

Nor was anyone in the house shooting back.

"Well?" Hunter demanded as he strode into the nursery.

"I can hear them, but I can't see them," Case said.

"Morgan," Hunter called. "What do you see?"

"Nothing."

Yet the gunfire came without pause.

"Army?" Case asked skeptically.

"No bugles," Hunter said.

"Maybe the raiders are fighting each other."

Hunter's grin was as savage as his crack of laughter.

Then there was only tense silence as men waited and listened and watched. They saw nothing but the burned land and the rich light of late afternoon.

Slowly a chilling sound swelled and drifted down to the ranch on the wind. Hunter and Case turned and looked at one another.

"Sounds like war cries," Hunter said.

"When the cat's away making maps and drinking whiskey, those mice sure do take advantage," Case said dryly.

"Maybe they'll kill each other off."

Saying nothing, Case raised his rifle, sighted down the barrel, and waited to see whether it was Indians or raiders who would come at the Ladder S next.

"Holler if you spot anything," Hunter said.

He turned and went through the house like a dark wraith, looking out every rifle slit, listening, waiting. Rifle fire and war cries came to him from all directions.

Hunter went back to Elyssa. Like Case, she was looking down the barrel of her gun, waiting to see which enemy survived. Unlike Case, she had propped the barrel on the bottom of the rifle slit, taking the gun's weight from her arms. Light from the slit made her eyes glow like blue-green gems.

Saying nothing, Hunter went to stand behind Elyssa. He put his hands against the shutter, leaned forward, and looked out over Elyssa's head.

After a few moments the lines of their bodies merged into one.

Without looking away from the land, Hunter breathed a kiss against Elyssa's hair. It was so light, so brief, that she wasn't certain it had happened at all.

"Indians heading for the cottonwoods," Case called from upstairs.

Hunter turned his head away from Elyssa.

"Hold your fire!" he yelled. "If they want to kill Culpeppers, I won't stop them."

Sporadic fire came from the cottonwoods, then shrill war cries followed by a silence that slowly expanded to fill the afternoon.

"Look alive, boys," Hunter called. "They could come at any moment."

Tautly Elyssa waited and watched the afternoon deepen into early evening.

Nothing stirred, not even the birds that usually flocked to the marsh for the night.

Just when Elyssa was certain that the Indians had gone away and left the Ladder S untouched, Case cried out again.

"Indians. Five of them." Then, in disbelief, "One is carrying a parley flag!"

"Hold your fire!" Hunter called.

Hardly able to believe what he was seeing, Hunter watched as four Indians stopped at the edge of the cottonwoods. The man with the parley flag rode on into the ranch yard.

"Ute," Elyssa said. "Painted for war, not truce."

Hunter went to the front door, where Morgan waited. Elyssa was right behind him.

"Go back," Hunter said. "It could be a trap."

"No. If you go, I go."

"Morgan."

Hunter said no more.

When the front door opened, Elyssa stayed inside for the simple reason that Morgan was holding her with wiry ease. She fought for a moment in bitter silence, then gave in with a weariness that tugged at Hunter's heart.

The front door shut behind Hunter, leaving him alone in a place of burned grass and churned dirt. There was no rifle in his hands, but there was a six-gun in his belt.

The warriors who waited at the cottonwoods were lean and hard and fit. Their ponies were the same. But it was the Ute with the ragged truce flag who had Hunter's attention.

Quick, flowing motions of the man's hands told Hunter what he hadn't dared to believe— the Utes had no desire to make war with the Ladder S. They had come to pay off a debt.

To Elyssa.

And only to her.

"Elyssa," Hunter called without turning away from the Utes. "Come out here."

An instant later the door opened and Elyssa came to stand beside Hunter.

The Ute began signing again. His hands were both graceful and powerful as he shaped concepts that were shared by white and native languages alike.

"He says that their headman owes a great debt to you," Hunter translated for Elyssa.

"But—"

"Wait," Hunter interrupted.

He watched intently, then began translating.

"His wife and son were taken by white men," Hunter said. "With the help of one, she managed to escape, only to be run to ground by the others like a rabbit by coyotes. Then a brave woman warrior came on a spotted stallion."

Startled, Elyssa looked at Hunter, but he was watching the Ute's hands.

"Though white herself," Hunter translated, "she shot a white man, took the son into her arms, and gave space on her horse to the wife. The white woman took the wife and son into her own lodge and cared for them as tenderly as a mother with her own babe."

The Ute paused and looked at Elyssa for a long moment before he resumed signing.

"He-Who-Speaks-First-at-the-Fire thanks the white woman," Hunter translated. "Let there be peace between our lodges."

"Yes," Elyssa said instantly.

The Ute understood. He made a sweeping motion with his arm.

Five more Utes galloped down from the slopes where cedar and piñon grew amid tongues of blackened ground. Three of the Utes led a string of three Appaloosa mares. They were beautiful animals, long-limbed and deep-chested.

"Hunter?" Elyssa whispered.

"Looks like you'll be raising spotted horses just like you wanted to," he said quietly.

Stunned, Elyssa gathered the lead ropes that were dropped at her feet as the Indians galloped by.

Then two more Indians came. One was leading the mare that the Indian girl had taken when she fled the ranch. A man was tied facedown over the mare's back.

The second Indian was riding double, holding another man upright in front of him on the pony.

A white man.

"Bill!" Elyssa cried.

The Indian released his burden, letting Bill slide onto the ground. As though that was a signal, the rest of the Utes whirled their ponies and galloped off.

The front door opened. Penny ran out and threw herself to her knees next to Bill.

Elyssa started to go to Bill as well. Then she froze as she saw that the man tied to the Ladder S mare had only one arm.

"*Mac,*" she said, shocked.

If Hunter was shocked, he didn't show it. He simply pulled his belt knife, cut Mac free, and caught him.

"Is he—" Elyssa began.

"Alive, barely," Hunter interrupted.

He carried Mac to the house. No sooner was Hunter through the door than he called out to Case.

"Take two men and see which raiders are left alive. If any."

Just after noon on the following day, Elyssa went silently down the stairs to the cellar. The house felt strangely empty to her. Most of the men were out rounding up cattle that had been held just beyond Ladder S land. At last count, more than six hundred head had been found.

The raiders were buried where they were found. Only one Culpepper had been found among the dead.

It wasn't Ab.

Case found mule tracks and followed them until they vanished on a slope of broken rock. Then he had returned to tell Hunter and pack his gear.

Elyssa knew that Case wouldn't be on the Ladder S come sundown.

Nor would Hunter.

I can't let my brother go against Ab Culpepper alone.

Only Bill and Mac remained in the dispensary. Bill wasn't badly injured. He was simply exhausted from being tied up, beaten, and left for dead by the Culpeppers on their way to raid the Ladder S.

Mac's condition was much worse.

At the bottom of the cellar stairway, Elyssa stopped and let her eyes adjust to the dim light. The flickering lantern revealed little. Mac's cot was on one side. Bill's cot was on the other, in a corner where the lantern light barely reached.

Penny was nowhere in sight.

Just before Elyssa turned to go back upstairs, there was movement from Bill's side of the room. As her eyes adjusted, Elyssa saw that there were two people on the cot. They were locked in each other's arms.

Words of passion and tenderness filtered through the darkness, telling Elyssa that Bill finally returned the love Penny had for him. Though Elyssa was happy for both of them, the sight of their love was almost painful to her.

Tomorrow at dawn Morgan, Sonny, and the vaqueros would drive cattle and horses to Camp Halleck, fulfilling the contract.

Hunter and Case would be going in the opposite direction, following Ab Culpepper's tracks.

I can't let my brother go against Ab Culpepper alone.

As Elyssa began to retreat, Bill called out to her in a low voice.

"Come on over here, Sassy. You can be the first to know that Penny has agreed to marry me."

There was a startled sound from Penny. She scrambled off the cot and stood beside it.

"Congratulations," Elyssa said.

"On finally getting smart?" Bill retorted.

"It's so rare in men," Elyssa said. Then she gave him a bittersweet smile, taking the sting out of her words.

Penny laughed out loud. Even Bill's eyes twinkled against his windburned face.

"How is Mac doing?" Elyssa asked.

Slowly Penny shook her head.

"I just checked on him," Penny said. "He drifts in and out, but each time he goes under . . ."

Penny shrugged and said no more.

In the time since Mac had returned so unexpectedly to the Ladder S, he had done nothing but fall deeper into the thrall of his wound.

"It's just as well," Bill said tersely. "Saves me the trouble of killing him."

"What?" Elyssa said, shocked.

"Mac was stealing you blind," Hunter said from the stairway behind Elyssa.

She spun around.

"What are you talking about?" she demanded.

Hunter looked at Bill.

"You tell her," Bill said, taking Penny's hand. "I'd rather kiss this little lady."

Penny's blush and smile of delight was like a sunrise in the dim room. She bent to receive Bill's kiss.

Elyssa looked away.

"Mac started stealing from you as soon as John Sutton died," Hunter said to Elyssa.

She simply shook her head, not understanding.

"Bill told me that Mac didn't figure a 'no-account daughter of an adulteress deserved the sweat of John's brow,' " Hunter explained. "So Mac started setting up his own ranch."

"With Ladder S stock and a Slash River brand?" Elyssa guessed.

"That's about the size of it."

"I suspected," Bill said a moment later, "but I was too drunk to care."

Penny made a low sound and touched Bill's face. He smiled at her gently.

"By the time Penny made me see the foolishness of my ways," Bill said, "the Culpeppers had started moving in. Mac didn't like it one bit, but he couldn't stop it."

"So he staged his 'death' and threw in with the Culpeppers?" Hunter asked.

Bill nodded.

Hunter threw a narrow look in Mac's direction.

"If he lives," Hunter said, "I should hang the son of a bitch."

Elyssa opened her mouth but could find no words to equal the icy rage in Hunter's eyes. The appalled sound she made brought his attention back to her.

"I won't see a man hanged for rustling," Elyssa said.

"Neither would I," Hunter said flatly. "But Mac tried to kill you three times that I know of."

"What?" she asked, shaken.

"He used that longhorn bull, and a landslide, and then took aim with a gun the night he salted your garden."

"Mac?" Elyssa asked in a strained voice. "He hated me that much? But why? What did I ever do to him?"

"It wasn't you he hated," Bill said. "It was Gloria."

"What do you mean?" Elyssa asked.

"Mac and John were partners until Gloria came along," Bill said. "Mac never forgave her for changing things."

"What does that have to do with me?" Elyssa whispered.

"You look so much like her, sometimes—" Bill hesitated and said simply, "Sometimes it's like being cut with a knife."

Elyssa shook her head, not wanting to believe that Mac had hated her enough to kill her.

"Sassy."

At first Elyssa thought she had imagined the whisper. Then it came again.

"Sassy."

Slowly she turned toward the corner where Mac lay dying.

Hunter reached the cot before Elyssa did. His hard arm barred her from coming within Mac's reach.

"I'm here, Mac," Elyssa said.

"Where?" he whispered. "Can't see."

Elyssa stepped around Hunter's arm and took Mac's hand.

"Right here," she said softly.

Mac's eyes focused on her.

"You know— my brand," he said painfully.

"The Slash River?" she asked.

"Give it— to you." He took a sharp breath. "Sorry."

"Don't talk," Elyssa said. "Save your strength for getting well."

Something close to a smile crossed Mac's face, shifting the line of his gray-streaked beard. When he spoke, his voice was stronger, as though he was drawing on a last reserve of strength.

"I'm dying, Sassy."

Elyssa caught her breath and squeezed Mac's hand gently.

"Damned whoring Culpeppers," Mac said, his voice hoarse and laced with contempt. "Just had to have a female. Stole a Ute gal."

Elyssa's eyelids flinched.

"Fools," Mac said. "Told 'em so. Then I— went to the marsh."

Mac drew several shallow breaths. Each one told of

the pain that was consuming him as deeply and finally
as death.

"It was you," Hunter said. "You shot Gaylord before
he could shoot Elyssa."

Slowly Mac glanced to Hunter and then back to
Elyssa again, focusing on her clothing.

"Looked like a man," Mac said painfully. "Fought
like one. Bravest thing— ever saw. Couldn't let them—
kill you. Ab figured it was me. Gutshot me— so I'd die
—slow— hard."

Mac's breath came out with a long, unraveling sound.
The hand Elyssa was holding went limp.

Tears she couldn't stop fell down her cheeks and
dropped onto Mac's hand.

Mac didn't feel it. He was finally beyond feeling anything at all.

In a way Elyssa almost envied him, for she knew her
greatest pain was yet to come.

When Hunter realized what had happened, he drew
the blanket over Mac's face and turned to Elyssa.

"Don't cry, honey," Hunter said roughly. "He isn't
worth your tears."

"I'm not crying only for him," she whispered. "I'm
crying for all of it, the pain and anger and betrayal of
the past. What a tangled, bitter legacy."

For a moment Hunter was silent. Elyssa sensed he was
remembering his own past, his own betrayal, his own
bitter legacy of pain and rage.

That was the most savage part of Elyssa's pain. She
could touch her own past, cry for it, even heal from it
in time . . . but she could not touch Hunter's past. She
could not heal him.

She could only lose him.

No, that's not quite true, Elyssa told herself with painful honesty. *I can't lose what I never had.*

Hunter never gave himself to me. He simply took what

I offered. And in return, he gave me pleasure.

Not his heart. Not his trust. Certainly not his love.

Just pleasure.

When Elyssa looked at Hunter again, her eyes were as empty as her heart.

"What did Case say about the mule tracks he followed?" Elyssa asked.

Hunter paused, surprised by the distance and lack of emotion in her voice. She was different in a way he couldn't describe, but he recognized it.

Being through a war changes you, Hunter reminded himself. *Finding out that your trust has been betrayed changes you, too.*

It sure as hell changed me.

Yet watching it change Elyssa was unexpectedly painful to Hunter. He would have given a great deal to replace the shadows in her eyes with the light of laughter and passion.

"Ab Culpepper is headed for the Spanish Bottoms," Hunter said finally.

"Then you and Case will be leaving soon."

Before Hunter could say anything, Bill did.

"Hunter isn't going one step off the Ladder S until he marries you," Bill said bluntly.

Startled, Elyssa turned toward Bill.

"I beg your pardon?" she asked.

"You heard me," Bill retorted. "From what Penny told me— and from what I can see with my own two eyes —it's past time a preacher came to the Ladder S."

"To marry you and Penny, yes," Elyssa said.

"It will be a double wedding," Bill said.

"There is no need."

"The hell you say," Bill shot back. "You and Hunter—"

"I'm not pregnant," Elyssa interrupted.

Hunter made an odd sound.

"You're certain?" he asked.

"Quite."

"The fact that he's asking," Bill said, "means it will be a double wedding. I'll see to it personally."

"No," Elyssa said.

"Sassy—" Bill began, exasperated.

"No," she repeated. "I won't."

"Why?" Hunter asked bluntly. "You know we're good together."

Elyssa turned to Hunter, confronting him and all that she hadn't lost, because it had never been given to her in the first place.

"A husband's first loyalty should be to his wife," Elyssa said neutrally. "Yours is to your dead children. And to Case."

Hunter lifted his hand as though to touch Elyssa, or to ward off a blow.

Or both.

"I want you," he said. "I can make you want me."

"Wanting isn't enough for marriage."

Hunter didn't disagree. Belinda had taught him that with cruel thoroughness.

"Marriage requires trust," Elyssa said, "for without trust, love isn't possible. You haven't trusted a woman since Belinda. I don't really blame you. Being badly burned teaches you not to trust fire."

Hunter looked away. He couldn't endure what he saw in Elyssa's eyes.

Then he wished he could stop listening as well, for what Elyssa was saying was more painful than what lay in her eyes. Her voice was an aching combination of exhaustion and understanding and regret that tore at him.

"I thought I could change your mind, or your heart," Elyssa said. "I was wrong. There is no room for the future in your mind and heart. Only the past."

From the upstairs came the sound of Case calling for his brother.

"Hunter? If you're still dead set on hunting Culpeppers with me, the horses are ready and the trail is getting cold."

Hunter stiffened. He looked at Elyssa and saw that she already knew he was leaving.

"Elyssa," he said hoarsely.

"Go ahead," she whispered. "There's nothing to keep you here. We were lovers. Just lovers."

Still Hunter hesitated, feeling as though he had lost something before he could even name it. In a haunted silence he searched Elyssa's eyes for what had once been there.

Just lovers.

Pain stabbed through Hunter as deeply as passion once had, as deeply as ecstasy, slicing all the way to his soul.

"Hunter?" Case called. "Where are you?"

"Good-bye, my autumn lover," Elyssa whispered. "I'll remember you each year when leaves turn to fire."

Hunter simply stared at her, unable to speak.

"Please excuse me," Elyssa said. "I haven't had any sleep worth mentioning in days."

Quickly she went to the stairs. When she emerged into the kitchen, Case turned toward her.

"Have you seen—" he began.

The look on Elyssa's face stopped Case cold. She went by him as though he wasn't there. He watched her go up to the second floor. The sound of a door closing came back down through the silence.

Hunter strode out of the cellar into the kitchen.

"What are you standing around for?" Hunter snarled. "The trail is getting cold."

Case whistled soundlessly through his teeth.

"Have you said all your good-byes?" Case asked.

"Yes."

"Then you're a damned fool. That's a fine woman you're leaving behind."

Hunter bared his teeth.

"Woman?" Hunter repeated sardonically. "She's a girl who doesn't know her own mind from one hour to the next."

Just lovers.

"Horseshit," Case said matter-of-factly. "She's a woman grieving for her man."

"She'll get over her tears."

"Sassy wasn't crying. She was grieving. If you don't know the difference, go upstairs and look at her face."

Hunter closed his eyes. They opened an instant later, cold and gray as the winter that follows autumn.

"Damn you, Case," Hunter said through clenched teeth. "Let it go."

"Just as soon as you do and not one moment before. If you take on Ab Culpepper the way you are now, we'll both be dead by first snowfall. So tell me again, brother. Why are you leaving the woman who loves you?"

"She said we were just lovers."

Case's left eyebrow lifted in a black, skeptical arch. "Was that before or after you told her you loved her?" Case asked.

"I never said any such thing."

"Well, that explains it," Case said agreeably, turning away. "I'm going out to talk to my horse. Its butt has more sense than you do."

Hunter glared after his brother, but even anger couldn't keep him from remembering Elyssa speaking of love.

And his own silence answering her.

Or even worse, his words.

Weren't you listening to me? Did I ever talk about anything but lust between us?

Elyssa had finally listened to him. Now she, too, was talking only about lust.

Just lovers.

Motionless, Hunter confronted what he had done to her, what she had described to him so calmly.

There is no room for the future in your mind and heart. Only the past.

Autumn lover. I'll remember you each year when leaves turn to fire.

For a time there was only silence in the house. Then Hunter turned and strode up the stairs to the second floor. With every step, he told himself that Case was wrong.

He had to be.

Otherwise it didn't bear thinking about.

Hunter reached the door to Elyssa's bedroom and hesitated, not knowing what to say.

Silence grew around Hunter. No sound came through the door. The quiet was unnerving. It was as though the room beyond was utterly empty.

Hunter knocked.

No one answered.

When Hunter's third knock was ignored, he tried the door. It opened soundlessly.

Elyssa was sitting on the bed in a room whose only illumination came from the rifle slits in the shutter. Her back was to the door and her arms were wrapped around herself as though to hold warmth inside.

Slowly Hunter walked to the bed. Elyssa neither turned nor spoke when the floor creaked beneath his weight. Hunter hesitated, then walked around the bed until he could see Elyssa's face.

His breath came in hard and stayed until it ached.

Elyssa no longer looked like a girl. Anguish lined her face, drained color from her skin, took life from her eyes, made her whole body rigid. Motionless, barely breathing, she simply endured each breath as it came, and with it the agony of being alive.

Case had been right. Elyssa was a woman grieving for the loss of the man she loved.

With a throttled sound of pain, Hunter sank onto the bed next to Elyssa. He lifted her onto his lap and stroked her face with fingers that trembled.

"It wasn't you I didn't trust," Hunter said in a raw voice. "It was me. I chose wrong and my children paid."

A shudder went through Elyssa. She turned and focused on Hunter. The anguish in her eyes made him flinch.

"Then I saw you," Hunter said in a low voice. "I wanted you until it hurt to breathe."

"Wanting isn't—"

"Enough," Hunter interrupted. "Yes. I know that as well as you do. Better. Belinda taught me."

Elyssa closed her eyes, unable to bear the memories in Hunter's.

"Then you taught me something far more important," Hunter said. "Love."

"Just—" Elyssa's voice broke.

"Just love," Hunter said softly. "Your love for me. My love for you. The love we will have for our children."

"Hunter—" Her voice broke again.

"I love you, Elyssa."

Hunter said it again as he kissed her, then he said it again and again.

The truth of Hunter's love swept over Elyssa like sunrise. With a broken sound she turned to him. Crying, laughing, Elyssa whispered her own love against Hunter's lips and heard her words returned.

Then they simply held one another, healing each other, leaving the past behind.

❧Epilogue

*H*unter and Elyssa stood next to Case in front of the ranch house and watched the preacher ride off toward Fort Halleck. Bill and the new Mrs. Moreland had already left for the B Bar, anxious to celebrate their own honeymoon.

The yard of the Ladder S was sunstruck and wild with autumn wind. Case's horse stood with ears pricked and head high. He tugged eagerly at the reins, wanting to be as free as the wind.

"I'll come by again as soon as Ab is taken care of," Case said quietly.

Elyssa flinched. She was haunted by what Hunter had said only last week.

I can't let my brother go against Ab Culpepper alone.

But Hunter was doing just that.

A husband's first loyalty should be to his wife.

To Elyssa, who was now Hunter's wife.

Tears stood in her eyes as she turned toward Case.

"Let the past go," Elyssa said huskily. "Please. Make your home here with us."

With a gentleness that still surprised Elyssa in a man whose eyes were so bleak, Case put one hand against her cheek.

"Don't cry, Sassy," Case said. "Hunter knows where his future is."

"It could be yours, too," Elyssa said.

Case's thumb stole tears from Elyssa eyelashes. Then he turned and mounted his horse with the lithe rush of a cat leaping.

"Name your first boy after me," Case said.

"Done," Hunter said quietly. "Send word if you need me."

Case nodded. Then he reined his horse around and headed southeast, toward the Spanish Bottoms.

"Wait!" Elyssa called.

Hunter put his arms around Elyssa and held her close.

"It won't work, honey," he said.

"But—"

"Case believes he doesn't have anything else to live for except hunting down Ted and Emily's killers," Hunter said heavily.

Elyssa knew Hunter was right. She also knew the truth hurt him more than it did her.

"Would it—" Her voice broke.

Elyssa took a breath and forced the words past lips that wanted to remain silent.

"Would it be easier on you if you went with him?" she asked painfully.

Hunter's eyes closed. He knew what the words cost Elyssa.

He knew, because they cost him just as much.

"I love you," he said roughly, lifting her in his arms.

"Hunter?" Elyssa whispered.

"Case said if I went with him, it would be over his dead body. He meant it. You're stuck with me, honey."

Case William Maxwell was born the following year, when autumn turned the aspen leaves to fire. Like his father, the boy grew tall and lithe, with unflinching eyes.

Like his mother, the boy had a deep feeling for the land and a gentle way with even the roughest horses.

There were other babies, too. Girls with wit and great determination. Boys with power and gentleness. Like their parents, the children thrived in the wild country at the foot of the Ruby Mountains.

At the end of the day, whether the hot winds of summer blew across the Ladder S or the wild storms of winter wrapped around the house, Hunter pulled his wife close, finding peace with her.

And each night Elyssa fell asleep with her autumn lover in her arms, knowing that all the seasons of love were theirs.

For All Readers Who Loved

AUTUMN LOVER

 by

Elizabeth Lowell

Look for the Sequel

WINTER FIRE

Coming in Fall 1996

An Avon Books Hardcover